CARLA CASSIDY

BY ORDER OF THE PRINCE

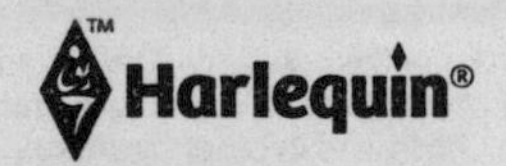

TORONTO NEW YORK LONDON
AMSTERDAM PARIS SYDNEY HAMBURG
STOCKHOLM ATHENS TOKYO MILAN MADRID
PRAGUE WARSAW BUDAPEST AUCKLAND

Special thanks and acknowledgment to Carla Cassidy for her contribution to the Cowboys Royale series.

ISBN-13: 978-0-373-69554-6

BY ORDER OF THE PRINCE

This edition published by arrangement with Harlequin Books S.A.

For questions and comments about the quality of this book please contact us at Customer_eCare@Harlequin.ca.

www.Harlequin.com

Printed in U.S.A.

"Beth, I don't want to scare you, but I thought you should know that I might have brought danger to you."

A hardness that had been around his heart cracked apart and fell away. "That means I don't want you staying here alone. That means I don't even want you out of my sight."

If somebody was after her because they thought she was his lover, there was no real way to disabuse them of that notion. He'd already made her a target and the best he could hope for was that he could keep her safe until he returned to Barajas.

But for tonight he didn't intend to go anywhere. And all he could think about was that they had been damned by what they weren't doing—so why not go ahead and do it? Why not become her lover?

He stood once again and took her by the hand and pulled her up from her chair.

"The coffee is ready," she murmured as he drew her into his arms.

"Hmm, suddenly I'm not in the mood for coffee." He leaned down and touched his lips to the warm flesh of her neck, then nibbled at the skin just beneath her ear. He felt the quickened beat of her heart against his and a faint tremor that stole through her. "I think it's time I made good on that earlier promise."

She didn't ask what promise he was talking about; rather she drew a shuddery breath and took him by the hand and led him down the hall toward her bedroom.

ABOUT THE AUTHOR

Carla Cassidy is an award-winning author who has written more than fifty novels for Harlequin Books. In 1995, she won Best Silhouette Romance from *RT Book Reviews* for *Anything for Danny.* In 1998, she also won a Career Achievement Award for Best Innovative Series from *RT Book Reviews.*

Carla believes the only thing better than curling up with a good book to read is sitting down at the computer with a good story to write. She's looking forward to writing many more books and bringing hours of pleasure to readers.

Books by Carla Cassidy

HARLEQUIN INTRIGUE

1077—THE SHERIFF'S SECRETARY
1114—PROFILE DURANGO
1134—INTERROGATING THE BRIDE+
1140—HEIRESS RECON+
1146—PREGNESIA+
1175—SCENE OF THE CRIME: BRIDGEWATER, TEXAS
1199—ENIGMA
1221—WANTED: BODYGUARD
1258—SCENE OF THE CRIME: BACHELOR MOON
1287—BY ORDER OF THE PRINCE

+The Recovery Men

CAST OF CHARACTERS

Beth Taylor—This hardworking beauty is drawn into danger by a handsome prince.

Prince Antoine Cavanaugh—He's determined to find out what happened to his friend and is unable to stay away from the pretty housekeeper, Beth.

Sheikh Amir Khalid—A bomb destroyed his car, but his body was never found. Where is the sheikh and who is behind the attack?

Jake Wolf—Sheriff of Wind River. Can the lawman be trusted?

Michael Napolis—Head of Security for Prince Antoine. Is he part of a bigger conspiracy?

Aleksei Verovick—Tied to the Russian mob. Is he behind the attacks on the royals?

Chapter One

It was creepy—packing away the personal belongings of a guest who nobody knew was dead or alive. Beth Taylor, head of housekeeping at the luxury Wind River Ranch and Resort, unlocked the door to one of the exclusive plush suites and pushed it open.

Just a little over three weeks had passed since Sheik Amir Khalid, one of the royals who had come to the hotel for a meeting, had gotten into a limo that had driven a short distance and then blown up. The driver had been killed, but nobody knew what had happened to Amir. The only witness to the event had seen the sheik crawl out of the wreckage and he'd been picked up by somebody. The problem was nobody knew if it had been friend or foe who had picked up the injured man.

"It's time to clear the room," Beth's boss had said to her minutes earlier. "It's been three weeks with no word and I can't hold the room forever. I'd like you to personally take care of it, Beth. We'll lock up the belongings in storage until somebody comes to claim them."

And so here she was, in a room where Sheik Amir Khalid had checked in as part of a four-nation coalition who had come here to discuss trade agreements that would benefit their individual countries. She pulled the luggage caddy she'd brought with her into the room and closed the door behind her.

The tasteful opulence of these suites never failed to amaze her. The thick carpeting beneath her feet, the subtle touches of gold trim in the woodwork and the oversized furniture all whispered of a kind of wealth Beth couldn't even begin to imagine.

Immediately after high school, Beth, who'd had a sickly mother to care for, had gotten a job as maid at the resort. Three years ago, after eight years of working hard, she'd finally been promoted to head of housekeeping, an often difficult but rewarding job.

She fought the impulse to kick off her high heels, peel off her pantyhose and dig her toes into the plush rug. Instead she headed for the bedroom. The king-size bed was truly fit for a king, with a rich navy bedspread and matching draperies that could either be drawn against the sun or opened to display the beautiful view of the Wyoming landscape.

Sheik Amir hadn't even spent a single night before the explosion had occurred, but his clothing had been neatly hung in the closet.

Her fingers lingered over the rich silks and other expensive fabrics as she carefully folded them and returned them to the suitcase she found on the floor in the closet.

With the closet once again empty she moved to the bathroom and quickly packed the personal grooming items that were scattered on the counter.

What had happened to Amir? It was the question on everyone's lips. Had he managed to get out of the limo alive only to be picked up by enemies and then killed? The area had been searched but no clues had been found to solve the mystery of the missing sheik.

Returning to the bedroom she beelined for the nightstands. Although she didn't think the sheik had been in the bedroom long enough to place anything inside the drawers, she wanted to be thorough.

The nightstands were tall and ornate, with marble tops and heavy drawers. She went to the one on the far side of the bed first. As she pulled open the top drawer she found herself thinking about how crazy everything had gotten since the dark-haired handsome sheik had taken the limo ride and never returned.

For the past three weeks the hotel had been turned upside down with the arrival of the royals. Reporters had flooded the area and there had even been local protests about the trade agreements. Since Amir's disappearance the air had grown even more intense as the various security teams scrambled to make sure the remaining leaders stayed safe.

With a shake of her head she focused on the task at hand. The nightstand drawers held nothing that belonged to Sheik Amir so she moved to the ones on the near side of the bed.

She gasped as she pulled the top drawer out too far and it fell to the floor. "Darn," she muttered, hoping she hadn't marred the beautiful wood. As she picked it up to put it back, she felt something odd on the bottom.

Frowning, she flipped the empty drawer over to see what her fingers had encountered. A white envelope was taped to the bottom. She stared at it in confusion as her heart stepped up its rhythm.

What was it? Had another guest at one time or another taped it there? Or had Sheik Amir wanted to hide something before he'd left the room for the night? There was only one way to tell.

She wasn't sure why but her fingers trembled slightly as she pulled the envelope from the drawer. It wasn't sealed. She pulled out the papers folded inside and opened them.

Her heart banged against her chest and a gasp escaped her as she saw the words printed on the first page.

DEATH WILL COME BEFORE YOU SEE SUCCESS WITH THE COIN COALITION.

She quickly scanned the next note.

BETRAYERS ALL OF YOU AND THE PRICE OF BETRAYAL IS DEATH.

There were a total of five and they were all threats to the visiting royals.

There was no question that the envelope had been placed there by Sheik Amir Khalid. COIN was the name of the partnership of the four Mediterranean nations led by the men who had arrived to make their trade agreements with the United States.

Had the person who had written the notes managed to achieve the goal of killing the sheik? And it was obvious from the notes that he hadn't been the only target. All members of COIN had been threatened.

She needed to take the notes to Jake Wolf, the sheriff of Wind River County. He'd know what to do with them and maybe could glean some clues from the content that would point to the person behind the threats.

Her fingers still shook as she carefully put the

notes back into the envelope and then shoved it into her skirt pocket. She bent down to put the drawer back into place and then stood with a deep sigh.

"Excuse me."

She squealed in surprise and whirled around at the sound of the deep male voice coming from behind her. Her heart tap-danced in her chest at the sight of Prince Antoine Cavanaugh.

She wasn't sure if her heart beat even faster because the envelope suddenly burned like fire in her pocket or if it was because the prince was the hottest-looking man she'd ever seen in her entire life.

"I was passing Amir's room and thought I heard somebody inside. I decided to come in and investigate." His pale blue eyes gazed around the room and then narrowed slightly as he looked back at her.

She felt a flush working up from the pit of her stomach to warm her face. From the moment she'd seen him, with his neatly cut light brown hair and those light blue eyes against his delicious dark olive skin, she'd felt a ridiculous teenage flutter in the pit of her stomach.

His white long-sleeved dress shirt fit perfectly across his broad shoulders and the black slacks he wore emphasized his slim hips. Even from this distance she could smell him, a wonderful blend of exotic spicy cologne that could dizzy her brain if she allowed it.

She suddenly realized she was staring at him and had yet to find her tongue to respond.

"Prince Antoine, I'm Beth Taylor, head of housekeeping," she began.

He nodded. "Yes, I know who you are, Ms. Taylor. I see you're packing up Amir's things. Has there been word about him that I haven't heard?"

"No, nothing like that."

"Then I don't suppose you found anything that might provide a clue as to what happened to him?"

The envelope in her skirt seemed to burn hotter. "No," she said quickly. "No, I didn't find anything like that. I'm just packing his things so we can move them to storage, but I didn't find anything. Unfortunately we can't hold this room forever. We have other guests to think about."

His eyes narrowed slightly. "When you finish in here would you mind coming to my room? I have something I'd like to discuss with you." Those blue eyes of his seemed to pierce right through her and her first instinct was to tell him she had other things to do. But she valued her job and the last person she wanted to upset was one of the visiting royals. She could just imagine having to tell her boss that she blew off Prince Antoine because he made her more than a little bit weak in the knees.

"Of course," she replied briskly. "It should only take me a few more minutes to finish up in here."

"Then I'll expect you in a few minutes." He gave her a curt nod and then turned on his heels and left the room.

Beth drew a deep breath, realizing that while he'd been standing there she'd scarcely breathed. The man wasn't just a royal prince, he was royal sin walking.

She hadn't missed the way other women in the hotel followed his movements with hungry gazes whenever he and his security team made an appearance. Antoine and his twin brother, Sebastian, had definitely been a special form of eye candy for the other guests.

Sebastian had left a week ago to return to the country of Barajas where he and Antoine were co-rulers, but Antoine had remained here.

As she continued checking the room for anything else that belonged to Amir, she tried to calm her frazzled nerves. Prince Antoine probably wanted to talk to her about some housekeeping service that he thought wasn't up to par, or maybe he needed something that wasn't normally provided.

There was absolutely no reason to believe that he wanted to talk to her about what she'd found. He couldn't have known that she'd found anything and there was no way she was turning those notes over to anyone but Jake Wolf.

Still, as she walked through the suite one last time, she couldn't help the nervous tension that coiled in her stomach as she thought about facing Prince Antoine again.

"YOUR HIGHNESS, YOU WORRIED ME." Michael Napolis, the head of Antoine's security team, met him at the door as Antoine returned to his suite. Michael's bulldog features displayed more than a touch of reproach. "One minute you were here and the next minute you were gone."

"Relax, Michael. I just stepped across the hall to speak to a member of hotel housekeeping. You can go to your own room now. I'm in for the rest of the night and will call you if I need you for anything."

"As you wish," Michael replied with a small nod of his big head, but it was obvious he wasn't happy. Antoine suspected that if Michael had his way he'd sleep on the floor next to Antoine's bed to keep him safe. Michael had been a nervous wreck since Amir's disappearance, at least giving the appearance that he was worried sick about Antoine.

Once Michael had left the suite Antoine sank into the large leather chair in front of the fireplace and stared unseeing at the neatly stacked unburned logs.

She'd lied.

Antoine had spent years in his country's military as one of the top interrogators. He'd been trained to find lies and break liars to get at the truth. The national security of Barajas had often depended on the information Antoine got from a particular prisoner.

There was no question in his mind that Beth Taylor had lied to him when he'd asked her if she'd found anything in Amir's room. He hadn't missed the subtle shift of her body weight away from him as she'd answered him, or the fact that she had expressed no real surprise at his question and instead had been far too verbose in her answer.

Bottom line—she'd lied, and Antoine was determined to find out what, exactly, she had found in his missing friend's room.

He looked toward the window where the sun had begun to make its descent. Another night would soon be upon them without answers about Amir. *Where are you, my friend? What has happened to you?*

With each day that passed, Antoine found himself growing more and more paranoid. He was unsure who to trust. Certainly not the local authorities, who had already proven to be untrustworthy. As much as he hated to admit it, he wasn't even sure he could trust his own security. It had only been a little over a week ago that Sheik Efraim Aziz, a fellow member of the coalition, had discovered that his own head of security had tried to kill him.

There were many people who had been unhappy with the COIN coalition's goals in working with the United States, many people who would love it if the COIN members simply disappeared.

Until a week ago he'd had his twin brother, the only person in the world he truly trusted, beside him, but Sebastian had gone back home where he belonged. He'd always been the stronger of the two when it came to the leadership of their small country. Barajas needed Sebastian and both the country and his brother would be fine without Antoine.

He glanced toward the door, surprised at the wing of anticipation that swept through him as he thought of Beth Taylor.

He'd noticed her the first day of his arrival. She'd been one of the hotel staff who had greeted him when they'd checked in. In that first moment he'd been struck by the soft curls of her shoulder-length blond hair, the bright green of her eyes and the lush fullness of her lips.

In the last three weeks of his stay here he'd seen her often, her long shapely legs moving her gracefully across the hotel lobby or down a hallway.

But, other than enjoying the sight of her, he'd had no other interaction with her.

Now he wondered how easy she'd be to break. He'd definitely faced more daunting adversaries and yet had always managed to get what he wanted out of them.

As a soft knock sounded at the door, he rose from his chair, the sense of anticipation growing stronger. He checked through the security peephole and then opened the door.

"Thank you for coming," he said. She gave a curt nod but made no move to step over the threshold and into the room. "Please, come in." There was no way he intended to have this conversation standing in the doorway.

She walked past him and he caught the scent of her, a soft floral that reminded him of a field of wildflowers. It was viscerally appealing and he was vaguely surprised by his immediate response. He pointed her to the sofa. "Sit," he said.

He hadn't realized it sounded like a command until she jumped and quickly sank down on the very edge of the rich burgundy sofa. "Would you like something refreshing to drink?"

"No, thank you. I still have a lot of work to finish up before I can go home for the day."

He sat on the opposite end of the sofa and noticed that not only did she tense slightly, but her gaze surreptitiously swept over him before focusing quickly on her hands folded in her lap.

Interesting, he thought as he read her nonverbal clues. It was possible she was attracted to him. Good, he could use that bit of information in trying to get the truth from her.

"Do you have family waiting for you to get home?" he asked.

She shook her head, her blond curls looking achingly soft and touchable in the waning golden light that danced in through the window. "No, there's nobody waiting for me, but I like to get home before night falls." She gave an uncomfortable laugh. "Although that rarely happens."

"Especially now," he replied smoothly. He hadn't missed the slight wistfulness in her voice when she'd told him there was nobody waiting for her at home. "I'm sure our presence here has only increased the workload for the housekeeping staff, for you."

"Not really," she countered. "Our high standard of service goes out to each and every guest, whether they are a prince or an accountant."

There was a ring of pride in her voice. He liked that. His grandfather had always told him that it didn't matter what you did, as long as you did it well.

Assessing what he knew so far, he recognized that she was a beautiful woman who was probably lonely and had embraced her work to fill the voids in her life. It was information he would use to determine the best way to get her to confide in him.

"It's been a difficult couple of weeks," he said and saw the flash of sympathy that crossed her pretty features. "Amir was a good friend of mine. With what happened, I don't know who to trust anymore."

"We're all sick about how things have gone," she replied. She shifted positions, turning her knees in his direction. "I hope you're being very careful."

"It's difficult to be careful when you don't know in what form danger might come. I find myself feeling very isolated." He flashed her the smile that had charmed more than one woman in his lifetime. "I'm sorry to take up your time, I was just feeling a bit lonely and then I saw you and needed a moment of company."

Her cheeks blossomed with color and one of her hands shifted from her lap to touch the pocket in her skirt. His heart stepped up its beating. Whatever she'd found in Amir's room was now in her pocket. He was sure of it. Now all he had to do was get her to share it with him.

"I'm sure you know my brother returned to our country," he continued.

"Yes, it must have been difficult for you to remain behind."

He nodded. "But I don't intend to return until I know what happened to Amir. He was like a brother to me. Do you have brothers or sisters, Ms. Taylor?"

"No, I'm an only child." Now it was not only her knees that faced him, but her entire upper body, letting him know she was open to him, perhaps just a little bit vulnerable.

With cool calculation, he leaned toward her, nearly closing the distance between them. He lightly touched her shoulder. "I can't rest. I can't sleep until we find out something about Amir. The local officials have been little help with their issues of corruption. I'm desperate to find something, anything that might give me a clue as to what happened and who is to blame."

Once again her hand touched her pocket and he saw an uncertainty in the depths of her beautiful eyes. His heart seemed to stop beating as he waited for her reply.

"I did find something in Amir's room," she finally said. For a moment she remained perfectly still and Antoine was struck by a quicksilver desire to stroke a hand across the smooth skin of her sculpted cheek, taste the full lower lip she was now nibbling in obvious indecision. She reached into her pocket and pulled out an envelope, but didn't immediately offer it to Antoine.

"I found it taped on the bottom of a drawer in the bedroom. I was going to turn it over to Sheriff Wolf," she said. "But I guess it won't hurt if you look at it first." Her slender hand trembled slightly as she held out the envelope.

He took it, his heart once again rapping an unsteady beat as he opened it and withdrew the pieces of paper. He read the notes, electrified by the contents. "You read these?" he asked.

She nodded, her eyes wider than they had been minutes before. "They're terrible."

There was now no question in his mind that the limo explosion had been meant to kill all of them, that it had been mere circumstance, a matter of sheer fate, that had placed Amir in that limo alone at the time of the bomb blast.

He placed the notes back in the envelope, but didn't return it to Beth. "Ms. Taylor, I have a favor to ask you. Please let me keep these and see what I can learn from them before you take them to Sheriff Wolf. I meant it when I told you I don't know who to trust."

She frowned thoughtfully. "What are you going to do?" she asked.

"A little investigating on my own, see if I can find out who is dirty and who isn't before I give these notes to anyone else."

Her frown deepened, the gesture doing nothing to detract from her beauty. "How are you going to be able to do that? You don't know any of the locals." She didn't wait for his response but instead continued, "You're going to need my help. I was born and raised here. I know the people who live here, and I also know the people who don't belong. The only way I'll give you the time you've asked for before going to Jake Wolf is if you let me help you."

She'd surprised him. The last thing he'd expected was her offer to partner up with him. His initial response was a resounding no, but there was no question that she could be useful.

"Okay, I accept your offer to help, but only on one condition—that if things get dangerous for you, then you step back."

"Agreed," she replied.

Antoine stuck out his hand and as they solemnly shook, he was aware of the softness of her skin against his, the delicate bones of her hands. A new flicker of something evocative and exciting swept through him. It had nothing to do with the fact that she might possibly be helpful to him in finding out who was behind the threats. Rather it was a flame of physical attraction.

"I've got to get back to work," she said as she quickly pulled her hand from his and stood.

"How much longer will you be?" he asked as they walked to the door.

She paused and looked at her watch. "Maybe another hour or so, why?"

"I'd like to make copies of these notes and then take them to somebody discreet and see if prints besides ours can be pulled from them, but I'm not sure where to go to get this done."

"Jane Cameron," she replied without hesitation.

He knew Jane Cameron was the forensic scientist who had been involved in processing the scene of the limo bombing. He also knew that she and Stefan Lutece, Prince of Kyros, had become involved in a romantic relationship. "And you trust Jane?"

"Absolutely," she replied. "Why don't I take the notes and make the copies in my office, then come back here when I'm finished for the day and we can go see Jane."

"Perfect," he replied. He gave her the envelope and then reached out to take her other hand in his. "I can't thank you enough for giving me some time to investigate this."

She squeezed his hand slightly and then pulled it away from him. "I just hope this isn't a mistake. I'll see you in about an hour." She flew through the door as if the hounds of hell were nipping at her heels.

Antoine closed the door behind her and tried

to ignore the scent of her that lingered in the air. He was attracted to her like he hadn't been to a woman in a very long time.

There was something soft, something inviting about her that called to him. But, it was an attraction he had no desire to explore.

Antoine never allowed himself to get close to a woman. He could enjoy their company and have sex with them, but his heart never got involved.

He would do anything to find out who was behind the threats made on himself and the others. He would do anything to find out who had been behind the attack on Amir. If that meant using the pretty housekeeper, it wouldn't be the worst thing he'd ever done in his life.

Chapter Two

She had to be crazy.

Somehow between the time she'd left Amir's suite and the time she'd left Antoine's, she'd lost her ever-loving mind. The minute Beth reached her private office she sank down at her desk and shook her head, wondering what on earth she'd been thinking when she'd given Antoine that envelope, when she'd offered to help him.

She should have kept her mouth shut and taken the notes to Jake like she'd intended. The problem was she hadn't been thinking. Instead, she'd been falling into the blue depths of Antoine's eyes, touched by the loneliness and the feeling of isolation he hadn't tried to hide.

She'd offered her help because she'd thought he needed it, which was a ridiculous thing for her to think. He was a prince, for God's sake. He had people to take care of his every wish, his every need. The last thing he needed was a simple woman who didn't know a thing about foreign politics and had only a high school education helping him investigate threats against members of royal families.

She checked her email and the voice mail on her phone to make sure there weren't any fires to put out with the housekeeping staff, then moved to the multitask printer to copy the threatening notes in the envelope. With both the originals and the copies back in her pocket she left her office to do a walk-through of the hotel before heading back to Antoine's suite.

The bulk of her work occurred in the mornings when she coordinated the staff to make sure all the rooms were cleaned and the guests' needs were met. She was not only responsible for the cleaning staff, but also for inventory of housekeeping items needed for the cleaning and maintaining of the guests rooms.

It was her routine in the evenings to walk through the hotel and be accommodating to any guest who might have a problem or simply to be a friendly face to both returning regular guests and new people who had come to enjoy the luxury resort.

She knew how important it was to offer a personal touch to the people who vacationed or came here for work purposes. She liked to think that her work here was at least part of the reason people chose to come back again and again.

When it was finally time to return to Antoine's suite a new tension began to well up in her stomach. The man definitely made her just a little breathless and she didn't like it. She didn't like it at all.

The last man who had left her breathless had not just broken her heart, but had shattered it into a million pieces. She'd never allow herself to be that vulnerable again. And she'd be a complete fool to entertain any feelings for a visiting prince who would soon return to his own life in his own country.

He'd obviously been waiting for her as he answered the door almost before her knock sounded. She stepped into the room and he closed the door behind her. "I made two copies of the notes," she said. "One for you and one for me." She handed him both the original and his copy.

"Why would you want a copy?" he asked curiously.

"In case something happens to yours," she replied and tried to ignore how her heart stuttered at his nearness. At five feet nine inches, Beth was unaccustomed to men towering over her, but Antoine was a good four or five inches taller. He made her feel small and feminine.

"If you'll get your driver, I'll give him directions to the forensic lab where we can find Jane," she said.

"You're going to be my driver," he replied smoothly. "I don't want anyone to know what we're doing, what we've found and that includes my entire security team. We must figure out a way to get me out of the hotel and to your car with nobody seeing me."

Beth stared at him, not only nervous at the idea of being alone with him but also by the fact that she would be responsible for him while he was with her. "But what if something happens? What if you get hurt?"

His sensual lips curved up in a smile that warmed the ice-blue of his eyes. "Unless you're planning on beating or maiming me, I should be just fine."

"But surely you should take somebody from your security team with you," she protested. She'd feel so much better if there was somebody big and burly and fully loaded with an arsenal of weapons.

The blue of his eyes paled to an icy silver and his lips thinned. "No. We go alone." His voice was laced with command and for the first time he looked and sounded like a prince accustomed to getting his way.

She frowned thoughtfully. "Okay, if you go down this hall to the end, there's another corridor, turn right and follow it and you'll see an exit door. If you give me five minutes I can pull up outside the door."

"Perfect, then I'll see you in a few minutes."

As Beth left the suite and headed back to the lobby nervous anxiety pressed tight against her chest. God forbid she had a wreck while driving the Prince of Barajas. Once again she found herself wondering when exactly she'd lost her mind and when she could hope for its return.

When she got into her car she quickly scanned the interior, noting the tear in the passenger seat, the faint layer of dust that covered the dashboard. Not exactly fit for royalty, but the ten-year-old car was paid off and still ran perfectly well. He'd just have to deal with the less-than-royal transportation.

She told herself that one of the reasons she wanted to help him was because this whole ordeal had hammered the hotel with negative publicity. But she suspected the truth of the matter was that she was desperate for something, anything that might fill the vast loneliness in her life, even if it was just for a single night.

She pulled up against the curb by the door she'd told Antoine to exit and watched as he strode toward her. Once again she was struck by his handsomeness and as he flashed a quick smile to her a crazy burst of heat momentarily usurped her nervous anxiety.

"Mission accomplished," he said as he slid into the passenger seat. "Nobody saw my escape."

"Won't somebody worry if you aren't in your room?" she asked as she pulled away from the curb.

"I have my cell phone with me and told my staff that I was retiring for the night and didn't want to be disturbed for any reason. Nobody will even know that I'm missing from my suite," he assured her.

Beth gripped the steering wheel tightly and headed toward the small town of Dumont. The scenery was spectacular with the last gasp of the sun sparking off the distant mountains and painting the landscape in lush shades of deep gold.

Antoine looked out the window and even though he was silent she felt a pulsing energy radiating from him. He turned to look at her, as if he'd felt her surreptitious gaze. "Do you think Jane will help us?"

"If anyone can pull a print from those papers, she can," Beth replied. "But, she's a by-the-book kind of woman. She might insist that the notes be handed over immediately to Sheriff Wolf."

"Then I'll just have to convince her that that's not in our best interest," he replied with an easy confidence.

"She's pretty tough," Beth warned.

"Yes, but I'm pretty charming," he countered.

Beth gave a rueful laugh. "You charmed that envelope right out of my pocket."

He sobered and she felt his gaze, intense and piercing on her. "I had a feeling you'd found something important and it was equally important that I convince you to tell me."

"Do you always get what you want?" she asked lightly.

"It's certainly rare that anyone tells me no."

"I would imagine that being surrounded by yes-men could get a little boring at times."

"Perhaps," he replied and then cast his gaze out the side window once again.

The town of Dumont, Wyoming, was a small, charming place with historic buildings that dated back to the early 1800s. It had been a town filled with good, hard-working people before the royals had arrived. Now the streets were clogged with news vans and strangers.

Beth drove down the main drag and parked in front of the brick courthouse. "Jane's lab and offices are on the second floor," she said as she turned off the engine.

Antoine glanced at his wristwatch. "Won't the offices be closed by now?"

"Security will let her know we're here and it's rare that Jane isn't at work this late in the evening," Beth explained.

Together they got out of the car and she noticed that Antoine did a quick sweep of the area with his narrowed gaze. Apparently he saw nothing to cause him alarm and they walked to the front door of the courthouse where Beth gestured to the security guard inside.

Within minutes they were in the elevator taking them to the second floor and Jane. She met them at the doorway of her office, her hazel eyes widening as she saw Antoine. "Prince Antoine, Beth... what's going on?"

Antoine glanced up and down the hallway and then gestured to her office. "Ms. Cameron, perhaps we could speak to you in private."

"Of course." Jane ushered them into the small office and closed the door behind them.

"I was instructed today to pack up Sheik Amir Khalid's items in his suite to be stored until we know what happened to him or somebody from his family came to claim them. While checking the nightstand drawers I found an envelope taped to the bottom of one," Beth said.

Jane's eyes filled with interest as Antoine held up the envelope but didn't offer to hand it to her. "We'd like to see if you can pull some fingerprints from either the envelope or the notes inside, but before I give this to you I would like you to promise to keep this strictly confidential between the three of us."

Jane frowned and raked a hand through her curly light brown hair. "I can't make that promise without seeing what you have." There was a hint of steel in her voice.

Antoine held her gaze for a long moment and then offered her the envelope. "What I'm hoping is that you can lift some prints and then give us a little time to do some investigating on our own before letting anyone else know about it."

Jane didn't take the envelope from him, but instead opened her office door and gestured them outside. "Bring it into the lab. I don't want to touch it without gloves. As it is I'll need to print both you and Beth so we can discount your prints on everything."

They entered a small lab where Jane grabbed a kit from one of the metal shelves against the wall and then stepped up to a work table and pulled on latex gloves. Only then did she take the envelope from Antoine.

As she read the notes her eyes widened once again and when she finished she stared at first Antoine, then at Beth.

"These need to go to Jake," she said.

"Eventually I'll hand them over to him," Antoine replied. "But let's be serious here. The local law officials haven't exactly proven themselves to be good, upstanding people. Even your own boss was proven to be untrustworthy."

Jane's face flushed and she looked down at the notes she'd spread out on the table. Amos

Andrews, Jane's boss, had not only tried to screw up her investigation into the bombing of the limo, he'd also tried to kill Jane. When he'd been arrested he'd made it clear that he was just a bit player in a larger conspiracy against the visiting royals, hired by somebody he refused to name.

"So, what exactly is it you want from me?" she asked with a weary sigh.

"Just a little time," Antoine replied.

"How much time?" she asked.

"Seventy-two hours," he replied after a moment of hesitation.

Jane said nothing. She opened the kit and withdrew several brushes and powder compounds in small bottles. As she began her work, Beth couldn't help but gaze at Antoine again and again.

He stood rigid and once again she felt the energy wafting from him. And why wouldn't he be tense? The stakes couldn't be higher. Somebody wanted him and the other participants in the COIN coalition dead.

They didn't know at this time if the people who were behind the conspiracy had already achieved the goal of killing one of them—Amir.

Antoine slid a glance at her and offered her a small smile that shot a hint of warmth in his cool blue eyes. Beth had always believed the term bedroom eyes meant dark and smoky and slightly mysterious, but she now recognized that bedroom eyes could be the cool blue of a mountain lake.

"I hope you find a useable fingerprint," he said, his focus back on Jane. "When I know the identity of the person who wrote those notes, I will make certain he's never a threat to anyone again."

His tone was light and easy, but with a chilling undertone. Yes, he might make a delicious lover, but she had a feeling he'd make an even more formidable enemy.

IT WAS ALMOST NINE when they finally left the lab after being printed by Jane. She'd managed to pull another print that didn't belong to either him or Beth and hoped that whoever had left it behind was in the Automated Fingerprint Identification System. If they were lucky she would have a name for them sometime the next day.

"I'm too wound up to go back to the suite and sleep." He turned to look at the woman driving the car. He'd been acutely aware of Beth even as he'd tried to focus on what Jane had been doing.

He knew that to be successful in her position she had to be a strong taskmaster. The resort was known for impeccable guest services and housekeeping. And yet he sensed a softness in Beth that drew the darkness that resided inside him.

And there was darkness.

She cast him a quick glance and then returned

her gaze to the road. "I'm a little wired myself," she admitted.

"Perhaps we could go back to your place, have a cup of coffee and talk about things."

He could tell he'd shocked her. "Prince Antoine, my home is small and simple. It's not exactly fit for a prince," she replied.

"A comfortable chair, some hot coffee and a little company is all I'd like. And please, call me Antoine."

"Then you can call me Beth. Coffee sounds good and then I'll be glad to take you back to the resort. My place is only ten minutes from there."

"Then it's settled, coffee at your house." He leaned back against the seat and stared out the side window into the darkness. *You're a cliché,* he thought ruefully. He was a prince who was afraid to trust anyone, with an aching depth of loneliness inside him and the mantle of power weighing heavily, definitely a cliché.

For the past three weeks Antoine had done nothing but worry and wonder about the attack, about what danger might come from what unexpected source.

He'd had long dialogues with the other men in the COIN coalition. Prince Stefan Lutece, Sheik Efraim Aziz, Sheik Amir Khalid and Antoine and his brother had all come here in the hopes of trade agreements with the United States that would benefit their small countries and instead had found nothing but treachery, danger and betrayal.

At the moment Antoine was sick of it all. The resort had become a place of intense stress, of people yammering at him and palpable tension that filled the air the moment he stepped out of his rooms. He was looking forward to a little more time away from the luxurious surroundings.

Beth turned off the road they had been traveling and onto a narrower road with deep embankments and thick trees on either side. "You drive this every night after dark?" he asked.

"It's the only way for me to get home. It's not too bad as long as you make sure you stay on the road."

A small laugh escaped him. "That would be an understatement. I'm sure it gets quite dangerous in the winter."

"I call this car my little engine that could." She tapped the steering wheel with a long slender finger. "Although I have to admit more than once in the winters somebody from the hotel has had to come to get me because I don't have four-wheel drive."

He could tell she was beginning to relax with each minute they spent together. He wanted that. For just a little while he wanted to be treated like an ordinary man and not like a prince.

"This feels very isolated," he said as the trees on either side of the road seemed to crawl closer.

"It is. It's a pretty big spread but most of it hasn't been cleared or anything. My grandfather bought the land years ago, long before there was a resort. My father and mother chose to make it their home after my grandparents died and I've always lived here. I like the isolation, the beautiful nature that surrounds me when I step outside my front or back door. Is your country beautiful?"

"White beaches, blue seas, lush flowers…yes, Barajas is very beautiful, but I find Wyoming to be as beautiful, just different."

She turned off the road and onto a driveway that led to a small cottage. A light shone from the front porch, a welcome beacon in the darkness that had fallen. Colorful flowers spilled from boxes under the windows. It looked like something from a fairy tale, an enchanted cottage in the middle of the wilderness.

"It's not much," she said with a touch of defensiveness. "But it's all mine and I love it here." This time her words held an obvious sense of pride.

The sense of welcome that the porch light had emitted continued on into the house. As Antoine stepped inside the living room the earthy burnt orange and browns of the décor instantly put him at rest.

"Please, have a seat." She gestured him toward

the overstuffed sofa. "I'm just going to get out of my uniform. I'll be right back to start the coffee."

She disappeared down the hallway and Antoine sank into the comfortable couch cushion and gazed around the room. Like subtle facial features that could give away internal emotions and weaknesses, he knew a room could speak volumes about the person who lived in it.

A bookcase stood against one wall, one of the shelves filled with framed photos of Beth with an older woman who appeared to be her mother. The television was small, as if watching it wasn't a top priority. A paperback lay on the end of the coffee table, the couple's clinch on the cover letting him know it was a romance novel. A wind chime tinkled a lovely melody from someplace outside the windows.

A lonely romantic who loved nature, he thought. There was no sign of a man's presence anywhere in the room. An old record player sat next to a stack of ancient LPs and it was easy for him to imagine her curled on the sofa with a book in hand while old, romantic music filled the house.

He looked up as she returned to the room, clad in a pair of jeans that looked slightly worn and hugged her long slender legs to perfection. Her mint-green T-shirt fit a little big but not so much that he didn't notice the press of her full breasts against the material.

He suddenly wished he was in a pair of jeans, on the back of a horse with her, her arms wrapped tightly around him as they rode carefree across a pasture. It was a vision that brought the first burst of pleasure he'd felt since arriving in Wyoming.

"Let's go into the kitchen and I'll make the coffee," she said.

He followed after her, unable to avoid noticing the way her jeans cupped her shapely buttocks. Why was there no man in her life? A woman like her should have a man to thrill her with his love-making and then hold her tight through the darkness of the night.

The kitchen was a surprise. Large and airy, with a breakfast nook that was surrounded on three sides by floor-to-ceiling windows, it was obviously the heart of the house. Gourmet copper-bottomed pans hung from a rack above the stove and a variety of cooking-aid machines lined the counters.

"You like to cook." He stated the obvious.

She flashed him a bright smile that warmed him in places he hadn't realized were cold. "I love to cook. It's my secret passion." She pointed him to the round oak table in the nook. "Have a seat. The coffee will be ready in just a minute and I have some leftover red velvet cake to go with it."

He sat and enjoyed the view of her bustling to get the coffee brewing. It had been far too long since he'd enjoyed the pleasure of a woman. For weeks before the trip to the resort there had been meeting after meeting to decide what to offer and what they needed from the trade agreements they intended to make. There had been almost no time for any kind of a social life.

"Hopefully Jane will have something for you tomorrow," she said as she placed a creamer and sugar bowl on the table. Then went back to the counter and returned with a platter holding a cake that looked as if it had just come out of a bakery.

"Hopefully," he replied. "But I don't want to talk about any of that tonight. Tonight I want to talk about ordinary things, things that don't set off a burn of anger in my belly. I noticed that you have a lot of pictures of you and your mother in the living room."

"Yes. My dad died when I was six and when I was thirteen my mom developed a severe heart condition. Unfortunately she passed away three years ago."

"My parents died when I was young." A long-remembered grief touched Antoine's heart. He thought about the horrific night of his parents' deaths often, recognized and never forgot the lesson he'd learned that night.

"I'm so sorry." She poured the coffee and carried the cups to the table, then sank down in the chair opposite his. "Was it some kind of an accident?"

"Actually, they were murdered." She gasped and he continued, "My father was initially my mother's bodyguard. He was an American, an ex-mercenary and they fell in love and married. Unfortunately my father had made many enemies in his past and that night those enemies found him and my mother."

"So, who raised you and your brother?"

"My mother's father, King Omar Zubira." A whisper of a smile curved his lips as he thought of the stern but loving man who had raised them. "He didn't approve of my mother's marriage and never really accepted my father, but he was a loving man to me and Sebastian, although I must admit we sometimes gave him a hard time."

"The twin thing?"

He grinned. "But, of course. Being an identical twin can be quite amusing and Sebastian and I definitely used it to our advantage whenever possible. After grandfather died I was grateful to have Sebastian by my side to share the responsibility of ruling Barajas."

"It must be a huge responsibility, to run a nation," she said as she sliced the cake and shoved a generous piece toward him.

"Probably no bigger than running the housekeeping staff at a luxury resort," he replied. "To be truthful Sebastian carries much of the weight. He's a good man with a knack for politics and he'd do fine without me. But enough about me. What I really want to know is why you don't have a man in your life. Surely you meet men during the course of your work."

He picked up his fork and took a bite of the cake and noticed that her features tightened slightly and a whisper of hurt filled her eyes. It was there only a moment and then gone, but it let him know that at some time in the not so distant past a man had hurt her…hurt her badly.

"I don't date hotel guests and besides, I stay busy with my work and I'm not particularly interested in a relationship right now."

It was a lie, he could see the deception in her features. "That's a shame, because you have lips meant for kissing."

Her cheeks flushed with a becoming color. "And you're rather impertinent for a prince."

He grinned, enchanted by her. "The last woman who called me impertinent was my mother. I was seven at the time. Now, tell me about your mother."

As Beth related moments from her past with her mother, Antoine recognized that Beth was not only beautiful, but loyal to those she loved.

She told him about having to forgo college to help support herself and her mother, but there was no complaint in her voice, merely a stating of facts.

He liked that about her. He had no patience for whiners. He and Sebastian hadn't been allowed to whine after the murder of his parents.

"So, what did you do before you became one of the rulers of Barajas?" she asked.

"I was a military man." He raised his coffee cup to take a drink, hoping a sip of coffee would wash away the sour taste that always sprang to his mouth when he thought of the things he'd done for the sake of his country.

"And you? When you were young did you dream of being a ballerina? Or perhaps a princess?" he asked.

She laughed. It was a pleasant sound that wrapped around his heart and momentarily held him captive. "Not at all. I have two left feet and I always wanted to raise horses so I dreamed of wearing chaps and a vest rather than a princess's tiara."

He had a sudden vision of her naked except for her long legs encased in a pair of leather chaps and her full breasts spilling out of a tiny vest. Hot blood welled in the pit of his stomach, spreading warmth directly to his groin.

He shifted uncomfortably against the wooden chair and reminded himself that he was here with her because he wanted to use her knowledge of the locals to further his investigation, not because he wanted to take her to bed and teach her everything he knew about sexual pleasure.

"You know horses?" he asked.

"I started riding at the resort stables when I was little and worked the stables until I got the job in housekeeping," she explained.

"You have enough land to raise horses. Why haven't you already done it?"

"It took me until six months ago to pay off the last of the medical bills that my mother had accrued. I'm hoping to realize my horse dream in about five years. It's almost midnight," she said with a glance at the clock on the wall. "I should get you back to the resort. I have to be back at work around six-thirty in the morning."

He leaned back in the chair and smiled. "I've already made up my mind. I'll stay here with you for the night."

Chapter Three

Beth stared at him in horror. The idea of this man, this prince, sleeping beneath her roof horrified her. As it was, the whole afternoon and evening had taken on the surreal aspect of some kind of weird dream.

"I don't want you traveling back and forth from the resort this late at night alone," he said. "The road that leads here is too narrow, too dangerous to drive in the darkness."

A nerve throbbed in the side of her neck, a nerve that always acted up when she felt anxious. "But the spare bedroom doesn't even have a bed in it. I've been using it as a home office."

"The sofa looked nice and comfortable. All I need is a pillow and blanket and I'll be fine. I'll call Sheik Efraim and let him know I'm with you in case a problem arises." He pushed back his chair and stood as if the matter had been decided.

It was a half an hour later when Beth closed the door to her bedroom and sat on the edge of her bed. What a night. She still couldn't believe that a prince was now on her sofa sleeping beneath one of the patchwork quilts her mother had made years ago.

She changed into her nightshirt and went into the adjoining bathroom to wash her face before going to bed. Initially when the royals had first arrived at the hotel all she'd been focused on was the extra work their presence might make for her staff. She hadn't really thought about them as being men, just ordinary men with the weight of power on their shoulders.

And now she couldn't stop thinking about Antoine being a man—a very hot, take-your-breath-away kind of man. But even though he looked at her with a bit of hunger in his eyes, she wasn't about to fall prey to ridiculous fantasies about life with Antoine or any other man.

She certainly wasn't about to become an American dalliance for him. She could just see the headlines—The Prince and the Chambermaid. She couldn't help the small giggle that escaped her at the very idea.

Her feet were firmly planted in reality, had been since she'd been young. With her mother's illness there had been little time for fantasies.

There had only been one time when she'd allowed herself to fall into a romantic fantasy and the result had been an ugly mess.

There was no way she intended to fall into Antoine's bedroom eyes. He was here only until he solved the mystery of his friend Amir's disappearance from the bomb site. Once he'd accomplished his goals here he'd be gone.

She got into bed and as always fought against a well of loneliness that had been with her for the past year. She was twenty-nine years old, longed for love and a family, but the next time around she intended to be smart, to be wary. She'd make sure the man she gave her heart to deserved the gift.

She'd expected to have trouble falling asleep, but the moment her head touched the pillow sleep claimed her. She was instantly plunged into an erotic dream.

She was naked and clinging to Antoine's broad dark shoulders as his mouth made love to hers. His kiss held a mastery she'd never experienced, a silent command that she respond with every fiber of her being. And she did. It was impossible not to.

His strong hands stroked up the length of her bare back and then around to cup her breasts. Sweet sensations cascaded through her at his touch. She was on fire with her need for him. It didn't matter that he would be gone before she knew it, she only knew that she wanted what he offered, longed to stay in his arms.

A moan filled her head, not her own but

rather his and not from her dream and not one of pleasure.

A louder, more tortured moan pulled her from her dream. Her eyes snapped open and for a moment she couldn't discern dream from reality.

Her heart pounded with a quickened rhythm as she sat up and shoved strands of hair away from her face. A glance at the illuminated clock next to her bed told her it was just after two.

The noise came again, this time louder, deeper and definitely not from her dream, but rather coming from someplace outside her bedroom door.

The prince!

Was he in trouble? Had somebody found out he was here and was now trying to strangle him or hurt him in some way? Oh, God, she knew having him here had all been a mistake!

She jumped out of bed and grabbed a flower vase from the top of the dresser, the only thing she could think of that might be used as a weapon, and then ran into the living room.

In the spill of the moonlight through the windows she instantly saw that there was no danger, that Antoine was not being strangled or beaten by an intruder. Rather he was obviously in the throes of a terrible nightmare.

She set the vase down at her feet and then crept closer to the sofa, trying not to notice how his powerful bare chest gleamed in the moonlight as he tossed and turned and emitted deep, mournful groans.

"Antoine," she whispered softly.

He groaned again, the intensity of it filling Beth with immense empathy. What sort of dreams could evoke the sounds of such pain, such an emotional outburst while sleeping?

She called his name again, this time louder, but it wasn't enough to pull him from his tortured sleep.

She stepped even closer to the sofa and lightly touched his shoulder—and found herself shoved against the wall, Antoine's hands wrapped around her neck as his eyes blazed with an unfocused fire.

He'd moved off the sofa in the blink of an eye. She would have screamed, but she couldn't. It had all happened so fast. Shock and the pressure of his hands against her throat kept her mute. For just an instant she wondered if he was going to kill her before he came fully awake.

Reaching up, she managed to touch his cheek and in that instant saw the flames in his eyes douse as a searing focus took their place.

He released a ragged gasp and dropped his hands to his sides. "Beth. Beth, I'm so sorry." He pulled her off the wall and wrapped her in his arms. His bare skin was warm and she burrowed into him as the shock of the moment slowly faded away.

"I might have killed you," he breathed into her hair as he tightened his arms around her.

She closed her eyes, delighting in the moment of being in his embrace. This wasn't a man who had gone soft with good living. He was all hard, lean muscle against her. "You should come with a warning label—dangerous when awakened," she murmured against his chest.

His hands smoothed down her back. "Why did you awaken me?"

She raised her head to look up at him. "You were moaning as if you were in terrible pain. It was obvious you were having a bad dream. I…I just wanted to get you out of your nightmare."

"It *was* a very bad dream." He reached up his hands and cupped her face. "Thank you for waking me and I'm sorry if I hurt you."

Before she could guess his next move, he'd made it, taking her mouth with his in a kiss that ripped her breath right out of her chest.

His lips plied hers with heat and even though in the back of her head she knew she should step away, stop the madness, she didn't. Instead she opened her mouth to him, allowing him to deepen the kiss by delving his tongue to battle with hers.

The fevered heat of his soft lips and the feathery touch of his tongue shot a well of want through Beth. His hands tangled in her hair as he pressed so close to her she could feel that he was aroused.

Instantly she knew this was a bad place to be—the middle of the night, a handsome prince holding her tight and a heart she didn't want broken again.

She stopped the kiss and moved out of his arms. "That probably wasn't a good idea." She was surprised by how breathless she sounded. "Hopefully you'll sleep okay now for the rest of the night," she said, her gaze not meeting his. "And now I'll just say good-night again."

She nearly ran back to the bedroom, grateful that he didn't try to halt her escape. Sinking down on the edge of her bed she tried to forget the taste of him, the feel of his warm body against her own.

He was sweet temptation, but she couldn't allow herself to get caught up in any kind of an intimate relationship with him. That was heartache just waiting to happen and she'd already been there, done that.

As she got back into bed she allowed her thoughts to go back in time, back to when she'd believed Mark Ferrer was the man who was going to be her happily-ever-after, when she'd believed that she was loved as deeply as she'd thought she had loved.

She'd learned a very important lesson from Mark—that men could take you into their arms, look you right in the eyes and lie to get what they wanted.

Beth didn't know how to have sex without meaning. She simply wasn't built that way. She wasn't capable of physical release without emotional connection.

Antoine's kiss had tasted of fevered passion, but she knew that's all he had to offer and that would never be enough for her. She finally fell asleep with the firm commitment to keep her distance from Antoine.

The next morning when she left her bedroom dressed in her uniform of the pencil-thin black skirt and the white blouse with a gold WRR on the breast pocket, Antoine was already up and dressed as well.

"Good morning," she said, hoping he didn't mention the kiss, praying for no awkward moments.

"Good morning to you," he replied. "I hope you don't mind that I took the liberty of using the shampoo in the bathroom when I showered."

"Not at all," she replied. "I don't usually cook breakfast, but if you want something before we leave I'd be glad to whip something up."

"That's not necessary. I can order something from room service when I get back to the hotel."

He seemed distant, antsy to leave, which was fine with her. Within minutes they were back at the hotel where she ushered him in through the employees' entrance so he wouldn't have to walk through the lobby.

"If Jane calls I can count on you to take me back to her?" he asked before they parted ways.

There was a part of her that wanted to back away from the whole thing, that needed to back away from him. The kiss they'd shared the night before had shaken her more than she wanted to admit.

But, there was a soft plea in his eyes and she realized she was probably the only person he trusted at the moment and it was impossible for her to tell him no.

"Just let me know if you hear anything and we'll figure something out," she replied. She turned to head toward her office but paused as he softly called her name. She turned back to face him.

His eyes glittered with a flirting light that instantly created a pool of warmth inside her. "I look forward to kissing you again, Beth."

"Definitely impertinent," she replied and then turned on her heels and quickly walked away to the sound of his amused laughter.

Once she was in her office the routine of the day quickly took over and the morning flew by. She checked the schedule and the time cards to make sure all her staff had arrived and by ten o'clock had left her office to do room spot checks.

She gave soft reprimands when necessary and praise when earned. She knew her staff respected her, but they also liked her as well.

Maybe Jane won't find anything, she thought at noon when she hadn't heard from Antoine. Maybe whoever had left that print on the papers wasn't in the AFIS system. Maybe last night was the end of their little partnership.

That would be good, she told herself as she returned to her office for a bite of lunch. He was far too charming, far too attractive and that kiss had dizzied her head and momentarily swept reason away. She was definitely better off keeping her distance from him.

Still, it was almost impossible for her to get him out of her mind. More than once she found herself staring unseeing out her window as her mind replayed the vision of his muscled bare chest in the moonlight. Her lips wouldn't easily forget the taste of his mouth against them. As crazy as it seemed, her body felt branded by the intimate contact with his.

It was just after two when her cell phone rang and Antoine's deep voice filled the line. "Jane called. She has a name. I'll be waiting for you by the back door."

He gave her no chance to reply, but instead immediately hung up.

As Antoine waited for Beth he was filled with tense energy. He hadn't asked Jane to give him the name over the phone, didn't trust that somebody else might be listening in. He couldn't be sure if her phones at her lab were bugged.

He'd spoken briefly with his brother that morning. Sebastian had sounded happier than Antoine had ever heard him and he knew it was because his brother had found love with a woman he'd helped protect against her ex-husband. She was the same woman who had witnessed Amir crawling out of the wreckage of the limo.

Jessica Peters had been reluctant to come forward since she and her little girl, Samantha, were in hiding from her ex-husband, a Russian by the name of Evgany Surinka. Eventually she'd come forward and her ex had found her. Sebastian had been forced to kill him and in the whole process he and Jessica had found love.

Love.

It was something Antoine would never allow for himself and he wasn't sure how Sebastian had managed to forget that enemies sometimes hurt the innocent people in one's life.

Antoine had made many enemies in his position as top interrogator for the military, enemies who would love to get to him by killing anyone he loved.

Antoine was determined not to make the same

mistakes his father had made. He would never allow anyone to get close enough to him to be used as a target for revenge. He would never forget that his father had been unable to protect his mother from the men who had been seeking revenge.

That's what Antoine had been dreaming about the night before, when Beth had awakened him. In his nightmare he and Sebastian had been children and had been hiding as angry men had killed his parents.

His thoughts slid from his dream to that moment when he'd held Beth in his arms. She'd been soft and warm against him, the thin material of her nightshirt barely a barrier between them. It had been a mistake to kiss her and it was a mistake he wouldn't mind repeating again and again.

Spending time with Jessica Peters's four-year-old daughter, Samantha, had shot a surprising desire inside Antoine, a desire for a woman to love and children to raise and a life much different than the one he'd led.

But, the choices he'd made for his country would forever keep him alone and with a loneliness deep in his soul that would never be assuaged.

As Beth's car pulled up against the curb he left the hotel and hurried toward her passenger door. He slid into the seat and instantly was enveloped by her floral scent.

"I hope I don't get you into trouble, taking you away from your work," he said.

She pulled away from the curb. "It's not a problem. The hotel manager is covering for me. I told him I needed to take some personal time off and since I rarely take any time off at all it was fine."

He nodded. "Good. The last thing I'd want would be to mess up your job, your life, before I return to Barajas." It was a reminder to himself not to get in too deep with her, not to think anymore about how sweet, how hot her kiss was and how very much he'd wanted to lose himself in her.

"I'm not about to let that happen," she replied firmly.

"You look tired."

"I am tired," she admitted. "I had trouble sleeping after I got back to bed." Her cheeks colored with just a hint of pink.

The kiss they'd shared had certainly made it difficult for him to go back to sleep. It had felt like it had taken hours for his body temperature to return to normal. "But your day has gone well so far?"

"A normal day. What about you?"

He tried to relax against the seat. "I spoke to my brother and also to Sheik Efraim."

"Did you tell them what we found?"

"No. I'm keeping this information to myself for

the time being and I would like to remind you to do the same."

She nodded. "The seventy-two hours Jane gave you is quickly ticking off," she reminded him.

"With a name from Jane I can hopefully find out what I need to help find Amir or at least know who might be behind those notes and the attacks." He turned to look at her. "You said you know the locals. What I'd like you to do for me is to make a list of anyone who has recently come to town, perhaps gotten a job at the hotel."

"We do pretty thorough background checks on all of our employees."

Antoine released a dry laugh. "Backgrounds can be hidden or made to look exemplary."

"I'll be glad to make you a list of the new hires," she replied as she pulled into the parking space in front of the courthouse. "And I'll make some subtle inquiries about new people who have come to town, but that's going to be a big task considering all the reporters who have camped out since you all arrived here."

"I think the person or persons behind these attacks would have arrived in town just before the reporters." He opened his car door, his stomach tight with nervous energy as he thought about the name Jane was about to give him.

Whoever had arranged for the limo explosion had also paid off local officials and henchmen.

There was money behind this operation—lots of money.

If he could get a name, then maybe he could figure out exactly where that money was coming from instead of the idle speculation they'd all indulged in up until now.

All thoughts fled from his mind as they took the elevator to meet Jane. At the moment he was focused only on getting the name of the person who had handled those notes before him, the person who had sent them to Amir.

Why his friend hadn't shared the content of the notes with the others in the coalition was a mystery. There was no way of knowing exactly when Amir had received them, if he'd gotten them before he'd left his country or after he'd arrived in the States.

Had the person who had written them been the one who had picked up Amir at the bomb site? Was Amir now a prisoner or had he been killed and his body buried someplace out in the Wyoming wilderness that surrounded them?

Jane met them at the elevator door and ushered them into her private office. "I still don't feel right about not taking the notes to Jake," she said in greeting.

"You promised us some time," Antoine reminded her. "And from everything I've heard about you, you're a woman of your word."

Jane's cheeks flushed red and she lifted her chin. "And I'll keep my promise, but if you find out something you need to take all this to Jake, and if you don't, I will." Her voice was filled with steel, letting him know she meant business.

"You said you have a name for me."

Jane nodded. "Aleksei Verovick."

Antoine stared at her in stunned surprise. "Are you sure?"

"It was a perfect match," Jane replied.

"Do you know him?" Beth asked.

"I know of him. Verovick is reputed to be the second-hand man in the Russian mob," he replied, his mind racing with supposition. This was proof that the mob was behind the attacks on the royals. Or was it? It was also possible that Verovick had gone rogue. Certainly he was a man who would be capable of anything if the price was right.

"But why would the Russian mob care if you all made trade agreements with the United States?" Beth asked in confusion.

"They shouldn't care," he replied. "Unless somebody has bought them and is paying for them to care."

"Today is Tuesday," Jane said thoughtfully. "I'll give you until Friday evening and then I'm taking this information to Jake."

He could tell by the look on her face that there was no more wiggle room, that he wouldn't be able to talk her into any more time. "Then I'd better find some answers before Friday evening." He touched Beth's arm and gestured toward the door. "Thank you, Ms. Cameron. I appreciate your cooperation."

"You only have it for three days," she reminded him as he and Beth left the office.

"What are you going to do now?" Beth asked as they left the building and headed for her car.

"Do some research into Verovick and see if I can figure out who's paying him and his men to destroy the coalition, to destroy all of us. Do you have a computer at your place?"

"Yes. You want to do the research on my computer?" Her voice held a touch of surprise. "Your suite has a computer and Internet access."

"If you don't mind, I'd rather use yours. I don't know who might enter my room when I'm not there, who could access the history on my computer to see where I've been. I have to be careful."

"Then we'll go to my place," she agreed easily. "You're welcome to use my laptop as long as you need to."

They got into the car and Beth started the engine. "I'm fairly ignorant about politics," she said as she backed out of the parking space. "I don't understand why anyone would want to stop what you all were doing here. A trade agreement between any of the COIN nations and the United States sounds like a win-win situation to me."

Despite the anxious burn in his belly, he smiled at her, unsurprised and charmed by her naïveté. "There are some people who believe that these trade agreements are just the first step of our nations being consumed by the United States. And then there are Americans who believe that we're all terrorists and this is just our way of attempting to infiltrate America's security."

"Small-minded bigots," she observed. "Not everyone from a different country is a potential terrorist and people who think that way are just ignorant."

He smiled at her again. "Too bad you aren't in charge of the world. I have a feeling if you were it would be a much nicer place."

She laughed. "I'm just in charge of laundry and cleaning supplies and that's enough for me, thank you very much."

Antoine shifted his gaze out the side window as she turned onto the narrow road that led to her cottage. "If it was somebody from the mob who picked up Amir the night of the bombing, then I can't think of any reason they would have of keeping him alive. I keep wondering if he's someplace out there, buried in the woods where nobody will ever find his body."

He was surprised by the sudden rush of emotion that welled up thick in the back of his throat.

Her hand, warm on his arm, pulled him back from where he teetered on the edge of grief. "You can't lose hope, Antoine. Until we know for sure, you have to keep hoping that he's still alive."

As she withdrew her hand from him, he smiled at her once again. "You're a good woman, Beth Taylor."

She smiled. "Not especially. I can be impatient with my staff at times." Her hands tightened on the steering wheel. "I lead with my heart and not with my head and that's caused me to make some bad decisions in the past."

"What sort of bad decisions?" he asked. He realized he wanted to know everything there was to know about her. She stirred a lusty passion inside him, but he was also curious about her as a person.

"It's not important right now," she replied and frowned as she gazed in her rearview mirror.

"Problem?" he asked.

"I don't know. There's a dark car coming up fast behind us. This road isn't meant for speed. I just hope he slows down before he tries to pass us on this narrow road."

He turned to look and saw the vehicle behind them approaching far too fast considering the road condition. "Surely he'll slow down," he said.

He turned back around and saw her eyes

widen in disbelief. At the same time their car was smashed from behind with a force that snapped his head back.

Beth struggled to gain control of the car, but to no avail. Antoine felt the car go airborne and knew they were in deep trouble.

"Beth!" he cried as the world went topsy-turvy and then everything went black.

Chapter Four

Grinding noise and splintering glass. Beth's world was a place of chaos and pain as the sky became the ground and top became bottom.

The car seemed to roll forever before finally coming to rest upside down. Beth felt dazed and unable to make sense of anything. Her heart pounded so loudly in her ears she could hear nothing else.

The scent of gasoline and motor oil filled the air. Her arms hurt from trying to wrestle with the steering wheel and her ribs ached from the tight grip of the seat belt. Everything that had been on the floor of the car was now around her head, confusing her even more as she tried to make sense of what had just happened.

Someplace in the back of her mind where rational thought still existed, she realized she wasn't badly hurt. She wiggled her toes and flexed her fingers and realized it didn't appear that anything had been broken. She was lucky to be alive.

And then she remembered her passenger.

She snapped her gaze to him as she worked to unfasten her seat belt. His eyes were closed and blood oozed from an ugly gash on his forehead.

Her heart felt like it stopped beating in her chest. Was he dead? Oh God, had she killed the Prince of Barajas? She became aware of a discordant sound and realized it was her own sobs.

"Antoine," she cried as she finally managed to get herself free of her seat belt. She reached over and grabbed his arm and shook it.

"Antoine, please wake up. For God's sake you have to be okay." She couldn't bear it if he were dead. She gasped in relief as he issued a deep-throated moan and slowly opened his eyes.

For a moment they stared at each other and then he groaned again. "Beth, are you all right?" He seemed dazed as he looked around the car.

"Yes, I think so. What about you? Your forehead is bleeding."

"I'm okay. I was just knocked out for a minute." He drew a deep breath and the faint fog in his eyes began to clear. He worked on unfastening his seat belt. "I smell gasoline. We've got to get out of here."

Thankfully the front window had exploded outward, affording them an escape route from the wrecked vehicle. After some difficult maneuvering Antoine finally managed to go out the window first and then leaned back in to help Beth escape the car.

They staggered away from the hissing, steaming car and collapsed on the grass. Beth looked up to the road, unsurprised to find that the car that had hit them was no place to be seen.

For a moment she felt too stunned to think as she stared at the car that might have become their coffin. She looked back at Antoine who was swiping the blood off his forehead.

"We need help," she said. "Do you have your cell phone?"

He patted his pocket and grimaced. "It must have fallen out in the car when we tumbled."

"Mine's in my purse, someplace in the car."

"I'll get it," he said and started to rise.

"No," she exclaimed quickly. "You sit still. You've had a head bang. Besides, I'm smaller and can crawl back through the window easier."

She pulled herself up from the grass and had only taken one step toward the car when the sound of a gunshot cracked and Beth felt the whiz of a bullet come precariously close to her head.

Antoine reached up and grabbed her by the arm and slammed her down to the ground. She hit the earth with a thud and Antoine instantly covered her body with his.

Her brain short-circuited. What was going on? Somebody had shot at her? She gasped as

Antoine pulled a gun from an ankle holster she hadn't known he wore.

"Wha…what's going on?" she finally managed to sputter.

"Shh, be still." His features were taut as he gazed in the direction where the shot had come from. His eyes were narrowed and pale—and utterly dangerous-looking.

His muscles tensed and he seemed to be holding his breath. Another shot split the air, the dirt near them kicking up in a whirl of dust.

He muttered a curse beneath his breath. "We're vulnerable out here in the open. We've got to move." He scanned the area. "See the trees behind us?"

She craned her neck to see and then nodded. "Yes." Her voice sounded two octaves higher to her own ears. Terror squeezed her throat and roiled in her stomach, making her feel as if she might throw up at any moment.

"When I say go I want you to run for those trees. Run as fast as you can and don't look back." He slowly moved his body off of hers.

Fear screamed through her as every muscle in her body tensed with fight-or-flight adrenaline. She didn't want to run. She didn't want to move. She just wanted to go back an hour in time, when everything was okay.

"Get ready," he whispered. "Go!"

As she jumped up and ran for the cover of the trees he stood and began to fire his gun in the direction of the shooter while he followed close behind her.

Beth stopped when she reached one of the large trees. She wanted to hug the trunk that was now an obstacle for the shooter to get around. Antoine slid in beside her and wrapped an arm around her waist. "Okay?" he asked.

Hell no, she wasn't okay. Still, she nodded, too breathless to speak. She felt like she'd stepped out of a nightmare and straight into hell.

Antoine's cold, calculating eyes scanned the area once again. She wanted to ask him what he saw…who he saw, but she was afraid to speak in case the shooter might hear her.

"We need to stay on the move," he said softly. "We'll go deeper into the forest and work our way toward the resort. Be quiet and stay close to me."

Stay close to him? If she could, she would have glued herself to his chest. The trauma from the wreck had momentarily shot her into a bit of a fog, but the fog had completely lifted now and she was consumed by a terror she'd never felt before.

The only thing that made her feel slightly better was that he seemed cool and calm, so completely in control and not afraid at all. She didn't know if it was just an act and at the moment she didn't care. She only knew it made her feel a little bit better.

"We're going to run to those trees," he said and pointed to the left of where they stood. "Stay low and move fast. Let's go."

As they raced toward the next stand of trees, Beth expected a bullet to slam into one of them, but there was no answering gunfire.

"Maybe he's gone," she gasped as they once again reached cover.

"Or he's on the move to get closer to us," Antoine replied, his words doing little to assuage the jagged fear that ripped at her. "We need to keep moving. We don't want to be static targets."

They moved from cover to cover, pressing their bodies against trees and crouching in the brush. Each chirp of a bird overhead, any rustle of a small animal in the brush momentarily stopped Beth's heart.

After making half a dozen moves, she felt Antoine begin to relax a bit. His eyes weren't as pale as they had been and his features were less tense.

"I think maybe he's gone," he said. "If he was still around he would have popped off another shot or two by now. But we still need to stay on guard."

"Maybe he was afraid somebody heard the gunshots," she said hopefully. "It had to be somebody from the sedan. Our wreck wasn't an accident.

He intentionally rammed us from behind." Fear once again raised a cold hand and gripped her in a deathlike vise.

"Let's get back to the resort and then we can figure it all out." He took her hand in his and together they began to head in the direction of the hotel.

Somebody had tried to kill them. First with the car collision and then with a gun. Had this been yet another attempt to kill one of the men in the COIN coalition? Did it have something to do with the notes they had given to Jane?

There were so many questions and no answers to make sense of what had just happened. All she knew was that she couldn't wait to get back to the safety of the resort and she didn't even want to think about the fact that her car was now destroyed and the insurance payment would be just shy of paltry for the old reliable car.

They walked in silence for what felt like hours. Every once in a while Antoine would signal a stop and as they stood still he listened to the woods around them, his gun at the ready.

When the resort property finally came into view Beth almost wept in relief. Antoine looped an arm over her shoulder, as if to offer some comfort as they made their way to a side door that would keep them from having to enter through the lobby.

"We have to call the sheriff," she said as they

entered his suite. “We can’t keep this to ourselves. We have to report this, Antoine.”

“You’re absolutely right,” he agreed and swiped at his forehead where blood still oozed from the gash. “But we don’t have to tell him everything. We don’t have to tell him that we were at Jane’s or about the notes, just that we were on our way to your place.”

She hesitated before replying. Lying was aberrant to Beth and she thought the time had come to tell Jake Wolf everything.

“Beth.” Antoine placed his hands on her shoulders and gently kneaded with his fingers. “You’ve been so incredibly brave and I know this all has shaken you up, but I need you to help me. I need you to trust me enough to let me do what I need to do. I need the time that Jane promised us.”

His eyes were soft pools of pleading and even though she knew she was probably all kinds of fool, she did trust him. “Okay, then we just tell him we were going to my house, that you wanted some time away from the resort,” she finally relented.

“Thank you,” he replied and dropped his arms back to his sides.

“I’ll call Jake and then we need to clean up your forehead. You should probably be checked out by a doctor. If you were unconscious for any length of time then you probably have a concussion.”

"Nonsense, I'm fine. No doctor." There was more than a little steel in his voice.

Minutes later, with the call made to Jake, Beth stood in the bathroom with Antoine. She tried to ignore his tantalizing nearness as she dabbed at his wounded forehead with a wet washcloth.

Even though they had survived a car crash and a shooter, despite the fact that they'd trekked through the woods to get back here, he still smelled of that wonderful cologne that danced delight in her brain.

"There's a lot of blood," she said, trying to stay focused on the task at hand. "You might need a stitch or two. I still think you should see a doctor."

"Head wounds always bleed a lot," he replied. "I'm sure it will be fine. I don't need a doctor." He was seated on the edge of the large tub, his face in a direct line with her breasts and she felt his gaze there, tightening her nipples beneath her blouse.

How could she be feeling so turned on after what they'd just been through? How could his nearness, his hand resting lightly on the small of her back, his simple gaze create such want inside her?

It had to be some sort of trick of adrenaline, she told herself. Hadn't she read something someplace about danger and sexual response? Something about endorphins or some hormone that made the two closely related?

"You have a soft touch." His deep voice was like a warm caress as his breath fanned her collarbone.

"And thank God you have a hard head," she retorted.

He laughed and stood and she suddenly found herself in his embrace. "Nothing like escaping death to make you want to affirm life, right? And what I'd like to do at this very moment is carry you into my bed and make love to you until the sun comes up tomorrow morning."

Her breath hitched as she stared up at him. She knew that making love with Antoine would indelibly mark her forever, that when he returned to his country and his people, he would take a little piece of her heart with him.

But at the moment none of that mattered. What mattered was that his strong arms around her stole away the chill of residual danger from her. What mattered was that she couldn't remember ever wanting a man like she wanted Antoine.

When his mouth sought hers, she answered with a hungry kiss of her desire. She tasted desire in his lips as well. His mouth demanded response and she gave, swirling her tongue with his as sweet sensations chased away the last of her fear.

She clung to him and wanted him to take her to his bed and make her moan with delight, gasp in sweet pleasure. She wanted to lose herself in him and not think about car crashes or crazy people chasing after them with guns.

His hands slowly slid down her back and cupped her buttocks and pulled her closer, tighter against him. He was aroused, but this time instead of pulling back from him, she wrapped her arms around his neck and pressed herself more intimately against his hard body.

"Sweet Beth," he whispered as his lips left hers and trailed a hot path down the length of her neck. "I want you." The simple words only increased her desire.

At that moment a knock fell on the door. Antoine groaned and with obvious reluctance released his hold on her. He stepped back, his eyes blazing with a hunger that threatened to devour her.

"This isn't finished," he said, his voice lower, deeper than usual. "I will have you in my bed, Beth Taylor."

The words were not a threat, but rather a promise that shot a shiver of anticipation up her spine as he turned on his heels and left the bathroom.

THE HEAT OF PASSION SLOWLY EBBED as Antoine walked to the suite door. He'd expected Sheriff Jake Wolf, but instead he saw Michael, his head of security, on the other side of the door.

Michael gasped in alarm at the sight of him.

"Your Highness, what happened? You've been hurt!"

"It's nothing," Antoine replied as he closed the door behind the big man. "I was in a car accident."

"A car accident? Why were you out in a car without your driver, without your security with you?" He didn't wait for Antoine to reply, but rather continued, "Your Highness, I can't keep you safe if you go off by yourself and don't let me know what's going on."

Michael's frustration was evident in his raised voice and the redness that filled his broad features. "These are dangerous times, Prince Antoine, and I take my job as head of your security team very seriously. I wish you would do the same."

"I'm sure Fahad Bahir, Sheik Efraim Aziz's head of security, took his job seriously as well," Antoine replied drily.

Michael sucked in a breath and froze. "You doubt my trustworthiness?" They both knew that Fahad had tried to kill Sheik Efraim but instead had been killed himself. "You wound me deeply. I would die to protect you," Michael exclaimed fervently. "You should know after all my years of service that your safety is my number one priority."

Suddenly Antoine was exhausted. The adrenaline that had pumped through him immediately following the crash, the raw, pulsing energy that had driven him through the woods to safety finally disappeared.

He sank down on the edge of the sofa as Beth returned to the room, looking as exhausted as he felt.

Michael raised a dark eyebrow at her appearance.

"Beth, this is Michael Napolis, head of my security team. Michael, Beth Taylor works here at the hotel as head of housekeeping." Beth nodded and slid down in the chair opposite the sofa as Antoine looked back at Michael. "We're waiting now for Sheriff Jake Wolf to arrive. We were forced off the road. We managed to escape the crash only to be shot at by an unknown person."

Michael's eyes narrowed. "I must insist that you use your security force whenever you leave these rooms. None of the members of the coalition who are still here are safe until we identify who is behind these attacks."

"We're safe for now. The sheriff is on his way and Ms. Taylor and I don't intend to leave this room for the remainder of the day. There are some things I want to go over with you later, but I'll call you when I'm ready."

It was an obvious dismissal and Michael knew it. He gave a quick bow and then left the suite. Antoine looked at Beth and for the first time noticed her clothes were dirty, her hose encasing her long legs were torn and she winced as she changed positions on the chair.

"You should go take a hot bath," he said. "You need to soak your muscles before they all tighten up. I have a clean robe hanging on the hook behind the door in the bathroom."

"Sounds like a plan," she replied but made no move to get up.

He stood and walked over to where she sat and held out his hand. "Come, it's been a difficult time and you look exhausted."

She took his hand in hers and allowed him to pull her up to her feet. "I'm more tired than I think I've ever been in my life," she admitted.

When they reached the bathroom, Antoine started the water running in the tub, added a liberal dose of scented bath salts and then walked back to her and gently cupped her face with his hands. "I'm so sorry about what happened."

She smiled, but it was obviously a forced gesture. "Don't you dare apologize. You aren't responsible for any of what happened. You didn't force my car off the road and you weren't the one taking potshots at us."

"I don't know what I would have done if you'd been hurt." Emotion welled up and pressed heavily in his chest as he thought of what might have happened to her. They'd been very lucky to walk away from not only the wrecked car, but also from whoever had been shooting at them.

"Thankfully the only real casualty was your head and my hose." This time her smile was more genuine, although still weary.

He held her gaze for another long moment, then let her go and stepped back. "Soak and relax. When Sheriff Wolf arrives I'll take care of the report to him. If he needs to speak to you I'll let you know." With that he closed the door to allow her privacy.

He would have loved to climb into the big tub with her, to feel her soap-slickened skin against his, but he had business to attend to and couldn't afford to allow himself to get distracted again by Beth's charms.

Although he'd been reluctant to use the computer in his room to do the search he wanted to run, he also didn't want to waste time. He needed to find out everything he could about Aleksei Verovick as soon as possible.

As he waited for the computer to power up he made a couple of phone calls, taking care of some business that needed to be handled and by that time Sheriff Jake Wolf arrived.

"Sheriff Wolf." Antoine ushered in the tall, Native American sheriff who had a reputation for being a straight shooter.

Despite his reputation, Antoine wasn't at all

sure whether to trust the man. According to what Antoine had heard, there had been whispers of corruption in the Wind River County law enforcement for many years.

"Prince Antoine, when Beth called me she said you needed to report a crime," Jake said.

"Please, have a seat." Antoine gestured him toward one of the easy chairs next to the sofa.

"Where's Beth?"

"She's in the bathroom cleaning up." Antoine shoved aside a quick vision of Beth in a tub of bubbles. "We've had a rather traumatic afternoon. It started when a black sedan intentionally rammed us from behind and forced Beth's car off the road and down an embankment near her cabin."

Jake sat up straighter in his chair, his dark eyes glowing with intensity. "Did you get a plate number? Maybe see who was behind the wheel?"

"Unfortunately no." How Antoine wished he'd seen who had been driving that car. How he wished he'd gotten an eyeful of the person who had been shooting at them. If he had, they would now no longer be a threat.

"It all happened so fast. The car plowed into us, we went off the road and flipped a couple of times, but Beth and I managed to climb out of the wreckage. Thankfully we were both wearing our seat belts so sustained simply bumps and bruises."

"And a pretty good gash on your forehead," Jake observed. "Do you need to see a doctor?"

Antoine raised a hand to the wound which had finally stopped bleeding. "No, it's fine. Anyway, by the time we managed to climb out of Beth's car, the other car was gone, but somebody started shooting at us."

Jake released a weary sigh. "And I suppose you didn't get a look at who was doing the shooting."

"I'm afraid we were too busy scrambling for cover to pay much attention. Eventually the shooter must have left the area and we made our way back here."

"You had no security with you?" Jake lowered his dark eyebrows in obvious disapproval.

"Beth and I were on our way to her place. I felt a need to escape everything and everyone, and that included my own security team."

Jake frowned. "You royals would make my life much easier if you'd either avail yourself of your own security or stay holed up here in your rooms. Better yet, perhaps it's time to wrap things up here and head back to your country."

"That's not going to happen until I find out about Amir's fate," Antoine replied firmly. "I understand the difficulties our being here has brought you and I apologize for that, but I have no plans to return to Barajas at the moment."

Jake waved a hand. "I guess it's all in a day's

work," he replied. "At least I can't say things have been boring around here lately. So, let's start at the beginning and you tell me exactly what happened again."

It was almost an hour later that Jake left the suite with what little information Antoine had been able to give him. Jake had made arrangements for Beth's car to be towed although Antoine was relatively certain it couldn't be salvaged for anything but junk.

The minute Jake left Antoine headed toward the master bathroom to check on Beth. She hadn't put in an appearance the entire time that Jake had been there.

He discovered the reason for her absence the minute he walked into the bedroom. Clad in his white robe, she was curled up asleep in the middle of his bed, a hand towel folded up and clutched in one hand. As he watched her sleeping he felt his heart constrict just a little bit.

During the entire trek back to the resort she hadn't complained. She hadn't worried about the fact that she now didn't have a car. She hadn't accused him of getting her into a bad situation. Her entire concern seemed to be getting him back to the resort so she could take care of the cut on his forehead.

She was unlike any woman he'd ever met before and she was definitely getting under his skin. She looked so beautiful with her long lashes dusting her cheeks and her lips slightly parted as if anticipating a lover's kiss.

Despite his words about taking her to bed, he knew the best thing he could do for both of them was to back away. When she woke up he needed to take her back to her cottage and then leave her alone.

The last thing he wanted was to bring danger to her doorstep and this afternoon had been too close a call for him to want to continue having her near him.

Antoine stared at her for a long moment. He'd never wanted to get too close to a woman because he'd never wanted to feel responsible for a woman's safety.

He'd never forgotten that his father's past had lunged up to destroy not only his own life, but Antoine's mother's life as well. Antoine was determined not to make the same mistakes as his father.

As quietly as he'd entered the room he left, more confused than ever about what to do with her.

They had gotten little sleep the night before and with the dramatic events of the day he knew the best thing for her at the moment was sleep. That would allow him to figure out whether he should cut her loose or keep her close.

He returned to his computer to find out what he could about Verovick. He didn't know how long he worked before darkness and hunger drove him back out of his chair.

He ordered dinner from room service and turned on lights against the night, then once again checked on Beth who was still sleeping soundly.

There was a part of him that wanted to get into the bed with her, to pull her warm sleeping form against him and allow himself to relax for the first time in hours.

However, Jane's clock ticked loudly in his head, reminding him that minutes were slipping by and he had only two days left before she'd take the information in the notes to Jake Wolf.

He returned to the desk and stacked the pages he'd printed off the computer. He leaned back in the chair and began to read.

There was no question that plenty of speculation swirled around Aleksei Verovick with little solid fact. He was reputed to be behind a scam that had stolen hundreds of credit card numbers and personal information that had yielded hundreds of thousands of dollars for the mob.

His name had been linked to kidnappings and killings, but a lack of solid evidence and plenty of palm-greasing had apparently kept him a free and very powerful man.

He picked up one of the printouts and stared at

a photo of the man. Verovick had a thick, beefy body and a square head with a prominent jaw. His hair was dark and cut with military precision and his eyes were round and black like those of a reptile. He looked like a formidable enemy to have.

Antoine frowned as he noticed the fountain in the background of the picture. It was large and made of stunning marble, with finely sculptured sea nymphs rising out of the huge base.

He knew that fountain, had stood before it many times when he'd visited the island of Saruk. In their area of the sea there were a total of five independent islands—Barajas, Kyros, Nadar, Jamala and Saruk.

Saruk was the largest of them all and the only one that had chosen not to participate in the COIN coalition.

So, why would a man like Aleksei Verovick be visiting in Saruk? More important, who had he been visiting while in that country? Antoine's mind raced with theories.

Kalil Ramat, the leader of Saruk, had made no secret of the fact that he disapproved of the COIN coalition and their goals, but surely his disapproval wouldn't go so far as to hire members of the Russian mob to destroy the leaders of the other nations.

Antoine picked up his phone and dialed his friend, Darek Ramat, Kalil's son.

"Antoine." Darek's deep voice held a warm welcome when he answered. "How are you, my friend?"

"Good," Antoine replied. He figured the fewer people who knew about the attacks against him and the others, the better.

"It's good to hear you're well."

"It's good to be well," Antoine replied with a touch of humor. "And how are things on the beautiful island of Saruk?"

"Wonderful. I have plans tonight to club it with a couple of beautiful women so life is definitely good," Darek said with a hardy laugh. "And when are you planning a visit here?"

"I don't know, Darek, things are still very much up in the air with nobody knowing anything about Amir."

"I pray for his safety," Darek replied. "There have been no new developments?"

"None," Antoine replied and felt the edge of grief he always suffered when thinking about Amir. "Aleksei Verovick, you know the name?" Antoine asked, getting to the point of the call.

"No, should I?" There was obvious confusion in Darek's voice.

"He's reputed to be a high-power player in the

Russian mob and he was recently a visitor to your country."

"Really? Well, I don't know the man. I have nothing to do with reputed mobsters."

"So you would have no idea what he was doing in your country?"

"Antoine, many people visit Saruk. This is a beautiful place where tourism thrives. Do you think this man has something to do with Amir's fate?"

"Perhaps," Antoine replied, not wanting to tell Darek about the notes that had been found, notes that were directly tied to Verovick.

The two men talked for a few minutes longer and then hung up. Antoine leaned back in his chair and fought against a new wave of exhaustion.

Was it possible that Kalil's disapproval had gone over the top? Had he taken his disapproval of the COIN coalition to the next level and actively worked against them by hiring the Russian mob to take them all out?

Antoine had a difficult time believing that about a man who had many times opened his household to him in welcome, a man who was the father of somebody Antoine considered a good friend.

Had Verovick simply been vacationing on the beautiful island of Saruk? He supposed even mobsters needed a vacation now and then.

A knock on the door pulled him from his

thoughts. Dinner had arrived. As the server left the suite Beth appeared in the doorway from the bedroom.

She had dressed back in her own clothes sans the ruined pantyhose and looked far more refreshed than he felt.

"Ah, sleeping beauty awakes. I hope you like steak," he said. "I took the liberty of ordering a late-night dinner for us."

"It smells delicious and right now I think I could eat anything you put in front of me." She walked across the room to the dining room table where the plates had been placed with meticulous care. "Did Jake come?"

He nodded. "He did. I made the report and Jake will be looking for a dark sedan with front-end damage. There's no way that car could have hit us with such force and not sustained some damage."

"I'm sorry I slept through it all. After the bath I sat on the edge of the bed and before I knew it I was out like a light."

"I had Michael pick up replacement cell phones for both of us," he said.

"Thanks."

She sat at the table. "And once we finish eating I'll call somebody on staff to take me back to my place."

"That won't be necessary," he replied. "I bought you a new Jeep, complete with four-wheel drive and all the extras. It's down in the parking lot now with a red ribbon tied to the antenna."

He'd expected joy to light her eyes, or at least a little bit of relief that she didn't have to worry about not having a vehicle anymore. He'd sent Michael to take care of the details and Michael had managed to get everything done while she'd slept.

But, instead of joy, her green eyes narrowed and her lips thinned with a hint of displeasure. "I didn't ask you to buy me a new car."

"No, you didn't," he replied easily. "That's not in your nature. But, you needed a new one and so I got you one."

"I can't accept a new car from you."

"Of course you can," he replied and sat next to her at the table. "It's already tagged and licensed in your name. It was because of me that your car was destroyed. Don't look at it as a gift, but merely a replacement of the one I ruined."

What he didn't tell her was that a tracking device had been placed on the Jeep to allow him to keep track of her movements by his computer. It was just a precaution, given what they'd just experienced.

Her cheeks were flushed pink as she stared at him. "I'll make payments to you until I've paid for it, every dime that it cost you."

Damn, but he wanted her now, this very minute

with her eyes blazing and her chin thrust forward in a show of stubborn defiance. But, as much as he'd like to think of his own wants, his own needs, he couldn't forget what had happened to his mother and father.

It was time to let her go.

Chapter Five

Beth sat at her desk the next morning with a cup of coffee in hand and thought about the night before. They had been halfway through dinner when Antoine had told her he didn't feel comfortable with her going back to her cottage alone.

Truthfully, she hadn't felt all that good about going home alone, either. The small house was far too isolated for her to be comfortable there alone after what had happened to them.

Antoine had told her she was welcome to stay in his suite, but she knew where that would lead and she wasn't willing to go there with him.

Once she'd slept good sense had prevailed and the desire she'd felt for him while the two of them had been in the bathroom had ebbed.

The fact that in the blink of an eye he'd bought her a new car reminded her of how very different their worlds were, how foolish she would be to think that there was any kind of future with Prince Antoine Cavanaugh.

She'd wound up spending the night in a hotel room that was available for staff and she always kept a spare uniform in her office.

She'd spent the night tossing and turning, thinking about what had happened with the car wreck and the shooting and ultimately her thoughts had returned to Antoine.

She took a sip of coffee and rose from her chair, ignoring the faint groan of muscles that had been overworked in the accident. She stared out the window, unseeing, lost in her thoughts.

People who stayed at the hotel were in transition. They were coming from somewhere or going someplace. They were conducting business or on vacation and had lives that had nothing to do with their stay at the resort.

Other than Mark she had never allowed herself to get involved in anything personal with a guest, aware that this was just a short stop in their lives that had little to do with reality.

There had been plenty of men who had flirted with her, who had made it clear that they might have pursued her given half an opportunity, but she'd shut them down easily.

Still, she was precariously close to losing her heart to Antoine. Not only was he handsome as sin, as sexy as satin sheets, but he was also a kind man and had a great sense of humor. He'd even started her bathwater for her. Damn, he was absolutely killing her.

If the knock on the door hadn't stopped them, they would have fallen onto Antoine's bed and made love. She'd been ready to succumb to him, to give herself completely with no thought of tomorrow. It would have been foolish to do so.

"Beth?" Barbara Kintell, one of the maids, stuck her head into the room. "Do you have a minute?"

"Of course," Beth replied, grateful to focus on work and not on the wondrous charms of Antoine Cavanaugh. This was where she belonged, dealing with hotel housekeeping business and not anywhere near a prince who had everything it took to break her heart.

It was noon when Beth realized she'd promised Antoine the night before to look at the personnel records and see who had been hired in the weeks before the royals had arrived.

It was possible somebody here at the hotel had seen Antoine and Beth leave together the day before and had been responsible for what had happened after they'd left the lab.

This thought brought with it a sense of personal betrayal. Beth had always considered the staff here at the resort part of her extended family. She didn't want to believe that anyone here could be guilty of such duplicity.

It was also possible somebody in town had seen them together and had decided it was a perfect opportunity to take out another member of the COIN coalition.

Beth spent most of her waking hours here at the hotel and rarely went to town for anything but groceries or to meet a friend for dinner.

There was one person who would probably know any newcomers in town and that was Beth's friend, Haley Jenkins, who worked at the most popular café in Dumont.

She dialed Haley's number and smiled as her friend's voice filled the line. "Hey girl, I haven't heard from you for a while. I was beginning to think you'd fallen off the face of the earth."

"I've just been really busy here at work," Beth replied.

"Rubbing elbows with all those hunky sheiks, I'll bet," Haley said.

Beth laughed although she felt the warmth of a blush on her cheeks. "Actually, a prince rather than a sheik," she admitted.

Haley squealed in delight. "Do tell all!"

"There isn't a lot to tell," Beth said hurriedly. "I've just been spending a little time with Prince Antoine Cavanaugh, but it's strictly on a professional basis. I'm helping him with a little investigative work."

"Beth, I've seen photos of him and his twin

brother. They are definitely the hottie twins. I hope some of your work is undercover…as in under the covers of one of those big, king-size beds."

Beth laughed once again and tried not to think about her and Antoine under the sheets of his bed, making love. "Not hardly. The reason I called is because I'm trying to get the names of people who came to town just before the visiting royals arrived, people who seem to have no real reason to be here."

"God, girl, that's a tall order. With all the reporters and journalists and all those kooky protestors, it's hard to figure out who has a reason to be here and who doesn't."

"This would be somebody who isn't a journalist, somebody who is probably a loner," Beth replied.

"Can I give it some thought and get back to you?" Haley asked.

"Of course," Beth replied. "And Haley, I really appreciate it."

"Whatever I can do to help. But, I will tell you that sooner or later I'm going to want details about you and the handsome prince."

Beth laughed again and when she and Haley hung up she typed in the password on her computer that would take her to the personnel files.

It took an enormous staff to keep a hotel and

resort of this size running smoothly and Beth intended to check new hires for any position on staff.

It took her most of the afternoon to plow through the records with interruptions to attend to normal housekeeping duties and coworkers popping in just to say hello.

There was very little turnover at the hotel. People who worked here liked what they did and knew that in this economy good jobs were hard to find. The hotel provided not only comfortable wages, but excellent benefits as well and there was definitely a certain prestige in working for the Wind River Ranch and Resort.

However, she did find one name, a member of her own staff, who had been hired a little over a month before the royals had come to the resort.

Janine Sahron had told Beth when she'd been hired that her husband was from a small Mediterranean island and that they had recently moved to Dumont. At the time the information had meant nothing to Beth, but now she had to wonder about it.

Was it possible they had moved to Dumont specifically to get Janine hired, specifically to infiltrate the hotel and gain access to knowledge about the movements of the members of the COIN Coalition?

Beth grabbed her cell phone and called Antoine. She tried to still the leap of her heart as he answered, his deep sexy voice washing over her in a wave of heat.

"Beth, I was just thinking about you," he said in a distinctly sensual tone.

She wanted to tell him to stop it, to stop thinking about her, and to stop saying her name as if he were making love to it. "I was just thinking about you, too. I have a name for you—a maid who was hired a month before you all arrived here. I also remember her telling me that her husband was from a small Mediterranean island."

"What's her name?" Antoine asked, all softness gone from his voice.

"Janine Sahron."

"Sahron," he repeated the name thoughtfully. "Doesn't sound familiar, but that doesn't mean anything. I would like to meet with her immediately. Can you arrange it for me?"

"Unfortunately today is her day off," Beth replied.

"You have her address?"

"Yes, but what are you planning to do?"

"You and I will pay her a visit at her home. I will interrogate her and her husband and get the truth from them."

A faint shiver walked up Beth's spine at the cool resolve in his voice. "Shouldn't you call them first and let them know you're coming?"

"Absolutely not. I would prefer the element of

surprise. So, when are you available to take me to them?"

She had told herself that she was done with Antoine, that what she needed more than anything was to distance herself from him, but she also knew that he had nobody he trusted as much as her. And the truth be told, she didn't want to distance herself from him—at least not yet and at least not physically.

"I can take off at about six this evening," she finally said and tried to ignore the dance her heart did at the thought of seeing him again. It didn't mean they would sleep together, she reminded herself. Helping him and sleeping with him were two very different things.

With arrangements made for her to meet him at the side door, they hung up. Beth directed her gaze out the nearby window where she had a view of the stunning formal gardens.

Was it possible that Janine and her husband were somehow tied to the Russian mobster who had written those threatening notes? It was so difficult to imagine the red-haired, blue-eyed, soft-spoken Janine involved in any kind of international intrigue.

But she reminded herself that lately the news had been filled with stories about spies living like the Joneses next door, people who looked like Sunday-school teachers and Boy Scout leaders who were actually planted for years as deep-seated spies.

Who would have thought that some of the local law could be bought off, that professional security teams could be compromised? She couldn't imagine living a life where you didn't know who to trust, where even the people closest to you could betray you in the blink of an eye.

Was it any wonder that Antoine found it easier to trust a virtual stranger like her than anyone close to him?

By the time six o'clock arrived nervous energy coursed through her. She was determined to take Antoine where he needed to go, support him in what he had to do, and yet try to maintain a healthy emotional distance from him.

That emotional distance was difficult to maintain the minute she slid into the interior of the new black Jeep. Despite the fact that Antoine had been suffering from a gash in his forehead and from the trauma of somebody trying to kill him, within minutes of getting to safety he'd thought about her and the fact that she no longer had a car she could use.

Sitting in the new beige leather seat, smelling the new-car scent that surrounded her and staring at all the bells and whistles he'd included, she felt a wave of emotion press tight in her chest and bring a haze of tears to her eyes.

Nobody had ever done anything so nice for her before and while she intended to pay off every dime, she couldn't help but be touched that he'd thought about what she'd lost, that it had mattered to him.

She sucked up the uncharacteristic sentimental tears and headed for the side door where Antoine awaited. As always her pulse raced at the sight of him.

Although he wore his customary black dress slacks, this evening he had on a pale blue short-sleeved dress shirt that both showed off his biceps and emphasized the blueness of his eyes.

As he slid into the seat next to her and gave her the smile that threatened to turn her into a puddle, she knew maintaining any kind of emotional distance from this man was next to impossible.

Somehow he'd managed to dig in beneath the defenses she'd erected after the debacle with Mark. The lyrics to a Mariah Carey heartbreaker flew through her head, a reminder that she desperately had to quickly rebuild the defenses to keep her heart safe.

"You slept well last night?" he asked once they were headed in the direction of the Sahron residence.

"I would have slept better in my own bed, but yes, I slept okay. What about you?" She cast him a quick glance and noticed that he looked tired.

The lines around his eyes appeared to cut deeper than they had the day before. “Nightmares?”

“No, no dreams. There were just too many thoughts in my head for me to sleep well,” he replied.

“You need to talk about your thoughts?”

He cast her a warm smile. “I’m not used to sharing my thoughts with anyone, except perhaps Sebastian.” He leaned back in the seat and a frown tugged his dark eyebrows downward. “I keep trying to figure out how to tie Aleksei Verovick to everything that has happened. I keep wondering if perhaps he’s here in town and pulling strings behind the scenes.”

“I called a friend of mine at a café in Dumont to see if she could give me a list of anyone who had come to town in the weeks before you all arrived. I haven’t heard back from her yet. But sooner or later everyone who comes to Dumont eats at that café.”

“You’re a very smart woman, Beth.”

She hated how she warmed at his words of praise. “If I don’t hear back from her today, I’ll give her a call first thing in the morning.”

“I don’t know what I would do without you, Beth. Without Sebastian here I have nobody else I can trust.” She felt his gaze on her.

“Do you really worry that you can’t trust your own security team?” she asked.

He frowned once again. "I want to trust them, but I'm naturally wary after what happened with Sheik Efraim's head of security. The promise of money and power can corrupt even the truest of heart."

"Money has never meant much of anything to me, except as a way to eventually finance my dream of owning horses," she replied. "I've never longed for designer clothes or fancy shoes. I love my simple life."

"A simple life sounds wonderfully attractive to me at the moment," he replied.

They both fell silent as she reached the Dumont city limits and she turned onto the street where the Sahron family lived.

"It should be just ahead," she said as she slowed to read the numbers on the mailboxes.

The Sahron house was a two-story that looked as if it was in desperate need of a face-lift. The white paint was peeling and weathered and some of the dark green shutters at the windows hung askance. The lawn was wild and dead bushes lined the sidewalk.

"Apparently money is an issue with the Sahrons," Antoine said drily as she stopped the car in the driveway.

"I'll go up and knock on the door," Beth said. Although she was relatively certain they had not been followed and hopefully nobody knew about her new vehicle, she didn't want Antoine standing on the porch and potentially making an easy target for somebody.

"We'll go together," he replied firmly and opened his car door.

So much for attempting to save a prince, she thought as she got out. Although Antoine definitely wasn't the kind of man who would ever need saving by a woman. With his military training and his quick mind he could probably take care of himself in most situations.

She felt a nervous flutter in her stomach as Antoine rang the doorbell. She didn't want to think that a member of her own staff might be at least partially responsible for the horrible things that had befallen the visiting dignitaries.

Janine Sahron was a hard worker and a team player. She was a soft-spoken woman whom Beth had instantly liked. Was it possible Beth had completely misjudged her character? Janine had melded seamlessly into the team which was why Beth hadn't thought about her until she'd looked over the files.

It certainly wouldn't be the first time she'd misjudged somebody. A vision of Mark filled her head. Mark with his charming smile and laughing brown eyes. Oh yes, he'd fooled her with his promises of love and marriage and she'd bought into each and every one of his lies.

Her attention returned to Antoine as he knocked on the door with an impatient rap. "I guess they aren't home," he finally said in frustration after knocking a second time.

"What now?" Beth asked as they returned to the car.

"I think we should park along the curb across the street and do what you call a stakeout."

"If that's what you want," Beth replied. "But, it's possible they're out for the evening."

Within minutes they were parked where he'd indicated with the engine off and the windows down to allow the refreshing evening air to flow around them.

"We'll give it an hour or so," he said. "And while we wait you can tell me about the man who broke your heart."

She looked at him in surprise and a small, uncomfortable laugh escaped her lips. "What makes you think some man broke my heart?"

His eyes gleamed a silvery blue in the waning light of day. "It's the only thing to explain why a woman like you is still alone."

She broke eye contact with him and stared unseeing out the front window as her mind drifted back in time. "I always had a firm policy not to date any of the guests who stayed at the hotel. It just seemed smart not to get involved with men who were there on business or on vacation and had lives to get back to."

"But, you made an exception," he said softly

She turned back to look at him and nodded. "Yes, I did. His name was Mark Ferrer. He was some sort of a medical salesman who worked the state of Wyoming and about every two weeks or so he'd spend a couple of nights at the resort. I ran into him in town one evening. He had just finished up a business call and I was in town to buy some groceries. We bumped into each other and he invited me to have a drink with him."

She thought about that night. It had been the one-year anniversary of her mother's death and she'd been filled with an aching loneliness. "On impulse I decided to take him up on the invitation."

"And that was the beginning." It wasn't a question but rather a statement of fact.

"Yes, we started seeing each other whenever he was in town and he'd call me during the time he wasn't in town. He told me he lived in a small town about three hundred miles from here." Once again she cast her gaze out the window. "He was very romantic, seemed to be head over heels in love with me and it wasn't long before I believed I felt the same way."

She removed her hands from the steering wheel and felt the faint tick of the errant nerve in the side of her neck. It was embarrassing to admit how incredibly foolish she'd been.

Antoine reached over and took one of her hands in his. As always when she looked at him she wanted to fall into his arms, lose herself in the blue waters of his eyes. "You loved him and he didn't love you back?"

She wished it had been that easy. Unrequited love would have been a cakewalk compared to what she'd been through with Mark. "No, he professed to love me desperately up until the very end when I told him to get out of my life and stay out forever."

Antoine looked at her in confusion. "I don't understand. What happened?"

Beth sighed. "One night Mark stayed with me and the next morning when he left I realized he'd forgotten his briefcase. That evening I looked up his home number in the hotel records and I called him. To my surprise a woman answered the phone, a woman who introduced herself as Mark's wife."

How well she remembered that moment of shock, of utter betrayal that she'd felt. Married? Mark was married? Worse than that, she'd heard the sound of young children in the background.

She would never forget how humiliated she'd felt at that moment, how her heart had ached not only for herself but also for the woman on the other end of the line.

"What did you tell her?" Antoine asked.

"That I was head of housekeeping here at the hotel and Mr. Ferrer had left his briefcase in his room. She thanked me and told me Mark would be in touch."

"And I'll bet he was," Antoine said drily as he gently squeezed her hand.

"He called me an hour later, told me that nothing had changed between us. He said he loved me and was grateful that the truth was finally out. He said his wife didn't understand him, that she was jealous and vindictive but ultimately he didn't want to divorce her because he had to think about his children. He told me that now that the truth was out, there was really no reason why we couldn't keep the status quo."

The words tumbled out of her. She'd never shared this with anyone. Not even her best friends had known about Mark's ultimate betrayal.

"He assured me that nothing had changed between he and I, that he still loved me, still wanted to be with me whenever it was possible. I was appalled. I don't do affairs."

"Of course you don't. So, that was the end of it?"

She frowned. "For the next three months Mark called me incessantly. He couldn't believe that I didn't want to be with him anymore. He sent me flowers and candy and other gifts. I finally changed my cell phone number, but he'd call me at work."

"Did you think about filing a restraining order of some kind?"

"No. I didn't want to destroy his life. I didn't want his wife to know what he'd done. I just wanted him to leave me alone. Finally one day he stopped calling, stopped trying to make contact. That was almost a year ago. He hasn't been back to the hotel since and I figure he found himself a new hotel and a new girlfriend who he's probably lying to like he lied to me."

"Men like that are predators," Antoine said with a touch of indignation.

"Women like me are foolish," Beth replied wryly. "I should have asked more questions, checked him out before getting involved with him. I was stupid just to take everything he told me about himself at face value."

One thing surprised her, talking about Mark didn't bring the pain she'd expected. She realized that whatever heartbreak he might have caused her had finally healed.

"Beth, you can't blame yourself for being a trusting, loving woman. Those are very positive traits for a person to have, they are the very traits that draw me to you."

She pulled her hand from his. "Now that's

enough about me. Why don't you tell me why you haven't found a woman to make your princess?"

"I will never marry." His voice rang with firm commitment.

She looked at him in surprise. "But why? Antoine, you're a good man and you deserve someone to share your life with." Not that she believed in a million years that woman could ever be her.

His eyes, which had been warm and inviting just moments ago, turned to pale ice. "I'm not a good man, Beth. I've done some terrible things in my life, things that I fear might put your life in danger."

Chapter Six

Her beautiful eyes widened at his words. “What are you talking about?”

He looked toward the Sahron house and frowned. “You say this woman is scheduled to work at the hotel early in the morning?”

“Yes, she should be in by seven. She’s never been late and never missed a day of work.”

“Then let’s go to your place. I’m in the mood for some peace and quiet and a cup of your wonderful coffee.”

She said nothing but started the engine and headed out of the neighborhood. He knew she had questions about what he’d said, but he didn’t intend to share any of his past with her until they were alone at her place.

He’d already had a difficult day. Thoughts of his friend Amir had plagued him, along with questions about the crash and the shooting he and Beth had experienced.

All day long he’d played and replayed the events

in minute detail in his head. What he couldn't make sense of was that after he and Beth had crawled out of the wreck, the gunman had shot at her when she'd stood to go back into the car and get their cell phones.

Why shoot at her? If Antoine had been the primary target, then why not wait for him to stand up and then take him out? The shot at Beth had served as a warning to him. Had it simply been an amateur mistake or something else, something darker and more devious?

The more he thought about it, the more concerned he'd become that it was possibly somebody from his past who had caught up with him, somebody with a burning need for revenge who had finally found him.

And that meant he might have put a target on Beth's head. By spending time with her, perhaps being seen in her company somebody might have gotten the impression that she would make a good vehicle for revenge against him. That was the only thing that explained the gunman shooting at her instead of waiting for a bead on Antoine.

Darkness was falling fast as they reached Beth's cabin. Antoine felt the same welcome this evening as he had the other time he'd come here with her. The house seemed to attempt to embrace him in a serene quiet but his mind was filled with too much chaos for that to happen.

"I'm going to get out of my uniform," Beth said as she headed down the hallway. "I'll be out in just a few minutes. Make yourself at home."

He didn't hang around in the living room but instead walked into the kitchen, where Beth's presence in the house was most vibrant.

He walked over to the bank of windows and stared out where the deep purple shadows of night were starting to pool beneath the trees and seep across the land.

In the distance he could see the faint sparkle of the dying sun on a stream. Despite all the troubles in his mind, he momentarily felt a peace he rarely enjoyed.

This place had a rugged beauty that called to something deep inside him. From its jagged mountains to the sparkling streams, he felt an elemental pull, a sense of being where he belonged.

Which was crazy. He belonged in Barajas, he reminded himself. That was his home, not this place.

"Now, coffee."

He turned at the sound of her voice. She'd changed into a dark pink sweatshirt and a matching pair of jogging pants. The fleece material hugged her body like a lover and the peace he'd felt earlier dissolved beneath a wash of desire that threatened to weaken his knees.

He sank down at the table, disturbed by how

profoundly Beth affected him, by how much he wanted her. He'd always been able to manage his emotions, his desires with little trouble. He was a master at manipulating others, but had always managed to stay completely in control of himself.

Until now.

Until Beth.

He narrowed his gaze as he watched her start the coffee. She moved with an efficient grace, despite her earlier claim of possessing two left feet.

"I tortured people." The words slipped from his lips, as if he knew these thoughts alone would drive any desire for her from his mind, would drive her away from him.

She gasped and turned to face him. He saw the nerve ticking violently in the side of her long, slender neck, letting him know she was anxious.

"What are you talking about?" Her voice was a soft whisper as she walked across the hardwood floor and sank down in the chair next to him.

He saw no fear in her eyes, only confusion and questions. The coffeemaker gurgled and began to drip its fragrant brew, but a cup of coffee was the last thing on his mind.

"It's what I did in the military," he said. "I was one of the top interrogators for my country. I broke people, sometimes mentally, sometimes physically."

The darkness that was never far from the

surface rose up inside him, filling him with the bitter tang of regret and a weight of sorrow he felt as if he'd never climb out from under. He was a thirty-five-year-old man who suffered nightmares because of his past. "I did terrible things, things that haunt me now."

"Antoine, you were in the military." She leaned toward him, her green eyes lit with the flame of conviction and holding a faint sense of redemption for him if he were willing to take it. "You were in charge of the security of your nation. You did what you had to do for your country," she said softly.

Unable to stand the easy acceptance in her eyes, he stood and returned to the window, his back to where she remained seated.

"I hate what I did." He spit the words out as his emotions careened out of control. "I hate who I had to become to get the job done. I found weaknesses and exploited them, I smiled with friendliness as I sought ways to destroy people, to break them to the point that I could get what I wanted from them."

He hadn't heard her rise from her chair, but suddenly her hand was on the small of his back. "The fact that you hate what you did shows me what kind of a man you are in your heart." Her soft voice soothed some of the rough edges in his soul.

He turned to face her. "It's what I dream about sometimes. It's the stuff of nightmares."

She tilted her head slightly and he realized the pulse in her neck had stopped its frantic beat. "Is that what you were dreaming about the night that I woke you up?"

He gave her a curt nod. "That and my parents' murder. Most of my nightmares are either of their murder or about the things I did in the name of national security."

"Antoine, you can't change what happened to your parents and you can't beat yourself up for doing your job for your country. You have to find a way to forgive yourself, to understand that you did what you had to do."

He wanted to fall into the softness of her green eyes, wanted desperately to believe he was the kind of man she thought him to be. She was so naïve, so accepting of not just his positive traits, but also of the dark side he'd tried to keep hidden from the world, from himself.

"What you don't understand is that I've made plenty of enemies. There are people out there who would like nothing better than to make me pay for what I did to them, or to their family members."

She frowned. "And you think that's who attacked us and not somebody out to destroy the coalition?" Her green eyes darkened slightly.

"I think it's possible and I also think it's possible they believe the way to hurt me is to hurt you."

"But why? I'm not your family." Her cheeks bloomed a dusty rose. "I'm just head of housekeeping at the hotel where you happen to be staying. I've just helped you out with some personal things."

"You know you're more than that to me," he said gruffly.

"But how would anyone else know what kind of a relationship you and I have?"

He led her back to the table and they both sat once again. "Somebody obviously saw us leave the hotel together, or as we drove to Jane's lab. Perhaps they drew certain conclusions about us being together in a more intimate way."

A frown once again sliced across her forehead. "But what makes you think it's somebody from your past?"

"There was no way the attack on us was done by professionals. It was clumsy and wrought with potential for errors. We could have seen the face of the driver, he might have wrecked his own vehicle in the process of trying to wreck ours. There were too many variables that could have made things go wrong. If he was trying to kill me after we got out of the crash, he shot too soon."

"He shot at me instead of you." Her voice was flat, as if she was just now starting to believe what he was trying to tell her.

"If it had been a professional wanting to stop

my participation in the COIN coalition, he would have waited until I stood to fire his first shot. That way I would have been clueless about his presence…and very dead."

The nerve in her neck reappeared and began to beat more distinctly and he reached out and tenderly placed a finger against the pulse. "Beth, I don't want to scare you, but I thought you should know that I might have brought danger to you."

Her eyes were amazingly soft as she gazed at him. "Then we'll just have to deal with it," she said.

A hardness that had been around his heart cracked apart and fell away. "That means I don't want you staying here alone." He moved his hand from the throbbing muscle in her throat and reached up and stroked a strand of her silky blond hair. "That means I don't even want you out of my sight."

"We'll figure it out," she replied, her voice a little breathless.

As he continued to look at her, his brain whirled with suppositions. If somebody was after her because they thought she was his lover, there was no real way to disabuse them of that notion.

He'd already made her a target and the best he could hope for was that he could keep her safe until he returned to Barajas. He felt confident that once he was out of the country the threat would follow him.

But for tonight he didn't intend to go anywhere. And all he could think about was that they had been damned by what they weren't doing—so why not go ahead and do it? Why not become her lover?

He stood once again and took her by the hand and pulled her up from her chair. He was immediately surrounded by the delicious scent of her that was as much a welcome as the aura of her home.

"The coffee is ready," she murmured as he drew her into his arms. Her body warmth radiated through the soft, fleece material.

"Hmm, suddenly I'm not in the mood for coffee." He leaned down and touched his lips to the warm flesh of her neck, then nibbled at the skin just beneath her ear. He felt the quickened beat of her heart against his and a faint tremor that stole through her. "I think it's time I made good on that earlier promise."

She didn't ask what promise he was talking about, rather she drew a shuddery breath and took him by the hand and led him down the hall toward her bedroom.

IT WAS LIKE A DREAM and she didn't ever want to wake up. Antoine's hand was warm and firm around hers as she led him into her bedroom.

This time it wasn't fear that caused her heart to crash wildly in her chest. It was a heady anticipation. She felt as if despite her internal protests to the contrary, they had been headed to this place when she'd first entered his suite after finding the notes in Amir's room.

They had danced around each other with sensual intent every moment they had spent in each other's company and finally it was time for them to reward themselves with a payoff.

She dropped his hand and walked over to the nightstand and turned on the light. A soft spill of illumination filled the room and in the glow she saw the ravenous hunger that lit his pale eyes as he gazed at her.

Waves of heat swept over her as her mouth went dry. The look in his eyes was like an exquisite form of foreplay. He didn't even have to touch her for her to feel him on her skin, deep inside her.

"Are you sure?" His voice was deeper than usual as he stood at military attention at the foot of the bed.

It was the first time since she'd known him that he appeared the least bit uncertain and that only made her more sure of what she wanted from him.

She walked to where he stood and laced her arms around his neck. "I want you to hold me, Antoine. I want you to kiss me until neither of us can think of anything but each other. I want you to make love with me and then hold me tight until morning comes."

Blue flames shot from his eyes. "I can do that starting right now." His mouth feathered over hers in a surprisingly light kiss that teased her senses and made her yearn for more...so very much more.

He wrapped his arms around her back and pulled her close and she didn't know if the rapidly beating heart she felt was his or her own.

His mouth blazed a trail down her jaw and to her neck, where his lips lightly nipped at the sensitive skin just below her ear.

She'd expected command and he gave her a gentleness that stole her breath away. "Sweet Beth," he whispered softly. "You are absolutely amazing."

He made her feel amazing, like she was the brightest, the sexiest woman in the world. Nobody had ever made her feel the way Antoine did and she had a feeling that nobody would again. This moment was magic. This man was magic and she wanted to savor it forever.

When his lips took hers again in a fiery kiss she was ready to rip her clothes off and get beneath the covers with him. But he seemed to be in no hurry. Languidly his hands stroked up and down her back as his mouth continued to ply hers with heat.

She didn't want to think about what would

happen when they left the bed in the morning. He was a hotel guest and had a country to return to and she knew in the very depths of her heart he would leave without her.

She would go back to being the highly efficient head of housekeeping with nothing but memories to keep her warm. But even knowing that she wanted him.

Perhaps someday in the distant future she could tell her grandchildren about the time she had shared with a handsome prince whose life had been in danger. Of course, she wouldn't tell them about this night of desire, but she'd tell them how she'd helped him in his quest to save his life and the lives of his friends.

All thoughts of grandchildren fled out of her mind. There was only Antoine and his fiery lips and the smooth slide of his hands down her back.

He finally released his hold on her and stepped back. As she stood frozen in place he leaned down and removed the gun that had been strapped to his ankle. He placed it on the nightstand, along with his wallet, and then began to unbutton his shirt.

With each button that was unfastened more of his dark, muscled chest was revealed. Beth felt her knees weaken as he finally shrugged the shirt off and it fell to the floor behind him. Taut chest muscles and six-pack abs attested to the fact that he was a man who worked out regularly.

It was only then that he approached her again. "You look adorable in that pink sweatshirt, but I have a need now to take it off you." The fact that he'd spoken his intent out loud only made her hotter.

Her heart hitched in her chest as he took the bottom of the shirt and effortlessly pulled it over her head and then threw it into one of the darkened corners of the room. She desperately wished she was wearing a sexy black or red lacy bra instead of the white cotton.

"Beautiful," he whispered.

She splayed her hands across his hard chest and smiled up at him. "Beautiful," she agreed as the heat of him warmed her palms.

"Do you have any idea how crazy you make me?" His fingers trailed a path across her bare collarbone.

"It can't be any more crazy than you make me," she replied breathlessly. "Antoine, nobody has ever made me feel the way you do."

He moved his fingers from her collarbone to her cheek. "I like that…and now I think we've talked enough."

She released a delighted gasp as he swept her up into his arms and carried her to the bed. He lay her down and then sat next to her and removed the slippers she'd put on when she'd changed out of her uniform.

When her slippers were gone he took the waistband of her jogging pants and pulled and she raised her hips to help him remove them.

Her heart now thundered as he once again stood and kicked off his shoes and then moved his hands to the waistband of his slacks. He hesitated. "Are you still sure about this? I need you to be sure, Beth. I don't want regrets from you, now or ever."

"I've never been so sure of anything in my life," she replied fervently. It was true. Right or wrong, she was going to make love to him tonight.

With surprisingly graceful movements, he took off his slacks, exposing black briefs beneath and long, muscular legs. He was perfection and the sight of him nearly naked only served to increase her desire for him.

As he joined her on the bed their legs wrapped together with the comfortable ease of longtime lovers. Their bodies fit perfectly, like yin and yang symbols.

Kisses became caresses and it wasn't long before both of them were impatient with the underwear that kept them separate. As he removed her bra his mouth eagerly covered one of her nipples.

She felt the pull of his lips deep in the pit of her stomach as her nipple responded to his touch, pebbling into a hard knot. She tightened her hands on his shoulders, loving the play of his muscles beneath her fingers.

He teased the tip of her nipple with his tongue, first licking and then nipping until she was gasping with the fiery sensations that coursed through her. Her blood was hot in her veins and she wanted more…more of him.

Within minutes the last of their clothing was gone and his hot caresses seemed to be everywhere…across the swollen rise of her breasts, down the flat of her stomach and whispering softly on her inner thighs until she wanted to scream with her need of him.

"I love the little sound you make in the back of your throat when I stroke you here," he whispered as he once again ran his hot, wicked fingers lightly over the inside of her thigh.

"And what kind of a sound do you make when I touch you here?" She moved her hand slowly down his stomach and encircled his hardness. A small moan escaped his lips and she smiled. "I like that sound."

"You are a wanton woman, Beth, and if you aren't careful this will be over long before I want it to be." Gently he shoved her hand from him and instead touched her where she most wanted him.

Instantly she tensed with pleasure. His fingers were magic and she felt the swell of not only her physical reaction to his touch but also the surge of emotion that accompanied her impending release.

Tears misted her eyes as the waves built up… up and then finally came crashing all around her and she cried out his name over and over again.

"Please," she said when she'd managed to catch half her breath. She knew she was begging but she didn't care. She wanted him fully, wanted him to possess her completely. "Please, Antoine, take me now."

He rolled over toward the nightstand and grabbed his wallet and withdrew a condom. A small relief flooded through her. She hadn't even thought about protection.

With the condom in place he moved between her thighs and entered her with an agonizing slowness that spiraled her upward once again.

When he was deep within her, she clung to his shoulders as she moved her hips to meet his thrusts. She was glad they'd left the light on, so that she could see the hunger in his eyes as he plunged into her faster and faster.

Suddenly he slowed and nearly stopped moving. She bucked beneath him as her well of want grew bigger. He smiled down at her and then resumed his movements.

He teased and tormented her, bringing her almost to the brink and then stopping. She could tell by the taut cords in his neck that he was teasing not only her, but himself as well.

She tightened around him, and saw his control snap with the blaze of his eyes. Wildly he moved against her, groans of pleasure escaping his lips.

She cried out his name as she shuddered with another climax. He stiffened against her in response as he found his own.

They clung to each other, breathless for several long moments. He finally got up and went into the bathroom while Beth remained sated and boneless beneath the sheets. When he returned, he turned off the light on the nightstand and then got back into bed and pulled her against him.

She snuggled into the warmth of his body, feeling safer, more content that she could ever remember feeling. He stroked her hair and pressed his lips against her forehead.

"That was amazing," he said in a soft whisper.

"You were amazing," she murmured drowsily.

"We were amazing together," he replied with a satisfied laugh.

She burrowed closer against his chest and as sleep reached out to claim her, she tried not to think about the fact that Prince Antoine Cavanaugh of Barajas was definitely going to break her heart.

Chapter Seven

They got up and drank a cup of coffee and shared a piece of cake together, giggling like teenagers in the middle of the night.

Antoine entertained her with stories about his and Sebastian's childhood antics, loving the sound of her laughter and the way amusement sparkled in her eyes.

He thought it possible that he could have a lifetime of her laughter and never tire of the sound. "You had a happy childhood?" he asked.

"I had a wonderful childhood," she replied. "The woods were my playground and before my mother got ill we spent lots of time exploring. We'd have wonderful picnics when the weather was nice."

"And you'd prepare gourmet food for the occasion?" he asked.

She smiled and shook her head. "I really didn't start getting interested in cooking until after my mother was ill. Her appetite wasn't good and so

I started trying new recipes to tempt her. That's what led to my love of cooking."

When the cake was gone and her eyelids were drooping with sleepiness, they turned out all the lights in the house and got back into bed.

She cuddled up beside him and he stroked her hair, more at peace than he could ever remember being. He could hear a faint night breeze through the window that tinkled the wind chime, and a rhythmic clicking from some kind of insect. The sounds only added to the peace that invaded his soul.

"Antoine, I know you said you'd never marry, but have you never wanted children?" Beth asked softly.

He hesitated a long moment before replying. "I never thought much about children until I spent time with Samantha Peters." His heart softened as he thought of the four-year-old little girl who would eventually call him Uncle. "She was quite a little charmer and I must confess for a moment I wondered what it might be like to have a child of my own. But, just like I have no place in my life for a wife, there's no place in my life for children."

"That's sad," she said softly. "You would make a wonderful father, Antoine."

He tried not to allow her words to ache in his heart. What kind of father would he make always looking over his shoulder, always worried that somehow, someway his enemies would find him? "What about you? You want children?"

"Definitely. At least two and I want them to know the kind of love my mother showed me." She snuggled closer against him and within minutes he knew she'd fallen asleep.

Antoine remained awake long after Beth had fallen asleep, watching her in the faint spill of moonlight that fell into the window.

He loved the feel of her in his arms. He hadn't expected making love to her to fill him with such a depth of emotion. He'd thought she'd be like all the other women he'd had in his life, easy to make love to and just as easy to walk away from and forget.

Was this how his father had felt about his mother?

Had his father known the danger of loving her but been unable to stop himself? Had he fought what he felt with all his might, only to realize that love was stronger than fear?

Surely what Antoine felt wasn't love. It was simply the pleasure of their lovemaking that had him feeling such craziness. He'd spent his entire life telling himself that his heart was not meant to love.

Perhaps his feelings for Beth were tied up with the fact that he had nobody else he could trust, that she provided a safe haven of sorts from the madness that had become his life here in the United States.

Perhaps it was time for him to consider returning to Barajas. He wasn't really accomplishing anything in his mission to find Amir. The COIN summit had been canceled and he certainly wouldn't be making any trade deals while he was here. That would happen at another place, at another time.

Was it time to go home? A tiny bit of rebellion burned in his belly at the thought. There had been times over the last three weeks that he'd considered not going back to Barajas. Sebastian was perfectly capable of carrying the leadership of the nation alone and Antoine had never truly been comfortable beneath the mantle of responsibility.

He loved this wild and beautiful state he'd found himself in, loved the idea of being a cowboy and settling into a different kind of lifestyle. But, he also wondered if this wasn't just a need to escape the intrigue that had surrounded him for the past couple of weeks.

Closing his eyes he breathed in the sweet scent of Beth and told himself that no matter what happened he couldn't love her. He was the master of his emotions, in total control of his feelings and he absolutely, positively refused to allow himself to love her.

He drifted off to sleep and the dream came

almost immediately. Big, muscular men clad all in black surrounded the bed where he and Beth lay, their dark eyes filled with intense hatred, with the bloodthirsty need for revenge.

Antoine could smell their rage in the room, an acrid scent that let him know they were dangerous, that he and Beth were in terrible trouble.

"You took my father's pride and he died a broken man," one of them said. "He was a farmer and had nothing to do with politics."

"You stole my brother's honor and now you're going to pay," another exclaimed.

All the men began to shout and Antoine found himself powerless to respond, unable to move a single muscle. Beth remained sleeping next to him, unaware of the danger that surrounded them.

Panic seared up the back of his throat as he struggled to respond. But, his efforts were to no avail, he remained mute and motionless, unable to defend himself or Beth against the attack.

"You took from us and now we'll take from you." One of the men gazed at Beth as he pulled a long, wicked knife from his belt.

Agony screamed through Antoine's head as he realized they intended to hurt her. *Kill me,* he silently screamed. *I'm the one who broke your father. I'm the one who hurt your brother. Take me and leave her alone!*

He awakened with a start and bolted up,

gasping for air as he gazed around the moonlit room. Alone. He and Beth were alone in the room. There were no men hovering next to the bed, nobody in the shadows. It had all just been a terrible nightmare.

He raked a hand down his face and drew several deep breaths. A cold sweat chilled him as the last of the horror of the dream faded away.

With a sigh he lay back down and looked at Beth, who was curled up on her side and still sleeping soundly. His heart crunched painfully in his chest.

He felt as if by involving her in his little investigation he'd damned her. By merely being in his presence he'd made somebody believe that she was important enough to him to be used as a weapon against him.

He didn't believe in the prophecy of dreams, but there was no question that the nightmare he'd just suffered had the aura of a warning. The problem was he felt as if it was too late to change anything where Beth was concerned. The dream and his knowledge of what had happened to his father only made him more certain that he would never have a woman, not even Beth, as a permanent part of his life.

Closing his eyes he tried to find sleep again, praying that it would be a slumber without visions, that if there were dreams they would be happy ones.

He had to believe that Amir would be found alive, that the rest of the coalition would be okay and that Beth would be all right when he eventually returned to Barajas.

He'd just about fallen back to sleep when he thought he heard the faint tinkle of breaking glass.

He froze. Was it part of a new dream? Or a trick of his imagination? Had the wind picked up and what he'd heard was the wind chime outside the window? There was no repeat of the noise that would make him believe it was simply the wind.

He tried to relax but after a moment sat up once again, knowing that he wouldn't be able to go back to sleep until he went to investigate what had made the noise.

Silently he slid out of the bed and pulled on his briefs and his slacks, then grabbed his gun from the nightstand, his heart beating unsteadily as he made his way out of the bedroom.

He paused in the darkened hallway and listened, and heard a faint sound he couldn't identify. He took several more steps and ahead he could see a faint flickering light coming from the kitchen area.

What the hell? He frowned and gripped the gun tighter in his hand as he entered the living room. He'd gotten halfway through the room when the acrid air reached his nose and he saw the dark swirl of smoke that waved ghostly fingers in front of the windows.

Fire!

The word exploded in his head in alarm. Shielding his nose and mouth with the back of his hand, he entered the kitchen. One of the breakfast nook windows was broken and fire danced up the curtains and ate at the wooden wall.

He smelled the distinct scent of gasoline and guessed that a Molotov cocktail had been thrown through the window and had exploded.

Dammit! Somebody must have followed them here. He'd assumed with the new vehicle they wouldn't be noticed for at least a couple of days.

He coughed as the viscous black smoke thickened, not only obscuring his visibility but also invading his lungs. They had to get out of the house. With the wooden structure to feed it, the fire would be completely out of control within minutes.

He raced back to the bedroom and flipped on the overhead light. "Beth, get up." He ran to the side of the bed and pulled at her arm.

She gazed at him in sleepy confusion. "What? What's wrong?"

"Quickly, put some clothes on. The house is on fire. We have to get out of here," he exclaimed.

The sleepiness instantly left her eyes. She

jumped out of bed but instead of grabbing for her clothes, she reached for the phone on the nightstand and called 911 to report the fire. Only then did she grab the sweatshirt and sweatpants and pull them on.

By this time the smoke had snaked down the hallway and had begun to drift into the bedroom. He shoved his gun into his waistband and stepped into his shoes while she pulled on her sneakers. He was aware that every second they wasted meant the fire was getting bigger, hungrier and the danger to them grew more intense.

"We should be able to get out the front door," he said as he took her by the hand and pulled her out of the bedroom. He got them halfway to the front door when he halted, his brain working to process the entire situation.

"Wait!" He stopped her from opening the front door as his brain snapped and fired. It was a perfect ruse. Set a fire in the rear of the house and then wait for the occupants to run out the front door. It would be easy to pick them off as they came out of the door.

"We can't go out that way," he exclaimed.

Thankfully she didn't take time to question his words. "The back door," she replied and started to tug him toward the kitchen.

He remained grounded and shook his head and then realized she probably couldn't see the action through the thick smoke that surrounded them. "It's too dangerous. The fire is near the back door." Besides, he had no idea if more than one person might be waiting outside for them.

Her hand clutched his in a death grip. "How do we get out?" she cried and then was taken over by a violent spasm of coughing.

"Come on." He pulled her back down the hallway and into the main bathroom where he closed the door behind them. "Don't turn on the light," he cautioned her. He didn't want to alert anyone outside as to exactly where they were in the house.

"Somebody is out there, aren't they?" she whispered. He felt her frightened gaze on him as he opened the bathroom window. When he turned to face her, she was barely visible in the faint moonlight that spilled into the window.

He placed his palms on either side of her face, his heart racing with a rush of adrenaline. His only desire at that moment was to keep her safe.

"Somebody *is* out there," he replied with a sense of urgency. "I think they set the fire and now they're just waiting for us to leave the house. We can't stay inside, the smoke is getting thicker and it's too dangerous."

She opened her mouth as if to say something, but he slid his finger over her lips to still her. "They will be expecting us to go out either the front or the back door. I'm hoping we can get out this window without being detected."

She nodded and he pulled his finger away from her mouth. "I'm going to go out first and you follow me. Once you hit the ground don't wait for me and don't look back. Just run like your life depends on it, because I'm afraid that it does."

Without waiting for a rcsponse, he slid his head out the window and looked around. Nobody. He saw nobody lurking in the darkness. He raised himself up and over the window ledge and dropped silently to the ground.

Gun firmly in hand, he once again scanned the area and then motioned Beth to climb out. Just as he'd instructed, she hit the ground and headed for the trees, not looking back as she ran.

He tightened his grip on his gun and went into a crouch position as he began to move along the side of the house and gave one last look toward the trees, praying this wasn't the very last time he'd see Beth.

SHE RAN THROUGH THE TREES like a rabid animal, darting first one way and then another as terror kept any rational thought out of her head.

Ladybug, ladybug, fly away home. Your house is on fire and your children all gone.

The nursery rhyme repeated itself over and over

again in her head and she felt a burst of hysterical laughter rise to her lips.

But she swallowed it, unsure who might be hiding behind a bush, who might be in the shadows of the night waiting to discern her location.

Who had seen them? Had somebody been hiding in the woods, watching her cabin and hoping to catch them here? On the drive she'd checked her rearview often, but had seen nobody following behind them. How had this happened? What would happen next?

She finally collapsed at the base of a tree and held her breath, listening for the sound of Antoine, for the sound of anyone who might be near. A stitch in her side burned painfully, but she ignored it.

Where was Antoine right now? Was he hiding in the trees or had he gone chasing the danger? She feared the latter and the only thing that made her feel the slightest bit better was that she hadn't heard the sound of any gunfire...at least not yet.

She didn't even want to think about her house... her home. It was just stuff, she told herself, and she didn't need stuff. What she needed was for Antoine to be okay. The last thing she wanted was for him to try to be a hero. Dead heroes held no appeal except in history books.

He had to be all right. She sent a dozen prayers toward the sky, praying for Antoine's safety. It would be tragic if anything happened to him, tragic for her and for all the people of Barajas.

Her heart banged so loudly in her chest she wasn't sure she'd hear if anyone snuck up behind her. Even though she was on the ground every muscle in her body was tensed for flight.

Who had done this? Was it somebody from Antoine's past, like he suspected? There was no doubt that this act had been meant to hurt not just him, but her as well. She sensed true hatred behind this, a hatred that went beyond political goals and into something far more personal.

Her heart leaped at the sound of sirens in the distance. Help was coming! She pulled herself back up to her feet and began to silently move in the direction of the cabin.

She hid behind a stand of trees that gave her a perfect view of the house and as she saw the flames eating at the kitchen, tears welled up in her eyes.

The kitchen, the place where she'd spent many happy hours. Had the fire broken the cookie jar that had belonged to her grandmother, burned the cookbooks that had been handed down through the generations? Had the dish towels her mother embroidered turned to char?

At that moment strong arms encircled her from behind and a hand shot over her mouth to still the scream that begged to escape.

"It's me," Antoine's voice whispered in her ear just as she was ready to whirl around and fight for her life.

He released his hold on her and she turned and threw herself into his arms. The tears she'd shoved back finally spilled from her eyes as he held her close.

Their heartbeats raced against each other as they clung together. "I was so afraid," she finally managed to gasp. "I was so afraid for you."

His arms tightened around her. "We'll be safe now. Sheriff Wolf is here."

The clearing around the house had become filled with firemen, lawmen and equipment. By the time she and Antoine left the cover of the trees the fire was under control and nearly out, although smoke still lingered in the air.

Jake Wolf stood near the back of the house, talking to the fire chief as they approached. When he spied them he left the man and came over to talk to them.

"Thank God you both got out safely," he said. He looked as tired as Beth felt. Soot dusted his high cheekbones and his eyes held a weariness. It seemed like an eternity since Beth had been sleeping peacefully in Antoine's arms.

"What happened?" Jake asked.

"We were sleeping and I woke up when I heard breaking glass. I got up to investigate and found the kitchen on fire. I think perhaps it was a Molotov cocktail that broke the window." Antoine placed an arm around Beth's shoulder. "We managed to get out through the bathroom window. I told Beth to hide in the woods and I went to investigate."

Jake's features tightened. "Prince Antoine, I would prefer you leave the investigating to me."

"In any case I didn't see anyone," Antoine replied, but it was obvious by his voice that he wished he had seen somebody.

Jake looked at Antoine and then at Beth and she felt the unspoken questions the sheriff had. She tried not to feel embarrassed about the fact that it would probably now be obvious to Jake that she and Antoine were in an intimate relationship.

"Are you okay?" Jake asked her, his gaze uncharacteristically soft.

"I'm fine," she replied and fought a new wave of tears as she looked at the house. Even though she'd told herself it was just things and not important, they had been *her* things and the fact that somebody had willfully destroyed them both made her angry and made her want to weep.

"It's not as bad as it looks," Jake said, as if reading her thoughts.

"I have insurance," she replied and stiffened her shoulders. "I'm sure it will all be okay."

Jake looked back at Antoine. "We'll know

more tomorrow when things cool down and the fire chief can get inside and take a look around. In the meantime me and some of my men will search the area and see what we can find. I'll also make sure somebody stays here on the property until arrangements can be made for Beth to return."

"Thanks, Sheriff. Can we go?" Antoine asked. "It's been a bad night and Beth needs to be someplace safe."

"I'll have a deputy drive you back to the hotel and another one to drive your car back there," Jake replied. "But I'm sure I'll have more questions for you in the morning."

Minutes later they were in the back of a patrol car. Beth could smell the acrid scent of smoke that clung to them as she leaned against Antoine's side.

"Try not to worry," he said softly. "I'll do whatever it takes to fix things."

"Insurance will take care of it," she replied wearily. It wasn't his job to fix things for her. He'd already bought her a new vehicle and she absolutely refused to accept anything else from him.

They were silent for the remainder of the ride back to the hotel, where the deputy insisted he accompany them to Antoine's suite. Thankfully at this hour of the morning the lobby was empty except for a few members of the staff who were cleaning the area.

They watched openmouthed as the three walked through and down the hallway that led to the suite. Beth could only imagine the gossip that would roar through the place in the next couple of hours. At the moment she was too tired to care. She'd deal with it in the morning.

A second deputy appeared to hand them the keys to the Jeep and then they were left alone. Beth stood in the middle of the living room area, unsure what her next move should be.

She was beyond numb. It had all been too much, the car crash, the bullets and now the fire. She was simply overwhelmed by it all.

"Come." Antoine took her by the hand and led her into the master bathroom. He started the water in the huge, glass-enclosed shower and then turned back to her and began to undress her.

Gently he pulled the smoky, soot-covered sweatshirt over her head and tossed it to the floor. When he pulled down her pants, she stepped out of them, still numb to the world.

There was nothing sexual about his actions. It was only tenderness she felt, along with his obvious need to take care of her. And she let him, grateful that she didn't have to think, didn't have to do anything but submit to him.

When they were both naked he pulled her into the warm spray of water. Using the clean-scented soap the hotel provided he quickly washed and rinsed himself and then began to wash her.

He dragged the soap-filled sponge over her shoulders and down her chest. She stood impassive and merely accepted, like a child being washed by a parent. He washed every inch of her until she was slicked with soap.

When he was finished he pulled her back beneath the warm spray and she closed her eyes as the scent of smoke finally disappeared down the drain. With her body cleaned, he used the shampoo and began to wash her hair.

She leaned with her bare chest and face pressed against one wall of the shower, the glass warm as she dropped her head back. His fingers worked against her scalp in a hypnotic fashion. Her brain was emptied of all thoughts as she completely gave herself to his care.

Slowly, she felt herself beginning to relax, leaving behind the terror that had filled her through the long, seemingly endless night.

By the time he was finished and her hair had been rinsed until it squeaked with cleanliness, she was beyond exhaustion. He turned off the shower, dried himself and pulled on one of the thick robes the resort provided, then dried her off and pulled his own robe around her.

She reveled in the scent of him that clung to the robe. It smelled like caring. It smelled like safety. He then picked her up and carried her into the bedroom where the bed had been turned down and was ready for sleep.

"I should make arrangements to return to Barajas and take you with me," he said once they were in the bed, with his body spooned around hers and his arm around her waist. "I feel responsible for you and there I can arrange for your safety without problems."

"Let's discuss it in the morning," she said and squeezed her eyes as tears once again burned. For in that moment she realized she didn't need him to fix her house. She didn't want to be his responsibility. The only thing she really wanted was for Antoine to love her.

Chapter Eight

Antoine awoke and knew by the cast of the sun slanting in through the windows that it was late morning. For several long moments he remained in the warm bed, reluctant to leave the comfort and the faint scent of Beth that filled the air.

He glanced over to the other side of the bed where she was curled up facing him. Her features were soft and his fingers ached with the desire to touch her cheek, to awaken her with a sweet kiss and then make love to her while her body was soft and warm and yielding.

She'd lost so much because of him. And last night she could have lost her life.

He fought his impulse to reach over and draw her into his embrace, repeat the lovemaking that had blown his mind. She deserved her sleep after all she'd been through.

But, it didn't take long before he grew restless, knowing that there were many things to attend to and staying in bed wouldn't accomplish anything.

With Beth still soundly sleeping, he slid from the bed, grabbed his robe and left the room.

The meeting with the housekeeper Janine Sahron would have to wait until later in the day. He knew there would be much business concerning the events of the night before to take care of this morning.

The first thing he did was order coffee and breakfast from room service and then arranged for housekeeping to dispose of the smoky clothing they'd worn the night before. Finally, he called the gift shop and ordered a pair of slacks and a blouse for Beth to put on when she awakened.

With the immediate needs taken care of, he sank down in one of the leather chairs by the fireplace and replayed the night's events in his head.

Why hadn't he considered that they might be in danger at her cabin? Had he allowed his overwhelming desire for her, his need to get her alone and make love to her to completely muddy his brain?

It was the only explanation for his foolish judgment and he hated himself for it. He'd allowed himself to be ruled by his emotions and that had nearly gotten them killed. It was definitely a mistake he wouldn't allow to happen again.

He could only hope that either the fire chief or Jake Wolf would be able to find some clue in the ruins of Beth's cabin that might lead them to arrest the person responsible for this latest attack.

He still believed the attacks he and Beth had suffered were too amateurish to be part of a bigger conspiracy with professional players in the mix.

Verovick wouldn't have used a Molotov cocktail, when he or his men could have planted an effective bomb in the car or in the house. There were any number of ways a professional killer could get to him without resorting to something as primitive as a gasoline-filled bottle stuffed with fabric.

Once again he suspected it was someone with a personal vendetta rather than anyone connected with the COIN coalition.

Who could it be? Who had the resources to follow him across the sea with the sole purpose of revenge? He didn't know how to begin to identify a person or persons who might be behind all this.

Dammit, he should have never pulled Beth into his drama. He should have insisted he take the notes from her and then left her to go on her merry way.

One thing was certain. She would not be returning to her home. She would not be going anywhere anytime soon. She didn't know it yet, but he intended to make her a prisoner in this suite until he knew for sure that the danger to her was gone for good.

He jumped as his cell phone rang and answered to hear Sebastian's voice. "My brother, how are things in Barajas?" he asked.

"Very well," Sebastian replied. "Jessica and little Samantha are settling in quite nicely and our people seem to be pleased that I finally have a woman by my side. What about there? Any news on Amir? Any other developments?"

"I'm afraid there's been nothing new on Amir," Antoine replied and then told his brother what had happened since last time they spoke. "I have a bad feeling, Sebastian. I don't think these attacks are related to our reason for being here in the States. I think it's somebody from my past and my biggest regret is that now I believe Beth is in danger as well."

The two brothers discussed what Antoine had learned about Verovick and speculated on the Russian mob's involvement in the conspiracy against the royals.

As he spoke with his brother, confessing all his concerns about Beth and how much his involvement with her had cost her, once again he was struck by her bravery. She was a woman unlike any other that he'd ever known. She would make some man a wonderful wife. She would be a courageous and beautiful mother and the fact that he wouldn't be around to see that broke his heart.

The conversation was interrupted by a knock on the door.

"I think breakfast has arrived," Antoine said into the phone as he got up from his chair.

"Then I'll let you go and enjoy your food. Stay safe, Antoine."

"I'm doing my best, my brother," he replied.

"And keep in touch," Sebastian added. With a promise to do just that, Antoine hung up.

At the door was not only breakfast, but also an employee from the gift shop with the items he'd requested for Beth. As the meal was being set on the table, he carried the clothing into the bedroom where he discovered that Beth was out of bed and in the bathroom.

He knocked on the door. "Beth, I have some clean clothes here for you."

She opened the door and he saw that she'd neatly brushed her hair and her face was dewy with a recent scrub. She looked achingly beautiful and for just a moment he wanted to pull her from the bathroom and back into the bed. He wanted to forget what had happened, not worry about what might happen and just hold her once again in his arms.

"Thank you," she said and took the clothes from him and then closed the bathroom door once again.

There had been a touch of distance in her eyes,

he thought as he quickly got dressed for the day. And could he blame her? She'd simply offered to drive him where he wanted to go and now she'd lost a vehicle, her house had been damaged and her privacy invaded.

He hadn't missed the shocked looks on the faces of the cleaning crew working in the lobby when he and Beth returned to the suite last night.

He knew the gossip that would be flying around the resort this morning, gossip about the prince and the head of housekeeping.

Long after he left here she would have to deal with the aftermath of her involvement with him. He had brought her nothing but trouble, was it any wonder her eyes had held a distance?

He returned to the dining area and poured himself a cup of coffee and by that time Beth had joined him. The navy slacks he'd bought kissed the length of her legs with perfection. The peach-colored blouse brought out the blond highlights in her shoulder-length hair and the bright green of her eyes.

Had it only been the night before when he'd tasted the sweetness of her lips? Felt the burn of her body next to his? Desire once again nibbled at him, like a voracious hunger that refused to be ignored, a hunger that would never be completely satisfied.

"Thank you for the clothes," she said.

"I didn't think you'd want to put the soot-covered smoky things from last night back on."

"Have you heard anything from Jake this morning?" she asked as she poured herself a cup of coffee and took a seat at the table.

"Not yet. If I don't hear anything from him by the time we finish our meal, I'll call him." He joined her at the table. "I'm hoping he'll have some news for us."

"You ordered enough breakfast for an army," she observed.

He looked at the food on the table. There were pancakes and eggs, fresh fruit and oatmeal and biscuits and bagels. He looked back at her. "I woke up hungry."

She must have seen something in his eyes that let her know he was talking about more than just an appetite for breakfast. Her cheeks grew pink as she speared a pancake and placed it on her plate.

He watched as she took banana slices and placed them on the pancake like eyes, then used an orange slice to make a mouth on the pancake. She looked up to see him watching her and a small smile curved her lips.

"My mother used to do this to my pancakes when I was a little girl and was being crabby. She'd say, 'Look, Beth, your pancake is smiling at you and he wants a smile back.'" She looked at him and her cheeks were pink. "Silly, I know, but whenever I was upset it always worked to bring a smile to my face."

He hated that the implication was that she was upset now and had reached back into the memories of her childhood to feel better. Again he mentally cursed himself for getting her involved in his mess.

He sought words to comfort her, but recognized at the moment he had none. He couldn't tell her everything was going to be okay when he didn't know what to expect next. He refused to mouth empty platitudes. She deserved so much better than that.

"Do you have happy memories of your mother?" she asked as they began to eat.

The most easily accessed memory Antoine had of his mother, Nephra, was of the night of her death. Certainly not a happy one.

He now fought past that particularly horrific memory in an attempt to find others more pleasant from his earlier childhood. And they were there, just waiting to be tapped into.

"She loved to sing," he said, surprised by the sudden recollection. "And she had the voice of an angel." His heart warmed as he thought about the lullabies his mother would sing to him and Sebastian before they drifted off to sleep each night.

And releasing that pleasant memory from his

past prompted others to spring free. "I remember her taking Sebastian and me to the beach where we built sand castles and played in the waves. She loved the water and swam like a fish. She taught both Sebastian and me to swim. She had a laugh that could fill a room and she loved us and my father to distraction."

Beth laid a hand on his forearm. "Those are the memories you should dream about, Antoine. Embrace the love your parents had for you and for each other and let it be your place of dreams."

It was at that moment that he knew that the most difficult thing he'd ever do in his life was tell Beth Taylor goodbye.

JAKE WOLF ARRIVED AT THE SUITE at the same time they finished breakfast. Antoine gestured him into the living area where Jake sat on one of the chairs facing Antoine and Beth who were seated on the sofa.

Beth looked at him anxiously, knowing he'd probably spent the morning at her place. "How bad is it?" she asked.

"The good news is the fire damage was confined to the kitchen area," Jake said. "There is some mild smoke damage throughout but a good cleaning company should be able to take care of all that."

A touch of relief filtered through her. Pots and

pans could be bought again and held no sentimental value. Of all the rooms in the house she could only be grateful that it had been the kitchen that had taken the brunt of the flames.

Jake turned his attention to Antoine. "You were right. It was a Molotov cocktail. We found pieces of the bottle near the window and gasoline was used as the accelerant."

"The type of bottle?" Antoine asked.

"An ordinary beer bottle that was loaded with gasoline and had what looks like part of a bed sheet as a wick," Jake replied. "We're hoping to pull some prints from the fragments of the bottle we collected." Jake looked formidable as his eyes narrowed. "If we lift a print, then I'll see to it that the person is behind bars for a long time to come. This wasn't a simple case of arson, it was definitely attempted murder. Whoever threw that bottle had to have known that you and Beth were in the house."

Antoine nodded, looking equally grim. "I have dispatched a couple of members of my security team to sit on the house and make sure there is no issue with looting. Beth will not be returning there until somebody is behind bars."

Jake nodded. "That seems like a wise idea to me."

"Hello?" Beth said in irritation. "I'm right here and I will make my own decisions." Both men turned to look at her. "And I won't be returning to the house until somebody is behind bars, although I would like to go there and pack some things."

"We also found some tire marks in an area near the house we think might belong to the perpetrator. We cast them and hopefully we'll be able to figure out exactly what kind of car it was," Jake added.

As the two men continued discussing all the events that had taken place over the last couple of days, Beth thought about what her next move should be.

The one thing she wouldn't do was pick up her life and go to Barajas where Antoine thought he could keep her safe. She wouldn't become a weighted ball around his neck, another responsibility he had to take care of. That was simply not an option.

She would stay in a room here in the hotel until her place was put back together. What she wouldn't do was stay in the suite with Antoine.

As crazy as it seemed in the short amount of time they'd spent together, she'd fallen in love with him, and now each minute that she remained with him only deepened her love. Somehow she had to cut her losses now, not get in any deeper than she already was.

She knew that when he left the country, when

all this was said and done, she would be left with a heart that wasn't just bruised, but rather battered.

"If you'd like, I can take you to get your things from the house right now," Jake said, pulling Beth from her thoughts.

"That would be wonderful," she replied and stood.

"I'll go as well," Antoine said.

Beth shook her head. "No," she said firmly. "I'll be fine with Jake and he doesn't need to worry about both of us." She raised her chin slightly and held Antoine's gaze. She needed some time away, wanted to see the damage to her home without him there.

"I would prefer you remain here, Prince Antoine," Jake said.

Antoine hesitated another moment and then gave a curt nod of his head. "Very well, but I insist you return to my suite when you have your things," he said to Beth. "I need to know that you're safe and sound."

"Okay," she replied. It was easier to comply for now than to argue in front of Jake. But, she had no intention of spending another night in Antoine's bed, another night of wanting him and loving him.

It was time she get back to reality and the reality was Antoine had made it clear to her that he wasn't interested in marriage and babies. Although she knew without doubt that he cared about her, that he wanted her physically, she also knew there was no future with him.

Minutes later she was in Jake's car and headed to her house. "How are you holding up through all this?" he asked.

"I guess as well as can be expected," she replied. "I certainly didn't realize what I was getting myself into by becoming friendly with Antoine. What about you? Your workload has certainly been crazy since all this began."

He gave her a wry smile. "I've definitely had to stay on my toes." The smile fell from his face. "I've never felt such frustration as I have over the last several weeks. I have a missing sheik and can't seem to find a clue that might tell me what happened to him. I've got attacks happening on everyone and no real suspects."

"I don't think any of us will be the same when the royals return to their countries and life gets back to normal." She gazed out the side window. She'd certainly never be the same. There would always be memories of Antoine and at the moment she couldn't imagine ever loving another man.

"I'm not sure any of us will recognize normal when it does happen again," Jake replied drily.

Within minutes they were back at her cabin. As she got out of the car her heart constricted in her chest. A big, burly man stood at the front door and wore a uniform that identified him as part of the security Antoine had provided. He was definitely big enough that anyone with half a mind would think twice about trying to get past him.

Jake flashed his badge and the man nodded at them and stepped aside as they approached the front door. Beth used her key to unlock it and then went inside.

The scent of smoke still lingered and the knot that was her heart tightened painfully. Hearing about the damage and actually seeing it were two different things.

The breakfast nook had been the focal point of the fire. The windows were gone, had exploded from the heat and the walls around the area were blackened. Still, it wasn't quite as bad as she'd imagined. The walls looked solid and the fire had been contained to the nook area.

Jake placed a large hand on her shoulder. "This will pass and all will be well again," he said.

She nodded, but she doubted that everything would ever be well again. She left the kitchen and went into the bedroom to pack a suitcase.

It was crazy, how in the space of three days Antoine had completely taken over her life, her heart. The fact that he'd told her he'd done terrible things as an interrogator for his country didn't taint the love she felt for him. It would be like blaming a soldier of war for having to kill his enemy in the middle of a battlefield.

The fact that he was tormented by what he'd had to do in the name of his country only spoke of the pure heart that beat in his magnificent chest.

When she had finished packing what she thought she needed for a couple of weeks away from the house, she and Jake got back into his car and returned to the hotel.

"We should have an official report on the fire within the next couple of days," Jake said. "Have you contacted your insurance agent yet?"

"Not yet. I'll do it sometime this afternoon," she replied.

"Beth, I don't know what your relationship is with Prince Antoine, but please take care of yourself. Bad things seem to happen around these royal visitors."

For a moment she had the urge to tell Jake everything, about the notes she'd found and about Aleksei Verovick, everything about Antoine's suspicions that the attacks weren't about the COIN coalition at all but rather about something more personal.

But, she would be betraying Antoine's trust if she told, and besides she reminded herself that by this evening he'd know it all anyway. Jane's deadline was quickly approaching and there was no doubt that she would stick to her word and pass the notes to Jake that evening.

When they reached the hotel Jake lifted her

suitcase from his trunk and insisted he walk her back to Antoine's suite.

Antoine opened the door and she saw the relief on his face. "Thank you, Sheriff," he said as Jake dropped the suitcase just inside the door.

"No problem," Jake replied. "I'll be in touch when I have more news and please, next time you decide to leave here, take your security with you or call me and I'll do my best to provide protection." With that Jake left and Beth turned to face Antoine.

"You can unpack your things in the dresser," he said, "and there's plenty of room in the closet."

Beth shook her head. "I'm not staying here, Antoine."

His handsome features pulled into a deep frown. "Of course you're staying here," he replied with a touch of that natural command in his voice. "It's the only place I can ensure your safety."

"I'm going to stay in the hotel room where I was the other night. I have to get back to my real life, Antoine. I have duties and responsibilities here and I can't just hole up here with you and forget everything else."

He walked toward her, his eyes pleading. "Beth, please. My heart will only be at peace if you're here with me, where I know no more harm can come to you."

She took a step back, not wanting him to touch

her in any way, afraid that he might be able to change her mind. What he didn't understand was that harm would come to her if she stayed here with him.

There was no doubt in her mind that they would make love again, that he would make her fall deeper in love with him. Then there was a chance that her heart might start believing that somehow, someway, they had a future. And it would all be a lie, a fantasy that would never come true.

"I'll be fine here in the hotel," she replied. "We have a good security team and I feel safe here in the confines of the hotel."

"Have I done something wrong? Something to offend you?" he asked and then didn't wait for her to respond. "Beth, you're the most important woman in my life. I couldn't bear anything happening to you."

"Nothing will happen to me," she replied, a lump rising in the back of her throat. He was breaking her heart even now, telling her how important she was and yet unable to speak any words of love.

She picked up her suitcase and started for the door. "Beth?" he called and she turned back to look at him.

"The woman, Janine Sahron. Can you still arrange for me to speak to her?"

With everything that had transpired she'd

forgotten all about Janine. She glanced at her watch and then back at him. "Give me a little while to get settled into my room and then I'll go to the office and call her in. I'll let you know when she's there and you can speak with her."

"Thank you. Unfortunately, I only have the remainder of the afternoon before the notes will become public knowledge."

She nodded and then left the suite. She realized as crazy as it seemed, she'd wanted him to stop her from leaving, she'd wanted him to break down and tell her that he was madly, passionately in love with her and she'd completely changed his mind about never marrying, about never having a family of his own.

She was such a fool. Funny, she could swear that there had been moments when she'd felt not just red-hot passion, but also real love emanating from him.

And if she were perfectly honest with herself she'd admit that deep inside her was a crazy little niggle of hope that somehow, when this was all over, they would find a way to be together.

And that little bit of hope almost scared her as much as everything else that had happened in her life since she'd handed those notes over to Antoine.

Chapter Nine

She seemed to take the very air out of the suite when she left. Antoine eased down in the leather chair by the fireplace and stared toward the bank of windows, his thoughts consumed with Beth.

How had she managed in such a short space of time to do what no other woman had ever done before—get so deeply under his defenses?

As he imagined leaving this place and returning to Barajas without her in his life, his heart ached with a pain it had never felt before.

He loved her.

The knowledge blossomed inside of him. He wanted to wake up each morning with her head on the pillow next to his. He wanted to hear her laughter every day of his life. He needed to go to bed at night and hold her in his arms.

He loved her.

And he intended to do nothing about it.

He sighed wearily and leaned his head back. She deserved a man with no baggage, children whose safety she would never have to worry about, and a life filled with happiness and nothing else.

He couldn't give her that.

All he could give her was bad dreams and fear, a lifetime of wonder and worry, looking over her shoulder and wondering when somebody from his past might find them.

No matter how much he loved her, he would never allow her to have a meaningful place in his life. She meant far too much to him. The best thing he could do for her was let her go so she could find a man who could love her the way she was meant to be loved, a man who could give her a future filled with nothing but joy.

He stood as a knock sounded at his door. It was Sheik Efraim Aziz. Antoine gestured the tall, dark-eyed man inside, grateful for the distraction from his thoughts.

"Would you like something to drink, my friend?" Antoine asked as Efraim sat on the sofa.

"No, I'm fine. I just wanted to check in, see how you were doing since your brother's return to Barajas."

Antoine eased down in the chair opposite Efraim. "Of course I miss him being here, but it was important that he return to Barajas and continue the job of running the country."

Efraim raked a hand through his black hair and released a sigh. "Who would have thought when we all got together and planned the COIN Coalition to benefit our nations that we would be sitting here now with one of us missing and betrayal surrounding us."

"You've learned nothing more from the other members of your security as to who Fahad might have been working with?"

Efraim frowned. "Nothing. The man took his secrets to his grave and I'm still not sure who we can trust at the local law-enforcement level."

"What do you think of Sheriff Jake Wolf?" Antoine asked, aware that within hours Jake would have the notes Beth had found in his possession.

"He seems an honorable man, but Fahad certainly blindsided me and that makes me wary of trusting anyone."

Antoine offered his friend a small smile. "I hear there's one woman you've come to trust pretty well."

A responding smile curved Efraim's lips. "Callie." He said her name with warmth. "Yes, she has become important to me."

Callie McGuire was Assistant to the Secretary of Foreign Affairs based in Washington, D.C. She'd come to Wyoming to help facilitate the COIN summit. Her family owned a ranch locally and it had been on her land that Fahad had tried to kill Efraim. It had been Callie's brother who had killed Fahad when he'd believed his sister was in danger.

"From what I know of her, she seems to be a good woman," Antoine said.

"She is my heart," Efraim replied in a surprising show of emotion.

"I'm happy for you." Antoine felt the lump that formed in his throat as he thought of Beth and all that he would never share with her. "Do you plan to take her with you when you return home?"

"We have no plans beyond today," he replied. "Right now it's one day at a time, but whatever happens, wherever I go I know that she'll be at my side."

"Do you have any new theories about who was behind the attack on Amir?" Antoine asked, wanting to steer the conversation away from matters of the heart.

A frown once again swept across Efraim's features. "I have worked any number of theories in my brain, but can't make sense of any of them. I have thought about this until my head hurts and I can't come up with any definitive answers. What about you?"

"I wondered about Kalil Ramat."

Efraim's eyes widened. "We all know the people of Saruk and Kalil himself were against the coalition, but we have all been guests at Kalil's home. His son is our friend. I can't imagine that Kalil would be behind a plot to kill us all."

Efraim only echoed what Antoine felt in his heart. "Beth Taylor, the head of housekeeping, found some notes in Amir's room taped to the bottom of a drawer." Antoine decided it was time to share what he knew.

"Notes?"

Antoine told Efraim what the notes contained and about he and Beth taking them to Jane for fingerprinting. "She managed to pull a print from them."

Efraim leaned forward in the chair, his features radiating a deadly calm. "Who?"

"A man named Aleksei Verovick. He has ties to the Russian mob."

"The mob would have no vested interest in us making trade agreements with the United States," Efraim scoffed. "What we need to do is find out who hired this Verovick."

"I agree. But that's easier said than done." Antoine released a weary sigh.

"You've given this information to Sheriff Wolf?"

"Not yet. He'll have the information tonight. If Verovick is here in town, then hopefully Wolf can find the man and get the answers we need."

"And find out what happened to Amir, although I must confess I fear the worst where he's concerned," Efraim said, his dark eyes filled with sadness. He stood. "I won't keep you any longer, I just wanted to see how things were going and if there were any developments since last we spoke."

Antoine walked him to the door, wishing he had the answers to who was behind all the attacks, and more importantly, what had happened to Amir. "We'll speak again soon," he said and clapped Efraim on the shoulder. "And we'll pray for our friend."

Efraim nodded and then left.

When he was gone Antoine walked to the window and stood staring out at the Wyoming landscape that spoke to a place in his soul.

When would this all end? When would they finally have the answers they sought? Frustration burned inside his gut. If the Sahrons were somehow tied to Aleksei Verovick, then he would find out and they would finally have a trail to follow to the source.

And then, he would leave here and try his damndest to forget about a woman named Beth Taylor and the pieces of happiness she had given him.

When Beth finally called him he was ready. He felt a cold, hard resolve as he left his suite and headed to her office. He knew it was possible that Janine Sahron and her husband had nothing to do with anything that had been happening, but he needed to assure himself of that fact.

He knocked on the office door and his heart sang at the sound of Beth's voice bidding him entry. When he saw her he felt as if it had been days rather than a couple of hours since he'd last seen her.

He wondered if she knew that her smile let him know how deeply she'd grown to care about him. He tried to rein in his own emotions as he greeted her.

"Janine is on her way," she said as she sat behind the desk and gestured him into one of the two chairs in front of her. "You won't be too rough on her, will you? She seems to be a very nice woman."

"Then I'll keep the whips and chains hidden until I think we really need them," he said teasingly.

"Good, because I can't have that sort of thing happening in this nice resort. We do have a reputation to uphold, you know."

He was glad to see the teasing light in her eyes but once again he was reminded of all that he would never have with her.

At that moment a knock sounded at her door.

The woman who entered was a thin redhead with big blue eyes that instantly became guarded when she saw him. "You wanted to see me, Ms.

Taylor?" A nervous twitch appeared at the corner of one of her eyes.

"Yes, Janine, please have a seat," Beth said. "This is Prince Antoine Cavanaugh. He'd like to ask you a few questions."

The nervous tick fluttered once again as she sank down on the chair. She nodded to Antoine and clutched her hands together in her lap and then looked back at Beth. "Is something wrong? Have I done something wrong with my work?"

"No, it's nothing like that," Beth quickly assured her. "Your work here has been exemplary." Janine seemed to relax a bit.

"Mrs. Sahron, I hope you don't mind me taking a few minutes of your time," Antoine said and gave her his most charming smile.

"Uh…no, I don't mind," Janine said.

Antoine could tell she was nervous not only by the eye twitch but also by the way her tongue slid over her lips, as if her mouth was unaccountably dry. It didn't mean she was guilty of anything. It was possible she was simply nervous because she was probably speaking to a prince for the first time in her life.

"Beth mentioned that your husband is from a Mediterranean island. Which one would that be?" he asked. He kept a light, easy tone to his voice.

"Nadar. Actually it's his parents who are from there. Hakim, my husband, was born here in the

United States," she replied. The tick at the corner of her eye stopped and although her fingers remained laced together he noticed that some of the tension had dissipated.

"Ah, Nadar is a beautiful place. Do you visit there?" Antoine leaned back in his chair and looked at her as if he was interested in learning everything about her.

Her cheeks flushed slightly and she nodded. "We've gone to visit family there several times over the years. It is a beautiful place but it's expensive to travel."

"And what does your husband do here?" Antoine asked. He was aware of tension wafting from Beth, but he kept his focus on Janine, seeking any sign of deception in her body language.

"He's a math teacher, but during the summers he works at a video store to make some extra money. The house needs a lot of work." Once again she looked from Antoine to Beth. "Is something wrong? I'm afraid I don't understand…"

"I just hungered to speak with somebody from my area of the world," Antoine said and once again infused his smile with warmth. "What brought you and your husband to Dumont? I understand you've only recently moved to the area."

For the first time since she'd arrived in the room Janine unclasped her hands and leaned back in her chair and he knew she was starting to fully relax.

"My grandparents are from Dumont. Five months ago they decided to go into an assisted-living facility and gifted Hakim and me their house. We were living in Texas, renting an apartment and trying to save up money for a house so it was like a gift from heaven." She was completely relaxed now, all signs of stress gone from her body language. "The house needs lots of work, so both Hakim and I are doing what we can to get extra money to make the repairs."

"Do you have sisters or brothers, Janine?" He leaned forward and gently touched her on the shoulder. She seemed to melt toward him.

"Two sisters," she replied.

"And you are very close to them, I can tell." He pulled his hand away from her shoulder but leaned into her, as if she were the most important person on the face of the earth.

A smile curved her lips. "Very close," she agreed.

"It's been a difficult couple of weeks for me," he said and saw the spark of sympathy that darkened her eyes. "I'm sure you've heard about the bombing of my friend Amir's car."

"Of course, everyone knows about it. It was a horrible thing that happened."

"He was a good friend to me...like my brother. If you'd heard anything about his whereabouts, if you had any clue as to who might have been behind the bombing, you would tell me, wouldn't you?"

Janine's eyes widened. "Of course. I'd want the people responsible brought to justice."

"And your husband? If he knew anything about it, he'd come forward to the authorities?"

Her brow crinkled in confusion. "Why would Hakim know anything about it? He knows about movies and math, but he doesn't know about what happens here at the resort unless I share it with him."

He believed her.

There were absolutely no signs of deception from her. If her husband was involved, then he was confident she had no idea about it.

"I appreciate you coming in to speak with me," he said as he stood. Just to be on the safe side he would give her husband's name to Jake Wolf and let him check out the man more thoroughly, but Antoine's gut instinct told him this was just another disappointing dead end.

Chapter Ten

Beth had watched him charm Janine, set her at ease with his warm, engaging smile and his gently orchestrated touch to her shoulder. A hard knot formed in the center of Beth's chest.

It was all so familiar, the way he'd manipulated her so easily.

Just like he'd manipulated Beth on the day she'd found the notes. She remembered that look in his eyes, the soft touch of his hand on her shoulder. Manipulation 101 and like Janine, Beth had fallen right in line and agreed to do whatever he wanted. And she'd continued to be manipulated by him.

He'd needed her. As Janine left the office Beth realized that the nice things Antoine had done for her, the caring she'd seen in his eyes, the passion she'd felt in his touch had probably all been a ruse to get what he wanted, what he needed from her.

That's what he did. That's what he'd been trained to do. He found weaknesses and exploited them and the biggest weakness she'd had was her aching loneliness and her overwhelming attraction to him.

"That was probably a waste of time," he said once Janine was gone. "I didn't detect any deception from her and my gut is telling me she doesn't know anything about Verovick or what's been happening."

"You're very good at what you do," she said as anger built up inside her.

He must have heard something in her tone for he closed the office door and then turned to face her once again. "I only asked her some questions."

"Oh, you did so much more than that." She remained on the other side of the desk as her anger continued to build. "That soft touch on the shoulder, that pain-filled gaze, so practiced and so effective at getting women to tell you whatever it is you want, to do whatever you need."

His eyes narrowed. "Beth, what is going on in that beautiful head of yours?"

"I think for the first time in days I'm finally seeing things clearly." She felt as humiliated and as stupidly naïve as she had when she'd found out that Mark was married. God, she'd been such a fool. He'd made her feel important, had acted like he was interested in every area of her life because he'd needed to use her to achieve his ultimate goals.

"And what is it that you think you're seeing

clearly?" He walked toward her and she steeled herself not to allow her thoughts to get muddied by the familiar scent of him, by his very nearness.

"I was easy, wasn't I, Antoine. I was lonely and already had something of a crush on you. I was just ripe for the picking when it came to you finding somebody to use." To her horror hot tears burned at her eyes, but she swallowed hard against them, refusing to allow him to see her cry.

He stared at her in surprise. "Beth, you've got it all wrong," he said. He rounded the desk and reached for her, but she held up a hand to stop him before he could touch her in any way.

"Really? You didn't use manipulation and interrogation skills when you called me into your room the day I found those notes?" She gazed at him belligerently, daring him to lie to her.

His cheeks reddened slightly and he opened his mouth to speak and then paused as if he were collecting his thoughts. "Of course I did," he finally replied and the hard knot in her chest expanded.

"I knew that you'd found something in that room that was important and I wanted to know what it was," he continued. "Did I like what I had to do? Absolutely not. Did it have anything to do with what we've shared since then? Absolutely not."

She didn't believe him. She was afraid to believe him. Any crazy fantasy she'd entertained about them somehow having a future together had died a final death as she'd watched him talk to Janine.

It was over. Her heart had finally shut down. She refused to be a fool any longer. "Antoine, I think it best if we just say goodbye to each other here and now. You should call Jake and give him the information about the notes and your suspicions. I've done everything you needed and so there's really no reason for us to see each other anymore."

His eyes were the soft blue that beckoned her to fall into their depths, but she knew she'd be foolish to allow herself to give him the benefit of the doubt.

"Beth, not like this." His voice was a soft caress that only served to break her heart a little more. "I can't let this end with you thinking this has been nothing more than what I needed to help solve Amir's disappearance. It was about so much more."

"Please, just go," she said as new tears begged to be released.

Still he hesitated, as if wanting to say more and for a moment she imagined what she saw in his eyes was love, but then he took a step backward and gave her a stiff bow. "As you wish," he said and then turned on his heels and left the office.

The minute he was gone Beth sank down at

her desk and allowed the tears to fall. She hadn't realized until now the tiny flare of ridiculous hope that had burned bright in her chest. And now it was gone and she was left feeling empty inside.

She hadn't really considered marriage to him, but she had desperately wanted to believe that when he'd made love to her it had been because he desired her to distraction and not because he'd needed to keep her on his side.

But, the truth of the matter was that he'd needed somebody who didn't have a stake in any of the intrigue that surrounded him. He'd told her again and again that he didn't trust the people around him. He'd needed a driver, a confidante, and she'd fit neatly into what he needed.

She could have been anyone…another maid, a member of room service or a clerk in the gift shop. And that's what hurt the most—that she could have been anyone whom he could manipulate into fitting what he needed.

She was grateful that nobody called or came into the office for the next hour; it took that long for her to shed the tears that had built up.

Antoine had been everything she ever wanted in a man. Her attraction to him had nothing to do with the fact that he was a prince. She'd loved him for his teasing sense of humor, for the soft heart she knew beat beneath his tightly muscled chest. She loved him for the way he'd made her feel—and that had been the biggest lie of all.

He'd warned her that he didn't want a wife, that he would never have a family. He'd at least been honest about that. And it was shame on her for thinking that what they had might make him forget his resolve to live alone for the rest of his life.

When her tears had finally been spent she went into the adjoining bathroom and fixed her makeup and at that moment her cell phone rang. She checked the ID and saw that it was Haley from the café.

"Hey, girl, sorry it's taken me so long to get back to you," Haley said.

"It's not a problem," Beth replied.

"You gave me a tall order," Haley continued. "I've been keeping an eye on the people who come in and I've got a couple of names for you."

"Hang on, let me get a pen and paper." Beth pulled a small notepad and pen from the desk. "I'm ready."

"The first name is Dimitri Petrov, he's a Russian who told me he's in town on business, but he was vague about what his business is. The second man told me his name is Abdul Jahard and that he's here in Dumont visiting relatives, but his relatives must not feed him because he's here for almost every meal. Unfortunately those are the only two I've identified as being slightly suspicious."

"How did you manage to get them to give you so much information about themselves?" Beth asked.

Haley laughed. "You know me, I could get a rock to confess its sins to me if I had enough time. I just struck up a conversation with them while they were waiting for their orders."

"Thanks, Haley, I really appreciate it," Beth replied.

"Are you okay?"

"Sure, why?"

"I don't know, you sound kind of funny…sad."

Darn. Beth should have realized her friend would pick up on her emotional state just by talking to her. "I'm fine," she said and forced more life into her voice. "Just tired, that's all."

"We need to do lunch sometime soon," Haley said. "It's been too long."

"I'll call you and we'll set something up." With that the two disconnected. Beth wasn't interested in meeting for lunch too soon. She needed to get over the pain of Antoine before she felt like going anywhere with anyone.

She looked at the two names she'd written down. She'd finish her day and then she supposed she'd take the names to Antoine. A couple of hours wouldn't make any difference as to when he got the names from her. At the moment all she wanted to do was get back to the work of running her staff and spot-checking rooms.

She left her office but stayed away from the suites, not wanting to run into Antoine until she was better prepared to see him again. If he hadn't already contacted Jake Wolf about the notes she had found and the fingerprint that Jane had pulled, within hours Jane would be talking to the sheriff.

There was nothing more to be done. Even though Antoine feared there were dirty people working for the Sheriff, he had no choice but to give up the information. Maybe she'd just give the names Haley had given her to Jake. That way she wouldn't have to speak to Antoine again.

She could only hope that if Antoine remained here he would be safe. No matter how much her heart ached because of him, it was important to her that he stay well and return to his home to rule his nation with his twin brother.

It was after five when she finally grabbed her purse from the desk and decided to call it a night. She'd called her insurance agent while she'd waited for Antoine and Janine to come to her office and he'd assured her that they'd work to get her back into her house as soon as possible.

Hopefully if she and Antoine had nothing more to do with each other, then she could eventually go home without worrying about her own safety and all she'd have to deal with was her broken heart and the fact that she felt like she'd been played for a fool.

Once she got to her room she'd call Jake and give him the names of the two men Haley thought might be suspicious and then the intrigue with the visiting royalty and any connection to Antoine would be over for her.

As she left her office, she was plagued by an exhaustion deeper than anything she could ever remember feeling. It was an emotional weariness that she feared would be with her for a long time to come.

Being a fool for a man seemed to come naturally to her, she thought as she started across the lobby. It would be a long time before she put her heart on the line again for any man.

She was halfway across the lobby when a slightly overweight brunette waved from across the room and hurried toward her with a bright smile.

Beth racked her brain frantically in an effort to identify the woman. A former employee? A returning guest? She came up blank but forced a responding smile as the woman reached her.

"Beth...Beth Taylor?" Faint shadows darkened the skin beneath her brown eyes, as if she hadn't been sleeping well.

Beth steeled herself, wondering if there was a

complaint coming over the quality of the pillows or the bedding or any number of other things that could keep a guest from sleeping well. "Yes, I'm Beth," she replied. "May I help you?"

The woman took a step closer, invading Beth's personal space. "Yes, you can help me, but more importantly you can help Prince Antoine and the other royals staying at the hotel."

Beth froze, her heart suddenly pounding a thousand beats a minute. "What are you talking about?" she asked in a half-whisper.

"Keep smiling, Beth," the woman said, her eyes like hard brown pebbles. "I've planted a bomb in the prince's suite and all I have to do to detonate it is flip this little switch." She opened her hand to show Beth what looked like a remote control of some kind.

Everything in the lobby faded away as Beth struggled to make sense of what she'd just said. A bomb? In Antoine's suite? "What do you want?"

"You have your car keys?"

Beth gripped her purse tightly and nodded. She wished there was a gun inside her purse instead of her keys, some lipstick and her cell phone.

"You're going to walk nice and slowly toward the door and we're going to get into your car." The smile never left the woman's lips. "If you move too fast, I'll push the button. If you try to get anyone else's attention or do anything at all, I'll blow the roof off this place. Do you understand?"

Beth wasn't sure if she nodded or not, but she must have for the woman nodded with satisfaction. "Good," she said. "Let's go."

Beth didn't know about bombs. She had no idea if this woman was lying, but she couldn't take that chance. She couldn't put Antoine's life at risk. Or anyone else's.

"Move it," the woman said, her voice rough despite the fact her smile never faltered.

Beth felt as if she were in a horrible dream as her feet moved her across the lobby toward the front door. They had considered the Russian mob, they'd worried about Antoine's security team and the local law officials. But, nobody had told her to be worried about an overweight brunette with tired brown eyes.

"YOU SHOULD HAVE BROUGHT THESE TO ME immediately when Beth found them." Jake Wolf was not a happy man.

Antoine had left Beth and come directly to his suite, more upset than he could ever remember being. But, instead of dwelling on what had just happened with Beth, he'd immediately called the sheriff to meet him.

"At the time that the notes were found I wasn't

sure who I could trust," Antoine replied. "And that included any local law enforcement."

"Even if you didn't trust me or my men, you could have taken them to the federal agents who have been working this case," Jake replied as he sat on the sofa.

"I know less about them than I do about you and your men," Antoine replied. "There was no way I was going to give them what I thought might be vital information."

Jake released a weary sigh and laid the copy of the notes he'd just read on the ornate coffee table before him. "When I became sheriff I inherited a corruption that had been in the ranks for years. Payoffs for a variety of things were common and I swore that I'd clean things up. Unfortunately, it's not done yet. I'm still working on it."

Antoine didn't know if he was a fool or not, but he trusted the man in front of him. Or maybe it was just the fact that he now found himself in a position where he was forced to trust him.

"In any case, Beth and I took the notes to Jane and she was able to lift a print that belonged to Aleksei Verovick." As he told the sheriff everything he had learned about the man, he tried to keep thoughts of Beth at bay.

He didn't want to think about the yawning pain he'd seen in her eyes, the utter sense of betrayal that had laced her tone. She'd been shattered by what she believed had been his lies and manipulations. Like one of the military criminals he'd once interrogated, he'd broken Beth.

"When I get back to my office I'll begin a search for this Verovick. If he's here in town I'll know about it," Jake said, his features hard with resolve. "Is there anything else you've been holding back from me?"

"No, that's it. And I apologize for not bringing the notes to you sooner." In trying to investigate on his own he had only managed to put Beth's life at risk and break her heart.

Jake pulled himself up from the couch. "I'll see what I can do with this and be in touch."

"Thank you, I appreciate it." He followed Jake to the door. "I was desperate to see if I could find out anything about Amir's disappearance. I had hoped he was still alive, but with each day that passes my hope gets more difficult to maintain."

Jake's eyes grew darker. "I hope we get some closure where Sheik Amir is concerned," he replied, but Antoine knew by his tone of voice that he, too, was having difficulty maintaining any real hope that Amir was still alive.

Once Jake had left, Antoine paced the living area of the suite, his thoughts once again on Beth. He figured he'd give her a little while to cool off and then he'd try to speak to her again.

He couldn't allow her to believe that she'd been

nothing but a pawn for him to manipulate and use and then discard when he was finished with her.

She'd been so much more than that and he needed to make her understand. The weight of what he'd done to her coupled with his own heartbreak nearly crippled him.

He needed her to understand that she deserved more than he could ever give her, that he loved her but sometimes love wasn't enough to overcome life's obstacles.

He finally threw himself in the leather chair and buried his face in his hands. There was nothing worse than to love a woman and be unable to allow her fully into your life.

Beth was everything he wanted, everything he needed. She was the woman he wanted beside him every day of his life, the woman who made him want to be a better man. But he'd made a vow to himself long ago and he couldn't, he wouldn't make the mistake his father made.

Perhaps it was best that she was angry and felt completely betrayed by him. Maybe this was the kindest way to end their relationship.

He held on to that thought until he could stand it no longer and then he grabbed his cell phone and called her. He couldn't allow it to end this way, with her thinking she had been stupid to believe in him and had meant nothing to him.

Her phone rang three times and then went to

voice mail. She was probably screening her calls and didn't want to talk to him. He tried a second time with the same result and then returned his cell phone to his pocket and decided to go in search of her.

He could not let it end this way. Somehow he had to make her understand that she hadn't been the fool, but perhaps he was.

He left the suite and headed for her office, hoping she would still be there despite the fact that it was just after five.

She wasn't in. He drifted back to the lobby, sickened with the overwhelming need to make things right with her, to somehow make her understand that he hadn't been using her.

He peeked into the coffee shop area, wondering if maybe she was getting a bite to eat, but she was nowhere in sight and he had no idea what room she was staying in here at the hotel. He also wasn't at all sure that anyone who worked at the hotel would give him that information.

He smiled as he approached one of the young, attractive women working the front desk. Her name tag read Julia. "Ms. Julia," he said in greeting.

"Prince Antoine," she replied with a touch of breathlessness. She was little more than a teenager and Antoine had a feeling she was not only intimidated by his presence, but also more than a little bit tickled. "How can I help, Your Majesty?"

If he hadn't been so worried about Beth, he might have found her grandiose title humorous. "I was looking for Ms. Taylor. Have you seen her recently?"

"Beth Taylor? She left for the day," the girl replied.

"Yes, I checked her office and I know she's gone from there, but I also know she's staying in a room here in the hotel and I really need to speak with her."

"Is this a housekeeping issue?" she asked. "I'm sure I can find somebody else for you to speak with if there's a problem."

"No problem," he replied smoothly. "And it's a personal issue."

"I'm afraid I can't help you. Ms. Taylor left the hotel a few minutes ago."

Antoine stared at her, certain that he must have heard her incorrectly. "What?"

"I saw her leave just a little while ago." She pointed toward the front doors.

Antoine's heart began a rapid beat. Why would Beth leave the hotel? She knew there was danger outside. She'd told him she was going to stay in a room here at the hotel. "Was she alone when she left?"

Julia frowned. “I think she was with another woman.”

Another woman? His mind raced with suppositions as he left the desk and hurried to the front door. Once there he checked the parking lot and saw that her Jeep was gone.

Why would she leave the hotel and who had she left with? Although there was no real reason to panic, that’s exactly what he felt—a screaming alarm that something wasn’t right.

He hurried back to his suite, his heart pounding as fast as his footsteps clicking against the marble floor. Once he got inside his suite he powered up his laptop, grateful that he’d thought about having the tracking device placed on her car.

Her Jeep was on the move, but it was not going toward her home, rather it appeared to be headed into an area where he thought from his trips back and forth to her place that there was nothing but woods.

He stared at the monitor screen as the alarm in his head screamed louder. She was in trouble. He had absolutely no facts to support his belief, but every instinct he possessed told him she was in danger.

He yanked his cell phone from his pocket and dialed Michael. “Get David to bring the car and meet me at the front door immediately,” he said to his head security man.

"Yes, sir," Michael replied without question.

Antoine grabbed his laptop and raced out of the suite, a frantic anxiety clawing at his insides. It made no sense. It made no sense at all that she would have left the hotel, that she would be heading into an area where there was nothing but wilderness.

He'd headed into battle many times over the years, but never feeling as if so much was at stake. When he ran out the front doors, David, his driver, had the car pulled against the curb with Michael riding shotgun.

Antoine slid into the backseat and slammed the door. "Beth Taylor is in trouble. We must get to her before it's too late." He handed Michael his laptop over the seat. "Find her. We have to get to her."

David looked at the screen, put the car into gear and headed for the hotel exit.

"What kind of danger are we facing?" Michael asked, his tone clipped and all business as he pulled his gun from his shoulder holster.

"I don't know. I only know she shouldn't have left the hotel. She knew she might be in danger if she ventured out and she's not a foolish woman. The woman behind the desk said she left with another woman."

"Could she not just be going with a friend for dinner or something?" Michael asked.

Antoine gestured toward the computer screen impatiently. "And where will they find food in the middle of nowhere?" He shook his head. "I feel it in my gut, Michael. She's in trouble."

"We'll find them," David said as he stepped on the gas. They couldn't go fast enough to ease the burn in Antoine's stomach.

It was Antoine's worst nightmare come true. He was certain that somebody from his past had taken Beth and they were going to make her pay for all his sins.

Chapter Eleven

"Who's paying you to do this?" Beth asked, trying not to lose it because the woman now no longer just held the remote control, but also a gun.

"Shut up," she snapped. "Slow down and turn in between those two trees on the right where there's a little trail."

Beth held the steering wheel so tight her fingers cramped. There had been a dozen times in the last five minutes of driving she'd thought about bailing out of the car, but she was afraid of that remote control, afraid that any wrong move on her part would mean Antoine's death.

And as if that wasn't worry enough, there was the problem of the gun in the woman's hand and the deadly intent in her eyes. She looked like somebody who wouldn't hesitate to pull the trigger.

Beth made the turn the woman had indicated and had to bring the car to a halt because of the grove of trees in front of them. The area was isolated with overgrown brush and thick trees crowding together.

The woman next to her seemed nervous. Beth noticed that her hands shook slightly and she chewed her bottom lip. That was the only thing that gave Beth a little bit of hope…that somehow she might be able to talk her way out of this mess.

"He won't care, you know," she said. "If you kill me he'll still eventually follow through and make trade agreements with the United States."

"I told you to shut up," the woman screamed, as if she were hanging on to her control by a very thin thread. "Get out of the car and don't be stupid. If you're stupid then I'll shoot you and blow him to smithereens."

Tears blurred her vision as Beth got out of the car. She had no idea what this woman intended, but it couldn't be good. They were in a wilderness area, where nobody would hear Beth scream, where nobody would blink at the sound of a gunshot.

Nobody knew where she had gone. She wasn't even sure anyone would know that she'd left the hotel. She was in deep trouble and she knew she could only depend upon herself to get out of it.

As the woman punched the barrel of the gun in the small of her back and ordered her to walk, Beth knew she had to be patient and wait for the perfect opportunity, pray that the perfect opportunity would come and she'd be able to take the woman down without getting killed in the process.

As they continued to walk deeper into the woods, Beth began to realize that she'd probably been a fool…again. She knew nothing about bombs, but she was beginning to think that there was no way a remote control could blow up the suite considering the distance they had traveled from the resort.

Still, she now had to worry about the gun and her own life. Was this woman somehow tied to Antoine's past? Was she seeking revenge against him? Was she a part of Antoine's nightmares?

She cried out as she stumbled over a fallen tree and fell to her knees. The woman grabbed her by the arm and yanked her up, muttering curses beneath her breath.

"Keep moving," she said as she once again pressed the gun painfully into Beth's back.

Beth felt as if they walked for hours, but in reality knew that it had probably been less than an hour since she'd made what might turn out to be a fatal mistake by walking out of the resort.

How she wished she could replay that moment when the woman had walked up to her in the lobby. How she wished she would have taken a risk and signaled for security instead of foolishly allowing herself to be put in the position she was in now.

The deeper they walked into the woods, the more the woman muttered unintelligibly beneath her breath. Maybe she was some crazy extremist, Beth thought. She definitely appeared unstable, but Beth didn't know if that was to her advantage or would ultimately work against her.

There was an unnatural silence in their surroundings, as if all of the woodland creatures sensed the danger that had entered their midst and held their breath in fear.

They finally reached a small clearing. "Stop," the woman said. "Turn around."

Beth slowly turned to find the gun now directed at the center of her body. "Are you working for the Russian mob?" Beth asked. She had to somehow make the woman talk. She needed to know who had hired the woman for her own sake, but more important she needed to buy herself some time to find a weakness and somehow exploit it.

The woman's eyes darted around the area and then settled back on Beth. "This is perfect. Nobody will ever find you here."

"Is this where you brought Amir? Is he buried somewhere in this clearing?" Beth didn't think her heart could beat any faster than it already was, but as she thought of the missing Sheik's body being buried in a grave in the clearing, it beat even faster.

The woman frowned and took a step back from

Beth. “I don’t know Amir and the only body who will be buried in this clearing is yours.”

“Please, don’t do this,” Beth said, her heart once again fluttering frantically in her chest. “Whatever you want, whatever you need, killing me isn’t the answer.” Tears misted her vision as she thought about never seeing Antoine again, about not living long enough to find true love, to have children and to achieve the dreams she’d always wanted.

“I have to kill you,” the woman screamed once again. The gun trembled in her hand, but didn’t sway enough from Beth’s center for her to make a move.

“You have to be gone,” she continued. “It’s the only way, the only way things will be better.”

Beth tensed, waiting for the perfect opportunity to leap forward and wrestle for control of the gun. “How does killing me make things better?”

“Because he’ll stop thinking about you, because he’ll finally stop loving you.” The woman spat the words as her features twisted with a rage that nearly took Beth’s breath away.

“Antoine doesn’t love me,” Beth exclaimed.

“Not him, you stupid bitch. Mark!”

The frantic beat of Beth’s heart paused as she stared at the woman. Mark? Mark Ferrer? “Who are you?” The question fell from her lips on a whisper even though in her heart she knew the answer.

"I'm Karen, you stupid cow. Karen Ferrer. I'm his wife, the woman who had his children. I'm the one who takes care of him, who loves him and you ruined it all!"

A hysterical burst of laughter rose to Beth's lips, but she quickly swallowed it down. They had been so worried that somebody from Antoine's past might use her to get to him. But, the real threat hadn't been somebody from his past…it had been somebody from hers.

THEY FOUND THE JEEP PARKED in a stand of trees and Antoine's heart leapt into his throat when he realized the vehicle was empty.

"What now?" Michael asked.

"We go hunting until we find her." Antoine got out of the car along with Michael. "David, you stay here with the car ready in case she's been hurt, and call Jake Wolf, tell him where we are and to get out here as soon as possible."

Antoine pulled his gun and looked at Michael who also had his gun at the ready. Which way? Antoine scanned the area carefully, seeking signs that the brush had been disturbed, that the grass had been tamped down by footsteps. Tension held him so tight he felt as if he might snap at any minute.

He knew if he didn't pick the right direction they would lose precious minutes…minutes that could mean Beth's death—if he wasn't already too late.

He mentally shook himself, refusing to allow his thoughts to go there. She had to be okay. He steadfastly refused to believe otherwise. He knew that if she wasn't he'd be forever destroyed.

Seeing some tall grass that looked slightly trampled, he motioned for Michael to follow him, praying that they were going in the direction that would take him to Beth.

As they moved with the silence of ghosts through the woods, Antoine wondered who in the hell had gotten to her, which of his enemies had managed to get her from the hotel and into these woods? What possible ruse could they have used to get Beth to walk out of the hotel?

Julie had indicated that she thought Beth had left with a woman. How clever. Beth would have never considered going anywhere with a man she didn't know, but a woman? Perhaps using some sort of a sob story?

God, part of what he loved about Beth was her trusting nature and it was possible that was the trait that might bring her to her death. He tightened his grip on his gun. He could shoot a woman as easily as he could a man if she intended to harm Beth.

Every few steps he motioned for Michael to halt and they listened for any sounds of other human presence in the woods. There was nothing, no noise to indicate there was either human or beast nearby.

The only sound Antoine could hear clearly was the frantic beating of his own heart. He'd done this to her. He'd brought danger to her doorstep and he'd never forgive himself if he'd ultimately gotten Beth killed.

They walked for what seemed like forever when Antoine thought he heard the faint sound of a voice coming from up ahead. He raised his hand to Michael and they stopped. Antoine strained to listen and his heart leaped as again he thought it was a female voice he heard.

He leaned toward Michael. "No sudden moves," he whispered. "We need to assess the situation before either of us makes a move."

Michael nodded and together the two men moved forward. The voice grew louder and after several more steps Antoine saw a clearing ahead and what stood in the clearing made his heart nearly stop beating.

Beth stood facing a woman Antoine had never seen before, holding a gun pointed directly at Beth. He noticed several things instantly—Beth's terror showed in the strain of her features and he could easily imagine the tick firing off in the side of her slender neck, a neck he wanted to save.

The woman with the gun was nervous. She

shifted her weight from foot to foot as her hand trembled. Antoine knew her nervousness made her even more dangerous.

"You ruined my life," the woman screamed. "We were happy and in love until you came along."

"I didn't know he was married," Beth exclaimed, her voice filled with her fear. "I haven't seen him or talked to him for almost a year."

Antoine frowned as his mind raced. This wasn't somebody who was after him, this was somebody seeking revenge against Beth.

Mark Ferrer's wife. The name of the man who hurt Beth was emblazoned on Antoine's brain. Antoine could only imagine the emotions raging inside the woman. It was obvious she believed that Beth had destroyed her marriage, ruined her life.

"You're lying," she screamed at Beth. "I knew something was wrong with him for a long time and finally a week ago he confessed that he'd had an affair with you, that he'd tried to break it off but you were obsessed with him."

It was obvious Mark Ferrer had lied to his wife, but it was equally obvious his wife wasn't going to believe anything Beth said.

As she grabbed the gun with both hands and steadied herself, Antoine knew he only had seconds to act. He shoved his gun in the back of his waistband and stepped out into the clearing. “Mrs. Ferrer.”

She jumped and thankfully didn’t shoot, but she whirled the gun in his direction. He immediately raised his hands to show her that he didn’t have a weapon.

“Don’t come any closer,” she yelled. She pointed the gun back at Beth. “If you come closer I’ll shoot her.”

The woman’s brown eyes were huge and filled with a combination of rage and fear and more than a little bit of crazy.

“I won’t come any closer,” Antoine said in a gentle tone. “I just want to speak with you, that’s all.” He knew that Michael had his gun pointed at the woman’s head, that if Michael sensed any imminent danger to Antoine he’d kill the woman without blinking an eye. But, Antoine hoped he could save both women who were suffering from the same fate—broken hearts.

“Mrs. Ferrer…can I call you by your first name?” he asked.

She stared at him as if he was the one who had lost his mind. “Karen,” she finally said with a shrug of her shoulders. “My name is Karen.”

“Karen, I’m Antoine.” He forced what he hoped was a charming smile to his lips. “Karen, I’m so sorry you’ve been having a rough time lately.”

Her narrow lips trembled and tears sprang to

her eyes. "You have no idea. Everything has been broken. She broke it!"

"I know. She was a selfish fool to mess with your husband," Antoine said smoothly. He kept his gaze focused solely on Karen and away from Beth. "It was you who tried to burn down her house?"

"She deserved to lose her house after she ruined my marriage. I ran her off the road, too." Her entire body shook with fury. "I would have made her pay that day but the two of you managed to get away from me."

"You said you have children? How many?" He needed to try to defuse some of the rage that made her entire body tremble.

A softness swept over her features. "Three. Jason is six, Matthew is four and Angela is three." The last of her words choked out of her on a sob. "We were a family, a happy family until she came along." The gun wavered and Antoine took the opportunity to take a step closer. "We were a family until she came along," she cried again, tears streaking down her cheeks.

"And you believe that if she's out of the way then you can be a family again," he replied.

"Yes! She has to leave him alone. She has to go away," Karen exclaimed and once again focused the gun on Beth.

"If you kill her then you'll go to jail, Karen. What about your children? Who will raise them while you're in prison?" Antoine took yet another step closer to the obviously distraught woman.

"Karen, let me help you," he continued, keeping his voice as soft, as non-threatening as possible. "I can make her go away. I'm the prince of a Mediterranean island. I can take her there and make sure she never returns to the States, that she never bothers you again."

At that moment hope flared in her eyes and she let down her guard. The tip of the gun lowered toward the ground and Antoine sprang.

Too late, his brain screamed as he saw the gun rise once again and point at Beth. Everything seemed to happen in slow motion. In his peripheral vision he saw a blur and at the same time he yelled Beth's name as the gun exploded.

He tackled Karen to the ground and wrestled the gun from her hand. Screaming and cursing, she fought him, but he easily got her under control.

A glance in Beth's direction nearly stopped his heart. A rush of relief whirled through him as he saw her still standing, but the relief was short-lived as he saw Michael on the ground at her feet.

At that moment his driver, David, arrived and Antoine thrust the still-cursing Karen at him. "Take her to the car," Antoine said, his gaze going to Beth who had crumpled to the ground next to the fallen Michael. As David took control of Karen, Antoine rushed forward and fell to his knees at Michael's side.

"I'm all right," Michael said as he struggled to sit up. He gripped his upper arm where a stain of blood had begun to appear on his shirt. "I think it's just a flesh wound."

Antoine helped him to his feet as sirens sounded in the distance. "Can you make it back to the car?" he asked. "It sounds like help is on the way."

Michael nodded and took off walking in the direction of the car. Antoine turned back to Beth, who was still on the ground and weeping softly into her hands.

It was only then that the complete relief began to wash over Antoine. She was safe. Thank God, she was safe. He crouched down next to her, wanting desperately to take her into his arms, but afraid of overstepping his boundaries considering what had taken place between them in her office.

"It's over," he said gently.

She dropped her hands from her face and gazed at him with tear-washed eyes. "She said she had a bomb planted in your suite and if I didn't come with her she'd blow it up. I thought maybe she was telling the truth and I couldn't take the chance that she'd hurt you."

Her words tumbled over themselves as her tears continued to flow. "I thought maybe she was working for the Russian mob, or maybe she was some kind of fanatic trying to stop the trade agreements. And then she had the gun and I knew there was no way for me to get away from her."

He could stand it no longer. He pulled her up and she came willingly into his arms and buried her face in the front of his shirt as he held her tight.

He closed his eyes, unable to believe how close he'd come to losing her. If it hadn't been for Michael the shot might have found Beth. He would never doubt Michael's trustworthiness again.

They were still standing in each other's arms when Jake Wolf and several of his men arrived. Jake shook his head as he approached them. "You two hotshots seem to be keeping me busy lately."

Beth stepped out of Antoine's arms and he felt not only the bereavement of her physical nearness, but her mental connection as well.

The danger was over and he realized they were back to where they'd been when he'd walked out of her office earlier in the day. He and Michael had managed to save her life, but nothing had really changed.

The night was endless. They all convened at Jake's office and statements were taken. Michael was treated and released with a bandage over his wound of courage and Karen was locked up to await trial on kidnapping and attempted murder charges.

When they were finally free to go, Antoine and Beth walked out of the building side by side. They had scarcely spoken to each other after Jake had arrived and throughout the long hours of interrogation.

During that time Antoine had reached a painful decision. As she headed for her Jeep in the parking lot he stopped her by taking hold of her arm.

In the illumination from the parking lot lights overhead he could see the weariness on her face, that faint pulse in the side of her throat and a raw vulnerability that would forever haunt him.

She pulled away from him, as if his very touch hurt her. He dropped his arms to his sides and fought his need to pull her to him and hold her close, hold her until she no longer fought him, until he'd convinced her of what she meant to him.

"I'll be returning to Barajas in the morning," he said.

She looked at him in surprise. "I thought you were staying until there was news about Amir."

"I'll leave the investigation in Jake's capable hands. I haven't been successful in helping anything. It's time I go home, but before I leave it's important to me that you understand that it was real, the emotions I feel for you are real and deep. I told you that I would never marry, but I will carry the memory of you with me for the rest of my life."

She studied him for a long moment. "You don't

have to worry about your enemies finding you to get revenge." The pain in her eyes became sadness.

He frowned, confused by her words. "What do you mean?"

"They've already gotten their revenge on you. You will forever be alone because you fear what they might do, what might happen."

She released a weary sigh. "We all have things in our past, Antoine. Tonight was a perfect example that danger can come from unexpected places and people. You can get hit by a car, or get a terminal illness. It's what you do with the life you're given that's important, not the things you don't do because you're afraid."

She didn't wait for his response but instead turned on her heels and headed for the Jeep in the distance. He remained frozen in place as she got into the vehicle and then a moment later disappeared into the darkness of the night.

At eight-thirty the next morning Antoine and his entourage were at the airport where the private jet was being readied for departure.

As they waited Antoine turned to Michael. "It will be good to get home," he said, as if the words themselves would be enough to convince him.

"I've had enough Wyoming to last me a lifetime," Michael replied.

Antoine studied the man for a long moment.

"Your job has always been to protect me from harm. Why did you risk your life by throwing yourself in front of Beth?"

Michael met his gaze evenly. "Because I knew how important she was to you."

Antoine swallowed around the lump that rose in the back of his throat. He had spent most of the night trying not to think about Beth, telling himself that the best thing he could do was return to Barajas and put his time in this beautiful state of America behind him.

He needed to forget the woman who had stood by his side through danger, kissed him with a passion that had stirred his very soul and made him think of dreams that could never be his.

"It's time to board," Michael said as one of the men on the tarmac motioned to them.

Antoine nodded, straightened his shoulders and headed for the plane.

BETH SAT AT HER DESK IN HER OFFICE and stared out the window. This morning the events of the night before seemed like nothing more than a bad dream.

Amir was still missing, Karen was in jail and Antoine was now winging his way back to where he belonged. It was time for her to put the last week away in her mind, in a place where it couldn't be accessed and create any more pain.

"Easier said than done," she muttered under her breath. She turned away from the window and looked at the inventory list in front of her.

For a moment her body recalled every moment of being in Antoine's arms. Her skin warmed with the memory and a wistful sigh brought the sting of tears to her eyes.

Funny, but in the brief conversation they'd had in the parking lot at the sheriff's office, she'd believed him. She'd believed that she had been more to him than somebody to use and then discard at will.

Even a man as good as Antoine was at manipulation couldn't have manufactured the look of love in his eyes when he'd gazed at her and didn't know she saw him. She'd tasted the desire in his kisses, felt the caring in his touch and had finally believed in her heart that he had loved her.

A lot of good it did either of them. He was a man tied to a tragic past that wouldn't allow him to move forward, a man who would forever be trapped by what he considered the sins of his father.

And what had his father done? Simply loved a woman, loved her enough to put his fears behind him and risk everything for that love.

Time for her to get back to her real life, she thought as she once again tried to focus her thoughts on the paperwork in front of her.

Fifteen minutes later a knock was heard on her door. “Come in,” she said. The door opened and for a long moment she stared, mouth agape at Antoine.

“You can’t be here,” she said in confusion. “You’re on your way back to Barajas.” He looked so incredibly handsome in a military jacket covered with metals and ribbons. He looked every inch the prince that he was and her heart squeezed tight.

She stood, her legs feeling ridiculously weak. “What are you doing here?”

He walked over to the window and stared out with his back to her. She held on to the edge of the desk, wondering what was going on, why he was prolonging her agony by attempting to speak to her again.

When she thought she might scream with anxiety, he turned and looked at her. “I had every intention of returning to Barajas this morning. I got to the airport where my plane was waiting and told myself it was what I wanted to do, what I needed to do. But, when it came time to actually get on the plane, I couldn’t.”

He stepped away from the window and walked close enough to her that she could smell that dizzying cologne of his, see the silver shards that glinted in his pale blue eyes.

“I never wanted to rule Barajas. Sebastian is

much better suited for the role of leadership. I've discovered that I've fallen in love with Wyoming. The land speaks to me and whispers that this is the place where I belong."

Is this what he'd come to tell her? That he intended to make a home here in Wyoming? In Dumont? God, the idea of running into him at the grocery store, seeing him on the streets was horrifying. How could she forget him if he was right here under her nose? It would have been so much better if he'd gone back to his island.

"You don't look happy," he said.

She mentally shook herself and pasted on a smile. "I want you to be happy, Antoine, and if you find happiness here then I'm glad for you."

His gaze seemed to pierce right through her as he took a step closer. "I've also been thinking a lot about what you said to me last night."

"Oh?" The word froze in her throat as he began to unbutton the dress military jacket.

"I think if I had the opportunity to ask my father if he had any regrets about loving my mother, about making her his wife, he'd tell me no. And my mother would have no regrets either. I remember their love for each other and know that even if they knew what the future held for them, they would have chosen to have the years that they did of love and family together."

She stared at him, her breath caught in her chest, afraid to try to guess where this all might lead.

"The past can be a tricky thing, Beth. It can bring you enormous joy or it can cage you like an animal at the zoo. I've been caged for a very long time." He shrugged off the jacket, exposing a white shirt beneath. He dropped the jacket to the floor and stepped so close to her she could feel the heat of his body warming hers.

"You take my breath away, Beth Taylor. For you I want to bend the bars of my cage and break free. I want to rebuild your house and make it big enough for a family. I love you, Beth, and I want to stay here with you and raise children and horses and embrace the happiness I know my parents would want for me."

Joy blossomed inside her, a joy that brought tears to her eyes as she threw herself into his arms. He wrapped her in a tight embrace that felt like love, that felt like safety, but more importantly felt like home.

"Antoine, I love you with all my heart, with all my soul," she said.

He released a sigh of sweet contentment and smiled. "You know that when we marry, you'll become a princess."

"I don't care about that," she replied. "Just being ordinary rancher Antoine Cavanaugh's wife is more than enough for me."

"Then I think we should go to the suite and start practicing to make the babies that you want," he said as his hands cupped her buttocks and pulled her even closer against him.

"Impertinent," she exclaimed, "definitely impertinent."

He laughed and his eyes blazed as his lips found hers and took them in a kiss that promised everything Beth had ever dreamed of, a kiss that spoke of love and passion and forever.

* * * * *

Don't miss
SOVEREIGN SHERIFF
by Cassie Miles
when Cowboys Royale *continues.*
Look for it wherever
Harlequin Intrigue books are sold!

COMING NEXT MONTH

Available August 9, 2011

#1293 SOVEREIGN SHERIFF
Cowboys Royale
Cassie Miles

#1294 STAMPEDED
Whitehorse, Montana: Chisholm Cattle Company
B.J. Daniels

#1295 FLASHBACK
Gayle Wilson

#1296 PROTECTING THE PREGNANT WITNESS
The Precinct: SWAT
Julie Miller

#1297 LOCKED AND LOADED
Mystery Men
HelenKay Dimon

#1298 DAKOTA MARSHAL
Jenna Ryan

HICNM0711

Praise for *Storming the Wall* by Todd Miller

"A well-researched and grim exploration of the connections between climate change and the political hostility toward the refugees it creates. Journalist and activist Miller (*Border Patrol Nation: Dispatches from the Front Lines of Homeland Security*, 2014) expands on his earlier focus on U.S.-Mexico border controversies with an alarming catalog of climatological effects on population movements, surveillance, violence, and other current issues."The theater for future climate battles," he writes, "will be the world's ever thickening border zones . . . vast numbers of people will be on the move, and vast numbers of people will be trained, armed, and paid to stop them." In eight punchy, discretely themed chapters, the author establishes that the destructive effects of climate change are already manifest and that the U.S. is establishing a violent, heavy-handed pattern of response to it, as seen in the ramping up of border security. Miller visited several locales to witness this bleak transition, including Honduras and the U.S.-Mexico border, and he argues that these developing strife zones, far from representing natural change, are fundamentally class-based phenomena: "In the climate era, coexisting worlds of luxury living and impoverished desperation will only be magnified and compounded". . . A galvanizing forecast of global warming's endgame and a powerful indictment of America's current stance."

—*Kirkuk Reviews*

"As Todd Miller shows in this important and harrowing book, climate-driven migration is set to become one of the defining issues of our time. We are at a political crossroads: continue hardening under the steadily creeping politics of xenophobia and the repressive militarization of border and immigration policy, or change course and plan for a just adaption to a hotter world. At stake is not only the well-being of immigrants but also the integrity and feasibility of democratic government itself. This is a must-read book."

—**CHRISTIAN PARENTI**, author of *Tropic of Chaos: Climate Change and the New Geography of Violence*

"*Storming the Wall* is essential reading in our climate-disrupted world. From conferences about the increasingly militarized security state to front-line interviews with climate refugees, Miller delivers a prescient and sober view of our increasingly dystopian planet as the impacts of human-caused climate disruption continue to intensify."

—**DAHR JAMAIL**, author of *The End of Ice*

"Nothing will test human institutions like climate change in this century—as this book makes crystal clear, people on the move from rising waters, spreading deserts, and endless storms could profoundly destabilize our civilizations unless we seize the chance to reimagine our relationships to each other. This is no drill, but it is a test, and it will be graded pass-fail."

—**BILL MCKIBBEN**, author of *Eaarth: Making a Life on a Tough New Planet*

"Todd Miller reports from the cracks in the walls of the global climate security state—militarized zones designed to keep powerful elites safe from poor and uprooted peoples. Weapons of war shoot to kill refugees from rising seas, superstorms, no rain and no food. Hyped-up fears morph climate justice activists into terrorists; the security state targets any and all of the poor and powerless. Despite growing millions of climate refugees caught in the crosshairs of border enforcement regimes, Miller finds hope—hope that may not survive in Trumpworld."

—MOLLY MOLLOY, Research librarian for Latin America and the border at New Mexico State University and creator of "Frontera List"

"Todd Miller takes us straight to the front-lines of our world transformed by climate change—to the tension points where those of us more protected from its disruptive impacts encounter those who are most vulnerable to them. Here is the largely untold back story to the thousands of people turning up on our borders, and challenging the very idea of those frontiers in the process."

—MARK SCHAPIRO, author of *The End of Stationarity: Searching for the New Normal in the Age of Carbon Shock*

"*Storming the Wall* demonstrates why the struggles for social justice and ecological sustainability must be one struggle. Todd Miller's important book chronicles how existing disparities in wealth and power, combined with the dramatic changes we are causing in this planet's ecosystems, mean

either we come together around our common humanity or forfeit the right to call ourselves fully human. If 'security' comes to mean only that the most privileged people on the planet can secure that privilege, then we are all, literally, doomed. Elites are planning how they will react to climate clashes. Miller explains why we have to as well."

—ROBERT JENSEN, author of *Arguing for Our Lives*

"Governments across the world today are planning for climate change. The problem, as Todd Miller ably shows, is that they're not planning mitigation, but militarization. *Storming the Wall* offers a dire report from what are literally the front lines of global warming: the razor-wired security zones and drone-patrolled borderlands where the Anthropocene's first human victims—climate refugees—are dying in droves."

—ROY SCRANTON, author of *Learning to Die in the Anthropocene*

Praise for *Border Patrol Nation* by Todd Miller

"Scathing and deeply reported . . . quite possibly the right book at the right time"

—***Los Angeles Times***

"At the start of his unsettling and important new book, *Border Patrol Nation: Dispatches from the Front Lines of Homeland Security*, Miller observes that these days 'it is common to see the Border Patrol in places—such as Erie, Pennsylvania; Rochester, New York; or Forks, Washington—where only fifteen years ago it would have seemed far-fetched, if not unfathomable."

—***Christian Science Monitor***

"Solid, absorbing reportage on the government's racist and constitutionally questionable notions of border security in the post-9/11 world. . . . An unsettling but important read."

—***Kirkus Reviews***

"Journalist Miller tells an alarming story of U.S. Border Patrol and Homeland Security's ever-widening reach into the lives of American citizens and legal immigrants as well as the undocumented. He describes the militarization of the Border Patrol and concurrent dehumanizing of 'unauthorized' persons; American citizens routinely harassed and arrested in Constitution-free zones that extend 100 miles from all borders; the expulsion of an exemplary Border Patrol agent for expressing his Mexican identity in casual conversation; and the Border Patrol's Explorer Academy for children, which,

with its lock-step marching, black boots, law-enforcement training, and indoctrination is eerily evocative of fascism and Hitler Youth. Miller reveals the 'complex and industrial world' looming behind the border patrol, spanning 'robotics, engineers, salespeople and detention centers' and the new generation of Explorers. 'It is the world in which we now live,' he states, 'where eradicating border violations is given higher priority than eradicating malnutrition, poverty, homelessness, illiteracy, [and] unemployment.' In addition to readers interested in immigration issues, those concerned about the NSA's privacy violations will likely be even more shocked by the actions of Homeland Security."

—***Publishers Weekly***, starred review

Storming The Wall

CLIMATE CHANGE, MIGRATION, AND HOMELAND SECURITY

Todd Miller

City Lights | Open Media Series

Cover design: Stealworks

ISBN: 978-087286-715-4
ebook ISBN: 978-087286-716-1

The Open Media Series is edited by Greg Ruggiero

Library of Congress Data
on file

City Lights Books are published at the City Lights Bookstore
261 Columbus Avenue, San Francisco, CA 94133
www.citylights.com

For William
This book is infused with a profound love that I would have never known without you.

Sometimes I recognize myself in others. I recognize myself in those who will endure, friends who shelter me, beautiful holy fools of justice and flying creatures of beauty and other bums and vagrants who walk the earth and will continue walking, just as the stars will continue in the night and the waves in the sea. Then, when I recognize myself in them, I am the air, coming to know myself as part of the wind.

I think it was Vallejo, Cesar Vallejo, who said that sometimes the wind changes its air.

When I am no longer, the wind will be, will continue being.

—Eduardo Galeano

CONTENTS

1. On the Front Lines of Climate and Borders *15*

2. Sustainable National Security: Climate Adaptation for the Rich and Powerful *37*

3. The 21st-Century Border *71*

4. Threat Forecast: Where Climate Change Meets Science Fiction *107*

5. Phoenix Dystopia: Mass Migration in the Homeland *131*

6. The Philippines and the Future Battle at the Frontlines of Climate Change and Global Pacification *171*

7. People's Pilgrimage: Toward a Solution of Cross-Border Solidarity *203*

8. Transition and Transformation *223*

Epilogue *235*

Acknowledgments 241
Notes 244
Index 263
About the Author 271

ONE

ON THE FRONT LINES OF CLIMATE AND BORDERS

> *I think the notion of dreaming in a time where we are told that it is foolish, futile or not useful is one of the most revolutionary things we can do.*
>
> —Harsha Walia

On the coast of the small Philippine island of Marinduque, a man in a black shirt and blue shorts walks up the shore carrying a baby in his arms. Just as has been forecast by climate scientists across the world, littered all around him are bits and pieces of the "future." There is a house so devastated by the rising sea and surging waves that its exposed frame looks like ribs puncturing its crumbling wall. An uprooted palm tree lies nearby like a corpse in the gravelly sand. Soon the sea will entirely claim the ruined house and, most likely, many more homes, farms, schools, and businesses farther inland. This small community, Balogo, which is on the island where my grandmother was born and raised, appears, like so many others across the globe, to be on the verge of being completely washed away.

The father and child look out into the gray, stormy sea. Typhoon Ineng's center is far away in the northern Philippines, but the waves still come crashing in. This storm will kill 14 people after battering communities with sustained winds of 80-plus miles per hour. The punishment includes tornadoes, flooding, and landslides that temporarily displace 34,000 people. Horrific as this may sound, by Filipino standards, this is a minor storm. Following super-typhoon Haiyan, everything is relative to that 265-mile-wide machine of wind and water that smashed the island of Leyte in November 2013, killing more than 10,000 people and uprooting hundreds of thousands more.

When I ask Edmund Oracion, a fisherman from Balogo, if the ocean is moving in, he doesn't hesitate: "Big time." Oracion wears a brown tank top and talks above the sound of rushing waves, which are as gray and stormy as the sky. Children are laughing and playing in the encroaching foamy sea behind him. Oracion tells me that he has been living here for 45 years—his entire life. The slow advance of the sea, of course, doesn't happen in one day. On the global plane, sea level reached its highest recorded level in March 2016, 3.48 inches higher than the 1993 average (with an overall trend of a 0.13-inch rise per year since 1993).[1] As of March 22, 2017, Arctic sea ice had melted down to its lowest level in recorded history.[2]

The fisherman points to a buoy that is rocking 25 yards away in the waves. "The shore used to be there. The water is getting close to us," he says. "It's a big concern." He says that the people of the region might have to relocate farther inland, a move that would not earn them climate-refugee

status, since such a status does not yet officially exist. Behind him, as he talks, sit long fishing boats under skinny coconut palms. Like fishing, coconuts are one of the primary sources of income on this island of more than 200,000 people, 40 percent of whom live below the poverty line. According to the book *Power in a Warming World*, people who live in the 48 "least-developed countries" are five times more likely to die in a climate-related disaster than the rest of the world.[3]

As I watch the waves consume the destroyed house, I realize that this is the first tangible casualty of sea-level rise that I have witnessed with my own eyes. And it was happening on my grandmother's island. In just a few days climate change went from the theoretical and futuristic to real, raw, and immediate. Even the night before, when I met with Rollie Josue of the Marinduque government's disaster management division, who explained all the potential hazards projected for the year 2050, the reality of it didn't hit me as hard as it did seeing the house as the sea ate away at it, and that small child in his father's arms, his black hair blowing around in the gusting wind.

As Filipinos reminded me day after day, their island homes are on the front lines of the world's most urgent issue. In his office, Josue told us that the projections for 2050 were dire. There will be more landslides. There will be more flooding. There will be ever-increasing possibilities for earthquakes and tsunamis. At least one Haiyan-strength typhoon is now expected to make landfall every year. The 2013 superstorm was so powerful and destructive that I thought that I must have misheard him. "One per year?" I

asked. He smiled, as if that was the only thing he could do. "Yes," he said.

According to a survey conducted by the Social Weather Stations in March 2013, 85 percent of Filipinos already believed that they had experienced impact from climate change, this was even before the devastation of the super-typhoon. Many in the Philippines, including Greenpeace's Amalie Obuson, credit the rapid increase in climate awareness to the devastation caused by the annual super-typhoons that have hit every year since Ondoy in 2009. The typhoon dumped more rain in Metro Manila in one day than ever before in the recorded history of the region. The capital, already used to being submerged in water, had never been so inundated. It was a "rude awakening," said Obuson. There was Megi in 2010, Nesat in 2011, and Bopha in 2012, which leveled Obuson's home province, Mindanao, a place known for U.S. military bases, not typhoons.

"We haven't had the experience of strong rains until recently," Obuson said. She shared a video of a man telling the tragic story of how he lost his infant son in Mindanao during Typhoon Bopha. The man described how he was cradling his son in his arms when debris struck and split the child's head open. He lay limp in his arms, not breathing. Seeing other family members caught in the swirling water and in need of help, the father released his beloved child and watched the water carry him away. In the video, he could barely tell the story. He could barely talk.

"It used to be just adaptation," Obuson said about the Philippines. "It's way past adaptation. It's really a question

of survival now." Since 2013, typhoons and storms have displaced nearly 15 million people.

The most common number now used by scientists to project sea-level rise, based on the accelerating pace of melting ice sheets in Antarctica and Greenland, is three feet over the next 80 years. If this projection holds true, Pacific islands such as Tuvalu, Kiribati, and Tokelau will soon be swallowed by the ocean. Kiribati's government bought 20 square miles of land in Fiji to relocate its people. Many people from the Marshall Islands have already migrated to the United States, and a good percentage live in the town of Springdale, Arkansas. In 2016, the United States government extended a $48 million grant to relocate 60 people from Louisiana's increasingly flooded island Isle de Saint Jean.[4]

According to the United States Geological Survey, Louisiana lost 1,900 square miles of land between 1932 and 2000—the equivalent, as journalist Brett Anderson describes it, "of the *entire state* of Delaware dropping into the Gulf of Mexico."[5] If trends continue, by 2064 rising water will take from Louisiana another landmass larger than Rhode Island.[6] The state's shape on today's maps is no longer accurate; the once familiar boot shape has increasingly appeared more chewed up and dissolved into islands. As it stands, the disfiguration will only accelerate.

The *New York Times* has called people from the Isle of Saint Jean the first U.S. climate refugees.[7] This is a disputable claim, of course, considering all the people who evacuated New Orleans after Hurricane Katrina and never came back; all those forced to leave their homes after Hurricane Sandy; and the unknown numbers who have

fled California to escape either the years of drought or the floods of early 2017.

Climate change means either too little or too much water, and we are already experiencing both. A March 2016 report titled "Contribution of Antarctica to past and future sea-level rise"[8] shows that future sea-level rise might even be more pronounced than originally thought. If greenhouse gas emissions are not sufficiently cut, the sea will likely rise more than six feet by 2100, double the commonly cited forecasts of the United Nations climate science body. If this occurs, due to atmospheric pressure that will accelerate the melting of polar ice, we will see an inundation of densely populated mega-cities and millions of acres of low-lying areas inland. "At that point it becomes about retreat" from cities, one of the lead co-authors, Rob DeConto, told *The Guardian*, "not engineering of defences."[9]

One-third of the world's population lives near a coast. Looking specifically at low-elevation areas most vulnerable to rising seas, that means close to 700 million people are at risk. To grasp what this means exactly for U.S. coastal cities and areas, there is an interactive map from the National Oceanic and Atmospheric Agency that visualizes the impact of rising water in places such as Miami, New York, San Juan, or the Florida Keys which, in a five-foot rise scenario, will completely vanish into the ocean. Miami, already spending millions of dollars on saltwater sea pumps, will eventually become the northernmost Key, much like nearby Biscayne. All this is happening now.

Sea level in the Hampton Roads area of Virginia has risen 18 inches since the beginning of the 20th century.

"Hundred year" flooding events are happening now with such frequency that a redefinition may be in order. One resident named Elisa Staton, whose house had lost half its value after being flooded, told reporter Brooke Jarvis, "I hate that house—that house has been my nightmare for ten years."[10] What Staton is describing is not only the most common, but the most expensive disaster in the United States—flooding. On a global level, floods are now impacting 21 million people worldwide annually. By 2030, a "double exposure to inundation"[11] is expected, and will impact more than 54 million.

The future potential for havoc becomes more pronounced when you add to the DeConto report another one titled "Ice melt, sea-level rise, and superstorms," whose lead author, climate guru James E. Hansen, is the person who famously brought climate change to the attention of the U.S. Congress in 1988 when he was a top scientist at NASA. Hansen's latest report focuses on how the incoming cool, dense water from melting ice sheets will impact the ocean's circulation patterns.[12] Such shifts will also likely further accelerate the speed at which the ice is melting. The result: faster-rising seas coupled with the most violent superstorms ever experienced in recorded history.

"I think the conclusion is clear," Hansen said after the report was released. "We are in a position of potentially causing irreparable harm to our children, grandchildren and future generations."[13]

Rising sea levels are just one of multiple ecological factors projected to dislocate unprecedented quantities of people. Though the numbers are often disputed, the most

common projection used by the United Nations is that 250 million people will be displaced by 2050. In a *New York Times* front page report in February 2017 about climate change and water shortages in Mexico City, Michael Kimmelman cited a report that suggested the number may be much higher: 750 million.[14] Another study referenced in Kimmelman's article predicts 10 percent of Mexicans between 15 and 65 could eventually migrate north due to rising temperatures, droughts, and floods.[15]

"Although the exact number of people that will be on the move by mid-century is uncertain," stated Koko Warner et al. in the report *In Search of Shelter: Mapping the Effects of Climate Change on Human Migration and Displacement*, "the scope and scale could vastly exceed anything that has occurred before."[16]

An average of 21.5 million people were displaced every year between 2008 and 2015 from the "impact and threat of climate-related hazards."[17] In the same time span, 26.4 million people are estimated to have been displaced each year by disasters more generally. This number means that one person is forced from their home every second, and according to the Internal Displacement Monitoring Centre, a person is more likely to be displaced by environmental forces than by war.[18] When you correlate the origins of the United Nations' 64 million "persons of concern"—a number that refers to refugees and has tripled since 2005—with the geographic locations of climate turmoil seen in data from NASA's Common Science Climate Index, as journalist Jessica Benko has done, the overlap is "striking" and vivid on a map.[19] And while many displaced people will try to stay

close to home, approximately 244 million people currently live outside their country of birth, up from 80 million in the 1980s (and a 41 percent increase from the year 2000). Since so many people are undocumented, and therefore uncounted, the actual number is likely much higher. People are traveling across borders in unprecedented numbers, and expectations—including those of people who live in vulnerable areas—are that this will continue. According to a 2010 Gallup poll, 12 percent of respondents—a percentage representing 500 million families[20]—stated that they thought environmental problems would force them to move within five years.

The upsurge has multiple factors, including, as described by sociologist Christian Parenti, a 30-year-long economic restructuring that has produced unseen levels of poverty and inequality. Volatile political and social situations often worsen economic processes that enrich a few while impoverishing many. Climate change will only intensify these inequalities and widen the gulf between those who are environmentally secure and those who are not. Parenti calls this the "catastrophic convergence."[21] The economic, political, and ecological factors are not separate; rather, they compound each other to create increasingly untenable situations over vast swaths of the Earth.

With the forecast, Koko Warner does not mince words: "In coming decades, climate change will motivate or force millions of people to leave their homes in search of viable livelihoods and safety."[22] It will be "staggering" and "surpass any historic antecedent." Despite predictions of such startling magnitude, there is no legal framework for climate

refugees. Not in international law, not in the laws of specific countries. Instead, there is more spending on border reinforcement than ever before in the history of humankind. And as the Donald J. Trump administration takes power in the United States, there is only more of this to come.

Back in Marinduque, Josue showed me the sea-level rise map where a red band—located smack dab in the middle of the Philippine archipelago—circled the heart-shaped island like a noose. Officials project that Balogo, where I watched the man hold his child near the crumbling house, will eventually be swallowed by the sea.

I was only on the island of Marinduque for three days, but it felt like I was there for a lifetime. This is the island from which my grandmother migrated to the United States in the early 20th century. She was only 16 years old when she left. I quickly became enchanted with the island's verdant green hills and the swaying coconut palms that I had heard about all my life but had never seen in person. Marinduque is the home of the annual Moriones Festival, in which residents re-create the Passion of Christ by dressing up in the garb of biblical-era Romans. As with the rest of the Philippines, you can still see indications of the U.S. occupation that date back to my grandmother's era. Roadside signs are in English in a place where everybody speaks Tagalog. In the small town of Santa Cruz, where my grandmother is from, a billboard advertises a cream promising "fresher and whiter underarms." The sign hangs over bustling market stalls where butchers chop meat on wooden slabs and bored fish vendors play poker on a cardboard sheet over the day's catch. As I walked through the market, I could smell the chicken

adobo—my grandmother's specialty, made with a sauce of vinegar, soy sauce, and a bay leaf—at every corner.

As I looked at the father tenderly holding his child, I knew that one day this boy, if he stays, could easily be one of the millions who will be displaced. It could be the slow, steady advance of the sea. It could be a violent superstorm that assaults his home, his community, and the landscape itself. It could be the impossibility of irrigating the rice fields with the inundation of saltwater that destroys freshwater supplies. It could even be a repeat of the copper mine spill of 1996, when 1.6 million cubic tons of toxic sludge poisoned Marinduque's river system and reached the small community of this child, oozing onto the beach and boats and palms and houses, killing animals and ruining harvests. Perhaps Balogo got off easy. Six feet of poisonous sludge buried a nearby town, displacing 400 families. With rising seas and surging storms, with skin disease and lead poisoning, my grandmother's island has become another tragic example of Parenti's "catastrophic convergence."

Up to this point I had only thought of Marinduque as a place in my family's ancestral past. But it wasn't until I set foot on this beautiful, verdant island of rice fields and jungle that I understood that I was getting an unfiltered glimpse into the future of an escalating crisis, not only for the Philippines, but for the world.

Families like those of the father and child I saw will increasingly move farther inland to the provincial capital Boac, or across the sea to Luzon to the expanding mega-city of Metro Manila. Perhaps they will dare to cross, like so many others, one of the many heavily armed border zones

proliferating across the world. Perhaps they will see the walls, the surveillance towers, the razor wire, the armed guards, detention centers, and refugee camps. Indeed, this is what I set out to explore in the pages ahead: an increasingly authoritarian world in which climate change, the displacement of people, and border militarization define the experiences of untold millions in the 21st century.

• • •

Just east of Agua Prieta, in the Mexican state of Sonora, is a section of the U.S. border wall that looks as if a gigantic hand tossed it a quarter mile inland in disgust. The Normandy-style barrier that the U.S. Department of Homeland Security (DHS) uses to stop vehicular traffic from crossing the Silver Creek Wash, is now covered with debris. It is covered with cobwebs. It is covered with dirt. The earth is slowly consuming it. Small purple flowers are growing on the metal structure once meant to keep the "unwanted" from entering the United States. It looks like an archaeological ruin destined to be included in a future museum on failed forms of social control.

In 2014, Hurricane Odile unleashed a torrent of rain over the Chiricahua Mountains. Unable to be absorbed by the southern Arizona land parched with drought, barren of vegetation, and overgrazed by cattle, a ferocious river raged through the region. As in many hurricanes of our day and age, the rain poured into Arizona with unprecedented force, and when the deluge arrived at the international divide, it swept a portion of the U.S. border wall deep into Mexico. It

was only one small section of the approximately 700 miles of wall along the 2,000-mile border, but it was an indication of how the wall is standing up to the primal forces of our changing climate.

The way the dislocated section of wall was situated, semi-buried, in the bed of the Silver Creek Wash, it was as if we were in the year 2218 and I had discovered a relic from a long-vanished civilization. If it was, it probably wouldn't take archaeologists too long to piece together the much bigger story: the half-buried piece of metal was just one vestige of a powerful regime that expanded from the Gulf of Mexico to the Pacific Ocean through the late 20th and into the 21st century. Perhaps a confused future archaeologist might think this massive apparatus had been meant to stave off the onslaught of heat waves, dust storms, wildfires, and drought hitting the region. However, such theories would quickly dissipate with the discovery of the guns and stockpiled ammunition, revealing the principal purpose: to keep people out by force.

Just like super-typhoons, rising seas, and heat waves, border build-up and militarization are by-products of climate change. Just as tidal floods will inundate the streets of Miami and the Arctic ice sheets will melt, if nothing changes we will find ourselves living in an increasingly militarized world of surveillance, razor wire, border walls, armed patrols, detention centers, and relocation camps. Such a world already exists, but the militarization will intrude ever more deeply into our everyday lives, our schools, our transportation, our communication, and our sense of citizenship, community, and humanity itself. A future

archaeologist will find not only a world deeply altered by the impacts of climate change, but also communities scarred with unprecedented militarization, and not only in the United States but throughout the planet, where more securitized borders divide the Global North and Global South than ever before. As it stands now, border enforcement is not only growing, but is increasingly connected to the displacement caused by a world of fire, wind, rain, and drought. These are among the most powerful dynamics that are reshaping places and the experiences of millions of people in the world today.

In a 2003 report commissioned by the Pentagon called *An Abrupt Climate Change Scenario and Its Implications for United States National Security*, authors Peter Schwartz and Doug Randall assess what they call the "unthinkable." In a world afflicted with climate cataclysms:

> The United States and Australia are likely to build defensive fortresses around their countries because they have the resources and reserves to achieve self-sufficiency. With diverse growing climates, wealth, technology, and abundant resources, the United States could likely survive shortened growing cycles and harsh weather conditions without catastrophic losses. Borders will be strengthened around the country to hold back unwanted starving immigrants from the Caribbean islands (an especially severe problem), Mexico, and South America.[23]

Since this crude Pentagon report was issued in 2003, the United States has more than doubled its number of armed Border Patrol agents. It has added over 650 miles of walls and barriers along the U.S.-Mexico divide, including the section that got swept into Mexico with the surge of storm water from the hurricane. The United States has poured billions into advanced technology, radar systems, drones, and tethered aerostats. Australia, too, has inaugurated a 6,000-strong border force. According to geographer Elisabeth Vallet, there were 16 border fences when the Berlin Wall fell in 1988. Now there are more than 70 across the globe, a number that accelerated after 9/11 and includes Hungary, Greece, Spain, Morocco, Turkey, and India, to name a few, among the countries that have also constructed border walls.

Border security is becoming a "globally sung mantra," says April Humble, a researcher from the Secretariat of the Earth League, and enforcement regimes are spreading faster and to more places than ever before. The reasons cited for these border build-ups are like the tripartite mission of U.S. Customs and Border Protection: stopping terrorists, stopping immigrants, and stopping drugs. However, now there is more to it. As Humble says, this is a "situation of border fortification in a warming world," a warming world where there is no legal protection for families who are suddenly displaced due to climate. It is a situation, she says, that is "highly toxic."

This suggests that the theater for future climate battles will be the world's ever thickening border zones and not, as national security forecasts constantly project, in

communities where individuals fight each other for scarce resources. "Battle," however, is probably an inappropriate term. While one side will deploy well-armed border guards to enforce borderlines (that in almost every occasion were drawn by colonial powers, dividing once unified communities), on the other side will be ever-larger masses of people fleeing from ecological, political, and economic catastrophes.

Thus, one of the most reliable forecasts for our collective future is that vast numbers of people will be on the move, and vast numbers of agents will be trained, armed, and paid to stop them.

"Border controls are most severely deployed by those Western regimes that create mass displacement," writes author Harsha Walia in the book *Undoing Border Imperialism*, "and most severely deployed against those whose very recourse to migration results from the ravages of capital and military occupation. Practices of arrest without charge, expulsion, indefinite detention, torture, and killings have become the norm in militarized border zones."[24] Walia's analysis takes into account the disturbing correspondence between the fact that the world's biggest polluters—including the United States, which has emitted more metric tons of greenhouse gas pollution than any other country since the Industrial Revolution—are the same countries constructing unprecedented border regimes.

In *Storming the Wall*, I report from the flashpoints where climate clashes are beginning to play out, and those places where future battles will most likely erupt. I have set out to chronicle the way a massive system of social and economic

exclusion militarizes divisions not only between the rich and the poor, but between the environmentally secure and the environmentally exposed.

The pages ahead explore how the idea of fixed and linear borders—and the categories of people borders are supposed to protect against—have changed. Border enforcement zones now claim wider swaths of territory and blend into the very real war being waged against an ever-shifting category of people who are deemed "unwanted."

At an August 2016 Republican presidential campaign rally in Tucson, Arizona, the crowd erupted into a loud cheer when Mike Pence stated that if elected, the Donald Trump administration would, without a doubt, build a border wall. I was in the process of writing this book when I attended that rally, and it was uncertain who would win. Outside it was baking in downtown Tucson, another day in the hottest year on record. Humankind is now, perhaps for the first time in history, truly the proverbial frog in a steady, but ever-quickening pot of boiling water.

Under the presidency of Trump, "wall" continues to be one of many bigoted code words thrown like red meat to a voracious constituency. While Trump may add sections—even in the form of an imposing cement fortification—to the preexisting border wall, he will not build a contiguous 2,000-mile barrier. What he will do is far worse: militarize the country with more cameras, radar, drones, roving patrols, guns, bullets, and checkpoints clogging every vein and artery that enters the United States, a process that has been going on now for many years that will gear up and go full throttle.

In a February 2017 communiqué titled "The Walls

Above, the Cracks Below (And To The Left)" the indigenous Zapatistas of Chiapas, Mexico, wrote that "Borders are no longer just lines drawn on maps and customs checkpoints, but walls of armies and police, of cement and brick, of laws and persecution. In the world above, the hunting of human beings increases and is celebrated with clandestine competitions: whoever expels, incarcerates, confines, and murders the most win."[25] Perhaps there is no better way to describe what is coming the world's way.

Indeed, as Trump nuked every single mention of climate change from the White House's website on inauguration day 2017, and then—a few months later—backed out of the Paris climate agreement, it could be understood that, as the Zapatistas surmise, from a U.S. presidential perspective, the crises caused by a rapidly warming world will be addressed with walls, bullets, drones, cops, and cages.

Border zones are increasingly far more expansive than any actual boundary line, such as in the United States, where border enforcement and immigration checkpoints extend 100 miles inland. The international boundary line is "neither the first nor last line of defense" says former Border Patrol chief Mike Fisher. The militarized atmosphere that results from this furthers the feeling that we are living in what the American Civil Liberties Union calls "Constitution-free zones."[26] In these zones, Homeland Security agents persistently stop and interrogate people even during routine and mundane daily events, such as when they are going to the grocery store or to school. In the event of massive upheavals in the United States—with vivid past examples that include the 1936 Bum Blockade set up on the California state

borders to stop Dust Bowl victims from crossing into the state, or climate catastrophes such as Hurricane Katrina that included Border Patrol agents policing black neighborhoods in New Orleans—a constellation of armed checkpoints can quickly attempt to establish authoritarian domination over a population. After all, as sociologist Timothy Dunn shows quite clearly in the book *The Militarization of the U.S.-Mexico border*, these border zones operate under a Pentagon doctrine of low-intensity conflict.

But the idea of homeland security is far bigger than this, connecting law enforcement and the military via an increasingly pervasive surveillance grid that serves and connects both. Border enforcement is but one component of many in this homeland security apparatus. As constitutional lawyer John Whitehead says, the United States is ruthlessly building a "standing army on American soil." With its 240,000 employees and $61 billion annual budget, Whitehead points out, the Department of Homeland Security is militarizing police units, stockpiling ammunition, building detention centers, and spying on American citizens. In the pages ahead I examine not just the booming homeland security business that serves border enforcement, but also its many components that can be used in a variety of ways, including crowd control, biometric ID readings, and surveillance. According to economic reports, the national security industry will mushroom into a $546 billion market by 2022. As it stands right now, accelerating climate destabilization goes hand in hand with accelerating militarization and border enforcement.

Among the many things that go underreported but

should be common knowledge, is the torrent of resources gushing into the global security apparatus and its industries, while only a trickle is marshaled to deter and prevent the human activities that cause global warming and climate change. As Ben Hayes says in the book *The Secure and the Dispossessed*, the "fundamental problem with 'security': at its core is the essentially repressive goal of *making things stay the same*—no matter how unjust they may be."[27] As Hayes writes, the very same institutions that issue warnings about the security implications of climate upheavals are "spying on perfectly legitimate and democratic activity to make sure that it doesn't get in the way of business as usual."[28]

This is why the image of a border barrier, semi-consumed by Mother Earth and covered with small purple flowers, is so important, for it is a testament that the course we are currently on is not the only option. In today's climate era—some are calling it the Anthropocene—there are millions of people who are opting for sustainable lifestyles and practices, opting to organize against climate change, against militarization, and against the suicidal business-as-usual scenario. There are environmental activists who have risked—and even lost—their lives to raise awareness about the urgency of the current ecological crisis, and to champion sustainable, just, and cooperative living.

As the world becomes more environmentally, politically, and economically volatile, and more and more walls go up, increasing numbers of ordinary people are coming forward to extend solidarity across borders of nationality, race, and class. Against all odds, hope, optimism, and solidarity drive great change. I was surprised and inspired multiple times

while researching and writing this small volume by the many people who have launched political, social, and economic projects at a grassroots level, often making connections between people on opposite sides of militarized borders.

One such cross-border project was happening where I stood just east of Agua Prieta. An organization known as Cuenca Los Ojos was using ancient water-harvesting techniques to restore diverse plant life, flowing ponds and creeks, and animal life in ecosystems shared by the United States and Mexico. Around where that discarded border barrier lay were galvanized wire cages, called *gabions*, on the banks and beds of the wash. The *gabions* were filled with rocks and went as deep as 18 feet into the ground. At first glance, they had the striking appearance of intricate stone walls. But instead of keeping people out, they were built to be sponges shaped to the contour of the riverbank, slowing the water and replenishing the soil with life, miraculously recharging the water table in a place stricken with a 16-year drought.

Another border wall, indeed, is possible.

It is in these sorts of acts of hands-on "imagination," in the term of the most preeminent nature writers in the United States, Barry Lopez, that hope is germinating. "Our hope," he states, "is in each other. . . . We must find ways to break down barriers between ourselves and a reawakened sense of power to do good in the world."[29]

As challenging as these times may be, despite the walls, the guns, and all the corruption, a reawakened sense of life, connection, and power is deepening and spreading. The little purple flowers continue to bloom. There are many ways to storm the wall.

TWO

SUSTAINABLE NATIONAL SECURITY: CLIMATE ADAPTATION FOR THE RICH AND POWERFUL

The grave danger is to disown our neighbors. When we do so, we deny their humanity and our own humanity without realizing it . . .

—Pope Francis

In late April 2015, when Kevin Watson of the National Aeronautics and Space Administration (NASA) spoke at the Defense, National Security, and Climate Change conference in Washington, D.C., he told the story of a climate refugee in a way that I had never heard before: from the perspective of the climate-security business.

The panel that Watson spoke on was titled "Geopolitics, Natural Resource Implications & Extreme Events." Next to him sat two other panelists, Paul Wagner, an ecologist for the U.S. Army Corps of Engineers, and John Englander, an independent consultant for Booz Allen Hamilton, the same top-tier security company that Edward Snowden was

working for as a cover for his employment by the National Security Agency. Just before Watson arrived at the podium, Englander had told the audience of a hundred or so conference participants, all sitting at round tables with white tablecloths, "We are about to have catastrophic coastline change. It's not a matter of if, it's a matter of when."

To illustrate his own presentation, Watson projected images of the space shuttle and an F-35, a single-seat all-weather fighter aircraft manufactured by Lockheed Martin, a four-star sponsor of the conference. "All are dependent on special engineering alloys," he said. Watson then highlighted the elements needed to make the alloys: chrome, columbium, and titanium that were extracted from mines in South Africa, the Congo, and Zambia. Watson said that the reason he was highlighting Africa was that it's one area of the world expected to experience "significant climate change effects into the next century."

Watson then projected images from the fourth report of the Intergovernmental Panel on Climate Change (IPCC). One image showed Africa divided into five parts: West Africa, Central Africa, North Africa, East Africa, Southern Africa, with bullet points indicating potential climate hazards and disasters in each place. Desertification and droughts dominated many of the regions where the elements required for the alloys were mined. There would be severe impacts on water, on agriculture. "So all of these are going to stress the continent, stress the population," he said.

Then Watson connected the climate crisis with migration. He said, "If these stressing factors result in increased migration, it will just increase the potential for instability

and conflict" both inside and outside of the continent. This could impact the ability maintain local labor conditions necessary to move the elements "critical to the alloys we need to support the system." In one sentence, Watson effectively insinuated how climate-driven migration crises directly threaten powerful U.S. military-corporate business interests.

To prove his point and underscore that it was already happening, he said: "All you have to do is look at the news every day and you see tragedies associated with illegal migration out of the African Mediterranean, boats full of refugees that are sinking and so forth."

As Watson spoke, news was still breaking about a rickety three-story boat that had capsized off the Libyan coast while carrying more than 850 people. There were only 28 survivors, one of them a 20-year-old man from Gambia named Ibrahim Mbalo who made a death-defying escape from the sinking ship. As should be anticipated, the predictions for climate disruption in Mbalo's home country are dire, a place of increasing windstorms, floods, droughts, and sea-level rise that could inundate 8 percent of its land area.[1]

Watson was speaking during what was to become the deadliest month of 2015, in a year that would register 3,771 known immigration-related deaths in the Mediterranean Sea alone. This was also the year when the extent of people on the move, and the danger and tragedy of their situation, finally dawned on the world. This was the year when the image of Aylan Kurdi, a three-year-old Syrian boy found face down on a Turkish beach after crossing the Aegean Sea, was widely circulated. At one point 2,000 people per day were attempting the voyage on rubber dinghies. According to the

International Organization on Migration, there were more than 18 deaths per 1,000 travelers.[2]

Although it sounded as though Watson, who spoke with a soft voice, may have personally felt sympathy for the people killed crossing borders and their mourning loved ones, he focused instead on migration as a threat, how it increased conflict. "Just last week there were incidents of violence in Southern Africa," he said, "because the local residents were concerned that migrants were taking economic opportunities away. . . . Migration definitely creates friction internally and externally."

As Watson spoke, I noticed that most in the audience had a blank expression. There were government officials, Washington insiders, private industry reps, and representatives from the Army, Navy, and Marines. There were chief scientists from private companies and senior analysts. There were people from the Department of Energy. Watson's emphasis on the connection between global warming, immigration, and conflict was accepted almost without question. Perception of the migrant threat now goes much deeper than the usual nativist intolerance; driven by escalating climate crises, it is now perceived by corporate America as a threat to a much broader socioeconomic political system and the military financed to protect and perpetuate it.

It might seem counterintuitive that a national security establishment known for its deep-seated conservatism would embrace the notion that human-induced environmental crises are increasingly shaping the future of civilization. This view was shared by at least one attendee in the audience, who spoke up at the end of a later panel titled "Nexus of Water,

Energy and Food Impacts on National Security." He said with full confidence that the panelists were ignoring the "elephant in the room." The military, he said, was entrenched in climate denial. Awkward looks shot across the room, as if the man had missed the memo. But he was just repeating a commonly held perspective found outside the conference, the dominant narrative that the U.S. government is still debating the science of whether or not catastrophic global warming is real, caused by humans, preventable or not, and that in the meantime we should just keep using cheap fossil fuels and living it up.

This was even more pronounced as President Donald Trump took office. On the very day he was inaugurated on January 20, 2017, the Trump administration's quiet deletion of all climate change information from the president's website recalls the Reagan administration's removal of solar panels from the White House. With Trump, all signs point to a radical shift from Obama-era policies around climate change. Just the appointments of renowned climate skeptic Scott Pruitt and former Exxon Mobil CEO Rex Tillerson augur a hotter world and a revved-up fossil fuel economy. Slated to head the Environmental Protection Agency and Department of State, respectively, both arrive at their positions with vested interests.

However, behind the scenes the military and the Department of Homeland Security (DHS) will continue to prepare for the future dislocations of people, global instabilities, and threats to U.S. political and economic interests due to climate destabilization. Indeed, Defense Secretary James "Mad Dog" Mattis, according to *Politico*, may "turn

out to be the greenest person in Donald Trump's cabinet."[7] And DHS secretary John Kelly, in charge of policing U.S. borders, is also a climate security hawk. On top of that, the Trump administration already works under the the climate security doctrine's core assumption, that migration is a threat.

Two questions I wanted to address by going to the conference were how did business as usual continue in the United States as climate change came to be identified as a top national security threat, and how did acknowledgment of this threat impact the border enforcement and homeland security regime? As I sat in meetings and workshops for two full days, it became quite clear that while military analysts were superb risk assessors who regularly do threat projections well into the future, their findings were not being used to ensure that the necessary changes would be made to prevent large-scale ecological crisis. Instead, as the world became shaken to its core with potential catastrophe, the security apparatus worked hard to keep things the same in terms of economic, political, and social centers of power.

Indeed, the massive adjustments were like a climate adaptation program for the rich and powerful. Those enriched by the politics of fossil fuel, money, and weapons seemed to want solutions, first and foremost, for how best to keep a world of more and more impoverished people either working for them or out of sight altogether. As environmental destabilization wields tremendous pressures on these people to survive, investments pour into weapons and surveillance systems as a way of perpetuating the current economic-political order (even as the order attempts to "green" itself).

To understand how ingrained the climate security nexus is—in the context of fringe, yet powerful, climate denialism in some Washington circles—it is best to turn to Brigadier General Stephen Cheney—a panelist at the same conference as Watson. In response to the man who earlier accused the military of climate denial, Cheney said, "The lance corporal in the forward operating base doesn't really care much about the wind or the sun or the drought. He wants his bullets and he wants his food and he wants his water. The mid-level guys and gals—the majors—go to West Point, and the lieutenant colonels go to the War College, and they all are learning about climate change and understand the impacts . . . and how it's driving international conflict."

And it is generals like Cheney himself, the higher-ups who implement policy and strategy, who most directly impact climate security. In January 2016, the U.S. Department of Defense issued Directive 4715.21: "Climate Change Adaptation and Resilience." According to *Foreign Policy*, Deputy Secretary of Defense Robert Work signed "one of the potentially most significant, if little-noticed, orders in recent Pentagon history. The directive told every corner of the Pentagon, including the office of the secretary of defense, the joint chiefs of staff, and all the combatant commands around the world, to put climate change front and center in their strategic planning."[4] And now, with "Mad Dog" Mattis at the helm of the DOD, this not-widely-known yet game-changing directive has not been, and is unlikely to be, removed—even as the Trump adminstration attempts, including via a marathon of executive orders, to roll back Obama's legacy on climate.

Climate change, according to analysts Caitlin Werrel and Francesco Fermia of the organization Climate and Security, has reached a level of strategic significance that "can no longer be ignored."[5]

THE OVERWHELMING WINNER

"I want to explain up front I'm a Marine," said Brigadier General Stephen Cheney as soon as he stepped up to podium. "Thirty years of experience. Marines like pictures. They don't like PowerPoint. So I'm going to show a couple of pictures up here. And we like to talk about war fighting." On his right a slide flashed on the screen that said "Hot Spots: The Middle East." To his left, up on a stage, his fellow panel participants sat at a table from which hung a banner that read "Defense, National Security, Climate Change Symposium." Cheney, who was CEO of the American Security Project, a nonpartisan national security think tank formed in 2005 by then-senator John Kerry, said, "I'm going to walk around the world a little bit. Talk about conflict and climate change."

Cheney's gruff, confident voice fit the portrait of a soldier who had spent years on distant battlefields. "No surprise to anyone here: extreme weather presents a direct threat to U.S. homeland security. Around the world this has a tremendous effect on our forces and our allies. And definitely our enemies."

Everyone in the audience seemed intent on Cheney's words. He came across as a straight shooter. At one point during his talk, a younger man from Lockheed Martin, the *Fortune* 500 military manufacturer that was on the "cutting

edge" of climate change, spilled coffee all over himself and the white tablecloth on the round table where he sat with four colleagues. Lockheed Martin had long ago leaped into the middle of the climate battlefield. In 2015, its CEO, Marilyn Hewsom, after winning an award for business management, said that the company "will continue its endeavor to create an environment-friendly world by combating the security and stability threats generated through climate change." Also, as the *Washington Post* reported, the 112,000-employee corporation known for unleashing "cataclysmic fury on America's enemies," was partnering with a small Hawaii fish farm so that, according to the farm's chief, Neil Sims, they can grow fish with "literally no imprint in the ocean." The massive border surveillance market has not eluded Lockheed Martin either; in 2013 it was recognized as one of the top 15 companies to profit from "border security" based on multimillion-dollar contracts for aircraft and data processing products.

Nobody noticed when the coffee spilled, except for a server dressed in a white shirt and black pants who beelined to the table to clean up the mess.

Meanwhile, Brigadier General Cheney was speaking at the podium about how an unprecedented drought from 2006 to 2010 had helped fuel the current conflict in Syria. He talked about Nigeria, Lake Chad, migration caused by water scarcity, and the Boko Haram terrorist group that formed in the region. And right when the coffee hit the white tablecloth, Cheney was talking about what he called the "poster child" of climate and conflict—Bangladesh. He talked about the 2,000-mile iron wall along

the Indo-Bangladeshi divide, and said that Indian border guards have "shoot to kill" orders. Indeed, from 2001 to 2011 the Indian border forces killed 1,000 people, turning these borderlands into, according to Brad Adams in *The Guardian*, "South Asian killing fields."[6]

Cheney said that current studies project that 5 million Bangladeshis will be displaced due to sea-level rise, but according to generals he has talked to, it may be more like 20 or 30 million people. When the young man from Lockheed Martin bolted for the bathroom, I couldn't help but notice the stark and racialized divide between the servers and the conference participants. Although I couldn't say for sure, it occurred to me that many of the servers at the conference, like the man who was scrubbing away the coffee, might have been from Bangladesh, Nigeria, Turkey, Tunisia, or from any one of the very climate-stressed places that Cheney was talking about right before my eyes. It was entirely possible, if not probable, that climate refugees, the very people that countries were building walls to stop, that Donald Trump travel policies were designed to ban, places where Lockheed Martin was unleashing its "cataclysmic fury," were also at the conference serving coffee to the mostly white, middle- to upper-class conference participants.

"There is no doubt," Cheney said as the young Lockheed Martin employee returned to his seat, "that climate change is going to increase the demands on military personnel. You're going to see more humanitarian interventions, more peacekeeping, and certainly more conflicts."

"Our military is preparing for climate change," Cheney said; it is a "stressor," a "threat multiplier," an "accelerant

of instability." At first the words themselves were difficult to understand. Yet they were part of the growing vocabulary of military generals and Washington officials that named emerging aspects of the current ecological crisis. And there were other surprising twists to older concepts. For example, I had never heard the expression "military environmental industrial complex." This came not from an activist, but from the executive director of the energy company Constellation, John Dukes, during a session called "Defense and Energy."

When U.S. Navy Captain Jim Goudreau first used the term "sustainable national security," my immediate assumption was that he was referring to the U.S. military and Homeland Security's goal to reduce their massive level of greenhouse gas pollution, including the U.S. Army's goal to get to net zero emissions (quite a spectacular one given that the Department of Defense was the largest greenhouse gas emitter in the United States, by far) and Custom and Border Protection's goal to reduce emissions by 28 percent.

But there were much deeper implications, I soon saw, to Goudreau's use of the term.

"When people typically hear the word sustainable, they automatically jump to an assumption that it's hugging a tree, it's saving the world, [but] it's more than the environmental piece. It's an absolutely legitimate and important piece from the environmental perspective, but there's an economic perspective to sustainability, there's a political perspective to sustainability, there's a cultural aspect to sustainability—we have to approach all of those."

And sustainability's most important piece, Goudreau

explained, is military-tactical. As he said it, I couldn't help but think of the countless surveillance towers dotting the Sonoran desert in the U.S. borderlands, powered by solar panels. Sustainable, renewable energy resources would not only cut down on emissions, Goudreau said, it would make the military "more lethal."

"We've always designed our systems to achieve victory. Not by small margins. But to crush the enemy . . . I never want to be in a close fight. I don't want it to be an even fight. I want to be," Goudreau stressed, "the overwhelming winner." Sustainable national security no longer seemed so pretty.

It was the same point that U.S. Defense Secretary James Mattis famously made when he was commanding troops in Iraq during the Bush era: "Unleash us from the tether of fossil fuel."[7] Mattis's wish has been coming true: Between 2011 and 2015 military renewable-energy projects tripled to 1,390, producing an amount of power that could supply electricity to 286,000 average U.S. homes. This has continued: on February 3, 2017 SunPower landed a $96 million contract with the Trump administration to power the Vandenberg Air Force Base in California until 2043. Indeed, the Department of Defense will "forge ahead under the new administration with a decade-long effort to convert its fuel-hungry operations to renewable power,"[8] senior military officials told Reuters in March 2017.

"We know for a fact," Cheney continued with momentum back at the podium in Washington, "that [climate change] is already driving internal and cross-border migration. We know that it is opening new missions and

responsibilities for the military. Just look at the Arctic and the potential up there. We know that it is going to destabilize unstable states and societies."

If there are problems anywhere, Cheney said, environmental crisis is going to exacerbate them.

"There will be more demand for already existing missions such as peacekeeping, conflict prevention, war fighting. . . . It will heighten tension between states. And it is going to draw us into wars that we don't want to be in.

"Fortunately, if there is any good news to this story it's that the military is really good at risk management and preparing. . . . So the U.S. military plans for the worst, plans for the most likely, and then hopes it is over-prepared." Thus, in an age to be defined by decreasing amounts of clean water, breathable air, and food-producing land, the United States, with the help of companies like Lockheed Martin, aims to be the well-armed, well-fortified, "overwhelming winner."

"IT WILL AFFECT EVERYTHING YOU DO IN YOUR CAREERS"

On a beautiful, breezy day in May 2015, President Barack Obama stepped up to the podium to give a commencement speech at the U.S. Coast Guard Academy in New London, Connecticut. It was the first time a U.S. president emphasized climate change in a keynote speech. Before Obama got to the crux of his message, in which he would stress that "climate change refugees"[9] would become a significant part of the Coast Guard's future, he spoke to the cadets of the importance of guarding U.S. territorial borders and interests—underscoring an important yet often overlooked point

about his presidency: the continued expansion in policies and practices of an already historic U.S. border enforcement and deportation regime. Obama stated that the Coast Guard will start patrolling in faraway places such as the Caribbean and Central America, in the Middle East alongside the U.S. Navy, and in the Asian Pacific. Obama said that the new patrol missions were meant "to help partners train their own coast guards," and "to uphold maritime security and freedom of navigation in waters vital to our global economy."[10]

Obama spoke about upgrades to Coast Guard fleets such as *Fast Response* and *National Security* cutters, "the most advanced in history." These cutters were a part of a $25 billion program to replace much of the Coast Guard's equipment, known ominously as the Integrated Deep Water System Program.

"And even as we meet threats like terrorism," Obama said shifting to his main point, "we cannot and we must not ignore a peril that can affect generations."

It was quite a remarkable moment. The president of a country that did not ratify the Kyoto Protocol—the 1997 treaty in which countries pledged to reduce greenhouse emissions—was about to lecture Coast Guard cadets about the perils of climate change.

"Our analysts in the intelligence community know that climate change is happening. Our military leaders, generals, admirals—active duty and retired—know that it's happening. Our Homeland Security professionals know that it's happening and our Coast Guard know that it's happening.

"The science," the president said, "is indisputable."

Obama told the cadets that the heat-trapping carbon

dioxide in the atmosphere was higher than it has been in 800,000 years. He said that 14 of the hottest 15 years ever recorded have already happened this century. He told the cadets that NASA reported that the ice in the Arctic was breaking up faster than expected and the world's glaciers were melting, pouring water into the oceans.

"Cadets," Obama said, "a threat of a changing climate cuts to the very core of your service. You've been drawn to the water. Like a poet who wrote, 'The heart of the great ocean sends a thrilling pulse through me,' you know the beauty of the sea. You also know its unforgiving power. Here at the academy, climate change, understanding the science and consequences is part of the curriculum, and rightly so. Because it will affect everything you do in your careers.

"You," Obama said, "are part of the first generation of officers who begin their service in a world where the effects of climate change are so clearly upon us. It will shape how every one of our services plan, operate, train, equip, protect their infrastructure, their capabilities, today and for the long term."

Obama addressed the future of conflict and instability. He talked about rising seas swallowing portions of Bangladesh and Pacific Islands. He talked about similar "vulnerable coasts" in the Caribbean and Central America. When he talked about people forced from their homes I imagined, for a moment, that he was talking about that father and son on that Marinduque coast.

Obama's clear articulation of climate security doctrine, however, didn't come out of the blue. More than 20 years before he spoke to the cadets, *The Atlantic* published an article

titled "The Coming Anarchy: How Scarcity, Crime, Overpopulation, Tribalism, and Disease Are Rapidly Destroying the Social Fabric of Our Planet," by Robert Kaplan. Usually a single article, especially with such a loaded mouthful of a title, wouldn't be worth discussing as a historic event, but *The Coming Anarchy* was immensely influential to the policy that led up to the Obama administration's 2010 assessment that climate change posed a direct threat to national security. Obama's speech was a sign that Kaplan's 1994 article had finally arrived in the foreground of U.S. foreign policy, even in the context of possible Trump-generated speed bumps.

Kaplan predicted that the environment would be the "national security issue of the 21st century."[11] At one point in the piece, he described an apocalyptic future from the vantage point of his taxi window in West Africa, a world where "hordes" of young men with "restless, scanning eyes" surrounded his taxi and put their hands on the window asking for tips. "They were loose molecules in a very unstable social fluid, a fluid that was clearly on the verge of igniting." According to Kaplan, this was the mixture of environmental degradation and migration: people moving from untenable rural areas, afflicted with drought, to the cities, where "they join other migrants and slip gradually into the criminal process."[12] He was describing in 1994 the same "climate refugees" that Watson was talking about at the 2015 climate security conference.

Kaplan's writing, a bizarre mixture of rancid Malthusian nativism and cutting-edge forecast of ecological collapse, anticipated much of today's militaristic climate doctrine.

"The political and strategic impacts of surging pop-

ulations, spreading disease, deforestation and soil erosion, water depletion, air pollution, and possibly, rising sea levels in critical, overcrowded regions like the Nile Delta and Bangladesh—developments that will prompt mass migrations and, in turn, incite group conflicts—will be the core foreign policy challenge from which most others will ultimately emanate."[13]

In their book *Violent Environments*, Nancy Lee Peluso and Michael Watts note that the speed in which policy makers and their advisers took up the security diagnosis from *The Coming Anarchy* was "astonishing."[14] Shortly after it was published, the undersecretary of state, Tim Wirth, faxed a copy of the article to every U.S. embassy across the globe. President Bill Clinton lauded Kaplan and Thomas Homer-Dixon, the environmental conflict scholar whom Kaplan featured in the article, as "the beacons for a new sensitivity to environmental security."[15] Vice President Al Gore championed it as a model for the sort of green thinking that "he assiduously sought to promote during the 1990s," according to Peluso and Watts. The U.S. government created a senior post for Global Environmental Affairs and an environmental program, because "it was critical to its defense mission." In 1994, Secretary of State Madeleine Albright said, "We believe that environmental degradation is not simply an irritation but a real threat to our national security."[16]

Describing these earlier models of environmental conflict, writer Betsy Hartmann points out that the "degradation narrative has proved particularly popular in Western policy circles because it kills a number of birds with one stone: it blames poverty on population pressure, and not,

for example, on lack of land reform or off-farm employment opportunities; it blames peasants for land degradation, obscuring the role of commercial agriculture and extractive industries and it targets migration both as an environmental and security threat."[17]

That same year that Kaplan's prescient article was published, the U.S. Army Corps of Engineers was using rust-colored landing mats from the Vietnam and Persian Gulf wars to build the first border wall in Nogales, Arizona, as a part of Operation Safeguard. This was part of a series of operations—such as Hold-the-Line in El Paso, Gatekeeper in San Diego, Rio Grande in Brownsville—that would remake the entire U.S. enforcement regime under a strategy called "Prevention Through Deterrence." Government officials called for a "strengthening of our enforcement efforts along the border,"[18] anticipating the impact of the North American Free Trade Agreement on immigration from Mexico, among other things.

In 1995, the U.S. Border Patrol even created mock mass-migration scenarios in Arizona where agents erected cyclone fence corrals into which they "herded"[19] people for emergency processing, then loaded them onto bus convoys that transported them to mass detention centers. The fake border enforcement scenarios included a makeshift border patrol camp with five olive green army tents, portable toilets, and water tanks that were bathed in floodlights—a drab futuristic lanscape that predicted free trade regime upheavals and perhaps, ultimately, ecological crises or even, in some places, collapse. Here Kaplan's dire predictions were already beginning to meet a Trump-era border zone.

From this moment on, over the next 20-plus years, the dynamics of both climate change and border militarization would increase exponentially.

When mass migration surged after NAFTA, people trudged through the vast borderlands deserts often with not enough water, not enough food, and no medical aid for the incessant hazards of the journey, ranging from dehydration to heat stroke to rattlesnake bites. By closing off traditional crossing points with a concentration of agents, technologies, and walls, the strategy funneled prospective border-crossers to places that were so dangerous, isolated, and "mortal,"[20] as the first "Prevention Through Deterrence" documents put it, that people would not dare to cross. This could be the Arizona desert, the Mona Strait, or, in Europe's case, the Mediterranean Sea. This border policing strategy, in which the desert, the river, and the sea itself become metaphorical hostile agents, was still in place when Donald Trump took office in January 2017.

In the book *The Land of Open Graves*, anthropologist Jason De León wrote that with the "Prevention Through Deterrence" strategy, border zones became "spaces of exception—physical and political locations where an individual's rights and protections can be stripped away upon entrance."

"Having your body consumed by wild animals," he wrote of conditions on the U.S.-Mexico border, "is but one of the many 'exceptional' things that can happen in the Sonoran desert as a result of federal immigration policies."[21]

De León further explained that the U.S. borderlands have become "a remote *deathscape* where American

necropolitics are pecked onto the bones of those we deem excludable."[22]

Indeed, the remains of more than 6,000 people have been recovered in the U.S. borderlands since the federal government implemented these policies in the mid-1990s. Scholar Mary Pat Brady described this as "a kind of passive capital punishment," in which "immigrants have been effectively blamed for their own deaths."[23] According to the report "Fatal Journeys,"[24] 40,000 people have perished crossing borders worldwide between the years 2000 and 2014. The International Organization on Migration, which issued the report, says there are probably many more uncounted.

Given the predicted increases of people displaced by environmental destabilization, we can only predict in turn that increasing numbers will brave hot deserts and hostile seas, circumventing the places where surveillance is constant. The changing climate, subsequent upheavals, and fortified borders are on course to geopolitically remake the globe in profound ways. "While there are examples of militarized borders in past eras—for example, the Eastern Bloc countries during the Cold War—most political borders have never been militarized," geographer Reece Jones wrote in the book *Border Walls: Security and the War on Terror in the United States, India, and Israel*. "Even the simple idea of using mutually agreed-upon borders to divide separate states is a relatively recent development."[25]

Now the militarized fringes of countries—with the injected xenophobia exemplified by the Donald Trump rise to power, or the United Kingdom's exit from the European Union known as Brexit, will result in the the 21st century

being defined by the refugee meeting the razor-wire wall guarded by the guy with the big gun.

While the Obama administration is given much credit for the institutionalization of global warming with the U.S. government and national security apparatus, it was the George W. Bush administration, after nearly eight years of climate change denial, that in its waning days laid the foundation for today's climate security doctrine, as crudely outlined by Kaplan. Right when money was flooding into the newly formed Department of Homeland Security and its border apparatus, in the exact period between 2006 and 2008 when the U.S. Border Patrol was in the largest hiring surge in its history—adding 6,000 new agents to its ranks—and just when bulldozers were cutting through pristine landscape to erect 650 miles of walls and barriers along the U.S. international boundary with Mexico under the Secure Fence Act of 2006, six new major unclassified documents came out of the military and intelligence communities. Their warning was that climate shifts would threaten U.S. national security and this time the reports had the backing of generals such as Stephen Cheney. There was the CNA Military Advisory Board report titled "National Security and the Threat of Climate Change,"[26] the United States Joint Forces Command report "The Joint Operating Environment, Trends and Challenges for the Future Joint Force Through 2030," the National Intelligence Council's "National Intelligence Assessment (NIA) on the National Security of Climate Change to 2030," and the Department of Defense's "National Defense Strategy" to name some of them.[27] Following the lead of *The Coming Anarchy* and

the Bill Clinton administration, Bush was setting the stage for Obama.

When Obama told Coast Guard cadets about the rising possibility of climate refugees, he did not say what he meant by "they will have to respond." One might think that he meant rescue operations. However, every other year the Coast Guard, other Homeland Security agencies such as Customs and Border Protection, and the U.S. military participate in a mass-migration simulation in the Caribbean, similar to the one done in Nogales in 1995, known as "Integrated Advance." This is part of Operation Vigilant Sentry, a mass-migration contingency plan that involves the "interdiction, screening, processing, detention, and repatriation" of people. In other words, mass detention and deportation are now rehearsed like war games on the high, rising seas south of Florida. As the 2014 addendum to the DHS Climate Adaptation Plan states: "A mass migration plan has been developed, and a plan for increased operations planning of mass migration is under development."[28] It was as if the border fortress described by Schwartz and Randall in the 2003 Pentagon assessment *An Abrupt Climate Change Scenario and Its Implications For U.S. National Security* was coming into being, the unthinkable already here. This was where the doctrines of Obama and Trump meet in the climate destablilization era: a machine of arrests, expulsions, and banishment from the United States.

DONALD TRUMP

The immediate U.S. response to one of the most devastating natural disasters to hit the Western Hemisphere in the 21st

century would have been befitting of U.S. President Donald Trump. Much like the scenarios fully practiced during Integrated Advance trainings, not only did 16 U.S. Coast Guard cutters prowl Haitian waters waiting to interdict anyone leaving the country, but the private prison company Geo Group set up a temporary detention center in Guantánamo Bay while Haitians were still digging themselves out of the rubble. The earthquake killed about 230,000 people and displaced more than a million. The message from U.S. Homeland Security was clear, and even broadcast over the country in the Kreyol language by a U.S. Air Force bomber: *If you leave, you will be arrested and returned.* "Please: If any Haitians are watching, there may be an impulse to leave the island and to come here," Homeland Security secretary Janet Napolitano pleaded, "Please do not have us divert our necessary rescue and relief efforts that are going into Haiti by trying to leave at this point."

When President Donald Trump took office, at his disposal was the most massive border enforcement apparatus in United States history, built on turbocharge for more than 20 years, even able to act with startling efficiency to faraway disasters such as in Haiti. At his disposal were more U.S. Border Patrol agents than ever before in U.S. history, approximately 21,000, a five-fold increase from 1994 numbers. Customs and Border Protection (CBP), at more than 60,000 agents had become the largest federal law enforcement agency in the country. Including Immigration and Customs Enforcement (ICE), the 2017 border and immigration enforcement budget was $20 billion, a significant jump from early 1990s annual budgets (from the Immigration

and Naturalization Service), which hovered around $1.5 billion. Such was the enforcement arsenal before Trump ever set foot in the White House. And at Trump's disposal were the relationships with untold thousands of local and state police through many collaboration programs with ICE and CBP, such as Operation Stonegarden and 287(g) agreements—accords between DHS and local police jurisdiction that deputized police officers as immigration agents—to name just two.

At his disposal was the capacity to extend the U.S. border to the shores of Haiti, to the Mexican divide with Guatemala, and to the Iraq border with Iran. On top of this, Trump promises to build a more chilling and ramped-up border and immigration control apparatus, capturing, whether he admits it or not, people coming from environmental catastrophes.

Indeed, Trump's climate change skepticism is well known. On November 6, 2012, he sent out a tweet that read "The concept of global warming was created by and for the Chinese in order to make U.S. manufacturing non-competitive."[29] On January 25, 2014, the president tweeted "NBC News just called it the great freeze—coldest weather in years. Is our country still spending money on the GLOBAL WARMING HOAX?"[30] On January 29 of that same day he tweeted "Give me clean, beautiful and healthy air—not the same old climate change (global warming) bullshit! I am tired of hearing this nonsense."[31] On January 6, 2014, Trump called climate change a "hoax" on *Fox & Friends*, and on September 24, 2015, he said, "I don't believe in climate change"[32] on CNN's *New Day*.

Finally, as part of his presidential campaign he said that he would "cancel the Paris Climate Agreement and stop all payments of U.S. tax dollars to U.N. global warming programs."[33] And in June 2017, he did exactly that, removing the United States from what some consider the most important international agreement ever signed, to the complete dismay of many people not only in the United States, but across the globe.

In mid-November 2016, a week after the election, the Climate and Security Advisory Group delivered to the president-elect a book of recommendations. This group was composed of 43 U.S.-based military, national security, homeland security, and intelligence experts, which included former commanders of the U.S. Pacific and Central Command and the former Special Assistant to President Ronald Reagan for national security—the same sorts of people who were at the "National Security, Defense, and Climate Change" conference discussed earlier in this chapter. The document stressed that the new administration needed to build off the "progress already made"[34] by both the Barack Obama and George W. Bush administrations around climate change and national security.

When I contacted the American Security Project's Andrew Holland, the senior fellow on Energy and Climate, to get his take on Trump's intentions with climate, especially regarding the extensively reported "hoax" comment, Holland responded (cautiously): "There's a lot of different moving pieces in a government: the President isn't everything! What the SecDef has to say is important—as apparently is what the President's daughter has to say!" Indeed, former

Exxon Mobile CEO Rex Tillerson stated in January after taking charge of the U.S. Department of State: "I think it's important that the United States maintain its seat at the table on the conversations around how to address threats of climate change, which do require a global response."[35] Even Trump himself has said and done wildly contradictory things, such as asking officials in County Clare, Ireland, to approve construction of a sea wall to protect his golf resort from global warming, and meeting with climate advocate Al Gore. Also at this meeting was Trump's daughter, Ivanka, who said that she wanted to "make climate change . . . one of her signature issues."[36]

In March 2017, Trump signed an executive order that sought to eliminate a number of Obama-era policy iniatives—such as the Clean Power Plan and the September 2016 presidential memorandum on climate change and national security. Little more than a month later, the U.S. intelligence community issued a "Worldwide Threat Assessment"[37] in which climate change is identified as a prominent national security threat. The Assessment, as presented by the Director of National Intelligence Daniel R. Coats to the Senate Select Committee on Intelligence, repeats the climate security doctrine almost verbatim: global warming is "raising the likelihood of instability and conflict around the world."[38] The report stated that "this warming is projected to fuel more intense and frequent extreme weather events " and that countries with large coastal populations would be the most vulnerable, especially those in "Asia and Africa."

When I asked Stephen Cheney at the 2015 conference about how climate change would directly affect the U.S.

southern border he told me that in fact the night before, in Las Vegas, he had had dinner with the commander of Southern Command, General John Kelly. Of course, he had no idea at the time of Kelly's future as Homeland Security secretary. What Cheney said was "We did talk border security and what's driving immigration and there is no doubt that climate change is having an impact there as well. As it gets hotter, as the catastrophic events become more frequent, it's having an impact on how they grow their agriculture in the Latin American countries, and employment is becoming a problem, and it's driving people up north. So he's seeing that problem."

Indeed, Cheney said in a November 2016 interview not only that Secretary of Defense Mattis "get[s] climate change"[39] but that John Kelly did as well. "I know both of them understand it. I've talked to them about it… They know, they get it."[40] In the same article Cheney said that he knew of not one top general, with access to the White House or Secretary of Defense who did not understand the climate situation, though he did admit that maybe there was somebody out there.

So it should be no surprise that then-commander John Kelly's Southern Command was in charge of the simulation "Integrated Advance," especially with so many future environmental projections of mass migrations from the Caribbean. In 2015, some of the more than 500 members of the Joint Task Force of military and Homeland Security agents disguised themselves as people attempting to breach U.S. borders and boarded rickety boats going north. From a distance, the boats rocking on the waves almost seemed

authentic, with only the orange life jackets giving them away. Soldiers also played the role of journalists and media outlets that peppered command with questions, including challenging and critical ones. They practiced setting up positions in Guantánamo Bay where camouflaged soldiers sat behind laptops and looked at live feeds to strategize in real time.

"A migrant operation is one of our most likely missions at Army South so we have to be prepared,"[41] said Major General Joseph P. DiSalvo. Using cameras from the private company FLIR (who has been given, over the years, extensive contracts with Customs and Border Protection) the same rocking, rickety boats showed up on the screens in the fake command post. Large, red-striped Coast Guard cutters patrolled the area, dwarfing the simulated boats moving north. "The main purpose of the exercise is to develop working relationships among different U.S agencies and departments to deter illegal mass migration."[42]

Even though President Obama said the words "climate change refugee," there was no legal framework, either in the United States, or internationally, that would give refugee status to a person fleeing a climate-induced event. The Coast Guard was subordinate to the Department of Homeland Security and its tripartite war on terrorists, drug traffickers, and immigrants.

Under the current U.S. border militarization regime, which will clearly be ramped up with the Trump administration, migrants are occasionally rescued and perhaps even given bits of humanitarian assistance, but these efforts are secondary to, and always followed by, interdiction, arrest, incarceration, and deportation.

CLIMATE ADAPTATION FOR THE RICH AND POWERFUL

South Carolina Congressman Jeff Duncan is getting frustrated. Three U.S. Homeland Security officials sit before him with stoic faces. They have been testifying for close to an hour in a hearing titled "Examining DHS's Misplaced Focus on Climate Change."[43] The South Carolina congressman scrutinizes the bureaucrats as if he can't believe he's sitting in the room dealing with this shit. This happens only weeks after 21-year-old Dylann Roof entered the Emmanuel African Methodist Episcopal Church in Duncan's state of South Carolina and killed nine people during a prayer service with the intent to incite a "race war." But he doesn't mention this.

Duncan, who wears a pressed white shirt with a light purple tie, looks at the DHS men intently. "Can you guys tell me why the Earth was warmer during the medieval times?"[44]

The Homeland Security men shuffle in their seats uncomfortably. Behind them is the audience at the hearing. In front are the members of the committee. The pause is awkward. Deputy Assistant Robert Kolasky, from the Office of Infrastructure Protection, finally makes a gesture that he'll take a stab at it. When Kolasky gave his testimony earlier, he could've been renowned climate journalist Naomi Klein when he quoted the 2014 U.S. Global Change Research Program's Third National Climate Assessment, which reported that the United States "will experience an increase in frequency and intensity of hurricanes, massive flooding, excessively high temperatures, wildfires, severe downpours,

severe droughts, storm surge, sea-level rise throughout the 21st century."[45]

Kolasky also told the committee that "extreme weather strains our resources, serves as a threat multiplier that aggravates stressors both at home and destabilizes the lifeline sectors on which we rely. Higher temperatures and more intense storms can cause damage or disruptions that result in cascading effects across our communities."[46] In other words, following the lead of the world's most respected climate scientists, the Department of Homeland Security projects that civilization as we know it will be difficult to maintain. The intelligence community knows that the sea is rising and will engulf entire swaths of territory, it understands the surges brought by hurricanes and the ensuing flooding, it anticipates the coming crises of wildfires and water scarcity.

However, to Duncan's question about the medieval period, Kolasky says, "I don't think any of us can speak to that."

"The Earth was warmer," Duncan interrupts. "Grapes grew higher on the mountains. The Earth was warmer. You're not going to refute that," Duncan says, extending his hand toward Kolasky, "I hope."

"I think that we got threats of ISIS, we got cartels shooting at helicopters, we got unaccompanied children coming into this country, we've got illegal aliens murdering beautiful, innocent lives in San Francisco, we've got a woman who had her head blown off in Los Angeles by someone," Duncan says, sounding similar to Donald Trump.

"There are events after events going around the world that are true threats to the United States. Folks that want to do great harm to Christians, that want to do great harm to

us. They come to this country to end the American way of life. [And] for whatever reason, we are spending our hard-earned dollars on climate science and this belief that it is one of the biggest threats to national security."[47]

In a measured, placating tone, Thomas Smith from the DHS Office of Policy Strategy, Plans, Analysis, and Risk explains to Duncan that U.S. authorities will continue to target the very types of people that Duncan mentioned. Homeland Security is not about studying climate science, he explains, it's about understanding the shifting global climate as a "threat multiplier"[48]—there's that phrase again.

The term "threat multiplier" first appeared in the 2004 United Nations report "Threats, Challenges, and Change" but didn't enter the common security lexicon until 2007. According to researcher Ben Hayes, "just as emphasis on the 'war on terror' was receding . . . influential security actors in Europe and the U.S. began to outline foreign policy options for addressing climate change as a security threat."[49]

The term "threat multiplier" hits a deeper chord, because the "threat" referred to much more than just severe weather, and gets back to Watson's point at the beginning of this chapter. More dangerous than climate disruption was the climate migrant. More dangerous than the drought were the people who can't farm because of the drought. More dangerous than the hurricane were the people displaced by the storm. The climate refugee was a threat to the very war planes required to enforce the financial and political order where 1 percent of the population wielded more economic power than the rest of the world combined.

At the global policy level, there are two principal

responses to climate change: mitigation and adaptation. Mitigation aims to reduce greenhouse gas emissions. Adaptation "seeks to lower the risks" posed by changing conditions. Climate adaptation could mean a wide range of things: building protections against sea level rise, improving quality of road surfaces to withstand hotter temperatures, rationing water, farmers planting different crops, businesses buying flood insurance. Through USAID, the United States has invested $400 million for worldwide climate adaptation programs, and in 2015 Secretary of State John Kerry committed the U.S. to double that amount. Often workshops focus on food security, health, humanitarian assistance, and water management, what the agency calls "key climate-sensitive sectors."[50] These State Department programs are on the chopping block in the Trump administration, and predicted to be slashed or gutted.

The climate "adaptation" plan that is rarely mentioned, but which drones silently over the globe, is the militarized security apparatus that is preparing to enforce "order"—including, in many ways, the suicidal fossil-fuel economy of today—even as it accelerates ecological crisis. Given that all environmental security assessments factor in the massive displacement of people, border militarization becomes one key component, among many others, to maintain the status quo.

Instead of, say, a sea wall's resistance to physical storms, a border wall envisions a sort of resistance on the part of the rich and powerful against the people whose homes and livelihoods were destroyed by those storms.

As David Ciplet, co-author of *Power in a Warming*

World, points out, there are choices regarding how money is spent. "Hundreds of billions of dollars each year subsidize fossil fuel industries globally—the main cause of climate change—and nearly $2 trillion are spent on the military."[51] And, of course, the military, even as it greens its own technology, provides the business-as-usual security for the fossil fuel industries.

Thomas Smith is one of the principal authors of the *2014 Homeland Security Quadrennial Review*, the main public doctrine that explains the DHS mission and now recognizes climate change as a central threat. Smith said earlier that experts in the Office of Policy Strategy did a number of activities to understand the threats and hazards facing the United States, and "the strategic environment we operate in." This collection of analyses was known as the Homeland Security Strategic Environment Assessment. It looks at risks, threats, and trends during a given time frame, in this case, the 2015–2019 window, and collectively identifies "natural disasters, pandemics, and climate change as key drivers of change to the homeland security strategic environment."[52] In the *Quadrennial Review*, Smith says, these associated trends continue to present "a major area of homeland security risk," and he specifically mentions that "more frequent severe droughts and tropical storms, especially in Mexico, Central America, and the Caribbean could increase population movements, both legal and illegal, toward or across the U.S. border,"[53] a tame version of the threat forecasts issued by officials worldwide.

To Duncan, Smith says: "We describe that climate change can aggravate stressors such as poverty, such as food

insecurity, such as causing population migration. For vulnerable populations with weak government institutions it may enable terrorism to take hold."[54]

The congressman from South Carolina is definitely not the only one fooled into thinking that discussions in Washington about climate change are limited to science and to laws regulating carbon emissions and debates about whether or not it exists. In the strategy rooms of Washington, a climate adaptation program for the rich and powerful is being created, and the walls and weapons to protect their systems of profit and politics as long as possible. The real threat is the inability to obtain alloying agents needed to make more fighter jets.

THREE

THE 21ST-CENTURY BORDER

If you ask us what's going to happen in the near future, we have no fucking idea. Sorry for using the word "idea."

—Subcomandante Marcos (now known as Galeano), at a press conference.

Three Honduran men sit by the train tracks in the small, broiling town of Tenosique, Mexico. They wait where hundreds of Central Americans congregate each night in hopes of jumping on the freight train notoriously known as The Beast, as it chugs north to the United States. In the distance, across the tracks, an army truck rumbles by. In the back, two soldiers stand poised with assault rifles, their faces covered with black balaclavas. The shiny Dodge Ram contrasts against the rusted machinery scattered in the overgrown grass and cement. It is as if we are on the set of a movie somewhere between *Children of Men*, a film that depicts the United Kingdom as an ultra-militarized police state rounding up and incarcerating refugees, and *The Road*, a tale of a

father and son who walk across a post-apocalyptic North America devastated by an unknown cataclysm.

The Honduran men's names are Luis Carlos, Santos Fernando, and Ismael. They have been living by the tracks in a small shack built of corrugated metal for several days. When I ask Ismael where he is from, he pulls out the identification card that is warped and fraying at the edges, as if it has been pulled out one too many times. I am not there to look for "climate refugees." I am there to investigate Mexico's upsurge in border policing since 2014, known as *Programa Frontera Sur*. The soldiers across the tracks are moving away from us. I wonder, as I watch them monitoring the train yard, if they are among the many military, police, and immigration officials who have been trained by the United States.

Ismael tells me that he is 17 years old and a *campesino*, a subsistence farmer. He tells me that they are headed to the United States, a thousand miles away. When I ask them why they decided to leave Honduras, his answer is simple, and similar to the case of many other farmers across the world in the climate era: "*No hubo lluvia*." There was no rain.

This is a border in the Anthropocene era: young unarmed farmers with failing harvests encountering expanding and highly privatized border regimes of surveillance, guns, and prisons. What I am witnessing is occurring in many places with many different manifestations—along the southern borders of Morocco or Libya, on the militarized divide between India and Bangladesh, between Syria and Turkey. Militarized borders are not only proliferating throughout the globe, they emanate from centers of power, such as the

United States and the European Union, that fund border infrastructure and train the guards.

This is the 21st-century border that I examine in this chapter. It is a border that is not solely defined by an international boundary line, nor even the most imposing Trump-era wall, but rather by a multilayered enforcement apparatus covering a wide swath of territory, defined more by political and economic power than by national sovereignty. There are many components to this, including complex surveillance networks, biometrics and big data, militarized police agents, border policing strategies, and "consequence delivery systems," to name a few elements of the totality of "border security." Perhaps, there is no better way to explore the emergence of a 21st-century border system vis-à-vis climate upheavals, than with a Central American's journey north. In many ways, and for many people, the imagined world of a degraded environment, combined with an authoritarian high-tech surveillance state, already exists. This is especially true if you are somebody traveling north from Honduras, without authorization to cross border lines.

Along the Mexico-Guatemala divide, expensive hardware such as underwater motion sensors, night-vision goggles, X-ray machines, and Black Hawk helicopters have come from the United States via a military aid package known as the Merida Initiative. U.S. Homeland Security agents have trained Mexican immigration authorities, police, and military in border policing. Customs and Border Protection agents from the United States are physically working in immigration detention centers along the Mexico-Guatemala border. Washington not only supports—but

insists on—Mexico guarding its borders since the upsurge of northbound Central American immigration of the early 2010s. Where Luis Carlos, Ismael, and Santos Fernando sit on the train tracks, 1,000 miles away from Texas, I understand that they are, as the Merida Initiative's third pillar indicates, just barely beginning their trek through the United States' "21st-Century Border."[1]

"WE'RE FACING AN UNPRECEDENTED CALAMITY"

In May 2015, many farmers throughout Central America sowed their seeds expecting rain that never came. It used to rain from May to November. People would take advantage of the first rains to plant corn, beans, and rice. In 2015 their seeds dried up in a drought that affected more than a million farmers spanning four countries—Guatemala, Honduras, El Salvador, and Nicaragua—in the Central American "Dry Corridor." Eleuterio Flores, one of the 400,000 farmers nailed by the drought in Honduras, told Agence France Press, "There is nothing to eat, the harvests are completely lost."[2] According to the Central American Agricultural Council, there was a loss of 80 percent of bean crops and 60 percent of corn. Where Flores lived, the small town of Texiguat, Honduras (population 12,000), 80 percent of the people live in acute poverty, 4 percent more than the national average; 54 percent of the people in Honduras live in severe poverty.

As 16-year-old Lesly Vasquez came to pick up a food packet that the Honduran government was distributing to the 82,000 families slammed by drought, she told AFP,

"We're here so somebody can help us, we have nothing to eat." The 16-pound bags of corn flower, manteca (lard), pasta, coffee, reminded me of the 100-pound sacks of rice I had seen distributed to typhoon survivors in the Philippines. "We're facing an unprecedented calamity," said the mayor of Texiguat, Lindolfo Campos.[3]

Climate scientist Chris Castro told me that the Central American northern triangle, right where Texiguat is located, is "ground zero" for global warming's impact in the Americas. One thing that is happening, according to Castro, is an "intensification of the mid-summer dry period." The *canícula*—the farmers' term for a "dip" in rainfall during the months of July and August, has intensified, "and that is critical for agricultural activities there, particularly for subsistence farmers." According to the regionalized climate model Castro is using in Central America,[4] the *canícula* is only predicted to get hotter and drier and could be devastating to agriculture and ecosystems attuned to the seasonal cycles of precipitation. "You might have threshold points where forests dry out, so they are more susceptible to fire, or where you reach drought conditions so that you can't plant certain crops, or they affect water supplies, or you have precipitation extremes that exceed design parameters for a system, then translate that to a population" in vulnerable socioeconomic conditions, whose "livliehoods are tied to the ability to interface with the the natural environment."

As Castro put it, "It's a paradigm of the wet gets wetter, the dry gets drier, the rich get richer, the poor get poorer. Everything gets more extreme."

In 2010, the American Security Project (of Brigadier General Stephen Cheney) issued a Latin America threat forecast in a report titled "Climate Change and Immigration: Warnings for America's Southern Border" in 2010.[5] Like the Department of Homeland Security's 2014 Quadrennial Report, the 2010 assessment foresaw the future of the three men at the rails in Tenosique: the heat waves, flooding, drought, and superstorms impacting what the government analysts called "impoverished and politically unstable communities." The pressure on "our southern neighbors to reach friendlier environments in the United States will grow stronger." There will be storms, soil erosion, run-off, and food shortages. Millions of people will be affected as coastal areas flood, particularly on Caribbean islands, which, they write, are in jeopardy of being swallowed by the sea, "both partially and completely."[6]

There will be an "environment ripe for migration."[7]

And if that were not enough, even "more problematic," according to author Lindsey Ross, are the "special interest aliens" that could be "potential terrorists from countries that are home to known networks."[8]

Indeed, as predictions of increasing numbers of climate refugees fill forecasts, the United States isn't planning to extend them any special status; rather, as the report stated, "climate migrants will place an additional burden on communities along the U.S. southern border. . . ."

PREVENTION THROUGH DETERRENCE

Increasing the speed of freight trains has been one of the many tactics the Mexican government has been using to

deter unauthorized immigration, since the declaration of the 2014 Southern Border Program. A fast-moving train can create suction between the cars that can pull a person onto the tracks, where they are chewed up or crushed alive. The train has injured so many people that there is a shelter in Tapachula, Mexico, dedicated to helping the mutilated and dismembered. The night before I met them, Ismael, Luis Carlos, and Santos Fernando had tried to jump on a train, but it was moving too fast.

The train was an example of "Prevention Through Deterrence," with the implicit threat of bodily harm or even death. This did, in fact, deter the three men. Remember, this was the strategy implemented on the U.S.-Mexico border that creates spaces of exception—in which the threat of the most terrible violence afflicts (and, according to policy makers, deters) migrants—and has been U.S. border policy since Gatekeeper-type operations started in the early 1990s. Now such a policy, whether explicitly stated or not, is in effect throughout Mexico. As Mexican analyst Marco Antonio Velázquez Navarrete put it, "The entire country of Mexico is now a border."

Even if they had been fortunate enough to get on the train, a mile down the tracks Mexican authorities ordered the train to a screeching halt. Immigration agents, accompanied by armed police, searched the train with blinding flashlights (in Mexico immigration authorities are unarmed, so they often conduct joint operations with police or military) and arrested everyone they could catch. Fray Tomás González Castillo, director of the nearby shelter known as La 72, tells me it is almost "impossible" for people to go

north. He says that there are "scandalous checkpoints" on the roads and that "organized crime" controls the trains.

As I talk to the Honduran men in the overgrown grass, I notice a train car with the graffiti, in Spanish, POR LA DIGNIDAD DE UN VIAJE SIN FRONTERAS, "*for the dignity of a journey without borders.*" Unfortunately for them, nothing could be further from reality. They sit in the first enforcement cordon of a three-tiered border policing system. Patrolling soldiers, fast trains, and immigration operations are all part of the first tier. The second layer is a series of mega-enforcement facilites, or "super-checkpoints,"[9] located on every highway headed into the interior of Mexico. They are each the size of a U.S.-style shopping mall. If you use public transportation, authorities force you off your vehicle and armed soldiers monitor you while you remove your belongings and submit them to an X-ray machine supplied by direct transfer from the United States government. Mexico also has backscatter vans with the controversial surveillance technology that can detect objects through walls and clothes, acquired through the 21st-Century Border program from the private company American Science and Engineering Inc.

Mexico has no walls with Guatemala and Belize, and people move easily over those borderlines. On the Suchiate River in Talismán or Ciudad Hidalgo, for example, people and merchandise freely cross back and forth on large rafts under the very eyes of the ever-modernizing official port of entry. I have crossed this slow, rippling river on a number of occasions, including once alongside a Guatemalan family on their way to the wake of a loved one in nearby Tapachula, Mexico. Since much of southern Mexico was

once a part of Guatemala, just as much of the United States was part of Mexico, there are many cross-border family and community bonds.

In 2010, an alarmed U.S. embassy official wrote in a leaked cable that they saw as many people "crossing the border illegally as legally,"[10] a sentiment that seemed to convey that the border is easy to cross. Nothing, however, could be further from the truth. Mexico's third tier of border enforcement extends for hundreds of miles into the country's interior. Checkpoint after checkpoint steadily halts all traffic going north, all the way to places close to Mexico City. Immigration agents, police, and military board buses and vans, interrogate people, and have the authority to remove passengers and detain them. I have seen this happen before my own eyes on multiple occasions. Every time since 2014 that I've traveled the 150 miles from Tapachula to Arriaga, I have counted more than 10 checkpoints. There are immigration agents who walk the aisles profiling passengers, soldiers who search through your bags. It has become a war zone where there is no war, a state of emergency where there is no invading army. Checkpoints have long existed in Chiapas, but now under the border logic they are the equivalent of a "wall" to be circumvented. Every single one of these checkpoints forces undocumented travelers off the roads and into dangerous areas such as La Arrocera, as documented by Óscar Martínez in *The Beast: Riding the Rails and Dodging Narcos on the Migrant Trail*, a network of 28 or so ranches where assault, rape, and killings of people moving through have become commonplace. Along the migrant trail, Central Americans speak of the "disappeared" with

similar horror as they did during the counterinsurgency conflicts of the 1970s and 1980s.

A group called the Mesoamerican Migrant Movement, composed of Central Americans searching for lost family members, claims that since 2006, approximately 70,000 people have disappeared while traveling through Mexico.[11] Since the Mexican government does not keep records of foreigners who have disappeared, the number is difficult to verify. If the claim is even remotely close to being accurate, a silent human rights atrocity is being perpetrated with little remedy or outcry.

In her book *Golden Gulag*, geographer Ruthie Wilson Gilmore writes that "racism, specifically, is the state-sanctioned or extralegal production and exploitation of group-differentiated vulnerability to premature death."[12] In many ways, Gilmore captures the 21st-century border's prevention through deterrence policy with precision.

Luis Carlos, the oldest in the group and the only one who has made the journey, says that he spent three months in a U.S. prison after he crossed the border a previous time. He has a distinct almost disfigured face, and reminds me of a Salvadoran man I interviewed at a migrant shelter the year before in Arriaga, Mexico, who had a deep purple bruises, dislocated fingers, and fresh stitches from being beaten with baseball bats and then thrown from a moving train.

With Luis Carlos, Ismael, and Santos Fernando I know I am catching the smallest glimpse of the colossal intersection of climate upheavals and the expanding zones of exclusion, what seems to be the coming future. These men, who can't get their plants to grow, now face a 1,000-mile space

of exception. They will travel over the unmarked graves of thousands before they even reach the towering border walls of the United States.

This state of exception, however, was at their doorsteps in Honduras before they even left.

HONDURAS: BETWEEN CLIMATE CHANGE AND ITS "SOLUTION"

Police agent Nuñez was no-nonsense when he got on the small, cranky bus that was traveling along the northern Honduran coast toward Tocoa. I was on my way to San Pedro Sula, often referred to as the most violent city in the world due to its homicide rate, to meet with one of Honduras's top climate scientists, Leonardo Lenin Banegas Barahona. I was coming from the small town of Vallecito, inhabited by the Garífuna, a people who were in constant struggle, I learned, with police officers like Nuñez, who tended to protect large landowners and corporate-driven mega-projects. The gruff agent of the Honduran Investigative National Police, an agency that the United States helped establish and the Colombian National Police trained, carried himself as if he didn't like anyone on the bus. This checkpoint was one of what seemed like dozens of roadside blockades throughout post-coup Honduras. Since former president Manuel Zelaya's forced removal in 2009, the country has been fraught with spiking violence, human rights violations, economic despair, and migrations that—from places like the shelter in Tenosique, Mexico—seem like an exodus. Honduras has never been a bastion of human rights and equality. Now, however, combined with

the above dynamics, Honduras has become one of the places across the globe that sharply exemplify where planetary warming and a global border enforcement regime overlap. At the checkpoints, if agents didn't stop the vehicle, they would eye it as it slowed down over a speed bump. Nuñez barked, "¡*Varones*! Off the bus!" Forcing males off buses for extended interrogation followed a long tradition of counterinsurgency practices in Central America.

When I stepped off the bus into the humid air, the view from where I stood on the crackled concrete was of African palm plantations that went on and on forever in this northern coastal plain. This monoculture was a modern crop, crowding and usurping communities, and their water sources, in order to irrigate the endless rows of palms, standing like erect soldiers in salute, whose oil would be used for cooking oils and soap. It can also be processed into a biodiesel, and, according to the Sustainable Palm Oil Transparency-Toolkit (SPOTT), "significantly reduce emissions from cars and trucks and thereby mitigate global climate change."[13] On the other side of the palm plantations, the sea creeps in like a simmering monster, eroding the coast, ready to surge again with the next mammoth storm, like Hurricane Mitch, whose floods and landslides killed 7,000 people and left 1.5 million homeless in 1998.

And this National Police officer—at least partially funded by the U.S. Central American Security Initiative (CARSI), a security package from the United States to Central American countries worth approximately $1.7 billion[14] since 2008—was there to keep "public order" in the midst of the powerful economic, ecological, and political

dynamics driving displacement. As with the Merida Initiative's 21st-Century Border, millions of dollars have been transferred to Central America from the United States in resources and training operations through CARSI. For example, U.S. Border Patrol's Tactical Unit, known by the acronym BORTAC, have carried out trainings in Honduras. Perhaps even Nuñez was trained by the Special Forces component of U.S. border policing that regularly trains foreign law enforcement and military personnel. In 2014 Cindy Carcamo reported in the *Los Angeles Times* that during an operation called "Rescue Angels," the Honduran National Police deployed roadside blockades in border areas to stop Honduran children from *leaving* their own country. As Carcamo reported, "Covered with bulletproof vests emblazoned with 'Police' and badges that read 'BORTAC,' the agents waved down a late-morning bus bound for Guatemala."[15]

The night before, in Vallecito, a young Afro-Honduran man named César spoke to a group gathered in the small community. His message was urgent. More youth were leaving than any other time since the Garífuna began inhabiting the northern Honduran coast more than 200 years before. As he talked about displacement (happening at breathtaking rates in Honduras), the super-low wages paid to people working in palm plantations, the internal youth migration to places like San Pedro Sula, where they worked for cheap in one of 200 factories, I could hear the sharp crack of a rifle fire in the distance. Round after round echoed as the dusk turned to night and the wind off the coast picked up and flapped the tarps. The sound was ominous enough to cause some of the people gathered to turn and look toward

where three soldiers were posted, about a quarter mile away. Earlier that day I had talked to the soldiers. One held an Israeli-made automatic rifle (a Tavor) in his hands. He had a distant look in his eyes, as though he didn't want to talk. He muttered that they were there to "protect" the community. The younger one, cradling an M-16, was friendlier and more energetic. They were new to this post, having arrived just a couple of days before after completing a seven-week urban-warfare training at the nearby city of Ciudad Trujillo.

Ciudad Trujillo was near the Honduran naval base in Puerto Castilla, where four U.S. Marines and one Naval officer were based and were assisting the Honduran military to form "professional military training centers." The six-month U.S. military deployment of 280 Marines to the Soto Cano air base in Honduras in May 2015, according to an article in *Military Times, was designed to ready* the soldiers to "assist with any humanitarian crises that emerged during the hurricane season." They also said they helped with infrastructure projects such as new schools for children. However, it was these "professional military schoolhouses" in which they were "definitely pioneers," according to Captain Juan Díaz. "We helped establish and start up an institution of sorts in this country."[16]

When I asked the young Honduran soldier how the Urban Combat training went, he described how awful it felt to receive a full plate of food only to have it be taken away just before he could take his first bite.

"But," he concluded, "I would die for my country."

Back in Vallecito, as rifle fire continued to crackle and echo into the night, César talked about his community being

unable to fish because multinationals were drilling oil off the coast, and how there were fewer places to plant yucca and corn because the mining companies had taken over huge areas inland. Seeing that I kept looking toward the distant rifle shots, someone from the group finally said it was probably just soldiers, bored, doing target practice. I imagined a soldier firing his M-16 into the African palm plantation located near their small outpost, run by a company of the late Miguel Facusse, the biofuel magnate who was known for hiring private security forces that continually attacked *campesinos* throughout the very region where I stood on the northern coast. When people uttered the name Facusse in Vallecito, they almost spat it out, as if they couldn't stand to have the word in their mouth. Facusse's armed forces, associated with his company Grupo Dinant, worked alongside Honduran police and military who have been used directly to expel communities.

According to Jennifer Kennedy, writing for Corpwatch, Facusse joined the biofuel rush, backed by bilateral and multilateral agencies such as the World Bank, to meet demand "by governments who want industry to reduce their dependence on fossil fuels like coal and petroleum in order to meet international obligations to mitigate global warming under the Climate Change convention."[17] Enriched by heavy subsidies, Facusse's company rose to the top in Honduras, clear-cutting and then commanding 22,000 acres of land.

Indeed, while most U.S. news continued to give uncontextualized depictions of gang violence in Latin America, the thugs I was hearing about on the Honduran northern coast were more of the corporate variety, including those

who aimed to profit from climate change. As César spoke, he simply reinforced what dozens of other community leaders from the Black Fraternal Organization of Honduras (OFRANEH) were expressing: they were facing the constant threat of compulsive eviction by state forces that were also working, in their own way, to reduce emissions.

The Garífuna people, descendants of Caribbean Native Arawak as well as Central and Western African people forcibly brought to this hemisphere by white enslavers, have a long history of resistance to European imperialism, a defiance so vexing that the British forcibly deported them from the Caribbean to the northern coast of Honduras in the late 18th century. Garífuna resistance has continued to this day against imperialism's various attempts at "systemic removal," as many in Vallecito described their situation. There was not only the advancement of African palm, but also mega-projects of commercial fishing, mining, drilling, and tourism (such as the resorts of Canadian Randy Jorgensen, who stood trial in November of 2015 for allegations of illegally seizing land in Garífuna territories).

The Garífuna talked about Economic Development Zones, or *ciudades modelos*, "model cities." These were the officially named Special Economic Development and Employment Zones, known as ZEDEs in Spanish.

Yilian Maribel David, one of the organizers for OFRANEH, said that the Economic Development Zones were like "a country within a country" where the state of Honduras no longer governed.

I had to ask for clarification to make sure I was understanding her correctly.

The ZEDEs—which are still in creation (and up for approval by the international Committee for the Adoption of Best Practices, according to an expert I talked to)—are conceived to be autonomous zones run by a technical secretary appointed by a committee that is in many ways separate from the sovereign country from which it was carved. Although committee members are appointed by the president of Honduras and confirmed by the Honduran congress, it acts almost independently. The zones each have their own laws and judicial systems, and their own government, serving the principles of free-market capitalism. Only the Honduran military has jurisdiction in the ZEDEs. Overseeing the creation and management of these zones is a 21-person committee that has included Grover Norquist of Americans for Tax Reform and Mark Skousen of the Foundation for Economic Education. Mark Klugmann, another member of the committee (and former speechwriter for Ronald Reagan and George H.W. Bush), wrote that "Central America could soon become—as southern China has been—the fastest-growing economic region in the world."[18]

Anthropologist Beth Geglia told me, "In short, the ZEDE is seen as an "exit" from the constraints of the Honduran nation-state for Honduran land-owning elites and foreign investors to practice new models of unchecked hypercapitalist growth." And like a supercharged trade agreement, it could be used for a wide range of "exploitative activities"—ranging from agribusiness to oil extraction—biodiesel meets fossil fuel.

Back in Vallecito, César, under the flapping tarp where I could smell—faintly—the sea air less than a mile away,

turned to what was to come for the coastal Garífuna: intensifying annual storm surges, flooding, and mass erosion. The sky was starting to darken; occasional distant gunshots still vibrated in the air. Like every other country on the Central American isthmus—places in the tight financial grip of neoliberal economics from years of structural adjustment programs via the World Bank, International Monetary Fund, and Central American Free Trade Agreement—Honduras is prone to just about every climate hazard.

When I asked a man from Vallecito named Guillermo, who was part of the OFRANEH gathering, about climate change in his country, he told me that the weather was changing the northern coast. And he could explain it in terms of the food supply.

"We used to have a place—a warehouse—to store the community's food."

"Our parents," he said, "had calculated quite well when to plant the seeds." The community, like so many across the world, had a sort of internal *Farmer's Almanac*; they knew when it would rain with precision. "We had corn, we had rice, and after the summer rains and harvest," when winter came, "everybody would be in their homes, relaxed, with plenty of food." Summer was work; winter was relaxation.

"But now. . . ." He paused for dramatic effect: "We don't have summer or winter!"

Honduras has been besieged by extreme weather for years. According to a report by the organization Germanwatch, from 1995 to 2014 Honduras was indeed ground zero, the country most impacted by severe weather.[19] During those 19 years, Hondurans endured 73 extreme weather

events and an average of 302 climate-related deaths per year. Other countries in the top 10 of this long-term climate risk index were Myanmar, Haiti, the Philippines, Nicaragua, Bangladesh, Vietnam, Pakistan, Thailand, and Guatemala, a list that often overlaps with the roster of border enforcement flashpoints. During the same period there were approximately 15,000 extreme weather events, according to its figures, that killed 525,000 people worldwide.

The Central American isthmus is a bridge between North and South America, bordered by two oceans. The region has demonstrated how vulnerable it has been to hurricanes and droughts. Over the last three decades Honduras has experienced a temperature rise of 0.7 to 1 degree Celsius, and rainfall patterns, Guillermo explained, have decreased. "Agriculture is very dependent on stable climate conditions,"[20] Germanwatch wrote. Like climate scientist Chris Castro, Germanwatch predicts ongoing severe conditions due to climate change in Honduras and beyond.

The 48 Garífuna communities on the northern coast of Honduras are caught between massive climate disruption, the "catastrophic convergence" of economic, political, and ecological forces, and the border. In April 2016 Miriam Miranda, the coordinator of OFRANEH, told journalist Heather Gies that "Hurricane Mitch demonstrated the vulnerability of the Central American Caribbean coast, especially in Honduras, a country where systematic deforestation destroyed watersheds. Now, 18 years since Mitch, we can say that the situation is tragic in the absence of climate change mitigation and adaptation plans."[21] According to Germanwatch, people "were resettled into the same vulnerable areas"

after Mitch. The underlying warning: it is only a matter of time before another super-cyclone smashes up the country.

In this, Miranda foresees the real climate adaptation plan in the Western Hemisphere as one exclusively benefiting the rich and powerful. Lacking the political and economic will to truly fight the impact of global warming, she argued, leaders are "preparing to avoid and control human displacement as a result of catastrophes" through, as her interviewer summarized, "ramped-up militarization and the so-called war on drugs in indigenous territories."[22] Add in the increased and increasing border controls in Central America, on the Mexican divide, and the ever-fortified U.S. border enforcement regime, and Miranda's analysis becomes as prescient as it gets.

She understood, as do officials and generals across the world, that displacement caused by intensifying environmental destabilization—or anything else—will be met with militarized borders, armed guards, surveillance, incarceration, and forced expulsions.

The next day, back at the checkpoint where Honduran Federal Police agent Nuñez ordered all the men off the bus, I wasn't sure I'd make it to a meeting I'd set up with Barahona, the climate scientist in San Pedro Sula. When Nuñez aggressively questioned me, I feigned that I didn't understand Spanish. But the people I was traveling with, journalist Jeff Abbott and a Garífuna man named Marcos, told Nuñez that we were journalists in a valiant attempt to appease the gruff police agent. "Let me see your credentials," Nuñez barked. Abbott showed Nuñez his international press credentials. With a gruff gesture, he signaled to Abbott to get back on.

Then he trained his eyes on me. He signaled for me to show him the identification papers that I did not have. He ordered me to stand off to the side, while he continued to interrogate the other men.

I knew that Honduras, since the 2009 military coup, had become an increasingly dangerous place for journalists, activists, and the LGBTQ community. In 2015, Honduras was ranked the second most lethal country in the Western hemisphere for journalists, after Mexico. In her book *Drug War Capitalism*, journalist Dawn Paley writes that "violence in Honduras is sometimes presented as random and wanton, or something involving drugs, but it can't be separated from the acute poverty imposed on the country's majority."[23] The country has also become one of the most dangerous places for environmental and human rights activists such as Bertha Caceres, who was gunned down in her home on March 3, 2016.

At the checkpoint, Nuñez wanted to know what I was planning to write about. I told him that I was looking at climate change and migration. He looked at me much the way an immigration agent might look at someone at the border saying there was no rain for the harvest: with a blank face. From the perspective of the border enforcement regime, it's immaterial whether or not there is a drought, whether or not there is a harvest, or whether or not there is sufficient food. Droughts do not matter. Persistent storm surges and sea-level rise do not matter. To the on-the-ground immigration authorities, when it comes to interdiction, incarceration, and deportation, it means nothing that a new era of climate instability has begun. All that matters is whether or not a person has the proper documents.

First, Nuñez checked my backpack. Then he pulled out one of my journals, and moved through my notes with such deliberation that I thought he might have understood English. I wondered what he was looking for, if there was a particular thought, idea, or reference that would trigger further interrogation. I realized that I was near Puerto Castilla, where the four U.S. Marines were stationed to "assist" Honduras when the next hurricane hits. I thought about U.S. regional presence backing brutal right-wing death squads during the 1980s, and William Walker marauding through Honduras before declaring himself king of Nicaragua in the 19th century. Finally, after scrutinizing my passport, Nuñez handed me my backpack. My experience pales, of course, in comparison to other horrific stories at checkpoints, but I felt a profound sense of humiliation and violation.

Onward to San Pedro Sula. By this point, my perspective had slightly shifted. I became hyper-aware of all the checkpoints, police, army, and private security guards that we passed along the way. It was almost as if I were traveling through the future: the coast line was ravaged; African palm, guns, and surveillance everywhere. At a gas station I watched an older security guard amble around with an automatic assault rifle almost as long as his body, while the driver filled the idling vehicle with gas. At one point, when the guard shifted his position, the gun's barrel was pointed right at the bus, in fact, it seemed like it was pointing directly at me. An hour later, at the San Pedro Sula bus station, military police armed with machine guns patrolled the area, but nobody gave them a second look.

As we moved through San Pedro Sula's congested

streets for the meeting with Barahona, another uniformed private security guard ran out of a fabric store with his finger poised on the trigger of his assault rifle. I had no idea who he was pointing the weapon at, because everything around us seemed so normal, especially pedestrians, who were walking by in a relaxed manner. As we continued, I knew, too, that San Pedro Sula had invested in a hyper-surveillance system, with plans to install 1,500 high-tech cameras throughout the city now so infamous for its lethal violence. The project is called *Ciudad Inteligente*, Smart City, and it's giving the city the feel of a privatized border zone. Ten years ago, such a program would have seemed outrageous. Today it is normal. In fact, San Pedro Sula just might become a model for a city of the future. Blame the poor. Blame the marginalized. Protect the Facusses.

In the Hotel Sula, where we had to pass through security guards to get to a sort of "Green Zone," the friendly, well-versed Barahona told me about the "desertification" in the central and western parts of Honduras. Of course, I remembered Ismael, Santos Fernando, and Luis Carlos in the Tenosique train yard. "This is having a tremendous impact on agriculture and on people's lives," he said, "forcing migrations from the countryside to the city."

And on the Atlantic coast where we sat in San Pedro Sula, and where we were with the Garífuna, there has been a "massive increase" of precipitation. "Small farmers lose their livelihoods. So people decide to look for better opportunities and they go to the bigger cities. They go to San Pedro Sula. They go to Tegucigalpa." And then maybe they go to the United States. At the end of the interview Barahona

said that, according to studies, today's gang problems in the city—the very gangs talked about consistently in U.S. security discourse—are tied to Hurricane Fifi's devastating impacts in Honduras in 1974.

THE REFUGEE MOVEMENT IS THE MOVEMENT OF TODAY

Before 2005, when Oxford ecologist Norman Myers announced that there would be 25 million climate-fleeing migrants by 2012, there wasn't the research to back it up. There was a steadily increasing stream of reports, sure, but according to what Koko Warner of the United Nations University and lead writer of several of those reports told me, there wasn't "the scientific methodological research that there is today."

As Barahona told me that day in San Pedro Sula, today's research confirms that massive migration—combined, as always, with a multitude of other effects—will be an inevitable consequence of global warming. Glacier melts are going to affect water flows and impact food production and migration. Heat and drought will also impact food production and migration. Environmental disasters are a major driver of short-term displacement and migration (though other studies have found that it is the gradual environmental degradation that causes movement in the long term). Saltwater intrusions, inundations, storm surges, and erosion from sea-level rise—all issues facing northern Honduras—will continue to impel ever larger numbers of people to move. "There is strong evidence that the impacts of climate change will devastate subsistence and commercial agriculture on

many small islands."[24] Warner et al. report that the Ganges, Mekong, and Nile River Delta are places where sea-level rise of one meter could affect 235 million people and reduce landmass by 1.5 million hectares. An additional 10.8 million people would be directly impacted by two meters of sea-level rise, which climate models now have to contemplate, given recent reports about feedback triggers and the accelerating disintegration of polar ice sheets. They report that "millions of people will leave their homes"[25] in the years ahead.

Serious impacts of climate change are already happening and can be projected into the future with certainty. There is now a lot of empirical research that melds climate with migration. In Satkhira, the coastal district of Bangladesh, 81 percent of the people reported a high level of salinity in their soil in 2012, compared to just 2 percent two decades earlier. Farmers planted a saline-resistant variety of rice when Cyclone Aila surged in 2009, but the increase of salt in the soil has been drastic. "Almost all farmers lost their complete harvests that year."[26] According to the United Nations University Loss and Damage report, while many farmers kept to salt-tolerant varieties, 29 percent decided to migrate. Remember, if they dare cross into India, they encounter a steel barrier and Indian border guards who have shot and killed more than 1,000 Bangladeshi people. In Kenya, researchers arrived after the 2011 floods, which followed a pattern of increased precipitation over past decades, washing crops away, drowning livestock, severely damaging houses, and causing an outbreak of waterborne diseases. Aid came, but it was not enough. Sixty-four percent of people migrated or moved to camps. The drought in the north bank of Gambia in 2011

affected 98 percent of 373 households interviewed, many of which lost entire harvests. People also attempted to find alternative income to buy food. They sold things in the informal economy, and borrowed money. Still, displacement or migration impacted 23 percent of the region's inhabitants. And although many people prefer to stay as close to home after displacement and do not cross an international border, the tales of people from many countries in Africa facing the European border enforcement regime, often referred to as Fortress Europe, are virtually endless.

As I wrote earlier, current estimates for climate refugees are wide-ranging, and go as high as one billion people displaced by 2050. No matter what the final number may be, it is worth remembering that most of those making projections say that human migration in the 21st century will be "staggering." The International Organization on Migration keeps their estimate around 200 million. The American Association for the Advancement of Science foresees 50 million mobilizing to escape their environment by 2020. As things stand, Honduras, and many countries in the global South, will contribute to those numbers significantly.

Harsha Walia wrote that "patterns of displacement and migration reveal the unequal relations between rich and poor, between North and South, between whiteness and racialized others."[27] And while visiting a refugee-occupied school in Germany in May 2015, renowned human rights advocate Angela Y. Davis said that "the refugee movement is *the* movement of the 21st century. It's the movement that is challenging the effects of global capitalism, and it's the movement that is calling for civil rights for all human

beings."[28] And it is, dare I add, the movement that will challenge fossil fuel consumption and its contamination of the living biosphere. It may be in refugees, and their experience, where the answer lies.

Michael Gerrard of Columbia University's Sabin Center for Climate Change Law told climate journalist Eric Holthaus: "I think the countries of the world need to start thinking seriously about how many people they're going to take in. The current horrific situation in Europe is a fraction of what's going to be caused by climate change."[29] Gerrard argued in an op-ed for the *Washington Post* that countries should take in people in proportion to the greenhouse gas emissions they pollute. For example, since between 1850 and 2011 the United States was responsible for 27 percent of the world's total carbon dioxide emissions, the European Union 25 percent, China 11 percent, Russia 8 percent—so each country should be obligated to take in an equal percentage of climate refugees.

Instead, these are the places with the largest military budgets. And these are the countries that today are erecting towering border walls.

"SUSTAINABLE" BORDER MILITARIZATION

If Ismael, Luis Carlos, and Santos Fernando ever reach the border of the United States, the world's largest greenhouse polluter, they will come face to face with the world's largest border enforcement apparatus. Walls of different shapes and sizes stand waiting for them in urban border areas such as Nogales or San Ysidro or El Paso, places poised to become even more barricaded during Donald Trump's presidency.

Also there to meet them are an army of Border Patrol agents in roving patrols on horseback, in Blackhawk helicopters, in fixed-wing aircraft, and at the controls of Predator B aerial surveillance systems. Depending on where they attempt to cross, they might encounter tethered surveillance balloons or any of hundreds of remote or mobile video surveillance systems strategically positioned to alert Border Patrol agents of their movements.

If they cross into the United States, they most likely will do so through a region much like Organ Pipe National Monument, a remote area in in southwestern Arizona where I stood talking to a U.S. Border Patrol agent. As the agent and I talked, we were surrounded by protected wilderness badly scarred with tire tracks by roving Homeland Security trucks whose national security mission trumps environmental protection.

The agent, who wished to remain anonymous, knew nothing about climate change becoming a greater planning priority for both the U.S. military and the Department of Homeland Security. He did know, however, about how border enforcement looks from ground level at a Forward Operating Base. Like those deployed in U.S. military operations in Iraq and Afghanistan, the strategy of a Forward Operating Base is to seize ground and maintain a presence in isolated areas and territories. There are now dozens of such bases in the U.S.-Mexico borderlands.

When I met with the agent I was with students of a border studies class from Prescott College. The agent was off-duty, wearing a blue shirt, a little bit out of breath because he had been jogging.

When we asked the agent what duties are performed at the desolate base his response was: "Depends how busy we are. Sometimes we're busy finding bodies." He paused.

"We found five just this week."

"Did you find any bodies yourself?" I asked.

"I found one," the agent said, then looked at his shoes. Besides the more than 6,000 remains found along the U.S. Mexico border since the 1990s, the Colibri Center for Human Rights has records of 2,500 additional missing people last seen crossing through the region.

"It's silly," the agent continued, "they keep walking until they don't have any food or water, and then they die."

As geographer Joseph Nevins points out in the book *Dying to Live: A Story of U.S. Immigration in an Age of Global Apartheid*, there are many reasons given, in the general broad analysis, why so many people die attempting to enter the United States. "To state what should be obvious," Nevins writes, "if migrants were allowed to freely cross the divide—and, by extension, to reside and work within the United States without fear of arrest and deportation due to immigration status—there would be no migrant deaths."[30] Nevins describes a system of exclusion that now extends well beyond the context of the United States. It is a system where the super-rich have luxurious enclaves on the world's sinking islands, able to jet there and claim, "It's so close!," while the world's impoverished majority, confronting more and more cataclysmic environmental changes, face constant impediments to their mobility. One person's "close" is many people's "never."

In the climate era, coexisting worlds of luxury living

and impoverished desperation will only be magnified and compounded. On one side are not only the super-rich who will want to continue to consume, possess, and waste without limits. There are those of the middle class, too, who populate U.S. suburbs and cities and live unsustainable consumer lifestyles.

On the other side are millions like Ismael, Luis Carlos, and Santos Fernando, deprived of the resources they need for subsistence living in their home communities. In the middle are the militarized border zones that, as Nevins writes, reinforce "an unjust world order."[31]

Behind the Border Patrol agent are solar panels that supply energy to this small base, part of Customs and Border Protection's effort to cut down greenhouse gas emissions by 28 percent, a practice that has continued under the Trump administration. Where we stood, the whole place seemed like it could be part of an active war zone in Iraq or Afghanistan, with the Forward Operating Base threatening to pounce—as Captain Goudreau put it at the Washington climate change national security conference—with the "lethality" of green energy.

The Department of Homeland Security's overall mandate, per an executive action by the Obama administration in 2009, is to reduce its massive carbon footprint by 25 percent. According to 2011 numbers, the DHS owns 50,000 vehicles (and leases another 8,000), more than the 48,500 FedEx vehicles used throughout the world. This environmentally efficient Forward Operating Base is one of close to 12,000 facilities owned by Homeland Security (with another approximately 2,000 leased), operating both in and outside

of the United States. The combined number of facilities was equal to the number of McDonald's restaurants that were operating in the United States in 2012—approximately 14,157. Reducing the degree of environmental degradation inflicted by such a massive department, with presence in places seen and unseen across the United States and the globe, is a monumental task.

According to the U.S. Green Building Council, the nearby Ajo Border Patrol station was one of the most energy efficient when it was built in 2014 with a "reduced light pollution" system and a "heat island effect" roof and parking canopies, intended to "minimize impacts on microclimates and human and wildlife habitats."[32] The "water use reduction" system creates a much lower flow of water, though it probably hardly matters in this station in the west Arizona desert that has increased from 50 to 500 agents in a very short period of time.

This is sustainable border militarization.

"Uncertain and unsustainable supplies of energy, water, and other resources, and the unpredictability of natural disasters and terrorism have a major impact on national security,"[33] a DHS document explains. And despite the enormous amount of greenhouse-accelerating pollution its operations dump into the atmosphere, the U.S. Department of Homeland Security presents itself as a setting "the paradigm for a sustainable, secure, and resilient future by demonstrating how efficiency and sustainability will enhance America's national security."[34]

Behind the agent at the Forward Operating Base were rows of solar panels, and farther on, a tall surveillance tower,

also powered by solar energy. Approximately 25 miles away from this simulated war zone was the international boundary where the Ground-Based Operation Surveillance Systems known as G-Boss, made by Raytheon company, gawk into Mexico through an 80-foot tower. From where I stood I heard not only the sounds of the desert, the distant rumbles of a monsoon thunderstorm that would bring with it the deep smell of creosote, but also the constant noise of sustainable militarization, including the distant buzz of another all-terrain vehicle.

All around were what conservationist Cyndi Tuell of the Sierra Club's Borderlands project calls "assaults on the landscape." This project has worked for years to advocate for borderlands ecosystems and against environmental destruction in the name of national security. One such assault, in front of my eyes, was a series of chained-together tires, discarded in front of the chain-link fence topped with swirling razor wire that encircled the Forward Operating Base. This was only one bit of evidence of the 12,000 miles of wildcat routes that have trampled the cryptobiotic soil—a thin cover that both holds dirt down and provides fertile ground for the ecosystem in both the Organ Pipe National Monument and the adjacent Cabeza Prieta Wildlife Refuge in the name of national, and now, we have to say, climate security. This environmental degradation of a U.S. national treasure is facilitated by the fact that the Department of Homeland Security can issue waivers to key environmental and cultural laws in order to install walls, roads, and surveillance technology.

For unwanted border-crossers, this once pristine desert

now fits the classic definition of dystopia: degraded, totalitarian, futuristic, filled with the sophisticated, and most likely privatized, surveillance gizmos of the state. "If we dare to approach this frightening geopolitical space," anthropologist Jason De León writes in *The Land of Open Graves*, "we can see how America's internal surveillance gaze functions."[35]

To this expanding surveillance state, as with my experience with Nuñez at the Honduran checkpoint, your story does not matter. The reasons you might arrive there do not matter. If Santos Fernando, Ismael, and Luis Carlos are ever caught there, the forms they fill out will not ask about clean water, food, or rain, though Homeland Security itself recognizes that droughts will displace people. If they get caught there, unlike a European tourist out for a hike in the desert, they will be transported by privatized Border Patrol agents working for the high-rolling U.K. company G4S. Their destination will be a short-term detention facility not unlike those used by the U.S. military in war zones. As researcher Blake Gentry writes, it's "deprivation, not deterrence."[36] Many will then be brought in shackles to a federal courthouse, where they will appear before a magistrate judge.

It doesn't matter whether the forces motivating them are ecological, economic, or political, the people walk in groups of five or eight, heads slightly bowed as if forced into a submissive pose. All of these people in the Operation Streamline proceedings in Tucson have been in the Sonoran desert, some near Douglas, some near Nogales, some near Sasabe, and some near the Forward Operating Base on Organ Pipe National Monument, and all have been caught by the U.S. Border Patrol. Operation Streamline represents

a zero-tolerance mass sentencing of undocumented border-crossers, and it is poised to become even harsher under the mandate of Attorney General Jeff Sessions. Unasked is the individual story of any of these people. If there are climate refugees in the bunch, you would never know. They have faces, but are faceless. All you see is their chained bodies shuffling up to the judges, the shackles clanking as they go; the only information that matters is where they entered the United States and whether their entry was properly authorized or not.

At one proceeding I attended in April 2016 at the Tucson Federal Courthouse, a man named Ignacio Sarabia broke the script and told magistrate judge Jacqueline Rateau exactly why he crossed the line without authorization:

"My infant is four months old and is a U.S. citizen," he told her. He was born with a heart condition. They had to operate. "This," he said, "is the reason I'm here before you." The man tried to gesture with his words but the shackles and chains restrained him from doing so. The magistrate judge responded that she was sorry for his predicament. She told him that he couldn't just come back here "illegally" and that he had to find a legal way to enter the country. "Your son, when he gets better, and his mother can visit you where you are, in Mexico," said the judge. "Otherwise he'll be visiting you in prison. You'll see how it will be for him—growing up visiting his father in a prison, where he will be locked away for a very long time." Then she sentenced him, along with the rest of the eight men standing side by side in front of her, to prison terms ranging from 60 to 180 days.

Throughout the whole interchange it never left my

mind, not even for a second, that his child, the one with the heart condition, was born the same exact month, and maybe even the same exact date, as my own child. His fate is that of the climate refugee, and as predictable as the Category 6 storms of displacement. He will be separated from his family in distress and locked up behind the razor wire of the Corrections Corporation of America—a privatized prison—that will earn $124 per day from his incarceration.

FOUR

THREAT FORECAST: WHERE CLIMATE CHANGE MEETS SCIENCE FICTION

[Elite] fear signifies their recognition that popular power is real enough to overturn regimes and rewrite the social contract.

—Rebecca Solnit

When asked what she thought the greatest challenges facing the field of crisis management would be in the next decade, Lina Kolesnikova, a homeland security researcher for the magazine *Crisis Response Journal*, hardly hesitated when she said refugees. Kolesnikova was one of a host of speakers at an international conference billed as "Climate, Geopolitics & Economics, Technological Advances." The presentations were held off to the side of a gigantic exhibition hall in Paris, in an enclosed room with large glass windows. Outside, you could see droves of people moving past from vendor to vendor in perhaps the world's biggest homeland security shopping mall, known as Milipol, in November 2015.

Every single time the door of the side room opened, the collective noise of more than 24,056 people from 143 countries—including representatives from 949 companies and official delegations from 115 countries—entered the room like a gale force wind. It became difficult to hear the speakers. Outside hung banners from companies of the world's burgeoning homeland security industry like Taser, Elbit Systems, Airbus, Atos, Verint, as well as companies with names right out of the pages of a William Gibson cyberpunk novel—Protecop, Visiom, Scopex, Ercom, and Ixiom. The SSI Groupe sign, as one example, advertised that the French company had superior "global response to multiple threats" with its audio and video surveillance, tracking and locating, jamming, and monitoring products. This futuristic world—a cacophony of visceral, booming white noise—can be overwhelming at first.

What Kolesnikova is beginning to describe is the threat forecast: escalating crisis is inevitable and amped-up surveillance is the answer   it can keep things under control.

The conference began in the immediate aftermath of the November 13, 2015, terrorist attacks in Paris that left 129 people dead. On November 18, just two kilometers away from where this big bonanza was happening, French authorities fired more than 5,000 rounds into an apartment in Saint-Denis, killing two people and collapsing the entire floor of the apartment. From the hotel where I was staying I could hear the early-morning mortar fire. France's violent state of emergency was colliding with what most people were calling the most important United Nations climate summit, the 21st Conference of Parties, or COP21, a little over a week

away. If world leaders didn't agree to reduce greenhouse gas emissions, climate impacts would become a runaway train. It felt like the future of the world was in the balance.

Guns and the companies selling them were everywhere. Pistols and assault rifles were elegantly presented so you could pick up a weapon, hold it, and caress it, as I saw so many people do with absolutely no embarrassment, just a concentrated, even serene look, as if the gun might purr when affectionately handled.

Kolesnikova, Russian with short blond hair and glasses, didn't even need to think about what the biggest threat was. She pinned it down quickly. It was the "influx of people to Europe" that would be a "huge challenge." Like many of the vendors peddling technologies, she was quick to make a bold declaration that there were "people who pretend they are refugees."

Her prescription was the "three Gs": "guns, guards, and gates."

What she meant was the deafening cacophony of surveillance equipment outside. We could predict not only—as they also discussed during the panel—a world of Category 6 winds, ravaging fires, devouring seas, and parched landscapes, but also a world of surveillance drones, crowd-control, and walls. And the most cutting-edge surveillance industries were there to deliver. Just as every climate projection showed more environmental crisis, market projections for homeland security surveillance revealed a world where Big Brother will dominate. In the 21st century, both dynamics are poised to become a part of people's everyday lives in ways that they have never been before.

You didn't even have to read the homeland security market's optimistic projections to feel its potential in the air at Milipol. Indeed, in 2014 this market surpassed 500 billion (US$558 billion) for the first time, according to an informational brochure handed out at the conference. Perhaps that's why in between militarized mannequins dressed in body armor, with gas masks and assault rifles, men and women in suits mingled, clinking glasses of wine and eating cheese. Everywhere there were monitoring cameras, drones of all shapes and sizes, armored cars, impenetrable border walls, and biometrics such as facial-recognition technology. At one point I took a "biometric selfie" that rendered my image in multiple separate squares, ranging from normal to thermal energy to green night-vision. I assumed that, as on the U.S.-Mexico border, the device retained my picture and added it to a remote database. Another company, called ISPRA, displayed a multi-barreled—crowd-control—weapon called Thunderstorm that could also be mounted to any of the many armored vehicles on display and launch tear gas, stun grenades, and smoke, either separately or at the same time. Preparing, I assumed, like many in surrounding booths, for the inevitable resistance of the displaced to Koleskinova's "three Gs."

And as Koleskinova spoke, when someone opened the door, the noise of this bustling marketplace was so deafening that I had to strain to hear her. I have been to many homeland security trade expos over the years, but never have I been to one with such energy, so much raw excitement. As global warming accelerates, there is a fortune to be made.

"WHICH OTHER MEANS DO YOU HAVE TO SOLVE YOUR BORDER ISSUES?"

British Rear Admiral Chris Parry summed up the international security consensus regarding climate refugees in perhaps the most vivid terms. The future climate migrations would be like the "Goths and the Vandals,"[1] the barbarian invaders who brought down the Roman Empire in the 5th century. Large immigrant populations, he said, would have little regard for their host countries and begin a sort of "reverse colonisation,"[2] a term similar to the *reconquista* used by members of border militia groups in the United States who fear that Mexico will take its territory back (the United States took over nearly half of Mexico after the Mexican-American war in the mid 19th century). Because of this, Parry laid out a prescient prediction (now backed by the dystopic Milipol floor): the increasing shift to robots, drones, nanotechnology, lasers, microwave weapons, space-based systems, and "customized" nuclear bombs.[3] These are the guards, gates, and guns necessary to protect the centers of political, economic, and social power that will really be under attack by the coming climate-induced "barbarian" hordes.

In her book *A Paradise Built in Hell*, Rebecca Solnit examined militarized responses to natural disasters, ranging from the 1906 earthquake in San Francisco to Hurricane Katrina in New Orleans in 2005. Following an essay in Social Forces by Lee Clarke and Caron Chess in 2008, Solnit and many other scholars called these sorts of heavy-handed responses "elite panic."[4] Solnit wrote, "Elites and authorities often fear the changes of disaster or anticipate that change

means chaos and destruction or at least the undermining of the foundations of their power."[5]

The findings that Solnit's work underscored would not be popular or profitable for the vendors on the Milipol floor. disaster sociologists' studies demonstrate not only that panic in the face of disaster "is rare," but that people in such situations are more inclined to engage in acts of mutual assistance, community solidarity, and altruism.

However, as Clarke and Chess write, "planners and policy makers sometimes act as if the human response to threatening conditions is more dangerous than the threatening conditions themselves."[6] They say that although it is the powerless, not the powerful, who are said to panic, it is the elite who exercise "hypervigilance." If the most heightened form of hypervigilance is panic, as they write, then down a couple of notches is the permanent anxiety at the foundation of the homeland security state.

It's not about the disaster happening now, but the disaster that could happen in the future. It is not the people panicking now, it is the anticipated mass panic in the future as the fires, floods, dust storms, and water shortages impact larger numbers of people over longer amounts of time.

Homeland Security is reacting to this perception of the future, preparing the world for human panic in the face of turmoil and upheaval before it actually happens.

It is preemptive pacification. The government anticipates that the coming crises will unleash movements that expose chronic inequalities and undermine the state's capacity to enforce a system that benefits the few and, although they might not admit it, disadvantages the many. The perceived

danger is not what imperils the whole of humanity, it is what endangers the power brokers of the very system that continues to poison the atmosphere and environment despite the assertions of a consensus of scientists that we must stop, or at least curb, human pollution.

The threat forecasts of human displacement and environmental destabilization in a warming world started well before Parry's barbarian descriptions, even preceding Kaplan's The Coming Anarchy, and well before there was the type of rigorous empirical research connecting climate change to migration that there is today. In 1990, after the first International Panel on Climate Change (IPCC) meeting, the initial assessment said that climate change "could initiate large migrations of people, leading over a number of years to severe disruptions of settlement patterns and social instability in some areas."[7] Joseph Romm, then of the U.S. Department of Energy, followed suit the next year by saying that climate change could lead to "conflict or ecosystem collapse," and then could be a "threat" to the United States "if refugees were allowed to flee in large numbers to this country."[8] The threat to the state, again, is not the ecosystem's collapse, but rather the people displaced by such a collapse. In 2001, German climatologist Herm Ott not only predicted that water and food shortages, rising sea levels, and changing precipitation would lead to "mass migrations," but also that there would also be "low- and high-intensity warfare in many parts of the southern world."[9] U.S. climate guru James Hansen stated climate-induced "forced migrations and economic collapse might make the planet ungovernable, threatening the fabric of civilization."[10]

If "elite panic" leads to overt militarized operations in moments of turmoil, this "elite anxiety" makes sure that the systems are in place—such as the build-up of homeland security regimes—so that such future overreactions will have a conduit.

In Israel, a 2012 report from more than 100 academics and experts asserted that to "combat increased waves of illegal migration that will likely accompany climate change," Israel must fortify its borders with "impassable barriers," including "sea fences" along the Mediterranean and Red Seas.[11]

A.K. Singh, a retired air marshal from India, might as well have been describing Rear Admiral Parry's "Goths and Vandals" when he stated that he "foresees mass migrations" that would start out with "people fighting for food and shelter. When the migration starts, every state would want to stop the migrations from happening. Eventually, it would have to become a military conflict."

He asked: "Which other means do you have to resolve your border issues?"[12]

THREAT FORECAST: HUMAN-MADE DYSTOPIA

The time frame of a national security planner is 30 years. It takes that long for a major military platform to go "from the drawing board to the battlefield,"[13] according to former assistant deputy secretary of state Kurt Campbell, editor of *Climate Cataclysm: The Foreign Policy and National Security Implications of Climate Change*. Based on a 2007 U.S. House of Representatives directive for the National Intelligence Council, top scientists and military practitioners in the United States began making serious projections connecting

climate change and national security. The intelligence estimate included estimates of food and water shortages, humanitarian disasters, and mass migration that will "tax U.S. military transportation and support force structures, resulting in strained readiness posture."[14] The United States must "plan for growing immigration pressures," the report said, too, in part because almost a fourth of the countries with the greatest percentage of low-level coastal zones are in the Caribbean.[15] Their projections were meant to help the Pentagon and Homeland Security visualize the world to come, so that the necessary surveillance, enforcement tools, and weapons could be designed to maintain control.

Migration models and borders were a significant part of these projections, which I will examine here. In the introduction, Campbell wrote, the "sheer numbers of potentially displaced people is staggering."[16] He pointed out that one recent World Bank report included calculations that, over the course of the 21st century, sea-level rise due to global warming could displace as many as one billion people from their homes between now and 2050.

Climate Cataclysm looked at three different scenarios: the "expected," a 1.3-degree Celsius temperature rise by 2040; the "severe," a 2.6-degree Celsius rise by 2040; and the "catastrophic," a 5.6-degree Celsius rise by 2100. Every projection of climate cataclysm underscored the threat of massive immigration coming to the United States. In the "expected" scenario, authors John Podesta—the 2016 campaign chairman for Hillary Clinton and former chief of staff to Bill Clinton—and Peter Ogden, from the Center for American Progress, a self-described nonpartisan educational

institute, said that a world of intensifying heat, reduced water availability, and severe weather will result in increased "border stress" both in the Southwest and in the Caribbean. The flow of displaced people, in their highly clinical words, will "generate political tension."[17]

In the severe scenario of a 2.6 degree Celsius rise by 2040, the "border problems" overwhelm U.S. capabilities "beyond the possibility of control, except by drastic methods and perhaps not even then," wrote Leon Fuerth, former security adviser to Al Gore. "Efforts to choke off illegal immigration," he continued, "will have increasingly divisive repercussions on the domestic, social, and political structure of the United States."[18]

In a later interview with journalist Gwynne Dyer in the book *Climate Wars*, Fuerth commented that "Governments with resources will be forced to engage in long, nightmarish episodes of triage: deciding what and who can be salvaged from engulfment by a disordered environment. The choices will need to be made primarily among the poorest, not just abroad but at home. We have already previewed the images, in the course of the organisational and spiritual unravelling that was Hurricane Katrina."[19]

The catastrophic scenario envisioned a world heated up 5.6 degrees Celsius by 2100. More than 100 nations will be "consumed by internal conflict, spewing desperate refugees, and harboring and spawning violent extremist movements," wrote Sharon Burke of the Center for a New American Security. Burke projected that, at that point, governance and infrastructure would become overwhelmed by the sheer mass of refugees crossing borders, "and in some cases armed

or extremist groups migrating into their territories." A "volatile mix" involving millions of "desperate people looking for safe haven" will overwhelm states, Burke said, and addressing this "will likely involve inhumane border control practices." The countries of the Global North will become "aggressively isolationist, with militarized borders." Burke added that the imposition of martial law was a possibility, gated communities would be more commonplace, and "the level of popular anger towards the United States, as the leading historical contributor to climate change, will be astronomical."[20]

Even if all participating countries hit the emission goals they pledged to achieve during the Paris Agreement of December 2015—and that's a big "if" (especially considering both its unbinding nature and the fact that the Trump administration has now backed out)—the Earth will still continue to warm and the biosphere will still experience severe destabilization. According to the above projections, arguably based on elite hyper-anxiety, nations of the world will be somewhere between between "border stress" and "beyond the possibility of control." Given the nonlinear progression of global warming and all its uncertainties, the likelihood of civilizational catastrophe is higher every day.

Climate scientist Kevin Anderson, who is known for not having flown for 10 years, calls the 2015 Paris Agreement a "triumph," on one hand, because limiting warming to a two-degree Celsius increase is "an obligation rather than a target."[21] According to scientists, 2°C would result in a manageable intensification of environmental crises. Beyond that, all bets are off. Many island nations are insisting

that 2°C is not safe, that temperature rise needs to be kept at 1.5 degrees Celsius. Otherwise, they say, they will be swallowed whole by the oceans.

The Paris obligation, Anderson says, at least creates a standard to which governments, businesses, and wider civil society can be held accountable. But then he puts his own praise in context. He claims that the "remainder of the 32-page document has no meaningful substance in delivering temperature obligations."[22]

In fact, it is not even close. According to Climate Interactive and MIT Sloan, even if the Paris Agreements are met, the Earth's living systems will experience a temperature rise of 3.5°C by 2100.[23] Anderson says that when you do the math, the allowance for greenhouse emissions is much "in excess of what is safe." He says that in order to reconcile this discrepancy there must be an anticipation of the "successful roll-out of highly speculative negative emissions technologies—technologies that do not exist yet, and may never exist."[24] But what we can be sure will exist is severe border militarization, required to counter much-anticipated social destabilization. Again, a 3.5°C increase is well above the "severe" scenario Fuerth projects above, and borders will impose severe methods of control.

No matter how the issue is approached, immediate and drastic change is required to prevent global warming from becoming a force that overwhelms human civilization and exceeds our collective ability to manage it. By immediate, I mean right now. By drastic change, I mean massive lifestyle changes for people in the United States, and not just an expedited phase-out of all gas-powered vehicles, but an

immediate restructuring of corporate America, industry, travel, environmental protection, and lifestyles based on consumerism, disposability, and convenience. Hitting zero emissions by 2025 means implementing intensive change right now. This urgency will only intensify while Trump and Pence are in power, and accelerated climate change prevention cannot be expected to begin in the United States until they are out of office. To top it off, the Paris Agreement is not set to go into effect until 2020 anyway, after another 200 billion tons of greenhouse accelerant will have defiled the atmosphere.

Climate journalist Eric Holthaus says unless the globe enacts the above drastic changes immediately, a 2°C temperature rise is unavoidable. It is therefore reasonable to think that by 2040 we will arrive at the threshold where all potential triggers will be pulled, and the trajectory of civilization becomes irreconcilably altered.

In her book *This Changes Everything*, Naomi Klein writes that if things stay the same, it won't be the "status quo extended indefinitely." Klein predicts a sort of evolving situation of "climate-change-fueled disaster capitalism—profiteering disguised as emission reduction, privatized hyper-militarized borders, and, quite possibly, high-risk geoengineering when things spiral out of control." The status quo is now developing into this scenario, as weapons and surveillance businesses make a mint selling products to governments that clearly seem to prioritize militarization over prevention.

For this reason, it doesn't even matter if any of these threat forecasts are actually true, a new military and

homeland security platform is already moving forward, anticipating and preparing 30 years in advance. "Over the next 20 years, worries about climate change effects may be more significant than any physical changes linked to climate change," according to the 2008 report *Global Trends 2025: A Transformed World*, written by the National Intelligence Council. Indeed, this center for strategizing in the U.S. intelligence community reports that "perceptions of a rapidly changing environment may cause nations to take unilateral actions to secure resources, territory, and other interests."[25]

However, in *Climate Change and Migration: Security and Borders in a Warming World*, scholar Gregory White writes that "securitizing climate-induced migration not only fails to solve the problem, but is also imprudent, because it enhances security against a non-threat." Not only that, he says, but the threat narrative "sets in motion a counterproductive, spiralling security dilemma and saps energy away" from the earnest search for real solutions to the ecological crisis before us.[26]

UNPRECEDENTED BOOM PERIOD: FORECAST TO THE FUTURE

When the dark-gray surveillance ball rolled on the blue carpet in the Phoenix Convention Center, it was hard to tell exactly what it was. It had two cameras on either side of its "head," which was covered with small domes that looked like miniature ears. Like a "chameleon," the cameras could look at two different places at the same time, boasted the manufacturer, GuardBot. It had forward motion and backward

motion; it could do 360-degree turns; it could travel off-road, on sand, on snow; it could swim. It was originally meant for NASA to explore Mars, but now the company's smiling vendor—impeccably dressed in shiny black shoes, pressed black pants, and a white button-down shirt—was explaining that his company had other ideas. These rolling potential robotic Border Patrol agents, another GuardBot employee explained to Cronkite News, could one day police the U.S.-Mexico divide, even in packs of 10, 20, or "maybe thirty."[27]

Similar to the scene at the Milipol convention in Paris, all around him were other robots: small tank-like machines cruising on the carpet, medium- and small-size drones (it's difficult to get the Predator Bs, the type of unmanned aerial systems deployed on the U.S. border, into the room.) They call it a Border Security Expo, but here was the crystal ball, here was the future, here you could see what the U.S. border—and increasing swaths of the interior—may look like in 20, 30 years, the ever-evolving "gates, guns, and guards." The dystopian futures foreseen by George Orwell and William Gibson have come to life in the matrix of high-definition surveillance, anti-ballistic towers, FLIR operational war rooms, acoustic technology, and crowd-suppression capabilities. The weapons of the authoritarian future have arrived, and are charging head first into climate change.

In other words, the GuardBot is not a tech nerd's fantasy. If deployed, its purpose will be to pursue, arrest, and possibly even fire weapons at people. Israel has already deployed "robo-snipers" in its operations against Palestinian communities and has made a series of "auto-kill zones"

that use remote-controlled machine guns, motion sensors, and drones. Barbara Opall-Rome of *Defense News* reported in 2007 that "initial deployment plans for the See-Shoot system call for mounting a 0.5-caliber automated machine gun in each of several pillboxes interspersed along the Gaza border fence."[28]

Also, on the South Korean side of the heavily militarized divide with North Korea, two Samsung-made, machine gun-wielding robots have surveillance, tracking, firing, and voice-recognition capabilities. They have grenade launchers that can target and kill people up to two miles away. "Automated machine guns capable of finding, tracking, warning and eliminating human targets, absent of any human interaction already exist in our world," wrote Simon Parkin in the article "*Killer Robots: The Soldiers that Never Sleep*."[29]

Down the hall from the exhibition hall, Mark Borkowski, from the U.S. Customs and Border Protection (CBP) Office of Technology Acquisition and Innovation, is pacing in front of the podium, clenching a pamphlet that is the agency's 2020 vision plan. Borkowski—wearing a tan jacket, white button-down shirt, and bow tie—is the guy you want to convince if you want to get a contract for your technology, if you want to sell a GuardBot or surveillance camera. Borkowski talks about people crossing the borders. He talks about technologies that will help him find terrorists. He carries himself with a certain pride. He is a rocket scientist and a mathematician and he makes sure the audience knows this. He talks about technologies that will help him find hidden weapons of mass destruction. "Innovation is highly visible in the 2020 plan." He is looking for the next great

border technology, the equivalent, he says, of the iPhone. He uses his daughters' iPhone as an example. "We didn't know we needed it until we saw it," he said. "Now we can't live without it."

Two years later, Borkowski discussed the Trump administration's January 2017 executive order on border security and its definition of "operational control." "'Operational control' shall mean the prevention of *all* unlawful entries into the United States, including entries by terrorists, other unlawful aliens, instruments of terrorism, narcotics, and other contraband." The emphasis on "all" was Borkowski's. Instead of expressing the impossibility of stopping all illicit entries across U.S. borders, which include international airports, Borkowski doubled down. He brought up a term that he said came to him when he was soaping himself in the shower 10 years before: "persistant impedance." CBP now had a definition for it: the "continuous and constant ability to deter or delay."[30] What they previously did on parts of the border, Borkowski said, they would do for the entire border under Trump.

Behind Borkowski's words loom a budget and a political will that dwarf those of the pre-9/11 U.S. border enforcement apparatus. He is in command of a technology budget for the largest law enforcement agency in the United States, with a budget that only seems to grow and grow. The 2017 CBP budget, at about $14 billion, is almost equal to the combined budgets of the FBI, DEA, U.S. Marshals, and ATF, which come to about $15.7 billion. If you add ICE's $6 billion budget to that of CBP, there is $20 billion for border and immigration enforcement, a twelve-fold increase over

the INS annual budgets in the early 1990s. The Trump administration is poised to pour in much more.

And even though Borkowski always mentions the limits of U.S. spending, the vendors that pack that room all know the forecasts. They know that the global border security market is in an "unprecedented boom period."[31] Vision Gain wrote that the global market was close to $24 billion in 2014 and will continue to grow exponentially, because of a "virtuous circle" that will continue to drive spending for a long time based on three interlocking developments: "illegal immigration and terrorist infiltration," more money for border policing in "developing countries," and "maturation"[32] of new technologies. The way Vision Gain lays it out, it sounds like a scientific projection for the climate-changed future. Another marketing firm, Sandler Research, projects that the border security market will grow 7.89 percent from 2015 to 2019. Its analysts say that borders not only "safeguard" national security and sovereignty, but also "economic prosperity."[33] And the broader global security market is poised to almost double between 2011 and 2022 ($305 to $546 billion), though the Milipol stats are more optimistic, indicating that $500 billion mark had already been surpassed. According to Homeland Security Research, the drivers of such markets include "cross-border illegal immigration, organized crime, smuggling of goods & narcotics, and terror."[34] Newer forecasts even have begun to include "climate-related natural disasters," a phenomenon that increased by 13 percent in 2013, making the "natural disaster preparation and responses" market poised to pass the $150 billion level.[35]

As these numbers show, worldwide budgets for border security are growing fast. In Europe, for example, budgets for its border guard FRONTEX jumped 67.4 percent between 2015 and 2016 and are "expected to grow to an estimated 322 million [US$359 million] in 2020,"[36]—50 times what it was in 2005. As the report "Border Wars: The Arms Industry Profiting from Europe's Refugee Tragedy" exposes, this has "led to a booming border security market,"[37] and the same industries selling weapons in the Middle East and North Africa, fomenting unrest and displacement, have also been "key winners of EU border security contracts." And, like the private industry sitting in that conference hall watching Borkowski, "the arms and security industry helps shape European border security policy, through lobbying" and "regular interactions with EU's border institutions."[38]

And now market forecasts are contemplating the Trump effect. Not only have stocks surged for construction companies—such as Martin Marietta Materials, Vulcan Materials, and remarkably the Mexican company CEMEX—on the hope that a massive border wall is in the works, but Homeland Security Research forecasts significant growth between 2017 and 2022 partly because "Trump promised, throughout his campaign, a tough fight against Islamist extremism at home and abroad, and to invest in law and order." The forecasts also mention "European terror and migration crisis" and "climate warming-related natural disasters growth."[39] In February, investors were betting on Israel companies reaping "a windfall" from Donald Trump securitization spending plans.[40] Companies such as Elbit Systems, Magal Security Systems, and Check Point Software Technologies

"have seen their share prices soar since Trump's election victory on Nov. 8."[41]

Everything is moving fast, like clouds gathering into a rotating super-cell. Even 20 years ago the Predator B unmanned aerial drones—large, pilotless, mosquito-shaped planes—might have still seemed like things from the pages of science fiction. So perhaps would an Israeli company—such as the stock-soaring Elbit Systems—that has invented a semi-sentient fortified "smart wall" capable of detecting human movement and touch. The company is now building a series of high-tech surveillance towers that are able to see night and day for a distance of up to seven miles. These towers are able to work in tandem with one another, in tandem with the drones, in tandem with the more than 12,000 motion sensors implanted along the 2,000-mile Mexican border. Twenty years ago, the idea of studying locust wings to develop miniature surveillance drones, or a robotic kiosk to detect if a person is lying, might still have seemed like things from a Ray Bradbury novel. Now even an amateur weather forecaster can see what's on the horizon. Although more barriers will surely populate the U.S. borderscape in select places, Donald Trump does not need to spend billions on a bricks-and-mortar wall when there is much more sophisticated technology available to weaponize the region.

On page eight of the strategic vision pamphlet in Borkowski's hand, under the subtitle "Innovation," is discussion about the commitment to innovation to make the paramilitary organization more "agile and adaptable." The text talks about the evolving "global challenges" and "leveraging

science, technology, and corporate innovation to ensure optimal capabilities development for peak performance." On page 21, graced with a picture of a blue-striped Predator B drone with a CBP agency insignia, it underscores the dedication to bringing more technology to the border enforcement regime as an "invaluable force multiplier to increased situational awareness." It talks about "securing the homeland" with information gleaned from "biometrics, mobile surveillance systems, radiation detectors, ground sensors, imaging systems, and other advanced technologies."[42]

• • •

Dave Gratton and Scott Carpenter of the EyeSite Surveillance company leaned back in their chairs in their Phoenix, Arizona office. Through the window behind them, I saw plane after plane taking off on that hot September afternoon. Behind them was a sign that laid out the layered strategy of their overt perimeter surveillance security system. Like a border zone, the "layers of protection" included, the sign explained, deterrence, detection, assessment, and apprehension. They too were at the Border Security Expo that April, near the GuardBot display, listening to the words of Mark Borkowski. There they promoted their covert technologies, or "concealments," as they are known. They are one of many companies turning cacti, or some part of the natural world, into organic surveillance camouflage.

Gratton described how EyeSite was an "American dream company" started in "Scott's garage." Gratton talked at length about how he had arrived at that Phoenix office

"the legal way" after being born and raised in Australia. They talked about a booming security market. They talked about how after 9/11 people were okay with being on camera, and mentioned that there were 26,000 security cameras in London alone. Gratton said that there was now "down sized privacy" and "upsized security." Like many in the so-called security sector they have had success. In this world there is a stark division between "good" and "bad," and the "bad guys run in packs."

If you take the future projections of the homeland security market and place them side by side with future climate projections, you can really begin to see the future come into focus inside the crystal ball. You see superstorms and surveillance cameras, droughts and drones. You see a warming planet with degraded landscapes, and now you see cacti filled with cameras like the ones they were describing at EyeSite.

The San Antonio company TimberSpy has even taken it a step further. They create fake cacti and tree stumps from artificial plastic used at Disney World. The barrel cactus can be stuffed with surveillance cameras. They have rockcams, perfect for desert *arroyos*, to see passing border-crossers. But clearly TimberSpy's speciality is tree stumps. Perfect, according to Kurt Ludwisgen, for patrolling the deforested "Montana border." There is the smaller "scoutout," which can carry cameras and transmitters. And there is the seven-foot "lookout" that can either be a "robustly equipped surveillance unit"[43] or fit an entire Homeland Security agent can fit inside. As Elizabeth Kolbert described in her book *The Sixth Extinction*, there have been five major mass

extinctions of life on planet Earth, and the sixth is happening now, right before our eyes. It is, Kolbert writes, a "truly extraordinary moment."[44] On U.S. borders, this vast loss of biodiversity, is being replaced with surveillance equipment that looks like the natural world.

FIVE

PHOENIX DYSTOPIA: MASS MIGRATION IN THE HOMELAND

Jumping cholla, la brincadora,
la viajera, la vela de coyote
—alight in a lightness of being, borderless.

—Logan Phillips

At the front of the July 2011 storm, cold air rushed down with powerful velocity and met a parched desert that had long been in drought. When the fast wind met the loose soil, it whipped up a wall of dust 5,000 feet high and 100 miles wide. The storm resembled the massive, blowing barrier of dust in the apocalyptic car chase of *Mad Max: Fury Road*. It engulfed the sleek silver bank buildings in downtown Phoenix, the domed baseball stadium, and the basketball arena; it blew over Interstate 10, reducing visibility to zero, and over the Maricopa County Sheriff Department's tent city for undocumented people. Climate change has made the U.S. Southwest hotter, drier, and dustier, with predictions of more to come. The wall of dust enveloped Sky Harbor International Airport and even penetrated the buildings

themselves, where passengers covered their faces as they waited for their luggage at the carousel. The storm dumped a thick layer of dust and debris over the entirety of what Andrew Ross calls the world's "least sustainable city." Ferocious storms once considered so rare as to occur only once every hundred years may soon become the annual norm.

More frequent dust storms are but some of the many climate changes expected to impact Phoenix, says William deBuys, author of *A Great Aridness: Climate Change and the Future of the American Southwest*. More than any other city in the United States, Phoenix "stands squarely in the crosshairs of climate change."[1] The dust storms embody everything that could go feasibly wrong for a community, large or small. Not only does drought dehydrate soil to such a degree that it becomes easily swept up by wind, it also threatens a population's fresh water supply, as it has threatened those who rely on Lake Mead, the largest freshwater reservoir in the West. In May 2016—again, the planet's hottest year on record—Lake Mead evaporated down to its lowest level ever.

"Arizona's 'bank' for 40 percent of its water supply, Lake Mead, is being drained faster than it can be filled," making eventual water rationing inevitable in the state, says the Western Resource Advocates.[2]

The same conditions that produce the dust storms also contribute to the raging wildfires that have tripled in frequency in the U.S. Southwest since the 1970s. One such fire was only 80 miles north of Phoenix, near the small town of Yarnell, in June 2013. In one day, a fatal mix of chronic drought, abnormal heat, and fatal winds drove the fire from 300 to 2,000 acres when it overran and killed 19 firefighters

from the city of Prescott. In March 2017, "wildfires raged across four states, fanned by winds and fueled by a drought-starved prairie," reported the *New York Times*, "killed at least six people and burned more than 2,300 square miles."[3]

And then there are the heat waves, "the greatest environmental killer," according to Giles Slade. He wrote in his book *American Exodus: Climate Change and the Coming Flight for Survival* that it may seem unlikely to "claim that heat waves will cause an exodus from enlarged cities of mid-century North America, but intense heat lasting through the long months of the summer will become a contributing factor to a prolonged urban exodus that may have already begun."[4]

There are six stages of heat stroke: heat stress, heat fatigue, heat syncope, heat cramps, heat exhaustion, and finally, heat stroke. In his book *The Devil's Highway*, Luis Alberto Urrea explains that the process can creep up on a person, starting with dizziness, then general disorientation, fever, cramps, headaches and nausea, and then vomiting, even vomiting blood. When people reach this point, Urrea writes, they might strip off their clothes, not because they are cold, but because they are no longer able to stand the feel of their own nerve endings. "Your muscles, lacking water, feed on themselves. They break down and start to rot. Once rotting in you they dump rafts of dying cells into your already sludgy bloodstream. Proteins are peeling off your dying muscles. Chunks of cooked meat are falling out of your organs, to clog other organs. The system closes down in a series. Your kidneys, your bladder, your heart. They jam shut. Stop. Your brain sparks. Out. You're gone."

What migrants have suffered for many years is now

coming to the world's cities. A 2003 heat wave in Europe killed 70,000 people. Temperatures in London hit over 100 degrees Fahrenheit for the first time in recorded history, while temperatures in parts of India exceeded 120°F in May 2016, melting roads and causing a spike in dehydrations, heat strokes, crop failure, mass migration, and even suicides. "Hundreds of people have died as crops have withered in the fields in more than 13 states," reported Alexandra Sims for the *Independent*, "forcing tens of thousands of small farmers to abandon their land and move into the cities. Others have killed themselves rather than go to live in urban shanty towns."[5]

In Phoenix, temperatures hit 100 degrees or more on approximately 100 days out of the year. According to calculations by Climate Central, if nothing is done to slow climate change, by 2100 Phoenix can be expected to endure temperatures in excess of 100 degrees 163 days out of the year. And trust me, it sometimes feels like this is already the case; in the summer, Phoenix is an oven. If anything knocks out the electricity grid for any length of the time, people bake in their homes. "If, in summer, the grid there fails on a large scale and for a significant period of time," William deBuys writes for *TomDispatch*, "the fallout will make the consequences of Superstorm Sandy look mild."[6]

When I followed up with deBuys in 2015, he took such a scenario one step further, and imagined the exodus of people from the city, clogging up Interstate 17 as they fled north to the White Mountains until conditions improved. Hundreds of campers would enter the tinderbox forests, where an ill-placed match or lightning strike could ignite a fire with

ease. Of course, there are an endless number of potential scenarios that could play out that could make the Valley of the Sun, as *Truthout*'s climate journalist Dahr Jamail put it, "uninhabitable by the end of the century." What happens if there is a mass upheaval in the United States? What happens if the word refugee no longer refers to a person who comes from outside of the United States, but to someone who is roaming from town to town and state to state within the country? What happens in this scenario, in the context of a border enforcement apparatus unlike anything we've ever seen before, under which agents are given free rein to patrol in the interior? Borders can be enacted quickly through road blockades and interrogating agents, and this has already begun. There is a strong probability that even Americans who support Donald Trump's "big, beautiful" border wall might soon be on the outside of an internal border, looking in.

THE BUM BLOCKADE

Members of a family in Oklahoma packed a rattletrap Ford with everything they owned and headed west. Since their intention was to remain within the United States, they did not expect that armed authorities would force them to halt. On being stopped, they wondered if they had accidentally gone off course and somehow ended up near an international border crossing.

The family was fleeing an Oklahoma suffering from statewide agricultural and economic collapse. It was five years before, in 1931, that the center point of a drought settled over the Great Plains, creating aridness comparable to the deserts of the U.S. Southwest. It would become the

worst drought in U.S. climatological history. It came with temperatures soaring to well over 100 degrees in Nebraska. Thousands died from the heat alone. Instead of precipitation, biblical clouds of grasshoppers descended upon what remained of the crops. It was after the drought had parched the land, already clear-cut in the name of agribusiness, that large air masses and low, sirocco-like winds began to lift enormous amounts of dirt, whipping up dust storms that towered 8,000 feet high and buried entire homes. One particularly powerful storm carried 350 million tons of dirt from Montana and Wyoming and dumped it on cities from Chicago to Atlanta. The dust appeared in different colors and gave off a variety of aromas. It created health problems such as "dust pneumonia" for people who inhaled it and then retreated indoors, but outside livestock and wildlife often suffocated. "I'm on my horse," one man responded to people who offered him a ride to another town, after seeing that he was covered up to his head with dust.

"The story of the southern plains in the 1930s is essentially about dust storms," historian Donald Worster wrote in *Dust Bowl: The Southern Plains in the 1930s*, "and not once or twice, but over and over for the better part of a decade: day after day, year after year, of sand rattling against the window, of fine powder caking one's lips, of springtime turned to despair, of poverty eating into self-confidence."[7] Worster argued that there is a close link between the Dust Bowl and the Depression—that the same society and system produced both, and for similar reasons.

In writing about the calamities that befell Midwesterners during the Dust Bowl, Worster might well have been

writing about our current Anthropocene era. He might well have been wrting about what's to come.

A study by NASA predicts a devastating drought to hit the U.S. Southwest and plains states by the end of the 21st century. "Recent droughts like the ongoing drought in California or in the Southwest—or even historical droughts like the Dust Bowl in the 1930s—these are naturally occurring droughts that typically last several years or sometimes almost a decade," scientist Ben Cook wrote. "In our projections what we're seeing is that with climate change, many of these types of droughts will likely last for 20, 30, sometimes even 40 years."[8] Forty years would be four times longer than the Dust Bowl. Cook was also the lead researcher for a study that found the drought that began in 1998 in the eastern Mediterranean Levant region—which comprises Cyprus, Israel, Jordan, Lebanon, Palestine, Syria, and Turkey—has been the most severe the region has endured in nine centuries. Such a drought might crumble a place like Phoenix entirely, and is as likely as the impending sea rise washing over Miami.

In 1936, the newly formed border guard had no sympathy for fellow Americans who were fleeing droughts and dust storms. The family from Oklahoma in the rattletrap car only had 10 bucks. The border they had reached was not the one with Mexico, but the one with California, and armed authorities were positioned there to make sure that people like them did not enter the state. The same was true if you arrived by train. Police, like immigration officials today in southern Mexico, patrolled the rails, shining their bright flashlights between the cars as the squeaky, slow-moving

freight trains trudged through an area that even 100 years earlier was not part of the United States. All of a sudden, where there had been no enforced border, an apparatus appeared solely to obstruct people's mobility.

In 1936, Rose Marie Packard reported to *The Nation* magazine that when she asked the police officer what they were doing patrolling the Arizona-California border, the officer said they were only fingerprinting those "who looked like criminals." Similar explanations have come from today's Border Patrol agents working checkpoints. Packard asked the officer if he "did not know that these people had a constitutional right to travel where they pleased?"[9] The officer responded that he was there on the orders of the chief of police. Packard said that she took two famished young men to dinner because they hadn't eaten in three days. They too were denied at the border when authorities saw they had no money and were unemployed. "This is as far as you go, young man."[10]

As with many borders in the world, there were the accusations of violence and abuse occurring at the California "bum blockades." Because the incidents took place far from the public eye, they were very difficult to later prove. As geographer Reece Jones demonstrates in his book *Border Walls*, "exclusion and violence" are inherent "to [securing] the borders of the modern state."[11] Or, in this case, the state of California.

In August 1935, Americans heading for California in search of work were warned by H.A. Carleton, director of the Federal Transient Service, to "stay away from California."[12] Carleton said: "California was carrying approximately

7 percent of the entire national relief load, one of the heaviest of any State in the Union. A large part of this load was occasioned by thousands of penniless families from other States who have literally overrun California."[13]

From the mid to late 1930s, two decades before scientists in Hawaii started to detect an increase of carbon in the Earth's atmosphere, about 350,000 environmental refugees entered California. As they did, the stereotypes quickly followed. They were shiftless, lazy, and irresponsible. They had "too many children."

Los Angeles Police Department Chief James E. Davis, sent an "expeditionary force"[14] to the California-Arizona border in February 1936. True to form, this particular stretch of Arizona border, according to the LAPD deputy chief was overwhelmed by a "flood of criminals,"[15] not an increased number of Americans fleeing environmental crises. These were the "trenches."[16] This was a "swift war" on "jobless, penniless winter nomads."[17]

The "bum blockade" strategy was similar to today's layered border policing strategy. In a paper titled "The Bum Blockade: Los Angeles and the Great Depression," sociologist Hailey Giczy wrote that the Los Angeles Police Department made it clear that it was based on "two lines of defense."[18] One of the enforcement layers was the city of Los Angeles itself, where authorities pursued, arrested, and fingerprinted "vagrants and beggars."[19] Police gave those they apprehended the option of doing hard labor in a prison camp or wholesale expulsion from the state. And much as in the "See Something, Say Something" campaign of today's Department of Homeland Security, Los Angeles

"housewives"[20] were encouraged to report all hoboes who come to their doors.

The other line of defense was the California state line. A mere 12 years after the U.S. Border Patrol was created, 136 Los Angeles police officers were deployed to "prevent undesirable migrants from entering the state."[21] And these "vagrants and beggars" were mainly white.

Chief Davis told the newly minted border patrol that, while they controlled the roads and railroad tracks entering the state, they would have much latitude, and "individual initiative is encouraged to determine the proper modus operandi" as they searched for fellow Americans, like the Oklahoma family, who went from "place to place without visible means of support."[22] Police were to "shake down" all adult males to make sure they didn't have any weapons.[23] They also fingerprinted them, and often sent them off on the next train going the opposite direction. Even though L.A. city councilman Parley Parker Christensen called Davis "our Los Angeles edition of Mussolini,"[24] and said that the "bum blockade" was acting against U.S. citizens' fundamental right to travel from state to state, the deployment of border guards on a state line occurred with official sanction. When pressed that the California border was out of their jurisdiction, the state governor said that L.A. County went "almost" to the boundary. Local police agencies also deputized the officers, and some police agents said it was their right to conduct citizens' arrests, the same claims made by border militia groups on today's U.S.-Mexico border. A state attorney claimed there was a historical precedent—the 1917 forced deportation of 1,300 striking mine workers and

their supporters by a 2,000-strong deputized citizen posse in Bisbee, Arizona. They expelled the workers from the state of Arizona en masse to the state of New Mexico.

At that time, border militarization was hardly as commonplace as it is now, yet was quickly mobilized and justified when the context was the security of the rich versus that of the poor. Indeed, the U.S. Supreme Court and the California Supreme Court were both on the record declaring that a state has a right to protect itself "against the spread of crime, pauperism or disturbance of the peace, by closing its borders to migrants not self-supporting."[25] The U.S. Supreme Court declared that a "State may exclude from its limits convicts, paupers, idiots and lunatics, and persons likely to become a public charge . . . a right founded . . . in the sacred law of defense."[26] Similar institutionalized discrimination can also be found in the Immigration Act of 1917 that stated that "undesirables," such as "idiots" and "alcoholics," along with "criminals" and "anarchists" were banned from the United States. Immigration law, history, policy, and rhetoric is low on empathy, high on name-calling. Environmental refugees could become, in the parlance of Donald Trump, as one example, people with "lots of problems, and they're bringing those problems with us. They're bringing drugs. They're bringing crime. They're rapists."

California has a history of enacting this type of enforced exclusion based on identity, race, or nationality. It was the state at the frontlines of enforcement of the federal Chinese Exclusion Act, the 1882 law that prohibited the entrance of all Chinese laborers into the United States. Giczy writes that the Chinese were considered a "perpetual, unchanging

and unchangeable alien element that could never be homog enous."[27] The 1930s—one of the crucial decades when the United States was moving to a voracious fossil fuel economy as the car industry took over streetcar systems and other public transportation works in Los Angeles and many other cities across the country—was also a dark period of round-ups, internment, incarceration, and expulsion of people of Japanese and Mexican heritage. Not only a "white paradise," (only for the right type of whiteness), but also also an enforcement model for potential future use.

On April 20, 1936, a headline appeared in a Colorado newspaper: "Troops Move into Action at Dawn to Prevent Invasion by Indigent."[28] The insinuation was that Colorado's entire southern border should be patrolled by soldiers because the low-income were coming. Florida initiated a "poverty quarantine,"[29] a border blockade established to keep out those with little money, people who the state claimed would "turn to crime for support." According to one newspaper report, Florida thwarted more than 50,000 "hitch-hiking, rod-riding, and flivver-driving itinerants."[30] Unlike in California, for Colorado and Florida it was the state governments that led the charge: in Colorado, the National Guard; in Florida, the state police.

Colorado even declared martial law along its southern border to "repel" people described as "aliens, invaders," and "indigents."[31] A sign on the Colorado state line read: "Martial Law—Slow—Stop."[32] If you weren't a Colorado resident and, say, were on your way to do seasonal work on a sugar beet farm, you would be stopped and physically blockaded from entering the territory, regardless of whether or not you

were an American citizen. Where there is no border today, there could be one tomorrow—even in the middle of your own country.

The point of writing this is to say that the patrolling of state borders could happen again, it could happen now, it could happen in the future, it could happen during mass internal migration, or it could happen during whatever. In March 2017, probably close to the same Arizona-California border location where the blockade halted that family in the rattletrap car from Oklahoma, after crossing the ever-dwindling Colorado River, I came to the booths where an agricultural inspector forced me to stop briefly, then waved me through. I looked behind him only to see a large, idling Border Patrol truck with an agent staring right at me. He didn't force me to stop, or stop anyone else at that moment, but he was clearly doing visual inspections and had the authority to do more.

Unlike creating comprehensive legislation to prevent climate change by eliminating greenhouse gas emissions, proposals that have languished in Washington for decades, laws aimed at stopping and expelling people have the ability to mobilize nations and states into sometimes dazzling rapid-fire action. For example, within one week of the Paris attacks of 2015, 32 U.S. states declared that they would not accept Syrian refugees in their territories. This reaction was based on Obama's advance commitment to resettle 10,000 Syrians into the United States in 2016, a small fraction of the total number seeking political asylum for their homes ravaged by war and drought. Leading the charge against them was Texas governor Greg Abbott, who said "American

humanitarian compassion could be exploited to expose Americans to similar deadly danger."[33]

One more step and Texas would be setting up a border blockade, not with Mexico but with Syria. Here climate change and immigration restriction would be meeting in the strangest of places, since any Syrian forced to be a refugee has not only faced off against a brutal political situation and constant international intervention in their country, but also most likely has experienced chronic drought. For Texas, it would not be hard to add an additional vetting protocol on its state boundaries, because the state already has its own Border Patrol. And, for that matter, so does South Carolina. The state's Immigration Enforcement Unit has its own insignia, uniforms, and vehicles. Arizona's Border Strike Force, formed in 2015, has an ominous rattlesnake on its flag, perhaps to remind would-be offenders of its lethal capabilities or its affiliation with the Tea Party. The force is led by the controversial sheriff of Pinal County, border hawk Paul Babeu, who was publicly shamed in 2012 when it was revealed that he threatened to deport his male lover, an undocumented foreigner, if he told anyone the details of their relationship. These enforcement units could not function without the Department of Homeland Security's resources that sustain and enable them. For example, Arizona's SB1070, the 2010 law that obligates police to check a person's residency status if they are suspected to be undocumented, could not function properly without the Border Patrol or ICE, the authorities that respond to the calls. It is that idling Border Patrol I encountered non the Arizona-California border that makes things happen.

Today's budgets for law enforcement, military, and the relatively new Department of Homeland Security dwarf those of the 1930s. If states were to put up such blockades, unless by a completely rogue move with little teeth, it would undoubtedly be in collaboration with the U.S. federal government and have access to the billions of dollars budgeted annually for this category of operations. When the levees, sea walls and dams burst and cities, towns, and homes go under, when wildfires scorch the land for miles and the people who flee for safety are themselves seen as a threat, the federal government will have the capacity to set up thousands of "bum blockades," enforcing the same exact security zones of exclusion—yet with much more modern force—that the states of California, Colorado, and Florida attempted to impose in the 1930s. Any student of borders knows how quickly and efficiently boundary lines put forth by a sovereign power can be normalized. Likewise, given their artificial nature, one also understands how quickly, as with the collapse of the Soviet Union, such man-made lines can simply disappear.

The bum blockade didn't last long. However, it lasted long enough to show what might happen when chronic environmental destabilization forces large numbers of people in the United States to flee, as is, indeed, predicted.

Or, as is already happening before our eyes.

CHECKPOINT TRAUMA

Joshua Garcia's pulse quickens every time he approaches a U.S. Border Patrol checkpoint. The staggered speed-limit signs on the side of the highway indicate that he should slow

down from 40 to 30 to 20 miles per hour. Due to his experiences in the past, and unlike most other drivers, he follows the speed limits exactly.

Garcia has done nothing wrong. He is also a U.S. citizen. But he feels that sense of dread. It is like that feeling of trepidation pulling into, say, that checkpoint on the Colorado border where armed, uniformed officials could order you to pull over. Maybe this time, as on many occasions, they would just wave him through. Perhaps he'd be able to continue on his way back to Tucson as the harsh afternoon light softens into dusk. He hopes that is the case, because he has two kids from the youth council with him.

Sebastian, who is 17, is asleep in the back seat. Fifteen-year-old Amelia is pointing to a sign that says there are dogs on duty. "I want to pet the dog," she says. Garcia looks at Amelia and jokes, "They're working dogs, you're not supposed to pet them."

In addition to feeling nervous about approaching the checkpoint, there is also exhilaration and afterglow from a great day. That morning, when they drove from Tucson to the Tohono O'odham Nation, a beautiful and muscular wildcat walked across the two-lane road in front of them. "A mountain lion," the kids murmured. They had to look twice to make sure. And then they were sure. It was the first time either of them had seen one. It was the first time for Garcia, too, the adult leader who had spent thousands of hours walking in the desert. There is something about seeing an elusive and endangered animal, free and wild in its own habitat, that stays with you a long time. Conversations about the lion dominated for the rest of the day. Garcia believes that

it was because of the lion that many in the group wanted to walk toward Baboquivari Peak, on a path that climbed to one of the caves where Itoi, the Tohono O'odham creator, resided. From the sacred cave there was a sweeping view of the O'odham aboriginal land that extended as far as the eye could see, including hundreds of miles into Mexico. For a moment there was no international border dividing the land, only the beauty one has of suddenly seeing a vast, inspiring landscape. At the cave they sang to the mountain. It was that sort of day, reconnecting with the living Earth with a sort of reverence that goes against the grain in much of the contemporary United States.

They can see the authorities wave another car forward. They can hear and smell the idling engines. It was another abnormally hot day during the year 2015, which would be the hottest year in recorded history up until that point (only to be surpassed by the very next year). Garcia puts his truck into gear and inches ahead. There are orange striped signs in the middle of the road. There is a stop sign with a trio of orange flags on top, slightly flapping around in the breeze. There are well-armed Homeland Security agents in forest-green uniforms observing his vehicle as he pulls forward into this modern-day bum blockade, located 45 miles north of the international border.

Of course, Garcia is not yet a climate refugee like the Dust Bowl migrants who were turned away from the California border in the 1930s, or the many people fleeing ecological, political, and economic disasters around the world today. A common misperception about border enforcement is that it targets only people on the other side. Lines like in

a bum blockade, however, can be drawn quickly and anywhere at any time, including on all paved roads leaving the Tohono O'odham Native American reservation, creating essentially an extra layer of border security around a particular group of people. Our borders are constantly changing, and the same is true of whom and what they apply to, including U.S. citizens.

Borders may seem passive and static, but they are actually agressive and dynamic. As evidenced by the Trump administration's January 2017 executive order that banned travel from seven countries, CBP—after multiple days of blockading people from those countries into the United States—demonstrated that it has the will, capacity, and infrastructure to respond swiftly to commands.

Sophie Smith, an activist scholar based in Arivaca, Arizona, has studied the checkpoints that surround her small town and in the broader region. Smith says checkpoints start out as temporary, as did many of them in the Southwest in the post-9/11 era, then become part of border policing strategy. The checkpoints have become, Smith stressed, a "model that is workable in the rest of the United States."

Authorities, Smith says, "know how the checkpoints would function. They know and have the infrastructure. They know whom to contract; they have all the relationships with the public and private sector. The protocols already exist and are constantly evolving depending on the security situation."

According to former CBP commissioner Gil Kerlikowske, "the border is a nexus to a continuum of activities that threaten the national interests of both security and

prosperity. In response, CBP will lead collaborative efforts that apply multidimensional pressure on those seeking to do us harm; outside U.S. borders, at the border, and into the interior regions of the country."[34] What Kerlikowske is saying: it doesn't matter where you are; Border Patrol will be there too.

Indeed, as Garcia inches toward the three green-uniformed agents, he is in the 100-mile border jurisdiction area, a "zone of security,"[35] in Kerlikowske's words, that wraps around the contour of the United States. This zone was determined in the 1940s and 1950s when Border Patrol was a fraction of what it is today. The Immigration and Nationality Act stated that they can patrol a "reasonable distance"[36] away from the border and the U.S. Supreme Court determined that reasonable distance was 100 miles. The expansion of the checkpoints happens like a heat wave. It happens gradually, then overtakes you. In fact, when I was doing the research for this book I could not pinpoint when exactly the Three Points checkpoint was installed. Nobody I asked knew. Was it 2006? 2007? The checkpoints appeared silently, with little fanfare. When asked, Homeland Security says that they are temporary, which in Arizona is technically true. According to the law, all checkpoints must be temporary. What "temporary" means is another issue, because the checkpoints that were installed around 2006 are, as of this writing, still there.

The Three Points checkpoint isn't exactly impressive—just a portable trailer with an attached tarp for shade—but it still qualifies, according to one of the Border Patrol's informational brochures, as "a critical enforcement tool for

securing the nation's borders against all threats to our homeland."[37] Authorities at the checkpoint stop every vehicle on the road, quickly look into each one, and then ask the people inside to verify their citizenship.

The surveillance dogs that Amelia wanted to pet sniff each car for traces of narcotics and explosives. According to the American Civil Liberties Union, this is one of the many ways that Homeland Security violates people's Fourth Amendment protection from search and seizure. According to the Border Patrol, such civil rights violations are worth it: "Our enforcement presence along these strategic routes reduces the ability of criminals and potential terrorists to easily travel away from the border."[38]

When Garcia lurches ahead and finally reaches the authorities, they just wave him over to secondary inspection. Garcia looks at the nearest agent to say something, but the official just waves his hand, now slightly irritated, as if Garcia were a pesky fly. Secondary inspection means that an agent has detected something that requires closer examination. Perhaps it is the dog. Perhaps it is the officially sanctioned "wide discretion"[39] an agent has to further invade your privacy. Perhaps it's your ethnicity, as Homeland Security is the only department officially permitted to use racial profiling as a pretext for detaining a person for questioning. When the Obama administration issued new rules in an attempt to curtail racial profiling, the one huge exception was DHS. As one DHS official told the *New York Times*, "We can't do our job without taking ethnicity into account. We are very dependent on that."[40]

Garcia slowly drives into the secondary inspection site.

He drives to where the armed agents are standing. He looks at Amelia and asks: "What happened to the phone that your mom gave you?" Amelia responds: "She took it back." Behind him, Sebastian is waking up, but his phone battery is dead.

Garcia does not, by his own admission, like conflict. He tries to avoid it. When he pulls into secondary he hears a forceful, a commanding voice yelling: "Get out of the vehicle!" The voice is urgent, as if there were explosives somewhere, as if there were a bomb, as if someone were in danger. The yelling has the urgency, the intensity of war. It is so urgent that Garcia briefly thinks that it must be something else. He finds it hard to believe that just a few minutes ago he was talking to Amelia about her dreams, about how she wanted to be a music teacher, about how she played in the orchestra, about how she wants to go to Japan. It was hard to believe that they were just talking softly about animals, remembering the mountain lion they had seen. The Homeland Security agent barks: "GET. OUT."

There is a term used on the Tohono O'odham reservation to describe the lingering side effects of a bad experience with Border Patrol: "checkpoint trauma." This is especially prevalent among little kids, says Amy Juan, a teacher and founding member of TOHRN (Tohono O'odham Hemajkam Rights Network). Kids could be playing, happy, smiling, laughing, but once they know they are in the vicinity of a checkpoint they shut down and become frightened. Although they are U.S. citizens, a massive enforcement apparatus encircles their traditional land and community, a modern-day "bum blockade."

RED DAWN

Now Garcia is thinking the worst. He remembers all the incidents that he's had with the Border Patrol since the upsurge in operations in the mid 1990s. He even remembers when this all began. Since he was young and growing up with his grandparents, he has always been very close to the land. He lived off the reservation, just west of Tucson, near Saguaro National Monument. Garcia loves to take long, slow walks in the desert. He knows the wildlife, the vegetation, and the saguaro fruit that his beloved grandmother taught him how to harvest. Garcia knows how to read the landscape, knows the subtle shifts of weather, when the nopal and the saguaro will flower and fruit. One spectacular October night in the 1990s, when he was a teenager, he saw bright flares light up the sky in a way he had never seen before. At first he was confused. Was there some sort of alien aircraft landing on the Tohono O'odham reservation? Then the sky filled up with helicopters and airplanes as if the flash opened a gate for the advent of homeland security.

"It was kind of like *Red Dawn*," he said referring to the movie that ridiculously depicts the invasion of the United States by North Korea. Garcia said that he knew something had, at that point, changed. This was confirmed a few days later, right after Halloween and the Day of the Dead, when there were trick-or-treater footprints coming and going all throughout his aunt's dirt lot. Border Patrol agents showed up, hyped up and in hot pursuit. At this point, there were more agents than ever before, though a fraction of what they are today.

When I first met Garcia, he would lay out very detailed

stories about how the dynamics of climate change and aggressive law enforcement were impacting the Tohono O'odham Nation. In the same breath he would talk about the massive Homeland Security presence, the unreliability of the rains, and the subsequent out-of-sync fruiting of the saguaro or the prickly pear cactus. Perhaps there is no better place to witness the convergence of climate change and border militarization than on this reservation, a territory bisected by an unwanted international boundary more than a century ago. In the age of global warming, the reservation has become, according to veteran humanitarian activist Mike Wilson, a "prototype police state" for the rest of the country.

The report "Record of Abuse: Lawlessness and Impunity in Border Patrol's Interior Enforcement Operations,"[41] describes in detail the components of this model "police state." Agents' brandishing of weapons during normal traffic stops of Tohono O'odham members, the report says, has become routine. Border Patrol agents have stopped and detained a school bus "more than a dozen times;" each time they forced students to stand out in the heat as they rifle through their personal belongings.[42] One family said that agents pulled them over after they returned home to retrieve a forgotten item, apparently, according to the agents, a "suspicious act."[43] For the O'odham, the result is similar to living under occupation, a term used often in their communities.

Over the years, I have heard stories from many O'odham, most of whom wish to remain anonymous. I have heard about a Tohono O'odham health worker whom Border Patrol pulled over after she picked up patients to transport

them to a dialysis center. I have heard about Border Patrol blocking a funeral procession and then showing up at the cemetery during the burial. I have heard about Border Patrol desecrating a burial ground—and other sacred places—by using it as a shooting range and by driving all over it with ATVs. A man told me that he was simply driving north from the international divide when Border Patrol pulled him over and six agents surrounded him, armed with high-caliber automatic weapons. They never informed him what it was that set them off. Tohono O'odham Nellie Jo David, a TOHRN member and student of indigenous peoples law and policy, put it this way: "We can't visit family, go to the store, attend meetings, participate in our culture, grab a bite somewhere, or say hi to our friends without being accused of something."

Using cases from heavily redacted documents obtained from Customs and Border Protection, the ACLU alleges that agents' "violent, reckless, and threatening" conduct is not that of just a few bad apples. The verbally and sometimes physically abusive routine conduct of the U.S. Border Patrol, according to the report, is not limited to the reservation. In one case, a Border Patrol agent told a woman to "put the fucking keys in the truck" at an interior checkpoint west of Tucson after a false canine alert. When she objected to the language, the agent responded by saying, "I can talk to you any fucking way I want." The agent then explained to his supervisor that he felt a "more forceful approach was needed in order to convey her need to follow my direction."[44]

In another incident, a woman asked why the Border Patrol had detained her in Tucson, 60 miles north of the

border, when she was driving in her car to drop off her two children at school in March 2011. The agents first told her that her Ford Expedition "was running low," and then: "We'll think of something."[45]

The ACLU called these practices a "de facto stop and frisk"[46] for border residents. It happens almost every single day, with very little attention or fanfare. The targeted mistreatment of indigenous communities is perhaps the most persistent form of racism in U.S. history, and harks back to white colonialism and Manifest Destiny. Such abuse offers a glimpse into what might one day become normal in the future of climate crisis and displacement. Worth stating again, the time is near when the very people who vehemently support a gigantic U.S. border wall may find themselves denied access to the other side.

Surveillance and racial profiling in the Southwest degrades millions of people from all walks of life. Former Arizona governor Raul Castro, for example, was detained and compelled to stand in 100-degree heat for more than 30 minutes while he was closely inspected. He was 96 years old at the time. Although the Border Patrol has made more than 6,000 arrests and confiscated 135,000 pounds of narcotics at checkpoints, records show that it was mostly U.S. citizens who were swept up, not criminals from other countries.

Surveillance and targeting of U.S. citizens is not new, and can only be expected to intensify under Donald J. Trump. For the 2018 U.S. federal budget, the Trump administration proposed to give a further jolt to already sky-high budgets for border and immigration enforcement. Trump plans to hire an additional 100 government lawyers and 1,500 new

ICE and Border Patrol agents. An extra $2.6 billion will be designated to "high-priority tactical infrastructure and border security technology, including funding to plan, design, and construct a physical wall along the southern border."[47] This is on top of existing budgets that already reach, it is worth remembering, about $20 billion annually (just counting CBP and ICE). A further $1.5 billion will go to expand incarceration, transportation, and expulsion of "illegal immigrants."[48] Add to this an extra $54 billion extra going to the Pentagon, a 10 percent increase, and slashing the Environmental Protection Agency by 31 percent, further entrenching these preexisting dynamics, ensuring the occurrence of future climate catastrophes and the militarization to corral their aftermath. The advent of a new sort of Red Dawn is upon us—except the invader isn't North Korea, but the U.S. government occupying its own communities..

Although it is not explicitly stated, the maintenance and expansion of the checkpoint system is implied, which means the policing of U.S. citizens and potentially blockading their mobility—and activism in future scenarios, and in places far away from the southwest border.

In 2008, for example, a Border Patrol agent forced Vermont senior senator Patrick Leahy from his car at a checkpoint 125 miles south of the New York state border. The ACLU unearthed a prototype plan for Border Patrol to operate checkpoints on all five Vermont highways. On the Adirondack Highway, rumble pads slow down traffic headed south from Plattsburgh toward Albany. Rarely are the Homeland Security agents there, but the infrastructure is there for them to commence immediately. At a checkpoint

near Watertown, New York, Border Patrol agents confiscated the car of a college student, pushed her to the ground, and electrocuted her with a stun gun.

In November 2016, the federal government deployed the U.S. Border Patrol at Standing Rock, North Dakota, where Native American groups accompanied by activists from across the country were trying to stop the construction of the Dakota Access Pipeline, which would carry oil from North Dakota to refineries and export terminals in the Gulf Coast and lock-in the equivalent of "30 coal plants"[49] worth of emissions. According to the statement of the U.S. Border Patrol Grand Forks Sector, the federal Homeland Security agency started its operation there, much more than 100 miles from the international boundary, on November 20—though activists made claims that Border Patrol had been setting up roadside blockades well before then. The statement said the Border Patrol presence "was requested to assist with preserving life and protecting property in and around the Dakota Access Pipeline (DAPL) protest location."[50]

One incident happened the morning of November 22, 2016, when a caravan of 200 cars set off on rural two-lane roads in North Dakota to do an action. About a half an hour in, police cars blistered past the caravan and set up a barrier, blockading the road. Two hundred cars had to suddenly brake to an abrupt halt, causing some rear-end collisions. People got out of the cars and engaged in a singing ceremony with plants in front of the police barricade. Ten green-striped U.S. Border Patrol vehicles pulled in. They told the people who were singing, according to student Nora Collins, who was present, "You are blocking off a public

highway, you must leave now or we will begin arresting people." When people responded that it was the police who were blocking off the highway, the Border Patrol was "dismissive," according to Collins.

What Josh Garcia and the passengers in his car were about to experience has become increasingly normalized in the United States. "GET OUT," the agent bellows. Garcia, Amelia, and Sebastian get out of the car into the already oven-like heat of the afternoon. There is a constant smell of burning exhaust, pollution, and simmering asphalt. An agent enters the car and rifles through Sebastian's backpack. Does the 17-year-old who wants to be a visual artist have something that threatens national security?

Garcia does not know what to do. He wants to assert his rights, but he doesn't want to make a scene in front of the kids. Finally he says it: "We don't consent to a search." Garcia's voice is soft, calm, and barely audible to the agent, who continues treating Sebastian's backpack as if there were a bomb inside. Another green-uniformed agent approaches Garcia. He is walking in a straight line, right at him. He reaches for the club on his gun belt. He yells, "Get back!" Several men in gray uniforms with black hats and boots from the company G4S, the same private security firm where Omar Mateen worked before killing 49 people at Orlando's Pulse nightclub in 2016, stand up and walk briskly to join the Border Patrol agent. One of the G4S cops is eating an apple. He throws it to the ground, and joins the action.

G4S has a quarter-billion-dollar contract to provide securitized transportation for the undocumented people whom the Border Patrol arrest in the desert. The for-profit

company has also identified extreme weather as a "potential source of business"[51] to the Carbon Disclosure Project. G4S sees potential profits in droughts and famines, and quotes a United Nations projection of "50 million refugees" as if this assures that they will continue their lucrative border contract and maybe even get a few new ones.[52] The privatized police force also deployed its agents during Hurricanes Katrina and Sandy and offered "security from social unrest."[53] While underscoring their lessening carbon footprint, G4S also wrote, "Climate change presents a risk to people and infrastructure across the globe. As an organization that specializes in managing risk, we recognize that the threat of climate change is an important and growing concern for our group, our customers and communities."[54]

In Three Points, the G4S agents are showing their ability to work checkpoints and intimidate young people. "We don't consent," Garcia says, backpedaling, along with the kids.

"Get the fuck back," the Border Patrol agent barks, pushing forward, flicking his wrist so that his billy club extends aggressively at Garcia, exposing the brute violence that underpins the border.

"We don't consent," Garcia tries one more time.

"Get. The. Fuck. Back."

The agent raises the club and pushes forward at Garcia as though he is about to strike. Garcia keeps walking backward. Sebastian is walking backward. Amelia is walking backward. The children, too, are bracing themselves to be assaulted by the grown armed men.

"Sit down," the agent barks.

The children immediately sit on the burning asphalt. Garcia doesn't sit. He is trying to articulate, now by his actions, that he doesn't consent. The pause is enough to irritate the agent again. "Sit the fuck down," the agent says to the U.S. citizen, again raising his billy club. Garcia finally complies. The border between these two sets of U.S. citizens is as powerful as the actual international border, and the threat of violence can emerge as suddenly and fiercely as an oncoming storm.

WE'RE HERE TO PROTECT YOU: THE LOW INTENSITY DOCTRINE

In New Orleans, a U.S. Border Patrol agent held a machine gun pointed downward, his hand poised so his index finger could quickly squeeze the trigger. He wore a forest-green flak jacket over his desert camouflage uniform, like the six other agents around him as they slowly walked down the stairwell of the hotel. There was anxiety on his face, as if someone might pop around the corner. They were from the Border Patrol Tactical Unit (BORTAC). The mission of BORTAC, the same unit that trained the Honduran Special Forces for Operation Rescue Angels, is "to respond to terrorist threats of all types anywhere in the world in order to protect our nation's homeland." That now includes threats that might present themselves from within the "homeland" itself, as in the communities of color that were ravaged by a hurricane.

The 2005 catastrophe gave a powerful glimpse into what could be a typical scene in the future. Outside, the damage was ruinous. The Category 3 storm came ashore

and pounded the population. The final body count would exceed 1,600 people. Everywhere there were flooded neighborhoods, splintered houses with their roofs ripped off. It was in the aftermath of the wreckage that agents in flat-bottom airboats patrolled these predominantly African American neighborhoods, as if they were on the slow-flowing Rio Grande between Texas and Mexico. Where there was less flooding, armed authorities conducted foot patrols, wearing flak jackets that said U.S. BORDER PATROL on the back, as if they were indeed on duty in Laredo securing the wall. News outlets such as CNN reported that "rampaging gangs" had taken control of the "unguarded city" of New Orleans, and the *New York Times* wrote that "chaos gripped" the city and "looters ran wild."[55] And James Ridgeway reported for *Mother Jones* that "what took place in this devastated American city was no less than a war, in which victims whose only crimes were poverty and blackness were treated as enemies of the state."[56]

As Naomi Klein wrote over 10 years later: "What does #BlackLivesMatter, and the unshakable moral principle that it represents, have to do with climate change? Everything. Because we can be quite sure that if wealthy white Americans had been the ones left without food and water for days in a giant sports stadium after Hurricane Katrina, even George W. Bush would have gotten serious about climate change."[57]

U.S. Customs and Border Protection deployed more than 600 personnel from Field Operations, Border Patrol, Air and Marine, and Information and Technology for 20 days of "intense operations."[58] The command base was

called a "Forward Deployed Operational Command Center."[59] CBP agents patrolled alongside other federal, state, and local law enforcement agencies as well as National Guard troops. Also on hand were mercenaries contracted by Homeland Security, including "soldiers" from Blackwater who, according to journalist Jeremy Scahill, hit the streets armed to the teeth with assault rifles and pockets stuffed with ammo.[60] Stalking the scene were roving bands of white vigilante groups whose leaders openly bragged to the local news about "shooting looters."[61] There was a "virtual martial law"[62] imposed on New Orleans, Ridgeway reported, and what writer Dave Eggers characterized as a "complete suspension of all legal processes,"[63] as in a border zone.

In a 1979 Pentagon-commissioned report on low-intensity conflict, a section called "A U.S. City in Revolt" envisioned an armed uprising by "a combination of poor and minority activist elements." Washington would react by sending in "regular Army units to restore order, disarm dissidents, and close all border traffic."[64] This was the scenario that sociologist Timothy Dunn laid out in his book *The Militarization of the U.S.-Mexico Border, 1978-1992: Low-Intensity Conflict Doctrine Comes Home*, illustrating that the Pentagon doctrine could and would be used on U.S. territory, in U.S. domestic law enforcement. Moreover, as Dunn convincingly argued, it has become the reality of enforcement on the border, and a proving ground for the rest of the country. U.S. doctrine on low-intensity conflict—what the Army has described as a "limited politico-military struggle to achieve political, social, economic, or psychological

objectives"—has applied to a number of U.S. military interventions throughout Central America in the 1980s (including El Salvador, Honduras, Nicaragua, and Guatemala), and not only in "countering revolution," but also with follow-up motivated by a "concern for maintaining social control in other unstable settings." And during "peacekeeping operations," there is the "notion that much of the world is threatened by endemic violence, and that the U.S. military's role is to act as an enforcer of global order so as to protect U.S. interests—however broadly these may be defined."[65] Scaffolding for the status quo.

Now there are national preparedness centers such as the Guardian Centers, dubbed "Doomsday Disneyland"[66] by CNN, where agencies such as Federal Emergency Management Agency (FEMA) prepare for disasters and the subsequent anticipated social unrest in fake, manufactured, sometimes flooded towns. FEMA's Center for Domestic Preparedness trains Homeland Security agencies and agents, as well as the military and national guard, in counterterrorism, responding to disasters, "crowd-control measures," and "understanding protester tactics" as forms of civil unrest.[67] In an article written by the Center, National Guard First Lieutenant Keith Frederickson even mentioned past experiences of protest from the Occupy Movement and public response to the killing of Trayvon Martin as examples of civil unrest. Vigilant Sentry, the Caribbean interdiction operation mentioned in Chapter Two, is another annual national preparedness exercise by Southern and Northern Command, again preparing itself not only for mass migration, but also for possible civil unrest

and crowd control. And, of course, Edward Snowden's revelations demonstrate quite clearly that surveillance operations by the National Security Agency target U.S. citizens with regularity. The amount of money required to stage all of this is staggering. As political scientist John Mueller and author Mark G. Stewart point out, domestic homeland security expenditures have increased by $1 trillion since the attacks of 9/11.

To return to the concept of "elite panic," disaster sociologist Kathleen Tierney's definition of the phenomenon, as quoted by Rebecca Solnit, show the parallels between disaster situations, border failure, threats to homeland security, and low-intensity military doctrine all in one fell swoop: "Fear of social disorder, fear of the poor, minorities and immigrants; obsession with looting and property crime; willingness to resort to deadly force; actions taken on the basis of rumor."[68] Because of this, during Hurricane Katrina, "officials and vigilantes . . . unloosed even more savage attacks on the public because the public was portrayed"[69] as barbarians like Rear Admiral Parry's Goths and Vandals.

If a hurricane or a succession of massive dust storms takes out a city such as Phoenix, if flooding leaves people homeless, if rising seas make entire swaths of territory uninhabitable, the country's largest federal law enforcement agency, U.S. Customs and Border Protection, will be there. It will bring its ability to carry out search and rescue operations. It will also bring its capacity to impose the low-intensity conflict doctrine upon large geographical areas, as described by Dunn, along with its ability not only to stop the mobility of people, but also to arrest, detain, and deport

them, in collaboration with ICE, if necessary. Instead of the serious yet ad hoc efforts of Colorado, Florida, and California, this is a sort of stealth power developed by a federal agency over the last 25 years to implement borders anywhere, with the U.S. Southwest as the model.

If infrastructure in Phoenix were to become overwhelmed due to water shortages or wildfires, it isn't too much of a stretch to imagine the checkpoints expanding only slightly north from where they currently exist in southern Arizona and surrounding Phoenix at all major veins and arteries, including Interstate 10 and Interstate 17. They could be set up quickly, without much fanfare, and under the guise of "public safety." It would be out of the 100-mile jurisdiction, but remember that the Border Patrol was operating road blockades in Standing Rock, North Dakota.

If Miami were to be inundated, it would be easy for Customs and Border Protection to roll into town, as it did for the Super Bowl in that city, in order to impose perimeter surveillance and deploy special forces units, Blackhawk helicopters, and interdiction operations at Greyhound and Amtrak stations. In all cases, the agents wouldn't go solo; they would work with the totality of the Department of Homeland Security, with other federal agencies like the FBI, with local and state law enforcement, and perhaps even with the National Guard and military.

During acute climate crisises that render the desert in the West uninhabitable or drown cities in floods, it is feasible for improvised border situations to be set up, accompanied by new lines of division and ever-changing protocol procedures for vetting and noncompliance. Such situations

can be expected to involve increasingly martial definitions of "legality" and "illegality" that incorporate militarized border vetting established to prevent mass entry. In other words, "defensive fortresses" might be set up not just on the international border lines of the United States, as mentioned in the report *An Abrupt Climate Change Scenario*, commissioned by the Pentagon in 2003, but also within the country—demonstrating how malleable and aggressive the borders really are. Say, if you are impoverished and from Oklahoma, you won't be admitted into California. Or if you are black you are contained in certain places, and not allowed to enter others. Or if you are Native American, your reservation could be "secured" by Homeland Security checkpoints.

Tohono O'odham teacher and resident Amy Juan told me that while the tribal government charges the U.S. Border Patrol $1 per month to use a massive multipurpose station on the border along with the Tohono O'odham police, it charges the organization Tohono O'odham Community Action (TOCA) $5,000 per month to rent a small office in the town of Sells. Juan says that these sorts of discrepancies are at the forefront of a problem of priorities. For example, TOCA does crucial work with traditional foods, "the only foods we'd be able to grow as the climate gets harsher," since they are adapted to heat and less water. TOCA is also promoting rainwater harvesting and flood farming, "very important if we are talking about sustainability and adaptation." At the same time TOCA is seeking to work in concert with the environment, Border Patrol is "out there messing up the land.

They're messing with the natural flows, the natural paths that water takes from the mountains, to the valleys, to the fields," Juan says.

TOHRN member and park ranger at Saguaro National Monument Tina Vavages-Andrews put it to me this way: "In terms of climate change and militarization along the border—all the Border Patrol vehicles, the technology they are using, the helicopters, definitely have an impact. Because we are already in a drought. We are already badly affected by climate change. And they're not helping reduce the impacts at all."

On the Tohono O'odham Nation, Juan explained, the elders have talked about the climate changes, "a bunch of little things that add up to big things." For example, the elders have talked about the changing rain patterns, how there wasn't as much rain as before; they said the good rains came from the south, and now the rain was coming from all directions. When you pick cholla, you have to pick on a day when it's not windy, otherwise you'll get blasted with thorns. Or at least you have to know the direction of the wind, so the thorns fly away from you, not toward you. "The wind's all over the place now, it's all crazy. You know that's just the observation I've had from my grandparents and other people."

Josh Garcia, detained and sitting on the ground at the Three Points checkpoint, is an environmental steward to the core. Amy Juan says he is "really close to the land" and has done a lot of walking in the Sonoran desert. At the 2015 climate summit in Paris, a global coalition of indigenous people gathered to put out the strong message that, as caretakers of the environment, they were not only on the

front lines of climate change, but also the people with the wisdom to lead the world out of this mess. Garcia would be one such person. He can read the land. Juan says he sent her a picture of a prickly pear fruit, noting that its shape, color, and the strange way it was growing amounted to something that he had never seen before, evidence that something was out of balance. Garcia also told me that the saguaro harvests were coming much earlier. It is this closeness to the land that makes Garcia such a valuable leader for the Youth Council, so that youth can get back in touch with O'odham traditions, and better know the beautiful land where they live. Garcia teaches youth environmental stewardship, traditional agriculture, how to harvest the saguaro fruit with long sticks, and sing songs to the mountains, as they move forward into a new generation.

As they sit on the hot pavement watching the U.S. Border Patrol ransack Garcia's truck, the wild mountain lion is still on everyone's mind. The sun is beginning to lower, giving the sky a certain radiance. The colors of the hills where the saguaros congregate take on a golden hue, almost as if the sun were streaking colors across the land, as if the sun herself were an artist. When the K-9 is done searching through the car, and the agent approaches the group, Garcia says, "I didn't consent to a search."

"I don't need consent," responds the agent. "Just go. Leave!"

At that point the two kids slowly get up and return to their vehicle. It would have been an exhilarating day, with the mountain lion, the land, the songs to the mountain at the cave, but now they will be traumatized by this incident

for months to come. Garcia intuitively knows this. He follows the agent and says, "I want the name and the badge number of the agent who assaulted me." But there he is, facing the most massive border enforcement apparatus ever created in the United States. As certain as the intensifying heat waves hitting nearby Phoenix, he is about to be told that nothing really just happened.

"Well," the supervisor says to Garcia, "I was standing out here this whole time and I didn't see an assault."

SIX

THE PHILIPPINES AND THE FUTURE BATTLE AT THE FRONTLINES OF CLIMATE CHANGE AND GLOBAL PACIFICATION

She's been betrayed time and time again, invaded, plundered, raped, and pillaged, colonized for nearly four hundred years by Spain and fifty years by the United States, brutally occupied from 1942 to 1945 by the Japanese army, bombed and pretty much decimated by Japanese and U.S. forces during an epic, month-long battle in 1945. In spite, or because of this bloody history, Manileños (her wild and wayward children) have managed to adapt, survive, and even thrive. Their ability to bounce back—whether from the latest round of catastrophic flooding, the ashes of a twenty-year dictatorship, or horrific world war—never ceases to amaze.

—Jessica Hagedorn[1]

It is not easy to plan for your own death, but that is what A.G. Saño is doing. The roof over his head is only barely there. It has been partially ripped from the hotel. The wind is so loud that it hisses and whistles like a howling monster through every hole and crack in the old hotel, located only a block away from the bay in Tacloban, Philippines. Water is cascading into his room. The old bones of the hotel are shaking. It feels as if "the monster can grab you and take you away." The water is rapidly rising. It is the worst windstorm ever recorded in the history of the Earth.

When I ask him to reconstruct that day, he tells me he can't. He tells me it would take eight full hours, because he remembers "every single horrific second."

He thinks of his family and friends nearby, the structure of the houses, and calculates how long they might be able to withstand the storm. He wonders how long it might take this shaking building to finally collapse. If he perishes, he hopes that his family will be able to find his body. He imagines in what pile of rubble his remains might end up. Saño, an artist, thinks about the hundreds of murals he's painted in this country of 7,000 islands. Saño's work has always had a focus on ecological stewardship. He has painted more than 23,000 dolphins on walls across the Philippines to pay them tribute. He was also the lead painter for the world's largest peace mural—3,700 meters long—on the wall surrounding Camp Aguinaldo, a military base built for U.S. forces in 1936 in Quezon City. In the mural, Saño wanted to depict a type of peace that was the accumulation of every single person doing small acts, for the benefit of all, on a daily basis. For him peace was not passive, but active. It was not

simply the absence of war, but a state in which people bring their best to the table and find meaning in mutual assistance and solidarity.

When Saño went to bed on November 6, 2013, he knew the storm was coming. That day, the sky was blue and the sea was calm. And that night Saño saw his good friend Agit Sustento, and that would be the last time the two would ever talk. The storm would claim the lives of his entire family, his little boy, wife, mom, and dad. With a force never witnessed before in human history, the "Category 6" typhoon would lift ships the size of small buildings and toss them onto the land. This is the exact type of violent superstorm that climate scientist James Hansen, with his report "Ice melt, sea level rise and superstorms," predicts for the future.

Tacloban is in the Cancobato Bay, on a strait that divides the islands of Leyte and Samar. The broiling town of approximately 200,000 people was a base for the U.S. military during that country's over 40-year occupation in the early 20th century. It is the place where General Douglas MacArthur came ashore during World War II. Tacloban is home of the former first lady Imelda Marcos, famous not only for the endless closets of shoes, but also the repressive martial law wielded during the dictatorship of her husband, Ferdinand Marcos's (his presidency from 1965 to 1986), that imprisoned 70,000 people, tortured 35,000, and committed 3,257 "extrajudicial" killings—2,520 of whom were "salvaged," that is, according to Chris Pforr, tortured, mutilated, and dumped on the roadside for public display. Saño's parents were among those imprisoned during the dictatorship.

As he watches water cascade down the side of the hotel

walls, A.G. Saño knows that the storm will slaughter thousands. He is located in the region of Eastern Visayas, a place that sociologist Dakila Kim P. Yee calls an area marked by "extreme poverty and political exclusion."[2] What Yee calls a "catastrophic consequence of an exclusionary political economy," is unfolding outside Saño's room in ways that are difficult to imagine. Waves the size of two-story buildings are slamming into the neighborhoods of the poor. Homes made of wood planks are collapsing; their galvanized metal roofs sail off in the ferocious wind.

This is happening mere days before the Warsaw Climate Summit, where A.G.'s brother, Yeb Saño, will speak in his role as the chief climate negotiator for the Philippines. When he does speak, Yeb's words are heavy with the tragic news of Tacloban. It seems that he is talking beyond himself, beyond his delegation, beyond even the Filipino people. He says,"To those who continue to deny [climate change], I dare them to get out of their ivory towers and go the islands of the Pacific and the Caribbean, the mountain regions of the Himalayas and the Andes, to the Arctic where communities grapple with fast-dwindling sea ice sheets." He invites people to see the Ganges, the Amazon, and the Nile, "where lives and livelihoods are drowned." He asks people to go to the hills of Central America, a region that faces "similar monstrous hurricanes," to the vast savannah of Africa, where, as devastating droughts persist, climate change has become "a matter of life and death."[3]

A.G., still in that room in the old hotel, doesn't know what to do. He thinks he's the only one left in the building. It's a stark moment, one of isolation, one of "helplessness

and hopelessness," he says. He thinks he has to face his death alone. He races down the stairs. He has absolutely no idea what to expect at the bottom.

Haiyan's winds are still coming through every crack and crevice with a high-pitched whistle. If it had been the first or even second floor, it would have been the rising water, flooded rooms, people dying. It sounds like a war outside. It sounds like a 260-kilometer-wide tornado. The heating planet is creating murderous storms. Storms that were not happening even 10 years ago, anywhere.

On the third floor a minor miracle happens. There are 60 or so frightened people crowded into the hallways and the rooms. First, it's just that there are other people who are alive. Then, A.G. recognizes one of the people in the group. He knows her from when he was little. As the storm howls outside and the water below continues to rise, this woman talks as if it were nothing. She was at his First Communion. She reminisces. What happens next is similar to a Buddhist death process meditation. A person embracing their own death simultaneously embraces a fuller appreciation of their life. The meditation, says scholar Arthur C. Brooks, is not as morbid as it might seem. It is "intended as a key to better living. . . . In other words, it makes one ask, 'Am I making the right use of my scarce and precious life?'"[4]

The woman is serene through the howling winds and shaking walls, and her serenity spreads to him. From that moment forward, A.G. follows his own core philosophical belief: small acts for the benefit of all.

Maybe that's why he stays in Tacloban after he survives and leaves the hotel. He first tries to get to his family's house,

but the streets are flooded and the roads are blockaded. Bodies of people and animals are strewn everywhere, some in piles, some mixed together. On his way to city hall, where he walks to try to see what he can do to help, he sees six firemen collecting the bodies. He immediately volunteers to help. Even though he has a ride out of town, he decides to stay. Carrying the remains of 78 people changes his life forever. He will now dedicate his life to sound the alarm about climate change.

HOMELAND PACIFICATION

While A.G. was gathering bodies, the U.S. Marines were beginning a massive deployment to Leyte. Defense Secretary Chuck Hagel issued a directive to U.S. Pacific Command to deploy rescue teams, helicopters to be used for airlifts, and cargo planes. They came, "at the request of Philippine armed forces, with P-3 Orion surveillance planes to help," they said, to "calculate the destruction and look for survivors." KC-130 cargo planes came from Japan, as did MV-22 Osprey aircraft, shaped like a cargo plane but with propellers, half-helicopter, half-plane. Assessment teams from USAID were issuing reports indicating that 90 percent of the housing was gone in some locations, and the cities of Tacloban and Ormoc were "wiped out."[5] President Obama said that he knew the "incredible resiliency of the Philippine people," adding, "I am confident that the spirit of the *bayanihan* will see you through this tragedy."[6] *Bayanihan* is a Filipino word that refers to the spirit of communal unity, work, and cooperation to achieve a particular goal. Maybe Obama didn't see it, but he should have. The *bayanihan*—in

terms of grassroots assistance and organizing—was going to be met with surveillance and military force.

Regarding the military operation, a U.S. embassy official later told me at a Manila restaurant, "There is no organization better able to deliver relief than the U.S. armed forces." There is nobody, he said, "quicker and better."

"Let's face it," the official told me in a moment of startling frankness, trying to explain that murky intersection where climate crises, militarization, and humanitarian missions become one, "soldiers landing on the beach do humanitarian missions the same way as soldiers landing on the beach to kill people."

As is well known, the U.S. military has a long relationship of colonial subjugation with the region, since the Philippine-American war in the late 19th century, a slaughter with a death toll between 250,000 and a million people. In some places U.S. soldiers set up "reconcentration areas," where the soldiers corralled members of the civilian population into "villages" surrounded by wire fences to prevent the Filipino soldiers from getting support. An estimated 100,000 people died in the camps. Outside these areas, the U.S. Army hunted down and killed Filipino guerrillas. U.S. General Douglas MacArthur called Filipinos an "inferior race."[7]

Less known is what historian Alfred McCoy reveals in his book *Policing America's Empire: The United States, the Philippines, and the Rise of the Surveillance State*; that the backbone of today's U.S. homeland security state was first tested, perfected, and exported from the Philippines. At the beginning of the book, McCoy describes the "15-year pacification

campaign" that the U.S. waged in the Philippines, during which time "its colonial security agencies fused domestic data management with foreign police techniques to forge a new weapon—a powerful intelligence apparatus that first contained and then crushed Filipino resistance. In the aftermath of this successful pacification, some of these clandestine innovations migrated homeward, silently and invisibly, to change the face of American internal security."[8]

To explain how this worked, McCoy correlates the U.S. invasion of the Philippines in 1899 with that of Iraq in 2003. A photograph published in April 2007 showed U.S. soldiers scanning the retina of an Iraqi that turned out to be one part of a massive Pentagon operation that collected iris scans and over one million Iraqi fingerprints in preparation for the deployment of "collapsible labs," which would then be linked by satellite to a biometric database in West Virginia. McCoy quoted the inventor of this "lab," who said: "A war fighter needs to know one of three things. Do I let him go? Keep him? Or shoot him on the spot?"[9]

Such eye and fingerprint biometric technology is currently in use at airports in New York City and Washington, D.C., and at the Otay Mesa, California, border crossing. The U.S. Department of Homeland Security plans to expand the program to 20 of the busiest airports in the country. It is also used for outbound pedestrian traffic.

In *Policing America's Empire*, McCoy quotes political theorist Max Weber, who famously said that a nation state is "a human community that (successfully) claims the *monopoly of legitimate use of physical force* within a given territory."[10] But McCoy made a crucial observation regarding one of the

important foundations of the modern homeland security state: "By emphasizing physical force, admittedly an important attribute, [Weber] overlooked a subtle yet significant facet of political power—the modern state's use of coercion not to enforce brute compliance but to extract information for heightened levels of social control."

At the lethal front lines of global warming, the now well-developed homeland security apparatus has come around again to the Philippines. The country has become a kind of proving ground for dealing with a world fraught with ecological disaster, a sort-of laboratory of "social control." Here the world can see the military-homeland security apparatus fire up in the aftermath of a superstorm using the rhetoric of aid and assistance, and then point its pacification arsenal at movements from below that challenge the status quo, that are trying to create a new world under new rules.

GRASSROOTS ORGANIZING AT THE CLIMATE FRONTLINES

Alfred Posadas stood on the mass grave next to the church to reenact what happened the morning of November 7, 2013, in Bislig, a community located on the Pacific coast just south of Tacloban. The night before, people gathered in the open-air church with a white tile floor to pray that the typhoon would change course. As Posadas talked, the murmur of waves a quarter mile away sounded like the rhythmic breathing of the planet. However, when he described the morning of the typhoon, Posadas spoke of waves so massive that they almost defied my capacity to imagine them, as if they could only be drawn by an artist or caricatured.

Posadas, who wore a black jacket with a Tasmanian devil ironed onto the back, depicted the day in vivid detail. He described how at one point people cowered in the church as the sound of rumbling outside kept getting louder, like an approaching freight train. "If you dared to look up, you could see the swirling, violent winds ripping up everything in their way." A tornado, he thought. "All you can do is close your eyes," he said in Tagalog. One man, he described, was sucked into the sky. "The wind," he said, "carried him away." But that was not the most horrific moment. Nor was it the moment when family members of a Philippine American woman tied her with thick rope to an iron post so she wouldn't be swept away, or when sharp-edged sheets of metal roofing began flying through the air. One man, Posadas said, had his head sliced open so "you can see his brain through the wound." Listening to Posadas talk was the first time I connected the raw, brutal violence of war directly with climate change.

Another man was trying to run to the church from the school, which was designated an evacuation site even though it was practically on the coast and now was completely blown apart and inundated with floodwater. He didn't see the metal sheet coming. It was flying through the air like shrapnel from artillery fire. The storm drove the metal into his thigh like a knife. "It went right through the bone," Posadas said. That man died later that day. But even that wasn't the most horrific thing, Posadas explained, now swept up in the descriptions, and still situated on the mass graves outside the church.

The most horrific part, he said, was the aftermath. When the sun came back out it revealed a level of decimation only

comparable to a scene from a war zone. Houses crushed, mere splinters flattened to the earth in a landscape of headless, bent palm trees. The devastation was worse than if a hydrogen bomb had been dropped. There was no food. There was no water. Contaminated water submerged the rice supplies with debris and soil and sand. Survivors found a broken pipe that was leaking yellow, brownish water that they boiled to drink. It was like the fetid black, bacteria-infested water that people sometimes drink out of desperation in the desert while attempting to furtively enter the United States. No food, water, or assistance arrived in Bislig for at least a week.

And so, as in most disaster scenarios across the globe, people organized. They cleaned the sludge off the rice as best they could and boiled it in the filthy yellow water. They ate this gross, pasty, tasteless stuff for five full days. People did not fight with each other. They did not struggle over resources. They searched for sustenance in the homes and stores that were not completely obliterated. Everything they found that was edible was cooked and shared. No one was hoarding, as the security projections insinuated that the poor would do. Posadas and others in the community began to organize a group that would walk toward Tacloban, where the warehouses were, to search for food, rice, and sardines. They knew the military would be deployed to prevent "looting." One of the first locations where the military set up, for example, was Robinson's Place, a huge air-conditioned mall in the center of town, with hip department stores like Oxygen, SwissTech, and Surfer's Paradise. The storms of climate change, as always, revealed priorities, the wounded world of acute inequalities, through its militarized internal borders.

The prevalent rumor in Bislig was that the soldiers would arrive with shoot-to-kill orders, as had happened many times in the past. Media reports had hyperbolic and unsubstantiated accounts of famished, armed people filling the streets and stopping aid trucks at gunpoint. Schoolteacher Andrew Pomada told Agence France Presse, "Tacloban is totally destroyed. Some people are losing their minds from hunger or from losing their families. People are becoming violent. They are looting business establishments, the malls, just to find food, rice and milk. . . . I am afraid that in one week, people will be killing from hunger."[11]

For Bislig, however, and many other communities, organizing searches for food were appropriate emergency responses. A small group of survivors walked toward Tacloban, where, Posadas told me, they began to see the dead. I asked Posadas how many bodies he saw with his own eyes. He paused. "Too many," he said in Tagalog. "Too much," he repeated, shaking his head as if trying to shake the image from his brain. He looked to his father, also in T-shirt and shorts, who crouched beside him on the grassy graves of the 26 who died in Bislig. "Too much," he said again, and then, he said, maybe they saw 200 bodies along the road on their way to the warehouse. There were bodies floating in the water. "You had no choice but to step on dead bodies," Posadas said. As they walked they kept hearing the stories of death. They passed a place named San Joaquin where the typhoon killed 300 children. In another place, the storm claimed the lives of 27 people from the same family. After time in the water, sun, and elements, the skin would slip off the bodies when survivors attempted to move them. It

was like "lechon," Posadas said, regretting the metaphor of a roasted suckling pig, but that was all he could come up with.

Despite all the horror, the group successfully returned with rice, water, and sardines for the traumatized community. Indeed, like most communities, they turned to the *bayanihan*—first locally, and then with a broader movement of survivors called People Surge. As we shall see, this sort of organizing for justice would concern the State more than looting.

At the same time, back in Tacloban, A.G. Saño continued to help the group of firemen recover people's remains. There were bodies everywhere, and as happened in Bislig, dogs began feeding on many of them. Bodies that were recovered went to mass graves. As A.G. worked, he communicated to his brother, Yeb, who was in Warsaw at the UN Climate Summit, that he was okay. A.G. still hadn't yet heard from his other family members.

Yeb Saño said that it felt as though something took him over as he spoke in the crowded hall, with hundreds of delegates sitting in long rows behind laptop computers.

"Now I wish to speak on a more personal note. Super-typhoon Haiyan made landfall in my own family's hometown. And the devastation is staggering. I struggle to even find words to describe the images we see on the news coverage. And I struggle to find words to describe how I feel about losses. Up to this point I anguish as I wait for words from my very own relatives. What gives me great strength and great relief is that my own brother indicated to us that he had survived the onslaught. In the last few days he has been gathering bodies of the dead with his own two hands.

He is very hungry and weary as supplies find it difficult to arrive in the hardest-hit area."[12]

The official death count was 6,300, but many believe it was closer to 10,000, if not more. The lethal scope of the typhoon's impact probably wasn't known as Saño spoke: 4 million people displaced from their homes, and 14 to 16 million people impacted in some way.

Even when Saño was on script, his voice lost any semblance of the dispassionate tone so common as such gatherings, and sounded instead as if he were having a painful epiphany. In the video of his presentation, you can see people gabbing at the start, but as Saño's emotional momentum increased, he had command of the room's attention. There was no way you could listen to him and not feel the immediate urgency of how the climate crisis is impacting lives, families, communities, and the world.

"What my country is going through as a result of this extreme climate event is madness. The climate crisis is madness. We. Can. Stop. This. Madness."[13]

Up to that point, there had been 18 summits, but humans and their institutions and corporations continued to increase the amount of greenhouse pollution they dumped into the atmosphere. Maybe Saño was mustering inspiration from the Australian group he told me about from a past summit that showed up to a closed-door negotiation in shorts and T-shirts with jokes, making a mockery of the negotiations themselves. Or indignation from all the times the United States had to make "another phone call" but was simply stalling, as it had for each of the 18 summits. But mainly Saño was thinking about the suffering of the people

in Tacloban, the people in Bislig trekking through the devastation in search of food, his brother piling up black body bags in mass graves.

"I speak for my delegation. But more than that, I speak for the countless people who will no longer be able to speak for themselves after perishing from the storm. I also speak for those who have been orphaned by this tragedy. I also speak for the people now racing against time to save survivors and alleviate the suffering of the people affected by the disaster."[14]

Yeb Saño was not planning to improvise or make any big declaration, nor was he planning to announce his fast. In fact, the night before he had gone to the grocery store and stocked up on two weeks of food. "There are moments when I feel like I should rally behind climate advocates who peacefully confront those historically responsible for the current state of our climate. These selfless people who fight coal, expose themselves to freezing temperatures, or block oil pipelines. . . . I'm in solidarity with my countrymen who are struggling to find food back home, and with my brother, who has not had food for the last three days." Yeb declared that he would fast for the climate, for the entire summit, "until a meaningful outcome is in sight."[15]

When he finished speaking he lowered his head and began to weep. A rousing standing ovation quickly crescendoed as people stood up, one by one, and clapped. It was as if in a heartbeat Saño had moved his faith from professional negotiators to ordinary people who were putting their bodies were on the line. It mattered little to him if by making the case for a more urgent environmental activism,

he might lose his job as climate negotiator (and he would). After all, according to a report by the organization Global Witness, "the environment is emerging as a new battleground for human rights."[16] There was a divide between official reform that left the polluting system intact, and the transformation to something new. There and then, Yeb Saño seemed to cross that turbulent border to where the real climate battle lay.

Perhaps this divide was best summed up in Bislig on the same day that Albert Posadas described the horrific scene at the church. I was on the beach talking with local farmer Marissa Cabaljao, the secretary general of People Surge, next to a large, splintered fishing boat that Haiyan had heaved onto the beach in 2013. I had met with Cabaljao the day before in the small office of People Surge in Tacloban, and she arranged the trip to Bislig. I wanted to know what Cabaljao thought about the aid that came into the region after Haiyan. The countries providing assistance since the typhoon—mainly European countries and the United States—weren't shy about putting up signs giving themselves credit. I wanted to know what she thought, since these same countries were both historic high-level greenhouse polluters and current lavish spenders on militarizing their borders.

There were examples of such signs right where we were in Bislig. As we walked around witnessing the devastation that was still evident, there were two small, green stores that stood out, with a sturdy architectural style distinct from all the others. Both stores had the same exact self-congratulatory signs. Though in two distinct locations, both stores had

signs reading: THIS SARI-SARI STORE WAS MADE POSSIBLE BY THE GENEROUS SUPPORT OF THE AMERICAN PEOPLE THROUGH THE UNITED STATES AGENCY FOR INTERNATIONAL DEVELOPMENT (USAID) IN PARTNERSHIP WITH PROCTER & GAMBLE AND COCA-COLA AND IN COORDINATION WITH THE TANAUAN MUNICIPAL GOVERNMENT.

Marissa Cabaljao cut straight to the chase, not stalling at the usual, almost cliché response of pundits and presidents that you can't attribute any one storm such as Yolanda—the local name for Haiyan—to climate change. Her answer was direct: "Yolanda happened because of the big industrialized countries. We at People Surge didn't say thank you for this. Because you have to pay. . . . You are the reason—big industrialized countries—why Yolanda came to the Philippines."

THE PEOPLE ARE SURGING

Jefferson Custodio had a way of driving to the basket. The thin, dark-haired farmer, 25 years old, played and practiced in the *barangay* hall—a neighborhood center and town hall—in the community of Carigara. His team won the regional championship in 2014, the year after Typhoon Haiyan. The wind pummeled and collapsed the house where he lived with his mother, father, and sister. They evacuated. Even though they were several miles away from the coast, the rising water almost reached their home, devouring everything in its way. It destroyed crops. It destroyed the coconut palms that take 5 to 10 years to produce their first harvest. The wind knocked them all down, scattering them on the ground like headless corpses. It destroyed the livelihoods of a place

where over 80 percent of the population were either fisher folk or farmers.

It was a struggle before Haiyan, but at least people could get food. After the storm, all across the region there was nothing. No food, no electricity. This propelled Jefferson to join the People Surge network of Typhoon Haiyan survivors who provided humanitarian aid and political action around climate change. Every day, Custodio traveled the countryside distributing farm tools, seeds, and seedlings throughout district eight, a verdant, hilly region on the west side of Leyte Island. Custodio was dedicated. Sometimes he was gone for several days.

In May of 2014, the Philippine military, 19th Infantry Battalion, began to camp at the *barangay* hall where Jefferson played basketball. At that point, they were fanning out, camping at a number of *barangays* throughout the region filled with farmers known for their history of organizing. "Our mission in the *barangays*," a representative from the 19th Infantry Battalion told my colleague Alex Devoid and me in an email, "is to facilitate delivery of basic services in partnership with the Local Government and other stakeholders."

One day after playing basketball, some soldiers approached Custodio and tried to recruit him. They asked why he was doing work for free, when he could be with them and earn a salary. According to Custodio's family, he rejected the offer. The military took a picture of him from the front and from the side, "as if he were wanted," a friend and fellow member of People Surge, Dolly (not her real name) told me. Custodio had been entered into the short list.

Soldiers from the battalion followed Custodio to his

house. They began to monitor his movements. At this point, the military was moving around the community and doing interrogations in households, "as if they were census takers," Rodolfo Custodio, Jefferson's father, sadly joked. They were roaming through the countryside, "making it difficult for us to get to some of our farmland." On the roads, the military set up checkpoints to stop vehicles and interrogate drivers and passengers, all while cradling high-powered rifles in their hands, much as in a border zone.

But Jefferson never saw it coming. According to Dolly, "He has too much of a pure heart." Besides, she said, he had no enemies in the region. Why would it even occur to him that his life was in danger?

Perhaps the real issue was the grassroots organizing that he was a part of. The People Surge had showed their power in January when 12,000 members and supporters marched through Tacloban.

Climate change exposed a world of vast inequalities that had long been reality: a world where the rich—who easily cross borders—sail on yachts and refugees drown in rickety boats, a world of vast mansions and clapboard houses, worlds where CEOs make 400 times more than their companies' workers, and pollute more than anyone else. Worlds that were completely unacceptable to people such as Jefferson Custodio and Marissa Cabaljio, like many in the People Surge, whose homes and livelihoods were drowned in the intensifying hurricanes. The People Surge's critique began with an analysis of the official disaster relief effort, then deepened into the intersecting issues of economics, colonialism, and militarism.

From a global perspective, the People Surge is one example of many. Across the world, at any given time, there are thousands of groups, organizations, and individual people putting forth proposals and working toward a new world that challenges this lethal status quo, one that promotes a discourse of "security" yet protects only a chosen few, and in this case, the polluters of the highest magnitude. These grassroots activist groups, community organizations, indigenous groups, social movements, scholars, and artists propose a wide range of tactics, from applying pressure on elected officials to nonviolent civil disobedience, to armed revolt. It is that "power from below" that, as disaster scholar Kathleen Tierney puts it, makes the elite fear the "disruption of the social order, challenges to their legitimacy." Thus, the cultivation and perpetuation of the "panic myth" that people freak out during disasters, when the real fear is of a true shift in this political, economic, and social order.[17]

As Rutgers sociologist Lee Clarke writes of Tierney's work: "Disaster myths are not politically neutral, but rath er work systematically to the advantage of the elites. Elites cling to the panic myth because to acknowledge the truth of the situation would lead to very different policy prescriptions. . . . The chief prescription is, she notes, that the best way to prepare for disasters is by following the command and control model, the embodiment of which [in the United States] is the federal Department of Homeland Security."[18]

A provocative framing for the emerging climate conflict comes from sociologist Alf Gunvald Nilsen, who describes a sort of "battle" between two camps: the "social movements from below" and the "social movements from above." The

social movements from below serve to remove "constraints" on human needs and capacities—by methods ranging from campaigns to curtail obstructions to basic services such as housing, health, or education, to the kind of grassroots survival organizing seen in the wake of disaster situations such as Haiyan.

The social movement from above "aims at the maintenance or modification of a dominant structure of entrenched needs and capacities in ways that reproduce and/or extend the power of those groups and its hegemonic position within a given social formation."[19]

Hence, emerging climate battles are being waged not just in the Philippines, but everywhere. Lines are being drawn between homeland security apparatuses and the people they protect; between social movements from above, including the very corporations most responsible for vast greenhouse pollution, and those from below that defy them, like the grassroots organizing of the People Surge, the "looting" expeditions of Posadas et al. in Bislig, or the countless millions who travel across lines of division without authorization, including climate refugees.

In other words, whether in the post-typhoon Philippines or on the U.S.-Mexico border, homeland security enforcement keeps these two groups apart. And if you dare defy these sanctimonious divisions, if you dare storm the wall, as Custodio was to find out, you may be putting your life in danger.

THE DISPLACEMENT PROVING GROUND

When the People Surge formed, a group of Typhoon Haiyan survivors traveled to Manila to ask for 40,000 Philippine pesos (a little less than $1,000 USD) for relief. President Benigno Aquino questioned why they came to the capital looking for money "instead of tending to their families in Eastern Visayas." Rehabilitation czar Panfil Lacson accused them of "being used by communists to destabilize the government." Marissa Cabaljao told me that they accused the movement of typhoon survivors of being affiliated with the New People's Army, a serious accusation since the government has been in an armed conflict with the insurgent group since the 1970s. Such accusations justified violence. Cabaljao told me that she, like Jefferson Custodio, was followed and monitored by the military.

"Do you ever fear for your life?" I asked her.

"No. If I'm going to die helping the survivors, I'm okay dying like that."

One of People Surge's founders, Dr. Elfleda Bautista, explained to the *Philippine Inquirer*, in response to the governmental accusations, that People Surge started in Tacloban and then the "movement spread to other municipalities, villages and even provinces."[20] Bautista explained that it was an alliance of farmers and ordinary people, including people from universities and religious organizations. Jefferson, a farmer from an outside province, showed just how far and wide the movement had spread.

The first demand of People Surge was the meager 40,000 pesos, Bautista said, because "the government

assistance has not reached us." They needed resources to send children to school. They needed resources for seeds on the farms. They needed resources because food prices had inflated 50 to 100 percent. They were the million displaced, who wanted to build their homes back up again. They did not want to migrate elsewhere.

Instead of offering meaningful aid, as Rodolfo Custodio, Jefferson's father, put it, "We got the military."

When we talked at the restaurant in Manila, the U.S. Embassy official told me that a "security situation" could arise from anything, especially a natural disaster. If there were a sudden disaster, he told me, it could result in "confusion and unrest." He said there were forces that might want to take advantage of the situation, and that in Mindanao, in the southern Philippines, there were "Islamic groups, indigenous groups." A group, he said, might move its agenda forward in a climate situation. The People's Army was an example of such a group. And this military wing of the communist party, deemed a terrorist group since the Cold War, was one of two groups specifically emphasized by U.S. Special Forces for counterinsurgency trainings with the Philippine army. The other was the Moro separatists, a secessionist movement in Mindanao.

These trainings in the Philippine proving ground—a powerful glimpse into how "the social movement from above" worked in a climate disaster scenario—were part of an upsurge of U.S. military aid to the Philippines following 9/11, after the George W. Bush administration called the country the "second front" of the global terror wars.[21] The

over $500 million of aid between 2001 and 2010 included helicopters, ships, and communications gear, much of it U.S. military surplus.

After that there was the "Asia Pivot." In 2011 President Obama told the Australian Parliament that "the United States is a Pacific power."[22] It was a move to make the region a top geopolitical priority, and would involve transferring military presence into the region from the Middle East. "We are here to stay," Obama said. The United States has enormous resources dedicated to the region, tens of thousands of troops, huge aircraft carrier groups, and mutual military treaties with South Korea and Japan. In the Philippines, the military budget went from $10 million to $30 million to $50 million from 2011 to 2013, following Obama's announcement and before Haiyan struck.

In a way, this was just a continuation of what had been true the entire 20th century. After World War II and the occupation, the United States operated 23 military bases in the Philippines. One was the Subic Bay Naval Base, which during the Vietnam War became one of the most important U.S. logistics bases in the world. Another prominent site was Clark Air Base, which, during its peak in the 1970s, had a population of 15,000.

But times have changed: in 2012, the same year the United States killed 15 people with a drone strike on the island of Jolo in Mindanao, and that Typhoon Bopha hit that southern state hard, U.S. Pacific Command ran a joint exercise with the Philippine military focusing specifically on disaster response. Commander Samuel Locklear said in a later interview that in the Asian Pacific a significant upheaval as

result of a warming planet "is probably the most likely thing that is going to happen," more than the feared Chinese or North Korean nuclear threats. Only months before Haiyan hit, the four-star general said, "You have the real potential here in the not-too-distant future of nations displaced by rising sea-level, [and] weather patterns are more severe than they have been in the past." Locklear warned that if it all goes badly "you could have hundreds of thousands or millions of people displaced and then security will start to crumble pretty quickly."[23]

The joint Philippine-U.S. exercise in Zambales looked like an act of preparation for what Locklear was alluding to—not a humanitarian mission, but a war scene straight from military crisis projections, and the description of the U.S. Embassy official in Manila. The idea was to create "interoperability" between the two forces "in the event of a disaster." However, U.S. Marines and their Filipino counterparts, wearing combat helmets and with their faces covered in green and brown war paint, stormed a "hostile shore." It was a disaster exercise, but they stormed the shore as if the climate-displaced people were not a population in need of assistance, but a mortal threat. It was these people, like the victims of Typhoon Haiyan and members of the People Surge, who would be desperate, hungry, dangerous, and eager to change the very polluting system these joint militaries, their commanders, and the political and economic elite who controlled them wanted to protect. It was an awesome and raw pacification exercise and a prelude to 8,000 U.S. troops landing on Philippine shores in the wake of Haiyan, opening the door to even greater U.S. influence in the region.

But the team presence was already felt. In just 2006, under a U.S.-instigated post-9/11 counterinsurgency strategy, the Philippine government killed one activist every 36 hours. The Melo Commission, the Philippine government's investigative task force, noted that victims were generally unarmed, alone or in small groups, and gunned down by two or more masked forces on motorcycles.

And in 2014 the People Surge did not get the 40,000 pesos it asked for.

"DO I LET HIM GO? KEEP HIM? OR SHOOT HIM ON THE SPOT?"

Jefferson Custodio never saw it coming. Maybe he should have known. A human rights organization known as Karatapan accused the Philippine government of waging war against a country of typhoon survivors, and especially those doing grassroots organizing. The first killing in 2014 was of Marcelo Monterona, a survivor of Typhoon Bopha in 2012. He and his community had begun to do rehabilitation projects. Using .45 caliber weapons, gunmen shot Monterona through the left side of his mouth. Monterona tried to escape from his vehicle, but the assailants shot him several more times before he could get to safety.

In August 2014, the same month Custodio found himself surrounded by masked men on motorcycles, seven other activists were targeted and killed in the Philippines. Gildegardo Hernandez, a leader of a farmer's organization who was doing relief work after Typhoon Glenda, was shot dead by assailants on motorcycles on August 7, 2014. On August 14, indigenous activist and leader Marcel Lambon was shot

and killed. Like Jefferson, he was under close government surveillance and had been interrogated by the military. He was also branded as a supporter of the New People's Army. According to Karapatan, who documented 229 such extra-judicial killings between 2010 and 2014, when small farmers organized their own relief efforts, they were often accused of association with the New People's Army.

The Philippines is just one example of a locale where the environment has become the new human rights battle-ground. According to Global Witness, an organization that campaigns to expose "the hidden links between demand for natural resources, corruption, armed conflict and environmental destruction," in 2015 alone, 185 environmental organizers were killed by the state, corporate security forces, or contract killers in places like Brazil and Colombia, DR Congo and India. "For every killing we document, many others go unreported," campaigner Billy Kyte told Reuters.[24]

The people are indeed surging, storming the wall. Not only in the Philippines, in every corner of the globe. There are countless examples of community efforts resisting environmentally harmful projects, including big-business gas pipelines, mines, and dams. In 2016, one of the most prominent cases was that of renowned environmental activist and Goldman Prize winner Berta Cáceres, gunned down in her home in Honduras by assailants with potential connections to U.S.-trained Honduran special forces, after leading the fight in her community against a dam project. In 2015, more environmentalists were killed in her home country than in any other country in the world. And in January 2017, Global Witness published a report showing that Honduras was

the "deadliest country per capita for land and environmental defenders."[25]

Like Honduras, the Philippines is also "one of the most dangerous places in the world to be an environmental or land defender."[26] This was the case both before and after Haiyan, and all signs show that this will continue to be the case under the President Duterte, who, as reported by Ana B. Santos, "once bragged that he was committed to killing 100,000 criminals and dumping so many of their corpses into the Manila Bay that the fishes would 'grow fat' feeding on them."[27] Indeed, the same military that had Jefferson Custodio under intense surveillance, continues to this day to monitor Eastern Visayas, under Duterte's orders.

"President Duterte, your military troops are illegally occupying our villages, harassing and vilifying our fellow survivors, and disrupting our still struggling livliehoods,"[28] the People Surge's Elfleda Bautista stated. The concern is valid: in the first five months of the Duterte presidency in 2016, more than 4,500 people were killed by his administration in what can only be termed a drug war rampage. This won praise from U.S. president Donald Trump, who said the Filipino strongman was conducting his drug war the "right way."[29]

On August 24, 2014, Custodio was going to the warehouse to pick up supplies. He parked his vehicle and was walking across the narrow paved street to the gate when first heard the buzz of the motorcycle. His other companion was already inside the warehouse. The motorcycle stopped. It had no license plate. The driver was masked. Remember, Jefferson was a committed activist, a humanitarian, and a

happy-go-lucky man. Despite the military surveillance, he didn't think there was a high risk of being assassinated. And remember what a war fighter "needs to know," as the inventor of collapsible biometric labs used in Iraq told author Alfred McCoy in his book *Policing America's Empire*: "Do I let him go? Keep him? Or shoot him on the spot?" The driver raised his arm and pointed his gun. He shot Jefferson three times. With the bullets lodged in his body, Jefferson ran through the outside gate into the warehouse area. He fell onto a soft grassy patch, where he lay bleeding to death. Behind him was a palm tree, its leaves drooping down.

REMOVE THE PRESENCE OF THE MILITARY

I went to Carigara, Leyte, to talk with Jefferson's father Rodolfo and other family members. Getting there, I traversed a landscape that was still suffering. On Roxas Boulevard, which ran along the bay in Tacloban, there were hundreds, if not thousands, of people lined up to get a 100-pound bag of rice donated by a Buddhist church in Taiwan. You could see people's muscles strain as they struggled to lift the large white bags and carry them off on their backs. Across the street, other people gathered in front of the semi-destroyed auditorium known as the "Astrodome." A group of women waiting in the grass for their numbers to be called told me that the storm had left them homeless. The government was granting 30,000 Philippine pesos (about US$600) to those who had "complete damage," but up to this point, after a full year of waiting, the women had not received a single penny.

As I entered the countryside outside of Tacloban on a small bus, I could see more destroyed houses and war-like

destruction. At one bus stop, written on the concrete post was the message SOS WE NEED FOOD. It was evidently written at the height of the disaster, and remained at the bus stop carrying the same sense of urgency as if the typhoon had just happened, testament to an aftermath that wouldn't be going away for a long time.

I traveled to Ormoc City, where I met Dolly from the People Surge. Three of us, including documentary filmmaker and journalist Alex Devoid, piled behind a driver on a single motorcycle, the preferred taxi in the area, and rode down narrow two-lane roads crowded with bikes transporting people in sidecars. We passed the warehouse where Jefferson was shot, and the grassy patch where he took his last breath. We walked through a verdant landscape of hills and homes until arriving at the compound of small houses where Jefferson lived. His parents and grandmother greeted us at a long picnic table. From the first question, I could see that they were still deep in the process of grieving.

"Jefferson is a good boy, he was my only son," his father Rodolfo said right off the bat.

I had come here following a story about climate change and militarization, but I don't think I knew entirely what this meant, knew it with my body and my bones, until this interview with Rodolfo, father of an assassinated activist. The interview was difficult from the start, it was obvious that they were sharing painful memories with me. Our talk was filled with many long silences and awkward pauses that at first I tried to fill with questions, but then I stopped, and gave them the space they needed, gave them the space for their grief. Rodolfo wore a purple shirt and cut-off jeans.

Rodolfo's mother, wearing a white flowered dress, with short gray hair, hovered about, as did a slew of little kids who would lean against the wooden table and quietly listen to the sad sounds of Rodolfo mourning.

At one point the assassinated man's father asked: "This interview, how can it help me?" He held my gaze across the table for a long time after he asked the question, his eyes brimming with tears. Behind him I could see the hills rolling all the way to the west coast of Leyte, and the distant ocean. It was down there, after the crops were ravaged, that he and his family—including Jefferson—were forced to forage for food, mainly root vegetables and snails. It was that same beautiful landscape where, he told us, the military had been roaming since they came into the region, patrolling, making it impossible to get out to some of the planted crops. They were roaming and interrogating, holding their high-powered rifles, "as if we were in a war."

Finally, he asked me, "Can I question you? Will there be justice for my Jefferson?" Tears began streaming down his cheeks.

"I am a poor man," he said. He told me that he didn't have the funds needed to pursue the case. The cost of transportation alone was creating a burden on the family. He knew that the murder, like so many others, wouldn't be solved. He said he didn't know what to do. I asked him what form of justice he'd like to see.

"Remove the presence of the military so there are no additional incidents."

This raw grief and pain was all I needed to know, in that moment, about climate and militarization. At that moment,

the mourning came from Rodolfo, but it could have been from any one of the people that gathered around us as we talked. He took out a picture of his son, who was slightly crouched and kneeling, with a slight, possibly mischievous, smile on his face. You could tell by the way Rodolfo placed the picture on the wooden table that this was a father who loved his child and missed him profoundly.

I remembered the Tzotzil Maya community of Acteal that I had just visited a month before in Chiapas, Mexico. There I met a man named Juan Carlos who lost eight members of his family, including his parents, in the 1997 massacre. He told me a story of his mother falling to the ground in a rain of bullets, and his father diving to hug her. When he hugged her, he realized that his beloved had died in his arms. He rose to his feet and said, "Forgive them for they do not know what they are doing," and pointed to the masked men with the guns, who shot him dead. When Juan Carlos stopped, I didn't know what to say, except that I was swept with emotion.

When Rodolfo stopped, silence fell between us. I thought about my pregnant wife on the other side of the globe, and that I was about to become a father. I didn't know what to say. But I did know that climate change would never be theoretical or abstract to me again. It would never be a term filled only with reports and statistics, however important they may be. From that moment on, before all else, the human face of climate change would be that of a father mourning the tragic assassination of his son, tears silently streaking down his cheeks, on a beautiful Philippine afternoon.

SEVEN

PEOPLE'S PILGRIMAGE: TOWARD A SOLUTION OF CROSS-BORDER SOLIDARITY

I tell you this to break your heart, by which I mean only that it break open and never close again to the rest of the world.

——Mary Oliver

A little over two years after A.G. Saño survived Typhoon Haiyan, he and his brother Yeb (I will use their first names to distinguish between the two of them), along with 20 or so other people, finished a 1,000-mile walk known as the People's Pilgrimage. The 60-day walk began in Rome with a blessing of Pope Francis, proceeded through the snowy Alps, and ended in Paris at the commencement of the 21st United Nations climate summit in 2015, deemed humankind's most important meeting ever.

Dressed in winter coats, A.G. and Yeb embraced each other in front one of Paris's popular outdoor cafés, where many people sat enjoying a cup of coffee despite the chilly

weather. The purpose of the People's Pilgrimage was to respond "from the human heart to the climate crisis."[1] The other pilgrims began to give each other weary hugs to celebrate, having accomplished their goal of walking all the way to Paris from Rome. Even I felt a sense of accomplishment while watching members of the group embrace, even though I had only walked the last 12-kilometer leg of their journey.

Suddenly a man emerged from the café, thrusting forward a copy of that day's newspaper with a headline picture of marching French soldiers. The man was aggressively extending the paper, putting it in front of people's eyes, putting it in front of the cameras documenting the moment of arrival. The picture was of an event commemorating those killed in the November 13 attacks in Paris, when 129 people were killed and many more injured. The man started to talk loudly at the chatting, embracing pilgrims. He talked passionately. He talked about terrorism. He told the Filipino group that people here in France were not concerned about climate change. He told them that the people of France were concerned about terrorism. Most of them, however, due to their jubilation and perhaps unable to understand French, ignored the man's outburst.

The pilgrims were already well aware of the declaration made by French president François Hollande on the same day of the brutal attacks. The nationwide state of emergency was the first one the country had declared since 1961, a policy that harks back to the Algerian war in the 1950s. The state of emergency gave the authorities exceptional powers. They could create lines of division and limit the movement of people. They could forbid mass gatherings, such as the

many planned around the coming climate summit. They could establish what they call "security zones,"[2] or enhanced surveillance zones, to monitor people. They could close places such as bars and museums and other institutions. And the police could act without judicial oversight; for example, they could conduct house searches or put people under house arrest at any time. In many ways it was like a border zone: you were suspected of being guilty until proven innocent. Paris, in November and December 2015, was where the climate justice movement met the militarized counter-terror apparatus.

When I first met the participants of the People's Pilgrimage, just outside Paris in a place called Choisy-le-Roi, the organizers were nervous. They had walked more than 850 miles, but the last seven miles coming into Paris were going to be the most challenging. They called the police for advance authorization, but were informed that France had banned political demonstrations, and they would risk arrest. Yeb Saño's initial reaction was to compare the situation to "martial law," when dictator Ferdinand Marcos ruled the Philippines with an iron fist, declaring that he was going to govern by public decree, enacting a nighttime curfew and banning public demonstrations.

Yeb's real first name, Nadarev, is the acronym for National Democratic Revolution, the group that his parents were involved with and whose political actions had landed them in prison for year. In a way, for both Yeb and A.G. Saño, the final leg of the 60-day pilgrimage from Rome was the end of a longer journey. The larger odyssey had begun with Yeb's forceful, emotional appeal to stop the madness

at the Warsaw Summit at the same moment that A.G. was helping gather the bodies in the aftermath of Typhoon Haiyan. The odyssey included Yeb's removal by the Philippine government from the negotiating team before the Lima Summit in December 2014.

After that, Yeb tweeted, "They can silence my mouth. But they can't silence my soul,"[3] crossing the line from the official climate negotiator to the front lines of climate-change activism.

In Choisy-le-Roi, the organizers' hesitance was surprising to me, because I had already been in Paris for a week and a half. I had arrived three days after the coordinated attacks.

There were two occasions when I had a sharp sense of heightened fear, and one of them was November 18, the day that the French National Police were pounding a residence in the Saint-Denis region of the city with 5,000 rounds of artillery. The barrage occurred not far from the Milipol homeland security expo that I was attending. Even though the French government prohibited the historic climate justice march planned for the eve of the summit's inauguration, Milipol proceeded as planned, and, as described in Chapter Four, with a turbocharged buzz. For the security corporations selling products at the expo, all the violence seemed to boost their pitch.

On the third day of the expo, as I was taking in booth after booth of guns, surveillance devices, armored cars, and drones, I reached a point where I couldn't take it any longer. I had to leave. I was in Paris, but I hadn't even seen the city yet. I felt the intense collective grieving. I wanted to commemorate the places that had been attacked, the Casa

Nostra, Le Carillon, La Belle Équipe, and the Bataclan, the historic music venue.

I was told to be cautious on public transportation and to not take the metro. I did so anyhow, boarding a metro B line headed south. A couple of minutes into the ride, the train stopped, the lights went out, and I immediately felt anxious. An announcement came on that an "incident" had occurred. We were near Saint-Denis, where the police were still attacking the residence with full force. Did the "incident" have something to do with that?

Just that morning I had seen footage of the actual November 13 attack, when assailants fired their Kalashnikovs at people in the Casa Nostra restaurant. The glass shattered with brutal force as the wait staff dropped to the floor all at once. And I couldn't get Lina Kolesnikova—the Russian woman from the climate part of the conference who talked about "gates, guards, and guns"—out of my head. In one part of her talk she went on about "soft targets," "the geography of attack," the "hardening" of soft targets, even about the Paris metro system. For a moment I was seized with the Milipol mentality that something terrible was about to happen. But nothing did. In fact, over the next few weeks I noticed the "incident" announcement came regularly. So I made vigils to the attack sites, where I saw bouquets of flowers with drips of water under a soft rain, gently flickering candles, and messages of solidarity and grief.

By the time I met the People's Pilgrimage at Choisy-le-Roi, I was riding the metro regularly and walking through its crowded halls and platforms, like almost everyone else. I went to the equally crowded Champs Élysées

holiday market, where throngs of people ambled amidst spectacular Christmas lights toward the glowing Arc de Triomphe—which made the denial of the pilgrims' passage seem ridiculous. Indeed, members of the People's Pilgrimage were not afraid of terrorists, but they feared the police. Due to the state of emergency in Paris, armed authorities were free to detain and question anyone at will. Yeb Saño's allusion to Filipino martial law during the times of Marcos was not so far-fetched.

In many important ways, the real tension between climate justice and climate security was summed up by the massive differences between the homeland security expo and the People's Pilgrimage: transformation versus fear, solidarity versus the status quo.

On that bitter cold and foggy morning in Choisy-le-Roi, Yeb Saño told me he saw a world "clamoring for change and transformation." We were on the southern outskirts of Paris near Mountrouge, the place where the police had found an explosive belt discarded in a garbage can, presumably from one of the escaping attackers. Given everything going on, the organizers wanted us to proceed in small groups. As we walked along the Boulevard de Stalingrad, you could tell Yeb was more bemused than irritated by the situation, but it was a little of both. There were bare trees in front of us, their branches stark against the cold gray sky. Wet leaves were flattened to the sidewalk as we walked at a fast clip. The organizers wanted to get to central Paris in less than three hours.

"I want to be candid about it. I don't know what's legal or what's not legal with the martial law here. But if they

arrest me for being a pilgrim, then they can do so. I have five cameras pointed at me," Yeb said, "to capture the moment."

Yeb, weighed down with a black winter jacket and a black hat, moved like a person who had been walking for a very long time. He said that the journey he was on was not just political, it was also spiritual.

"It allows you to learn so much about yourself, what you are doing in the world and how you must respond to things that are happening in the world," Yeb said against the sound of cars and buzzing motorcycles.

A.G., wearing a heavy orange winter coat, walked next to Yeb. Both brothers had on glasses. The former climate negotiator said that a pilgrimage "changes you." You begin as one person and you end as another. Along the way you create strong bonds with the people you walk with, "bonds that will stay there forever." The whole ritual of pilgrimage, Yeb said, went back to ancient times, when "there were no planes." He laughed as if to say, how can we begin to fathom such a world. It was "a ritual that every person goes to be transformed."

We walked through the cold streets, past multistory concrete apartment buildings; some of the balconies had clustered Christmas decorations and hanging wreathes, evidence that we were entering the festive season. We passed old cars and a construction site separated from the sidewalk by corrugated metal walls that were tagged with graffiti and put together like rows of crooked teeth. Walking with Yeb and A.G., I didn't forget how deadly these sharp-edged metal sheets had become during Haiyan. Just to be careful, we stopped at every intersection and waited for the lights to

change for us, even if there was no traffic, and even if traffic was stalled and other pedestrians were crossing during the opportunity. Each decision we made was a political one, a strategic response to the state-induced fear that slowly crept into your head.

"I'm a law-abiding rebel," Yeb joked.

Yeb said that the 1,000-mile pilgrimage helped him realize the convergence of all the ideas and experiences he had been absorbing for a long time. It wasn't about viewing the world in strict black-and-white terms, he said. Rather, the journey "gives you a bigger sense of connectedness with others that pushes you to fight for a world with no borders, with no prejudice, with more harmony and caring."

Sometimes, he said, you begin a journey with a negative outlook that we are up against something "really, really vicious." But then you realize it was the "real people"—the people you met along the way, the people in the communities, the people who gave you their beds so you could sleep at night who "give you hope."

"Solidarity is not an alternative, it is not an option, it is our only chance," Yeb told me. "Our only hope of ever moving forward and confronting this climate crisis."

Indeed, climate change doesn't know human political boundaries, it doesn't only occur in one bounded territory and not impact another. However, as Reece Jones wrote in *Violent Borders: Refugees and the Right to Move*, "while climate change is global, its solutions are bounded by state borders and limited by the concept of private property." There are two things that Jones underscores. One is that borders create "pools of exploitable resources, with rules on extraction

and access that differ across territories." The second is the damage "absolute state sovereignty over environmental decisions"[4] does to our collective world. In other words, each country pursues its own interests brings first and foremost, and for countries like the United States, these have been more often than not beholden to a poisonous fossil fuel industry. Trump's "economic nationalism" is a forceful demonstration of this point. As mentioned earlier, on March 29, 2017, President Trump, "flanked by company executives and miners, signed a long-promised executive order . . . to nullify [former president Obama's] climate change efforts and revive the coal industry, effectively erasing whatever gains the United States had made in the international campaign to curb the dangerous heating of the planet."[5]

The problem of global warming doesn't call for the further fortification of borders between countries, between people, or between the rich and the poor. If anything, it calls for a dissolution of those borders. As Yeb passionately stated, what we need most is cross-border hospitality and grassroots solidarity, even with all the messiness.

As we continued walking toward the center of Paris, I was reminded of an annual pilgrimage called the Migrant Trail Walk, a 75-mile, seven-day walk through the Arizona desert, from the border town of Sasabe to Tucson, in commemoration to people who have died crossing. There was a meditation that went along with the walk that I have done on four occasions. Day after day, you would just keep walking even when you felt the pain, the strained muscles, the sweltering heat, the endless chafing between the legs, the burned eyeballs (yes, one year I burned my eyes). Although

it was nowhere near the pain experienced by those who are crossing without enough food, without enough water, and in fear of the Border Patrol and criminal predators, the pain was still there. There was always a part of the walk where I ceased to be only myself and became part of a bigger whole, the bigger community that was walking. All you had to do, every day, was take a step forward, along with everyone else, toward a collective goal. During every walk, there was a point, whether it was day three, day four, or day five, when I would feel a deep solidarity with all those who have walked in these places, those who have lived and those who have died. It becomes a holy journey through an intensely policed landscape and a vast unmarked graveyard.

I sensed the same spirit from Yeb Saño as he spoke to me. He was on a holy journey. A journey that had begun not in Rome but at the moment he experienced a sort of transcendental intervention in Warsaw, and then broke from the script. One of the big takeaways, as we walked toward the center of Paris, was the exact opposite of the Milipol conclusion: an innate belief in the goodness of others. This was one of the ultimate tension points between climate justice and climate security.

"Pilgrims benefit from the goodness of others," he says, "we couldn't have done this pilgrimage without people embracing us."

In an article in News Deeply, humanitarian Paul Currion quoted the 20th-century Norweigan explorer Thor Heyerdahl: "Borders? I have never seen one, but I have heard that they exist in the minds of some people."[6] Currion laughed at the assertion, given the unprecedented number

of borders and border walls we have in the world right now. He highlighted a number of them, including Turkey's new "smart border" with Syria, which had a tower every 1,000 feet with a three-language alarm system and "automated firing zones" supported by hovering zeppelin drones. Currion wrote, "It appears that we've entered a new arms race, one appropriate for an age of asymmetric warfare, with border walls replacing ICBMs," the intercontinental ballistic missile. The vibrant buzzing corporate world making a mint selling techno-borders across the globe is the bread and butter of Milipol. The idea of strangers being friendly, extending hospitality, breaking bread together, offering a bed, seemed radical in this context, yet nothing could be more ancient.

Hardened militarized borders are a recent development of the late 20th and 21st centuries. Now this "global classification system," as April Humble of the Secretariat of the Earth League described the worldwide border regime, determining who does and doesn't receive hospitality, has become institutionalized. In the 21st century, border walls have become a perfectly "reasonable" way to express xenophobia without having to admit to it. It was "reasonable" to treat someone with contempt rather than kindness, with dismissal rather than respect, to use violence, based on the way a person looks, the color of their skin, the language they speak, or the money they don't have.

As we walked toward Paris, we passed gigantic colorful murals that took up entire sides of buildings. We also passed huge billboards; in one place the digital screen was advertising the climate summit, right in front of a McDonald's.

Yeb told me about his children—Yanni and Amira—11 and 8 years old—who understood "the climate issue very well," and when they were asked about Yeb's work, said, "He is doing it for us." He talked about the deep homesickness he has felt for them as he walked, but then said: "Homesickness is a great sign of being human. Humanity, it's something you get in touch with on a journey like this. And that's what we've lost, our civilization has lost their humanity."

We entered the city center and crossed the Seine. The Notre Dame cathedral was in the distance, an ancient display of beauty in the still soft morning light.

"I would to say that it is through every small act of caring, through every small act of kindness and love, that we build a future that is safe, peaceful, harmonious, and free from climate change," Yeb said. "This is the kind of mindset that we must embrace, so that we are able to work together. This movement must be strengthened and built despite, DESPITE, our world leaders."

When Yeb declared that was he was going to fast that day in Warsaw in 2013, he didn't know that thousands of people, all across the world, would fast with him. It was an action meant to express solidarity with the plight of the people of Tacloban who, like Albert Posadas, were eating rice boiled in filthy yellow water and were forced to skip meals. Then, for a year, on the first of every month, people fasted. In 2015, during the 365 days leading up to Paris, one person somewhere on the globe fasted, every single day. One day, the entire country of Tuvalu, an island that is sinking to the sea, refused food in solidarity with those adversely impacted by climate change across the globe.

At the end of the pilgrimage it was hard to believe that the man who came to the corner waving the paper and asserting that terrorism was the real issue knew why the people there were hugging each other, or that they were close to capping off a 1,000-mile, 60-day walk from Rome. It was unlikely that the man knew that A.G. Saño, contemplating the headline he insisted we read, planned for his own death during a typhoon and, after he survived, gathered the bodies of the dead. Despite the fact that Paris was the focal point of the media world at that moment, there were no media outlets or television cameras, just a handful of small documentary filmmakers with handheld cameras. Through mainstream eyes, this significant moment was occurring off the grid of history.

There were plenty of news outlets, however, in Paris, set up in the Place de la République under white tarps. This was the area targeted by attackers two weeks before. I watched news pundits from NBC speaking to the cameras every single day, prattling about U.S. politics and the sudden spike in stateside xenophobia about refugees, with a monument giving an austere look to the backdrop. They didn't cover the surveillance, weapons, and homeland security convention that took place directly after the attacks. They didn't cover the arrival of the People's Pilgrimage in Paris amid the state of emergency. They missed the true conversation about the future of the world between climate justice and climate security. And they would miss it the next day, too, when the police started to swing their clubs at the climate justice activists converging on Paris.

RUNNING

In front of me was a line of heavily armored police. They had helmets on. They were banging their shields loudly with their clubs. They were marching slowly but surely toward us. They were pushing us away from the Place de la République in central Paris. Behind the long, impassable line, I saw a coagulation of white police trucks with blue stripes. In the distance, plumes of tear gas wafted around the bronze monument of Marianne, who was holding aloft an olive branch, while simultaneously leaning on a tablet engraved with the words "*Droits de l'homme*," the "Declaration of the rights of man and of the citizen." Around the monument the piles of flowers and burning candles left by thousands of people in commemoration of the people killed in the attack were being crunched as the police marched forward in the plaza, pushing people out. As they swung their billy clubs into the bodies and bones of the climate justice activists, you could hear the sound of glass and crunching candles under black combat boots. In front of me the police continued to march, banging on their shields. Soon the line of police would charge, sprinting at full speed to where I had just been standing. I ran with a massive jolt of adrenaline.

A few hours before I ran from the French National Police, I watched NBC take down its tarp in the Place de la République where the climate activists were gathering on the day before the summit. Despite the fact that the climate march was banned by the French government because of the state of emergency, 11,000 people from all corners of the globe filled the plaza, first with shoes and signs, and then

with defiance. And even though these activists were going to march, and subsequently clash with police, the day before what people were calling the most important climate conference ever, NBC was packing its cameras and microphones in boxes and heading to the next hot story. The climate justice activists filled the plaza and spilled onto the streets all around, extending up Voltaire to the Bataclan. A group of mourning angels—with wide, white wings—walked solemnly by the cordoned-off Bataclan, where the sidewalks, like those near the other attack sites, were strewn with flowers, some wilted in the rain, with flickering candles and commemorative messages for the 80 people killed at the concert that night. A sign advertising the Eagles of Death Metal still ominiously hung over the vintage venue as an eery reminder. Another young man held a sign that said, WE NEED LANDSCAPE. The NBC departure was even more baffling since, on this day, 178 heads of state from around the world were arriving, including President Obama, who would leave a bouquet of flowers in this very spot. The police presence was building up, and you could feel the tension in the cold air.

Later, the banging of billy clubs against plastic shields was surprisingly loud, jolting, and the rhythm felt increasingly ominous. I was in a random group of people, many of them climate activists, some of whom were taunting the line of cops as we backpedaled. Behind them was a quaint autumn scene; the barren trees leading up to the plaza had shed most of the orange leaves that lay on the street. A grey sky behind the trees made them look like bones. I was with another journalist, David Schwenk. I was there to witness

and document a defining political moment, and now multiple issues were converging.

From behind the police line a cop emerged carrying a bullhorn. He barked several times in a loud metallic voice, "*Dispersez-vous.*" Even I understood that one. I still didn't know what would happen. Then they charged at us hard and fast.

They charged running at full speed, like runners in a track meet. Journalist or not, I knew I had to run. It didn't matter why any of us were there; our mere presence meant that we were doing something wrong. I turned quickly and blindly, camera in hand, and sprinted away. I never thought I'd find myself in the streets of Paris running away from cops. My mind raced back to the Milipol expo. The very same French National Police that I had watched demonstrate to businesspeople how to take down assailants were now charging at ME.

As I ran I realized that I had arrived at the true climate summit. The police were in full combat mode, and activists, journalists, whoever gave a shit about the climate was being violently disciplined. In the plaza the authorities brought out their clubs and swung at anyone in their way; and there is footage of the police smashing an elderly man directly in the knees, sending him crumpling to the ground. Paris was in a state of exception. The state could do anything. It could assault you and nothing would happen. So I ran. This was the other moment when I was truly scared in Paris, a good week and a half after the metro train stopped and we sat for a moment in pitch blackness.

It was as if the everyday world of border zones had

arrived in Paris. You weren't quite sure what you did wrong, but that didn't matter. Likewise, it didn't matter if your house was washed away or engulfed in a mudslide. It was a version of a "constitution-free zone." It didn't matter if you lost your beloved in a terrible howling hurricane, or in heat so hostile that your world had become uninhabitable. It didn't matter if your crops dried up in a drought. In the security business, all those are "threat multipliers," and *you* are part of the threat. The true climate war is not between people in different communities fighting each other for scarce resources. It is between those in power and the grassroots; between a suicidal status quo and the hope for sustainable transformation. The militarized border is but one of many weapons deployed by those in power.

In addition to banning all protest, France preemptively placed 24 climate activists under house arrest. The French interior minister said this was done to prevent them from demonstrating before the summit, just as the Philippine forces did during martial law. Amnesty International accused the French government of abusing the state of exception. France accused three of the arrested of belonging to a "radical opposition movement." The French government called lawyer Joel Domenjoud, for example, a member of the legal team for a coalition of protest groups planning the march, the "principal leader of the ultra-left movement."[7] He arrived home to find his apartment building crawling with cops from the first to the third floor.

Alleen Brown of *The Intercept* wrote on November 30, "Paris was supposed to be a launching point for activists to build a more coordinated international movement in the

coming months and years against the systems that produce climate change."[8] Yet, on this day, the launching point was met with walls of police.

Just when I thought I was going to be engulfed by those walls and battered by clubs, the sprinting police stopped. They grabbed one activist, who struggled mightily, and pulled him into their lines.

Later it was revealed that we were hardly alone. Solidarity with the protesters in Paris was expressed across the globe. More than 600,000 people in 175 different countries marched around the world to call for a strong climate deal. In Melbourne and in London they numbered 60,000 and 50,000, respectively. Los Angeles, Vancouver, Ottawa, Mexico City, Rio de Janeiro, and Manila, to name some of the many places. As Yeb said during the walk into Paris, there was a grassroots "clamor" for change and transformation.

IT IS GOING TO COME FROM THE PEOPLE, THE GRASSROOTS

The next day, I went to Le Bourget, where the actual United Nations summit was happening. It was cold, but the security guards wouldn't let us anywhere near the negotiations. The shuttles kept exhaling impeccably dressed people, and the highly fortified negotiation zone sucked them in. Those with access moved with the confidence of the included. The agreement that world leaders and diplomats were about to hash out was no doubt one of the most important international agreements ever to be put into words. Perhaps the deepening climate crisis could be averted, and civilization would evolve to be sustainable and just.

According to David Ciplet et al. in *Power in a Warming World*, there was an unsaid mandate that tied negotiators to the status quo so that "governmental representatives, who were structurally dependent on private sector profitability, may anticipate resistance from powerful business and related interests at home to initiatives that threaten established industries."[9] The same authors also note, and this merits repeating, that people in the 48 least-developed countries were five times more likely to die from climate-related disasters than the rest of humanity, while accounting for less than 1 percent of the emissions that contribute to global warming.

As Andreas Malms wrote for *Jacobin* right before the Paris summit started, each year the climate conferences (COPs) produce a "tidal wave of bureaucratic logorrhea. . . . As COPs have degenerated into annual exhibits in the latest innovations of officialese, no tangible measures other than the construction of various vacuous carbon markets have materialized; CO_2 emissions from fossil fuels have not declined, not leveled off, not increased a little more slowly, but soared by 50 percent."[10] Malms continues by saying that ever since Copenhagen, when spontaneous demonstrations erupted in the center of the negotiations and climate movement activists threatened to turn it into a "People's Assembly," authorities had begun to ban climate movement people and demonstrations from negotiation grounds and started to patrol venues with soldiers and police. This, according to Malms, was happening well before the attacks of November 13, 2015.

In front of Le Bourget, soldiers in full battle gear were deployed on a small hill that had a sweeping view over the

surrounding landscape. One was crouched and staring out over northern Paris, seemingly on the lookout for possible incoming threats. No one without authorized access was going to get past them.

There was at least one survivor from Typhoon Haiyan on the grounds, but A.G. Saño wasn't among those authorized to attend. He could not talk about the urgency, the shaking walls in his hotel room, how he expected to be killed. Since he wasn't allowed entrance, Amy Goodman from *Democracy Now!* interviewed him outside the exclusion zone. While the accords were called a "triumph" of diplomacy—and there are important ways that they were—the indigenous were inadequately represented, and neither the poor nor the people on climate's front lines were represented at all. There were no plans made for reparations to be offered for loss and damage. There was no concrete proposal to provide shelter and assistance for people displaced.

A.G., at the end of the interview, looked at Goodman and said, "Well, to be brutally honest, I don't really care about what's happening in the COP, because if the world leaders really cared, it won't take 20 years. It won't take 20 years. They've been talking since the 1990s, but what's really happening?" He explained, "I'm a person who would rather believe in the bottom-up process, where you can make change from below."[11]

EIGHT

TRANSITION AND TRANSFORMATION

The unexpected action of deep listening can create a space of transformation capable of shattering complacency and despair.

—Terry Tempest Williams

It's an interesting story how I ended up in front of that discarded border barrier—the one covered with purple flowers—where this book begins. At the Paris climate summit I went to an end-of-day briefing panel that paired John Liu, a Chinese American filmmaker best known for a film titled *Hope in a Changing Climate*, with French anthropologist Barbara Glowzecski and Rob Hopkins, from the United Kingdom, of the Transition Network. Liu began to address the difference between "transition and transformation" in the spacious basement of a Paris hotel where they were giving a daily press conference.

"What is wealth? Wealth is not having more stuff but having more time so we can work less and spend more time with our families." Liu said this after explaining that the

whole global system was out of whack. There was economic value placed on things, often "useless things," that were bought and sold, but the natural resources that we depend on to sustain life were not given any value at all. "We've devalued the source of life," he said. Things like fresh water, soil, and biodiversity are where true value lies. If human economy were based on ecological function, he said, human efforts would be radically different than they are now.

"We need more time so we can have lemonade under the fig tree," he told the audience in Paris to spontaneous, enthusiastic applause.

When I heard that Liu was going to be in the hypermilitarized U.S.-Mexico borderlands, I drove south from Tucson to Patagonia, Arizona, with David Hodges of Cuenca Los Ojos, the project Liu had come to see and directly experience. It was through this project, using the ancient traditions of water retention, that residents have transformed a good swath of land where native grasses, water, and animals were returning. It was on this transforming land where the discarded border barrier lay festooned with little purple flowers.

In her book *Hope in the Dark*, Rebecca Solnit states that people often aren't even conscious of their successes, or how the world can change in unimaginable ways in short periods of time. She talks about a type of activism in which people expect instant gratification, a type of civic engagement that focuses so much on the negative that we might miss the accomplishments, big and small.

Liu's documentation of ecological restoration in the age of climate disruption fits Solnit's vision quite well. In the film *Hope in a Changing Climate*, one part showed a parched

area of the Loess Plateau in China. After the community came together and replanted trees and natural vegetation, stabilized the soil, and started using terraced agriculture, a sort of lush miracle emerged. The results told a new tale, reversing for a moment the Anthropocene-era narrative of degradation and doom. The vegetation created conditions such that water didn't run off but was retained by the soil, via slow absorption. The plants and trees sequestered the carbon in the atmosphere. Agricultural yields increased to a much higher level than before. Liu went to Rwanda and Ethiopia and found similar miraculous tales of restoration. At one point the film depicted the rush of freshwater in a creek in Ethiopia that Liu said spontaneously emerged with the success of vegetation and water retention. His message was not only that it *is* possible to restore a degraded landscape, but that around the world people were coming together to do just that in an age of climate devastation.

This sort of ecological restoration was just one of countless ways that people could come together to create something new. Other ways could include the solidarity and humanitarianism of projects epitomized by—to take southern Arizona as just one example—No More Deaths, Samaritans, Humane Borders, and others that reject militarized borders and their global classification system, and offer hospitality and assistance to people who find themselves in dire circumstances, no matter who they are. In the era of intensifying climate change, such cross-border mutual assistance will be more important than ever before. However, it is in cross-border organizing—which rejects the nation-state frame—the real hope for change is located, defying a world

that is artificially divided, coming together in potentially miraculous ways.

Now John Liu stood on top of a ridge in southern Arizona, near the town of Patagonia. There was a cool breeze that accompanies the late afternoon sun in March, painting the grass a golden hue. In terms of climate impacts, this was a place where large wildfires have become commonplace, where water issues were perennial, and where climate disruption and the most massive border surveillance structure collide. Alas, where we stood thinking about the ocelots, bobcats, mountain lions, and even jaguars that were at home in an environment dotted with mesquite, ash, hackberry, and walnut trees, we were only 30 miles away from the U.S.-Mexico border, and on aboriginal Tohono O'odham land. It was here that a muscular, spotted jaguar known as *El Jefe* was caught on a wildlife camera, at the time the only known jaguar in the United States. It didn't elude me that the jaguar could have been watching us as we looked across the corridor to the Santa Rita Mountains and its highest peak, Mount Wrightson. "The jaguar," Randy Serraglio of the Center for Biological Diversity said, "is a border issue."

In the corridor there were hawks and vultures, kingfishers and kingbirds, hummingbirds and the magnificent elf owl that could be watching us with its ever-inquisitive face. It was wild, truly wild. The landscape seemed to drift off forever until it finally hit the mountain range. As in much of Southern Arizona, the landscape had the ability to break open the mind, create a sense of spaciousness, and induce new ways of thinking and perceiving.

"Is the meaning of life," Liu asked an audience later

that night in a Patagonia theater, "to buy and sell?" He answered himself: "I don't think so. The Earth is beautiful. The people here are beautiful. All living things are sacred." Liu described the Chinese pictographic characters for crisis that contained, he told the audience, "danger and opportunity." This was a time of grave danger, Liu said, but it was also the opportunity to change.

"So you CAN'T go on in the way it is happening now. On a planetary scale, humanity is going to have to shift, there is going to be transformational change. And it will either happen consciously and carefully in a way that the best things about civilization can be saved, or it will be a really dangerous period in which some horrible things are going to occur."

A TALE OF TWO WALLS

Professor Zoe Hammer of Prescott College asked a question in her Masters of Social Justice and Human Right class that made her students laugh. "What if the U.S. Border Patrol were put to work making community gardens?" At first the comment seemed outlandish. I imagined a border landscape of flowers and vegetables instead of barriers and Border Patrol. Never had the idea of two countries being so neighborly seemed so foolish. But there was a deeper undertone to Hammer's question. When you looked at the overall budget, the money and resources allocated to the Border Patrol and its accompanying apparatus, couldn't the money be spent more wisely? Couldn't housing, education, health, or other human services use a boost in resources?

And Hammer's comment went even further—was there

a way to transform the border walls to something else, recapacitate the labor force performing that one task, and have its members dedicate their time and energy to the creation, production, and reproduction of another task? If you interpret community gardening to mean ecological restoration, and understand that this needs to happen on massive levels, including cross-border areas, to begin to restore degraded landscapes, then the suggestion suddenly doesn't seem ludicrous at all. In fact, it seems like a reasonable, rational possibility with at least enough merit be seriously debated and discussed. Hammer's point was that it was possible to imagine a new world, to transform the old into something new. Things can no longer stay the same.

As writer Betsy Hartmann asks: "Might the challenge of climate change provide an opportunity to rethink the meaning of development and economic growth in ways that promote redistribution of power and wealth while simultaneously protecting the environment?"[1]

Liu insisted that the whole nature of the economy needs to be changed from a transactional economy to a trust economy, from the lever of money to the lever of ecological function. According to Liu, our current economy is destabilizing the climate conditions on which all livings things depend. Instead of addressing the root problem, border militarization simply reinforces the destabilization by reinforcing the status quo.

It was about a month after I met with Liu that I arrived where we began, at the border barrier that had been ripped from the ground by Hurricane Odile and become covered with cobwebs and flowers, almost like a beautiful work of

art. About a quarter mile up the wash known as Silver Creek, on the actual Mexico-U.S. boundary, Homeland Security had erected a new barrier to replace it. Behind the barrier, I could see an idling green-striped Border Patrol vehicle, and inside it an agent seemed to be watching us. I was at the San Bernardino Ranch in Sonora, just east of Agua Prieta.

For a moment, I realized I had in the same eyeshot both the border barrier (backed by the agent) and the gabions—the galvanized wire cages packed with rocks, embedded 18 feet deep to shape the contour of the streambed and riverbank. The gabions almost looked like intricate stone walls themselves. They were part of an ancient technique of strategically piling rocks to slow down the flow of water across the land. For the region, after years of mechanized farming, cattle production, and now a nasty drought, this once parched and barren landscape could begin to absorb this precious water, replenish the soil with life.

I was looking at two walls. One barrier was meant to keep people out. The other was based on the economy of ecological function that Liu was talking about. Before the gabions were built, rushing water from monsoon storms would take topsoil and leave cutting erosion. Now, there was water year-round.

I was with Juan Manuel Pérez, the foreman of the organization Cuenca Los Ojos (CLO) and in charge of 45,000 acres of restoration projects spread throughout the region. He was dressed in jeans and a white cowboy hat. While the Border Patrol agent eyed us, Pérez gestured to the reviving landscape around him. It was not only what was on the surface—the native grasses and sprouting desert willows and

cottonwoods—that was so remarkable. It was also what was below: a water table that had risen 30 feet in the middle of a brutal 15-year drought that everywhere else was sucking the land dry. All throughout the borderlands and Arizona, after years of hotter weather and less precipitation, the grass had withered, the earth had cracked, and animals had died. Yet, water was recharging even 10 to 15 miles downstream from San Bernardino Ranch into Mexico, to places where people hadn't seen it for decades. From brown to green, from completely dry to lush: to me, it seemed like a miracle.

In this microcosm along a remote area of border, it was clear that these two contrasting visions embodied the future struggle that was upon the world. As the Trump administration moved forward with promises of hyper-racialized border building, you could say what I saw that day on this ranch was a tale of two walls: one about restoration, the other about exclusion.

We were in a place where the Rocky Mountains meet the Sierra Madre, where the Chihuahua and Sonoran deserts merge, a place of wondrous biodiversity. This habitat was home to the most species of bees in the world, and the most species of butterflies in North America.

However, due to the drought and degradation, it was an area where, according to most U.S. national security assessments, water shortages and other climate shocks could propel mass migrations of people to the United States from this region, from places like the community of 29 families located approximately 10 miles upstream called 18 de Agosto. When resident Alberto Teran started farming there in 1976, he told me, "We had very little water." They had dug

wells in the parched land, but it was difficult to get the water they needed for harvest and animals. Because of this, when the Cuenca Los Ojos (CLO) projects began in the 1990s, 18 de Agosto was dead set against it, thinking, as Teran put it, that the 40,000 *trincheras* (small rockpile dams) and 50 gabion dams "were going to leave us without water."

Who could blame them for thinking this? Mexico had just entered the NAFTA era; the country's natural resources were put up for sale to the highest bidder, and the Mexican government was cutting subsidies and credit to small farmers like Teran. Add to this the aridity of the changing climate, and you had a classic example of sociologist Christian Parenti's "catastrophic convergence," a fusion of political, economic, and ecological displacement. People started to leave—including Teran's four children—for factory work in the city, or for the United States.

Then the miracles started to happen. A year later, the community began to notice that they had more water, and it was retained for longer periods of time. Water started to appear in places it had never been found before. Teran told me the river began to run year-round again. He told me again the miracle: in the middle of the drought, the water table in the San Bernardino Valley began to rise, while everywhere else water tables were falling.

And the water table, as Perez said back at the borderline, "doesn't respect the international boundary." It rose on the United States side as well. On both sides of the border, there was a return of biodiversity, biomass, and accumulation of organic material, the essence of ecological function.

Behind the discarded border barrier, David Hodges—

pointing out not only the cottonwoods and willows, but also the native grasses—said that we had passed the "tipping point." The wording struck me, because in the literature of climate projections, tipping point is almost always used in reference to a catastrophic point of no return—accelerating methane release, ice sheet disintegration, mass extinction, intensifying superstorms, and endless droughts. For Hodges, the tipping point meant that diversity was overcoming the barren blight, that water was coming year-round, that birds were present, even the glossy ibis with its beautiful curved bill. "We need to do this for future generations," Pérez told me.

This was just a small, increasingly fertile example of the possibilities, but there was something about this ruined border wall—filled with arachnids, surrounded by a restoration project, and menaced by an idling Border Patrol vehicle—that provided a glimpse of the common crossroads, not only in the U.S. borderlands, but throughout the world.

The second time I stood at the Silver Creek Wash, instead of the Border Patrol I saw a distant surveillance tower that hadn't been there a few months before. I assumed it was the Elbit Systems tower, one of 52 such towers (as part of a potentially billion-dollar contract for the private Israeli company) that DHS was constructing in the southern Arizona borderlands, equipped with high-powered night-vision and thermal energy cameras as well as complex radar systems.

This time I was with Alberto Teran from 18 de Agosto. This tower was in my view as he told me about the water now flowing year round in the stream through his community,

how they were going to continue the water restoration project there, how they were trying to revive the agriculture.

Back in Tucson later that week, thinking of that surveillance tower and 18 de Agosto, I asked one of the founders of Cuenca Los Ojos, Valer Austin, given the success of the restoration at San Bernardino, what could CLO and other restoration groups in the borderlands do with the close to $20 billion designated to border and immigration enforcement each year? When she heard that number she, like many others, said, “Oh my God.” Then quickly, “That money could be put to better use.”

Austin said that CLO had invested millions and had restored a big swath of flora and fauna.

“But what if you had a hundred times that money? You would get a whole river system to run. It would expand like ripples, out and out and out. It would touch people for miles on either side of this river.”

“With that kind of money,” Austin continued, “we could restore a lot of streams that on the ground would alter climate change in the region. It would make a huge difference. It would change the economics [of the region]. It would change health. It would change everything on the border.

“It would make all the difference between life and death.”

EPILOGUE

It is a serious thing
just to be alive
on this fresh morning
in this broken world.

—Mary Oliver

When I began this book, William, you were still in your mother's womb. When I saw you then—your tiny heart thumping in colorless ultrasounds—I was mesmerized by your beauty, your innocence, your potential. I never thought I would have a child, but there you were before my eyes. At this point, I could only make out the vague shape of your body, I didn't know the color of your hair, I didn't know your sex, I didn't know anything about you, except that I had never felt such tenderness.

In November 2015, the *Tucson Weekly* asked me to write a letter. The idea was for the letter to be to a loved one, and would address the future of the world undergoing climate change. I accepted the invitation and chose to write you a letter meant to be read in the year 2050, the year you will turn 35, an important year, I remember, for

climate projections on your great-grandmother's island in Marinduque.

I was staying in a small apartment in Paris when I began to write to you. It was one week *after* the city had been traumatized by an attack that had killed 130 people. And it was one week *before* the most important global climate summit that had been organized up to that point. The purpose of the letter was to predict the summit's outcome, because there was so much at stake. In many ways this book has been an extension of that letter to you, my child.

On the day I began to write you, things seemed bleak. Outside my small Paris apartment the sky was grey and a cold rain was falling. There had already been 20 previous such summits over 20 years. Despite our growing scientific understanding of its impact, civilization kept pumping billions of metric tons of heat-trapping pollution into the atmosphere every year. Even after the urgency of the situation became palpable, humans could not seem to rein in the pollution. Eventually some began to say that we were fast approaching—if not already past—the point of no return. Way back then, we had already locked into a trajectory that scientists deemed unsafe and unmanageable for you and your future.

I wrote a lot to you in that first letter, much of which has appeared in the pages in this book. I wrote about all the climate pressures predicted for the area, how they compound each other and cause catastrophe. I wrote about heat waves and dust storms and water shortages and wildfires, all the elements of the southern Arizona where you will grow up, that could force increasing numbers of people to flee.

Predicting 2050, I wrote about homeland security checkpoints deployed on the interstates going in and out of Phoenix and Tucson, and the officials who claimed to erect them as temporary measures for "the protection of the people." I speculated about a new United States, carved into exclusion zones, with militarized lines of division and new blockades only allowing the passage of people with certain papers. I wrote that the likelihood of the world becoming a militarized surveillance state was probably as predictable as all the other consequences of climate change. And it is true, the dynamics of global warming and militarization may shape the world you inhabit more than any other, my child.

But now I want to describe another moment to you, when I was leaving Marinduque, the island of your great-grandmother.

As the ferry pulled away from the island, kids shrieked in joy as they swam toward our boat. The fresh smell of the sea was exhilarating. As we pulled out, I thought of my grandmother moving away slowly from the same island in the 1930s. The island looked startling, a mist graced the green hills topped with coconut palms that swayed in the wind. Slightly rusted boats rocked back and forth in the harbor. Those were the boats that head out into shifting seas, more moody than ever in the age of climate change.

Then, for a moment, the sky and the sea were the same color, and the division between land and sea was indistinguishable. There was a momentary sense of the possibility that there was a world out there that was miraculous, and that a miracle could indeed happen—a miracle of the spirit, a miracle of politics, a miracle of economics, a miracle of the

human imagination a sense that the ordinary was pregnant with the extraordinary that was always there, just waiting to be called into being.

I hope, my child, that when you read this in 2050, if nothing else, you find that these words help rev your spirit, kindness, and generosity to join with others to transcend boundaries and borders. I want you to visit this island. I want you to see where your great grandmother grew up. I want you to meet the beautiful child I saw in the man's arm on the beach, his black hair tossing in the wind of that distant typhoon as I watched the foamy waves smash into the shore.

After all, it was there in the land of our ancestral past that I may have found our common future.

I wasn't sure what I'd find in Marinduque. Yes, I found an island in danger of being engulfed by the sea or destroyed by typhoons, but I also found a deep tenderness. I felt your great-grandmother, whose whispers graced this small island at every corner. I could imagine when she was in her mother's womb, William, the way you were when I was there.

Feelings of tenderness bring love and power, and I felt all three, William, as I left the island and felt connected to our past and future. Perhaps I was touching what the poet Mary Oliver means when she writes, "Always leave room in your heart for the unimaginable." It's a feeling I experienced right when we sailed off from Marinduque, when the color of the sea briefly and magically matched the color of the sky. As we sailed away and I deeply inhaled the intoxicating sea air, William, I knew something was shifting inside. A tenderness had softened my brittle places, and how I envisioned the future—your future.

Every journey is a process of change. You start as one person. You end as another. People still treat you like you are who you were. They may not be able to see the transformation.

Perhaps we who are born in the Anthropocene era are doomed. The rising seas may indeed swallow islands and inundate coastal mega-cities. We may perish from droughts, superstorms, or the bullets of the elite. Civilization is dying. The unsustainable system is collapsing now under its own weight. It may be too late to organize for change. But even so, you should not stop from daring to imagine something new. You should continue to be a counterforce for the common good.

The possibilities are endless. There are hundreds, if not hundreds of thousands of groups, individuals, communities, and movements putting themselves on the line, putting themselves in peril, in order to imagine something new. In *Hope in the Dark*, Rebecca Solnit shows that there have been so many events that have happened, even just in the last 30 years—from the fall of the Berlin wall to the advance of LGBT rights—that have significantly altered our world. There have been so many successes of grassroots movements, achievements that have gone by without sufficient recognition. And I imagine that by the time you read this in 2050, there will be many more such victories to celebrate. There has to be hope. Hope with teeth and muscle, like the grit of ordinary people who join together to protest, march, and challenge injustice.

The living world, my child, is calling on us to make bridges, not borders. The world is calling us to build bridge

across language barriers, gender barriers, social barriers, racial barriers, generational barriers. I think we can even cross borders of time and speak with the past, as I did with your great-grandmother; and also speak to the future, as I am speaking with you right now. There is a slight chance in this crossing that we can break the notion that we are threats to each other, and that we have to surround ourselves with militarized borders we have created for ourselves in the Anthropocene.

We need each other more than ever, for the living world teaches us that all things are connected. Maybe we will learn to live in harmony with this beautiful planet, and become our own salvation.

ACKNOWLEDGMENTS

This book was hatched in a diner in midtown Manhattan after a conversation with my editor at City Lights, Greg Ruggiero. Safe to say that without his vision, creativity, and masterful editing, this book would not exist. Gratitude to everybody at City Lights in San Francisco, including Elaine, Robert, Stacey, Chris, Linda, and of course the institution's great poet-painter-publisher founder, Lawrence Ferlinghetti. Elizabeth Bell deserves special thanks for her exceptional copy editing.

I would also like to give my deep gratitude to the many who have helped me with this book in a multitude of ways—from research assistance to offering feedback and insight to financial support—including my long time mentor Joseph Nevins, Alex Devoid (who came with me on many trips and is creating an accompanying documentary), Miriel Manning and Nora Collins (whose exceptional research was indispensable), the brilliant writer John Washington (who trudged through an early version of the manuscript), Jeff Abbott (who accompanied me on multiple trips through Southern Mexico and Central America), Jill Williams, Isabel Ball (a great researcher from Tucson, Arizona), Isabel Ball (an exceptional guide and interpreter from Marinduque, Philippines), Tita Agnes Apeles, Felix Perez, Ka Noli Abinales, Patricio Abinales, Tony Veloso, Yilian David and La Organización Fraternal Negra Hondureña (OFRANEH), Beth Geglia, Louise Misztal, Randy Serraglio, Dahr Jamail (not only offering his generous time to talk about these issues, but his incisive monthly reports on climate destabilization at Truthout), NACLA Report on the Americas and its column

"Border Wars" (for years of support), the Tucson Samaritans, the Green Valley Samaritans, No More Deaths, Randy Mayer and the Good Shepherd United Church of Christ, Joshua Garcia, Amy Juan, Nellie Jo David, and Tina Vavages-Andrew of the Tohono O'odham Hemajkam Rights Network, Larry Gatti and Tucson Community Acupuncture, The Historic Y, Blake Gentry and Laurie Melrood, Cyrina King, Tom Engelhardt and TomDispatch, Megan Kimble and Edible Baja Arizona, David Hodges and Cuenca Los Ojos, Mari Herreras and the Tucson Weekly, John and Molly Knefel with Radio Dispatch, Jessica Stites and In These Times, Marissa Cabaljao and People Surge, Richard "Dick" Erstad, John "Lory" Ghertner and the Greater Rochester Coalition for Immigration Justice, Eric Holthaus, Ben Beachy, Norma Price, Mary Goethals, Raquel Rubio-Goldsmith, Guadalupe Castillo, Isabel Garcia, Victor Braitberg, Crystal Guerra, Gabriel Schivone, Chris Castro, and Steve Teichner. Dora Rodriguez's crucial role—not to mention lovely friendship—should not be underestimated. Yeb and A.G. Saño deserve a special shout out, as does the People's Pilgrimage. Jim Cohen, gratitude for the warm hospitality in Paris. Zoe Hammer and Prescott College, including all the wonderful people who have helped me with my research—Maddox Wolfe, Ashleigh Hall, and Alissa Stutte. And, of course, the students who put up with me when I designed a border studies class around the exact topic of this book: Zoe Reeves, Sierra Reinertson, Isaura Lira Greene, Danielle Davis, and, of course, again, the great Miriel Manning. Dan Millis, Cyndi Tuell, Scott Nicol and the Sierra Club Borderlands program have supported me on so many occasions that I can no longer count them, as has the educational organization BorderLinks. Geoff Boyce

has always a source of insight and conversation, especially over late-night drinks, and the Earlham Border Studies program has not only been a source of support, but has also given me excitement for the incoming generation. Of course there are countless friends, impossible to list in their entirety, with whom I've had so many conversations with about this subject matter, not to mention the many books and experts from whose work I have drawn from extensively in these pages.

Special thanks to Lauren and William for their endless support, and for putting up with my all-nighters and long trips. William's birth happened when I was writing this book. Watching the miraculous strength of both Lauren and William in that small room at the birthing center breathed hope and love into this book perhaps like no other event could. Lauren, I thank you for reminding me of the strength, imagination, and potential of humankind. I hope that this spirit has faithfully showed up in the words in this book.

Special thanks go to Peggy and Dennis, Tom and Shannon, and Wes and Kim. And I can't say how much I owe to my parents—literally everything—and brother Mark for always being there.

My grandmother, of course, although she passed away many years ago, was very influential to this book—in countless ways. It was so wonderful and heartening to connect with family in the Philippines for the first time, and not only experience their wonderful hospitality, but eat the delicious adobo and flan!

Always a special thanks goes to my co-conspirator Reina the cat, who even at 20 years old still sat by my side as I wrote, day after day.

NOTES

CHAPTER ONE

1. NASA Goddard Space Flight Center NASA, "Satellite Data: 1993-Present," Global Climate Change: Vital Signs of the Planet. Accessed February 22, 2017: https://climate.nasa.gov/vital-signs/sea-level/

2. Henry Fountain, "Arctic's Winter Sea Ice Drops to Its Lowest Recorded Level," *New York Times*, March 22, 2017. Accessed March 28, 2017: https://nyti.ms/2mRhtdl

3. David Ciplet, J. Timmons Roberts, and Mizan R. Khan, *Power in a Warming World: The New Global Politics of Climate Change and the Remaking of Environmental Inequality* (MIT Press, 2015).

4. Coral Davenport and Campbell Robertson, "Resettling the First American 'Climate Refugees,'" *New York Times*, May 3, 2016. Accessed February 22, 2017: https://www.nytimes.com/2016/05/03/us/resettling-the-first-american-climate-refugees.html?_r=0

5. Brett Anderson, "Every Map of Louisiana Is a Lie—What It Really Looks Like Should Scare You," *Business Insider*, Sep. 17, 2014. Accessed February 21, 2017: www.businessinsider.com/louisianas-coast-is-sinking-2014-9

6. Ibid.

7. Coral Davenport and Campbell Robertson, "Resettling the First American 'Climate Refugees,'" *New York Times*, May 3, 2016. Accessed Februrary 22, 2017: https://www.nytimes.com/2016/05/03/us/resettling-the-first-american-climate-refugees.html?_r=0

8. Robert M. DeConto & David Pollard, "Contribution of Antarctica to past and future sea-level rise," *Nature*, April 5, 2016. Accessed April 20, 2017: www.nature.com/nature/journal/v531/n7596/full/nature17145.html

9. Damian Carrington,"Sea levels set to 'rise far more rapidly than expected,'" *The Guardian*, March 30, 2016. Accessed February 21, 2017: https://www.theguardian.com/environment/2016/mar/30/sea-levels-set-to-rise-far-more-rapidly-than-expected

10. Brooke Jarvis, "When Rising Seas Transform Risk into Certainty," *New York Times*, April 18, 2017. Accessed April 20, 2017: https://www.nytimes.com/2017/04/18/magazine/when-rising-seas-transform-risk-into-certainty.html?hp&action=click&pgtype=Homepage&clickSource=story-heading&module=photo-spot-region®ion=top-news&WT.

nav=top-news&_r=0

11. Evan Lehman, "Extreme Rain May Flood 54 Million People by 2030," *Scientific American*, March 5, 2015. Accessed April 20, 2017: https://www.scientificamerican.com/article/extreme-rain-may-flood-54-million-people-by-2030/

12. James Hansen et al., "Ice melt, sea-level rise and superstorms: evidence from paleoclimate data, climate modeling, and modern observations that 2°C global warming could be dangerous," *Atmospheric Chemistry and Physics*, March 22, 2016. The full report can be accessed here: www.atmos-chem-phys.net/16/3761/2016/

13. James Hansen, "Ice Melt, Sea-level rise and Superstorms: The Threat of Irreparable Harm" (video transcript), March 22, 2016. Accessed February 23, 2017: http://csas.ei.columbia.edu/2016/03/22/ice-melt-sea-level-rise-and-superstorms-the-threat-of-irreparable-harm/

14. Michael Kimmelman, "Mexico City, Parched and Sinking, Faces a Water Crisis," *New York Times*, February 17, 2017. Accessed February 22, 2017: https://www.nytimes.com/interactive/2017/02/17/world/americas/mexico-city-sinking.html

15. Ibid.

16. Koko Warner et al., "In Search of Shelter: Mapping the Effects of Climate Change on Human Migration and Displacement," May 2009. Accessed February 23, 2017: http://ciesin.columbia.edu/documents/clim-migr-report-june09_media.pdf

17. Internal Displacement Monitoring Centre, "GRID 2016: Global Report on Internal Displacement," 2016. Accessed February 28, 2017: www.internal-displacement.org/globalreport2016/#ongrid

18. Internal Displacement Monitoring Centre, "Global Estimates 2015: People Displaced by Disasters," July 2015. Accessed February 28, 2017: www.internal-displacement.org/assets/publications/2015/20150713-global-estimates-2015-en.pdf

19. Jessica Benko, "How a Warming Planet Drives Human Migration," *New York Times*, April 19, 2017. Accessed April 20, 2017: https://www.nytimes.com/2017/04/19/magazine/how-a-warming-planet-drives-human-migration.html?WT.mc_id=SmartBriefs-Newsletter&WT.mc_ev=click&ad-keywords=smartbriefsnl&_r=0

20. Gallup World Poll: The Many Faces of Global Migration, IOM Migration Research Center & Gallup, 2010.

21. Christian Parenti, *Tropic of Chaos: Climate Change and the New Geography of Violence* (Nation Books, 2011).

22. Warner et al., "In Search of Shelter."

23. Peter Schwartz and Doug Randall, "An Abrupt Climate Change Scenario and Its Implications for United States National Security," October 2003. Accessed April 13, 2017: http://eesc.columbia.edu/courses/v1003/readings/Pentagon.pdf

24. Harsha Walia, *Undoing Border Imperialism* (AK Press, 2013).

25. Subcomandante Insurgente Moisés and Subcomandante Insurgente Galeano, "The Walls Above, The Cracks Below (And To The Left)," *Enlace Zapatista*, February 14, 2017. Accessed February 28, 2017: http://enlacezapatista.ezln.org.mx/2017/02/16/the-walls-above-the-cracks-below-and-to-the-left/

26. American Civil Liberties Union, "Customs and Border Protection's 100-Mile Rule." Accessed February 28, 2017: https://www.aclu.org/other/aclu-factsheet-customs-and-border-protections-100-mile-zone?redirect=immigrants-rights/aclu-fact-sheet-customs-and-border-protections-100-mile-zone

27. Nick Buxton and Ben Hayes, *The Secure and the Dispossessed: How the Military and Corporations Are Shaping a Climate-Changed World* (Pluto Press, 2016).

28. Ibid.

29. William E. Tydeman, *Conversations with Barry Lopez: Walking the Path of Imagination* (University of Oklahoma Press, 2013).

CHAPTER TWO

1. Malanding S. Jaiteh, Baboucarr Sarr, "Climate Change and Development in the Gambia: Challenges to Ecosystem Goods and Services," Columbia University, March 3, 2011. Accessed March 3, 2017: www.columbia.edu/~msj42/pdfs/ClimateChangeDevelopmentGambia_small.pdf

2. "IOM Counts 3,771 Migrant Fatalities in Mediterranean in 2015," International Organization for Migration, January 5, 2016. Accessed March 3, 2017: www.iom.int/news/iom-counts-3771-migrant-fatalities-mediterranean-2015

3. Eric Wolff, "Mattis: Trump Cabinet's lone green hope?," *Politico*, December 19, 2016. Accessed March 3, 2017: www.politico.com/story/2016/12/james-mattis-climate-change-trump-defense-232833

4. Keith Johnson, "Obama Says Climate Change Is a Security Risk. Why Are Republicans Laughing?," *Foreign Policy*, March 21, 2016. Accessed March, 2 2017: https://foreignpolicy.com/2016/03/21/obama-says-

climate-change-is-a-security-risk-why-are-republicans-laughing/

5. Caitlin Werrel and Francesco Femia, "How the U.S. Military's Not Waiting to Find Out If Cimate Change Is an Existential Risk," Center for Climate and Security, March 24, 2016. Accessed March 3, 2017: https://climateandsecurity.org/2016/03/24/how-the-u-s-militarys-not-waiting-to-find-out-if-climate-change-is-an-existential-risk/

6. Brad Adams, "India's shoot-to-kill policy on the Bangladesh border," *The Guardian*, January 23, 2011. Accessed March 2, 2017: https://www.theguardian.com/commentisfree/libertycentral/2011/jan/23/india-bangladesh-border-shoot-to-kill-policy

7. Wolff, "Mattis: Trump Cabinet's lone green hope?"

8. Timothy Gardner, "U.S. military marches forward on green energy, despite Trump," *Reuters*, March 1, 2017. Accessed March 2, 2017: www.reuters.com/article/us-usa-military-green-energy-insight-idUSKBN1683BL

9. "Remarks by the President at the United States Coast Guard Academy Commencement," *obamawhitehouse.gov*, May 20, 2015. Accessed March 4, 2017: https://obamawhitehouse.archives.gov/the-press-office/2015/05/20/remarks-president-united-states-coast-guard-academy-commencement

10. Ibid.

11. Robert D. Kaplan, "The Coming Anarchy: How scarcity, crime, overpopulation, tribalism, and disease are rapidly destroying the social fabric of our planet," *The Atlantic*, February, 1994. Accessed March 4, 2017: https://www.theatlantic.com/magazine/archive/1994/02/the-coming-anarchy/304670/

12. Ibid.

13. Ibid.

14. Nancy Lee Peluso and Michael Watts, *Violent Environments* (Cornell University Press, August, 2001).

15. Ibid.

16. Ibid.

17. Betsy Hartmann, "Rethinking Climate Refugees and Climate Conflict: Rhetoric, Reality, and the Politics of Policy Discourse," *Journal of International Development* (2010), Vol. 22, Issue 2.

18. Joseph Nevins, *Operation Gatekeeper and Beyond: The War On "Illegals" and the Remaking of the U.S. Boundary* (Routledge, 2010).

19. Sam Dillon, "U.S. Tests Border Plan in Event of Mexico Crisis," *New York Times*, December 8, 1995. Accessed March 4, 2017: www.ny-

times.com/1995/12/08/us/us-tests-border-plan-in-event-of-mexico-crisis.html

20. Jason De León, *The Land of Open Graves: Living and Dying on the Migrant Trail* (University of California Press, October 2015).

21. Ibid.

22. Ibid.

23. Mary Pat Brady, "The Homoerotics of Immigration Control," *S&F Online*, Issue 6.3, Summer 2008. Accessed March 4, 2017: http://sfonline.barnard.edu/immigration/brady_01.htm

24. Tara Brian and Frank Laczko, "Fatal Journeys: Tracking Lives Lost During Migration," International Organization for Migration, 2014. Accessed March 4, 2017: https://publications.iom.int/system/files/pdf/fataljourneys_countingtheuncounted.pdf

25. Reece Jones, *Border Walls: Security and the War on Terror in the United States, India, and Israel* (Zed Books, 2012).

26. Caitlin Werrel and Francesco Fermia, "New Briefer: Why the U.S. National Security Community Takes Climate Risks Seriously," *Climate and Security Briefer* (2016). Accessed March 4, 2017: https://climateandsecurity.org/2016/12/21/why-the-u-s-national-security-community-takes-climate-risks-seriously/

27. Ibid.

28. "DHS Climate Action Plan Addendum," June 2014.

29. Louis Jacobson, "Yes, Donald Trump did call climate change a Chinese hoax," *Politifact*, June 3, 2016. Accessed March 4, 2017: www.politifact.com/truth-o-meter/statements/2016/jun/03/hillary-clinton/yes-donald-trump-did-call-climate-change-chinese-h/

30. Ibid.

31. Ibid.

32. Ibid.

33. Ibid.

34. Caitlin Werrell and Francesco Femia, "Military, Security Leaders Deliver Climate Change Briefing Book to President-Elect," The Center For Climate and Security, November 14, 2016. Accessed March 4, 2017: https://climateandsecurity.org/2016/11/14/climate-and-security-briefing-book-for-the-president-elect/

35. Rebecca Leber, "There's More Than One Way to Blow Up the Paris Climate Deal," *Mother Jones*, January 23, 2017. Accessed March 4, 2017: www.motherjones.com/environment/2017/01/trump-tillerson-paris-climate-deal

36. Jeremy Schulman, "Every Insane Thing Donald Trump Has Said About Global Warming," *Mother Jones*, December 5, 2016. Accessed March 4, 2017: www.motherjones.com/environment/2016/11/trump-climate-timeline

37. Daniel R. Coats, "Worldwide Threat Assessment of the US Intelligence Community," May 11, 2017. Accessed May 31, 2017: https://www.dni.gov/files/documents/Newsroom/Testimonies/SSCI%20Unclassified%20SFR%20-%20Final.pdf

38. Andrew Freedman, "Trump's intel agencies tell Congress that climate change poses national security threats," Mashable, May 11, 2017. Accessed May 31, 2017: http://mashable.com/2017/05/11/trump-intel-report-cites-climate-change-risks/#qqhfcKwCPiqx

39. Karl Mathiesen, "Trump defence secretary favourite 'gets climate change,'" *Climate Home*, November 30, 2016. Accessed March 4, 2017: www.climatechangenews.com/2016/11/30/trump-defence-secretary-favourite-gets-climate-change/

40. Ibid.

41. Sgt. Mahlet Tesfaye, "U.S. Army South plays a vital role in mass migration exercise," U.S. Army website, March 10, 2015. Accessed March 4, 2017: https://www.army.mil/article/144159/us_army_south_plays_a_vital_role_in_mass_migration_exercise

42. Ibid.

43. "Subcommittee Hearing: Examining DHS's Misplaced Focus on Climate Change," July 18, 2015. Accessed March 4, 2017: https://homeland.house.gov/hearing/subcommittee-hearing-examining-dhs-s-misplaced-focus-climate-change/

44. Ibid.

45. Ibid.

46. "Examining DHS's Misplaced Focus on Climate Change," 2015.

47. Ibid.

48. Ibid.

49. Nick Buxton and Ben Hayes, *The Secure and the Dispossessed: How the Military and Corporations Are Shaping a Climate-Changed World* (Pluto Press, 2015).

50. "USAID Climate Change Adaptation Plan for FY15," *USAID climatelinks*, June 2014. Accessed March 4, 2017: https://www.climatelinks.org/resources/usaid-climate-change-adaptation-plan-fy15

51. David Ciplet, "Whose Lives Matter? A Crisis of Solidarity at the Climate Talks in Paris," *Truthout*, December 10, 2015. Accessed March 4,

2017: www.truth out.org/opinion/item/33983 whose lives matter a cri sis-of-solidarity-at-the-climate-talks-in-paris

52. Thomas Smith, "Homeland Security Strategic Environment Assessment": Written testimony for a House Homeland Security Subcommittee on Oversight and Management Efficiency hearing titled "Examining DHS's Misplaced Focus on Climate Change," Department of Homeland Security website. Accessed March 4, 2017: https://www.dhs.gov/keywords/homeland-security-strategic-environment-assessment

53. "Quadrennial Homeland Security Review," Department of Homeland Security website, 2014. Accessed March 4, 2014: https://www.dhs.gov/quadrennial-homeland-security-review

54. "Examining DHS's Misplaced Focus on Climate Change."

CHAPTER THREE

1. U.S. Department of State, "Merida Initiative," state.gov. Accessed March 20, 2017: https://www.state.gov/j/inl/merida/

2. Noe Leiva, "Campesinos hondureños pasan hambre por la sequía," *Agence France Presse* (translated into Spanish and reposted by El Faro.net), August 1, 2015. Accessed March 20, 2017: www.elfaro.net/es/201507/internacionales/17241/Campesinos-hondureños-pasan-hambre-por-la-sequ%C3%ADa.htm?st-full_text=all&tpl=11

3. Ibid.

4. Through the Nexus program of the U.S. Fulbright program.

5. Lindsey R. Ross, "Climate Change and Immigration: Warnings for America's Southern Border," American Security Project, September 2010. Accessed March 20, 2017: https://americansecurityproject.org/wp-content/uploads/2010/09/Climate-Change-and-Immigration-FINAL.pdf

6. Ibid.

7. Ibid.

8. Ibid.

9. Adam Isacson, Maureen Meyer, and Hannah Smith, "Increased Enforcement at Mexico's Southern Border: An Update on Security, Migration, and U.S. Assistance," Washington Office on Latin America (WOLA), November 2015.

10. "Mexico: Tapachula Arms Conference Focuses on Southern Border Problems," U.S. Embassy cable (posted by Wikileaks), January

25, 2010. Accessed March 20, 2017: https://wikileaks.org/plusd/cables/10MEXICO77_a.html

11. Marta Molina, "Central American mothers organize to find their missing migrant children," *Waging Nonviolence*, November 6, 2012. Accessed March 20, 2017: http://wagingnonviolence.org/feature/central-american-mothers-organize-to-find-their-missing-migrant-children/

12. Ruthie Wilson Gilmore, *Golden Gulag: Prisons, Surplus, Crisis, and Opposition in Globalizing California* (University of California Press, 2007).

13. "Transport and biofuels," Sustainable Palm Oil Transparency Toolkit (SPOTT). Accessed March 20, 2017: www.sustainablepalmoil.org/transport-biofuels/

14. Peter J. Meyer, "U.S. Foreign Assistance to Latin America and the Caribbean: Trends and FY2017 Appropriations," Congressional Research Service, February 8, 2017. Accessed March 21, 2017: https://fas.org/sgp/crs/row/R44647.pdf

15. Cindy Carcamo, "Elite Honduran Unit Works to Stop Flow of Child Emigrants to U.S.," *Los Angeles Times*, July 9, 2014. Accessed March 20, 2017: www.latimes.com/world/mexico-americas/la-fg-ff-honduras-border-20140709-story.html

16. Gina Harkins, "Marines help Central American troops develop training," *Military Times*, November 22, 2015. Accessed March 21, 2017: https://www.marinecorpstimes.com/story/military/2015/11/22/marines-help-central-american-troops-develop-training/76003594/

17. Jennifer Kennedy, "Deadly Conflict Over Honduran Palm Oil Plantations Spotlights CEO," *CorpWatch*, December 31, 2012. Accessed March 21, 2017: www.corpwatch.org/article.php?id=15802

18. Fergus Hodgson, "Honduras: Free Marketeers Dominate ZEDEs Leadership," *PanAm Post*, February 18, 2014. Accessed March 21, 2017: https://panampost.com/fergus-hodgson/2014/02/18/honduras-free-marketeers-dominate-zedes-leadership/

19. Sonke Kreft, David Eckstein, Lukas Dorsch & Livia Fischer, "Global Climate Risk Index 2016: Who Suffers Most From Extreme Weather Events? Weather-related Loss Events in 2014 and 1995 to 2014," GermanWatch, 2016. Accessed June 8, 2017: https://germanwatch.org/en/11366

20. Ibid.

21. Heather Gies, "COP21 Dooms Indigenous Communities to Climate Displacement," *Telesur*, April 22, 2016. Accessed March 17, 2017: www.telesurtv.net/english/opinion/COP21-Dooms-Indigenous-Commu-

nities-to-Climate-Displacement-20160122-0016.html

22. Ibid.

23. Dawn Paley, *Drug War Capitalism* (AK Press, 2014).

24. Koko Warner et al., "In Search of Shelter: Mapping the Effects of Climate Change on Human Migration and Displacement," May 2009. Accessed March 21, 2007: http://ciesin.columbia.edu/documents/clim-migr-report-june09_final.pdf

25. Ibid.

26. "Fact Sheet: Pioneering study shows evidence of loss & damage today from the front lines of climate change: Vulnerable communities beyond adaptation?," United Nations University et al., November 2012.

27. Harsha Walia, "The Making of the Migration Crisis," *Telesur*, June 19, 2016. Accessed March 21, 2017: www.telesurtv.net/english/opinion/The-Making-of-the-Migration-Crisis-20150619-0019.html

28. Tosco Berlin, "Angela Davis: 'The refugee movement is the movement of the 21st century,'" *Vimeo*, May 14, 2015. Accessed March 21, 2017: https://vimeo.com/127986504

29. Eric Holthaus, "Rising tide of migration accompanies sea-level rises, as predicted," *Columbia University Law School Magazine*, May 2016.

30. Joseph Nevins, *Dying to Live: A Story of U.S. Immigration in an Age of Global Apartheid* (City Lights Books, 2008).

31. Ibid.

32. "Heat island reduction," U.S. Green Building Council, usgbc.org. Accessed March 21, 2017: www.usgbc.org/credits/ss7

33. Homeland Security Advisory Council, "Sustainability and Efficiency Task Force Recomendations," dhs.gov, February 2010. Accessed March 21, 2017: https://www.dhs.gov/xlibrary/assets/hsac_sustainability_efficiency_task_force_recommendations_2010.pdf

34. Ibid.

35. Jason De León, *The Land of Open Graves: Living and Dying on the Migrant Trail* (University of California Press, 2015).

36. Blake Gentry, "Deprivation, not Deterrence," Guatemala Acupuncture and Medical Aid Project, October 2014. Accessed March 21, 2017: www.academia.edu/16985511/Deprivation_not_Deterrence

CHAPTER FOUR

1. Peter Almond, "Beware: The New Goths Are Coming," *The Sunday Times* (UK), June 11, 2006. Accessed March 11, 2017: https://www.amren.com/news/2006/06/beware_the_new/

2. Ibid.

3. Ibid.

4. Lee Clarke and Caron Chess, "Elites and Panic: More to Fear than Fear Itself," *Social Forces*, December 1, 2008.

5. Rebecca Solnit, *A Paradise Built in Hell: The Extraordinary Communities That Arise in Disaster* (Penguin Books, 2009).

6. Clarke and Chess, "*Elites and Panic*."

7. Preface to the IPCC First Assessment Report Overview, 1992. Accessed March 11, 2017: https://www.ipcc.ch/ipccreports/1992%20 IPCC%20Supplement/IPCC_1990_and_1992_Assessments/English/ ipcc_90_92_assessments_far_overview.pdf

8. Joseph Romm, *Defining National Security: The Nonmilitary Aspects* (New York: Council on Foreign Relations Press, 1993).

9. Hermann Ott, "Climate Change: An Important Foreign Policy Issue," *International Affairs*, Vol. 77.

10. Eric Holthaus, "Earth's Most Famous Climate Scientist Issues Bombshell Sea Level Warning," *Slate*, July 20, 2015. Accessed March 11, 2017: www.slate.com/blogs/the_slatest/2015/07/20/sea_level_study_ james_hansen_issues_dire_climate_warning.html

11. Sharon Udasin, "Defending Israel's Borders From 'Climate Refugees,'" *Jerusalem Post*, May 14, 2012. Accessed March 11, 2017: www. jpost.com/National-News/Defending-Israels-borders-from-climate-ref- ugees

12. Tom Gjelten, "Pentagon, CIA Eye New Threat: Climate Change," NPR, December 14, 2009. Accessed March 11, 2017: www.npr. org/templates/story/story.php?storyId=121352495

13. Kurt M. Campbell, *Climate Cataclysm: The Foreign Policy and National Security Implications of Climate Change* (Brookings Institution Press, 2008).

14. Ibid.

15. Ibid.

16. Ibid.

17. Ibid.

18. Ibid.

19. Gwynne Dyer, *Climate Wars: The Fight for Survival as the World Overheats* (Oneworld Publications, 2010), 22.

20. Campbell, *Climate Cataclysm*, 155.

21. Joseph Nevins, "Plant Something So Something Bigger Might Emerge: The Paris Agreement, An Interview With Kevin Anderson,"

Flying Less, February 29, 2016. Accessed March 12, 2017: https://academicflyingblog.wordpress.com/2016/02/29/planting-seeds-so-something-bigger-might-emerge/

22. Ibid.

23. Ellie Johnston, "Paris Agreement Pledges Must Be Strengthened in Next Few Years to Limit Warming to 2 degrees C," *Climate Interactive*, April 19, 2016. Accessed March 14, 2017: https://www.climateinteractive.org/analysis/deeper-earlier-emissions-cuts-needed-to-reach-paris-goals/

24. Nevins, "Plant Something So Something Bigger Might Emerge."

25. "Global Trends 2025: A Transformed World," National Intelligence Council, 2008.

26. Gregory White, *Climate Change and Migration: Security and Borders in a Warming World* (Oxford University Press, 2011).

27. Bill Slane, "Firms showcase products aimed at boosting border security," *Cronkite News*, April 23, 2015. Accessed March 14, 2017: https://cronkitenews.azpbs.org/2015/04/23/firms-showcase-products-aimed-at-boosting-border-security/

28. Noah Shachtman, "Robo-Snipers, 'Auto Kill Zones' to Protect Israeli Borders," *Wired*, June 4, 2007. Accessed March 14, 2017: https://www.wired.com/2007/06/for_years_and_y/

29. Simon Parkin, "Killer robots: The soldiers that never sleep," *BBC*, July 26, 2015. Accessed March 14, 2017: www.bbc.com/future/story/20150715-killer-robots-the-soldiers-that-never-sleep

30. "CBP Acting Commissioner Testifies on Plans for Border Security and Progress to Date," cbp.gov, November 12, 2013. Accessed April 22, 2017: https://www.cbp.gov/about/congressional-resources/testimony/ahern-border-progress

31. Reportlinker, "Border Security Market Outlook 2014-2024," *PR Newswire*, June 3, 2014. Accessed March 14, 2017: www.prnewswire.com/news-releases/border-security-market-outlook-2014-2024-261679721.html

32. Ibid.

33. Sandler Research, "Border Security Market to Grow at 7.89% CAGR to 2019," *PR Newswire*, November 11, 2015. Accessed March 17, 2017: www.prnewswire.com/news-releases/border-security-market-to-grow-at-789-cagr-to-2019-545638842.html

34. "Global Homeland Security & Public Safety Market—2015-2022," *Homeland Security Research*, January 28, 2015. Accessed March 14, 2017: http://homelandsecurityresearch.com/2015/05/glob-

al-homeland-security-public-safety-market-2015-2022/

35. Ibid.

36. Mark Akkerman, "Border Wars II: An update on the arms industry profiting from Europe's refugee tragedy," Transnational Institute, December 19, 2016. Accessed April 22, 2017: https://www.tni.org/en/publication/border-wars-ii

37. Ibid.

38. Ibid.

39. "Homeland Security and Public Safety Market Will Go Through a Growth Period, Sustaining a 2016-2020 CAGR of 5.7%, Says a New Research Report from Homeland Security Research Corp.," Homeland Security Research, November 29, 2016. Accessed March 10, 2017: http://homelandsecurityresearch.com/Press-release-homeland-security-and-public-safety-market-will-go-through-a-growth-period-sustaining-a-2016-2020-cagr-of-5-7-says-a-new-research-report-from-homeland-security-research-corp/

40. Steven Scheer and Tova Cohen, "Investors bet on Israel tech stock windfall under Trump," *Reuters*, February 21, 2017. Accessed March 10, 2017: www.reuters.com/article/us-usa-trump-israel-economy-idUSKBN1601KL

41. Ibid.

42. "Vision and Strategy 2020: U.S. Customs and Border Protection Strategic Plan," Customs and Border Protection. Accessed March 14, 2017: https://es.slideshare.net/BenjaminWebb/cbpvisionstrategy2020

43. TimberSpy: secure and stealth surveillance, Products, timberspy.com. Accessed March 14, 2017: http://timberspy.com/products

44. Elizabeth Kolbert, *The Sixth Extinction: An Unnatural History* (Henry Holt and Co., 2014).

CHAPTER FIVE

1. William deBuys, "Phoenix in the Climate Crosshairs: We Are Long Past Coal Mine Canaries," *TomDispatch*, March 14, 2013. Accessed March 17, 2017: www.tomdispatch.com/blog/175661/william_debuys_exodus_from_phoenix

2. "Western drought watchers eye Lake Mead water level," *Associated Press*, January 17, 2017. Accessed March 22, 2017: www.mercurynews.com/2017/01/20/western-drought-watchers-keep-wary-eye-on-lake-mead-level/

3. "Across the Parched Prairie, Fires Scorch 2,300 Square Miles,"

New York Times, March 8, 2017. Accessed May 31, 2017. https://nyti.ms/2m3M6wB

4. Giles Slade, American Exodus: Climate Change and the Coming Flight for Survival (New Society Publishers, October 2013).

5. Alexandra Sims, "India's roads melt as record-breaking heat wave continues: Temperatures hit a record-breaking 51C in the city of Phalodi, Rajasthan on Friday," *The Independent*, May 23, 2016. www.independent.co.uk/news/world/asia/india-s-roads-melt-as-record-breaking-heat-wave-continues-a7044146.html

6. William deBuys, *Phoenix in the Climate Crosshairs.*

7. Donald Worster, *Dust Bowl: The Southern Plains in the 1930s* (Oxford University Press, 25th anniversary edition, 2004).

8. Michael Mcintee, "NASA Predicts 20-40 Year Megadroughts in U.S. Because of Man-Made Climate Change," *The Uptake*, February 12, 2015. Accessed March 22, 2017: http://theuptake.org/2015/02/12/nasa-predicts-20-40-year-megadroughts-in-us-because-of-man-made-climate-change/

9. Rose Marie Packard, "The Los Angeles Border Patrol," *The Nation*, Vol. 142, No. 10, March 4, 1936.

10. Ibid

11. Reece Jones, *Border Walls: Security and the War on Terror in the United States, India, and Israel* (Zed Books, 2012).

12. "Stay Away from California Warning to Transient Hordes," *Herald-Express*, August 24, 1935. Accessed May, 17, 2017: http://newdeal.feri.org/tolan/tol09.htm

13. Ibid.

14. "Indigents Barred at Arizona Line," *Los Angeles Herald-Express*, February 4, 1936.

15. Ibid.

16. Ibid.

17. "Rule Guard at Border Legal," *Los Angeles Herald-Express*, February 6, 1936.

18. Hailey Giczy, "The Bum Blockade: Los Angeles and the Great Depression," *Voces Novae: Chapman University Historical Review*, Vol. 1, No. 1, 2009.

19. Ibid.

20. "Report All Beggars Is Plea," Los Angeles Herald-Express, February 12, 1936.

21. Giczy, "*The Bum Blockade.*"

22. Elisa M. Alvarez Minoff, *Free to Move?, The Law and Politics of Internal Migration in Twentieth-Century America*, PhD dissertation Harvard University, Department of History.

23. Ibid.

24. Ibid.

25. Giczy, "*The Bum Blockade.*"

26. Ibid.

27. Ibid.

28. Alvarez Minoff, *Free to Move*.

29. Ibid.

30. "Florida Bars Out 2,000 by 'Poverty Quarantine,'" *New York Times*, November 20, 1936.

31. Alvarez Minoff, *Free to Move*.

32. . Jennifer Anne Meredith, "Colorado Governor Edwin Johnson: Politics and Race," *Utah Historical Review*, Vol. 2 (2012).

33. Ashley Fantz and Ben Brumfield, "More than half the nation's governors say Syrian refugees not welcome," *CNN*, November 19, 2015. Accessed March 23, 2017: www.cnn.com/2015/11/16/world/paris-attacks-syrian-refugees-backlash/

34. R. Gil Kerlikowske, "Vision and Strategy 2020," cbp.gov, April 8, 2015. Accessed March 24, 2017: https://www.cbp.gov/document/publications/vision-and-strategy-2020

35. Ibid.

36. "U.S. Border Patrol's Interior Enforcement Operations," ACLU Border Litigation Project. Accessed March 24, 2017: https://www.aclusandiego.org/wp-content/uploads/2014/11/100-Mile-Zone.pdf

37. "Border Patrol Checkpoints," U.S. Customs and Border Protection informational brochure. Accessed March 24, 2017: https://www.cbp.gov/sites/default/files/documents/bp_checkpoints_2.pdf

38. Ibid.

39. "Border Patrol, Checkpoints Contribute to Border Patrol's Mission, but More Consistent Data Collection and Performance Measurement Could Improve Effectiveness," Government Accountability Office, August 2009. Accessed March 24, 2017: www.gao.gov/new.items/d09824.pdf

40. Matt Apuzzo and Michael S. Schmidt, "U.S. to Continue Racial, Ethnic Profiling in Border Policy," *New York Times*, December 5, 2014. Accessed March 24, 2017: https://www.nytimes.com/2014/12/06/us/politics/obama-to-impose-racial-profiling-curbs-with-exceptions.html?_r=0

41. James Lyall et al., "Record of Abuse: Lawlessness and Impunity in Border Patrol's Interior Enforcement Operations," ACLU, October 2015. Accessed March 24, 2017: https://www.acluaz.org/sites/default/files/documents/Record_of_Abuse_101515_0.pdf

42. Ibid.

43. Ibid.

44. Ibid.

45. Ibid.

46. Ibid.

47. Office of Management and Budget, "America First: A Budget Blueprint to Make America Great Again," whitehouse.gov, March 2017. Accessed March 25, 2017: https://www.whitehouse.gov/sites/whitehouse.gov/files/omb/budget/fy2018/2018_blueprint.pdf

48. Ibid.

49. Lorne Stockman, "The Dakota Access Pipeline will lock-in the emissions of 30 coal plants," *Oil Change International*, September 12, 2016. Accessed March 25, 2017: http://priceofoil.org/2016/09/12/the-dakota-access-pipeline-will-lock-in-the-emissions-of-30-coal-plants/

50. Kerry Picket, "Border Patrol Expected to Assist Police Near Dakota Access Pipeline Protests, *The Daily Caller*, November 21, 2016. Accessed March 22, 2017: http://dailycaller.com/2016/11/21/source-border-patrol-expected-to-assist-police-at-dakota-access-pipeline-protests/

51. Jeremy Schulman, "How 19 Big Corporations Plan to Make Money Off the Climate Crisis," *Climate Desk*, April 20, 2016. Accessed March 25, 2017: https://www.climatedesk.org/warming-world/2016/04/20/how-19-big-corporations-plan-to-make-money-off-the-climate-crisis

52. Ibid.

53. Ibid.

54. "Securing our Environment," G4S USA website. Accessed March 25, 2017: www.g4s.us/en-US/Who%20we%20are/Social%20Responsibility/Securing%20our%20environment/

55. Rebecca Solnit, *A Paradise Built in Hell: The Extraordinary Communities That Arise in Disaster* (Penguin Books, 2009), 237.

56. James Ridgeway, "The Secret History of Hurricane Katrina," *Mother Jones*, August 28, 2009. Accessed March 25, 2017: www.motherjones.com/environment/2009/08/secret-history-hurricane-katrina

57. Naomi Klein, "Why #BlackLivesMatter Should Transform the Climate Debate," The Nation, December 12, 2014. Accessed March 22, 2017: https://www.thenation.com/article/what-does-blacklivesmatter-

have-do-climate-change/

58. U.S. Customs and Border Protection, "CBP Responds to Hurricane Katrina," CBP In The News, Video uploaded on January 27, 2012. Accessed March 24, 2017: https://youtu.be/u1VdhSNxN1w

59. Ibid.

60. Jeremy Scahill, "Blackwater Down," *The Nation*, October 10, 2005. Accessed March 25, 2017: https://www.thenation.com/article/blackwater-down/

61. Ibid.

62. Ibid.

63. Ibid.

64. Timothy J. Dunn, *The Militarization of the U.S.-Mexico Border 1978-1992: Low-Intensity Conflict Doctrine Comes Home* (Center for Mexican American Studies Books, 1996).

65. Ibid.

66. Jason Evans, "Take a tour of the 'doomsday Disneyland,'" *CNN*, March 31, 2014. Accessed March 24, 2017: www.cnn.com/2014/03/30/us/guardian-center-disaster-response-training/

67. "Military Police Company Prepared to Support State," Center for Domestic Preparedness. Accessed March 24, 2017: https://cdp.dhs.gov/news-media/article/military-police-company-prepared-to-support-state/

68. Solnit, *Paradise Built in Hell.*

69. Ibid.

CHAPTER SIX

1. Jessica Hagedorn, "The Ultimate Femme Fatale: Noir in Manila," *The Margins*, July 16, 2013. Accessed March 28, 2017: http://aaww.org/manila-noir/

2. Dakila Kim P. Yee, *Dialogues of Sustainable Urbanization: Social Science Research and Transitions to Urban Contexts* (University of Western Sydney, 2015).

3. Brad Johnson, "In Tearful, Amazing Speech, Philippines Climate Delegate Announces Hunger Strike," climatebrad *YouTube*, November 12, 2013. Accessed March 28, 2017: https://youtu.be/S6RXGGFBdlo

4. Arthur C. Brooks, "Be Happier, Start Thinking More About Your Death," *New York Times*, July 9, 2016. Accessed March 28, 2017: https://www.nytimes.com/2016/01/10/opinion/sunday/to-be-happier-start-thinking-more-about-your-death.html?_r=0

5. Sunshine de Leon and Barbara Demick, "Relief teams rush to ty-

phoon-devastated Philippines," *LA Times*, November 10, 2013. Accessed March 28, 2017: http://articles.latimes.com/2013/nov/10/world/la-fg-philippines-storm-20131111

6. Obama White House Archives, "Statement on Typhoon Haiyan," November 10, 2013. Accessed March 28, 2017: https://obamawhitehouse.archives.gov/the-press-office/2013/11/10/statement-president-super-typhoon-haiyanyolanda

7. Paul A. Kramer, "Race-Marking and Colonial Violence in the US Empire: The Philippine-American War as Race War," *Asia-Pacific Journal*, June 1, 2006. Accessed March 28, 2017: http://apjjf.org/-Paul-A.-Kramer/1745/article.html

8. Alfred W. McCoy, *Policing America's Empire: The United States, the Philippines, and the Rise of the Surveillance State* (University of Wisconsin Press, 2009).

9. Ibid.

10. Ibid.

11. "Typhoon Haiyan: Thousands feared dead in Philippines," *BBC*, November 10, 2013. Accessed March 28, 2017: www.bbc.com/news/world-asia-24887337

12. Brad Johnson, "*In Tearful, Amazing Speech, Philippines Climate Delegate Announces Hunger Strike.*"

13. Ibid.

14. Ibid.

15. Ibid.

16. Global Witness, "Deadly Environment: A rising death toll on our environmental frontiers is escaping international attention," April 15, 2014. Accessed March 28, 2017: https://www.globalwitness.org/en/campaigns/environmental-activists/deadly-environment/

17. Solnit, *A Paradise Built in Hell*.

18. Ibid.

19. Alf Gunvald Nilsen, *Dispossession and Resistance in India: The River and the Rage* (Routledge, 2010).

20. Kristine Angeli Sabillo, "In the Know: What Is the People's Surge?" *Inquirer.Net*, February 25, 2014. Accessed March 28, 2017: http://newsinfo.inquirer.net/580604/in-the-know-what-is-people-surge

21. Walden Bello, "A 'Second Front' in the Philippines," *The Nation*, February 28, 2002. Accessed March 28, 2017: https://www.thenation.com/article/second-front-philippines/

22. Obama White House Archives "Remarks by President

Obama to the Australian Parliament," November 17, 2011. Accessed March 28, 2017: https://obamawhitehouse.archives.gov/the-press-office/2011/11/17/remarks-president-obama-australian-parliament

23. Bryan Bender, "Chief of US Pacific forces calls climate biggest worry," *The Boston Globe*, March 9, 2013. Accessed March 28, 2017: https://www.bostonglobe.com/news/nation/2013/03/09/admiral-samuel-locklear-commander-pacific-forces-warns-that-climate-change-top-threat/BHdPVCLrWEMxRe9IXJZcHL/story.html

24. Anastasia Moloney, "Violent 2015 sees three environmental activists killed each week," *Reuters*, June 19, 2016. Accessed March 28, 2017: www.reuters.com/article/us-global-landrights-violence-idUSKCN0Z601U

25. "Honduran Government Must Counter Smear Campaign Against Land and Environmental Defenders and Protect Those Under Threat," Global Witness Press Release, March 15, 2017. Accessed March 27, 2017: https://www.globalwitness.org/en/press-releases/honduran-government-must-counter-smear-campaign-against-land-and-environmental-defenders-and-protect-those-under-threat/

26. "Filipinos on the Front Lines," Global Witness. Accessed March 27, 2017: https://www.globalwitness.org/en/campaigns/environmental-activists/filipinos-front-line/

27. Ana P. Santos, "The Widows of Duterte's Drug War: As the death toll in the Philippines soars, those left behind confront a different life," *The Atlantic*, December 1, 2016. Accessed March 27, 2017: https://www.theatlantic.com/international/archive/2016/12/rodrigo-duterte-philippines-drugs-widow-human-rights/509030/

28. "People Surge hits Duterte's defense of militarization in rural areas," People Surge, November 30, 2016. Accessed March 27, 2017: https://peoplesurgephils.wordpress.com/2016/11/30/people-surge-hits-dutertes-defense-of-militarization-in-rural-areas/

29. Emily Rauhala, "Duterte: During phone call, Trump praised my drug war as the 'right way,'" *Washington Post*, December 3, 2016. Accessed March 27, 2017: https://www.washingtonpost.com/news/worldviews/wp/2016/12/03/duterte-during-phone-call-trump-praised-my-drug-war-as-right-way/?utm_term=.4ee6e537c6b8

CHAPTER SEVEN

1. The People's Pilgrimage Web. Accessed March 28, 2017: http://peoplespilgrimage.org/about.html

2. Daniel Severson, "France's Extended State of Emergency: What New Powers Did the Government Get?, *Lawfare*, November 22, 2015. Accessed March 28, 2017: https://www.lawfareblog.com/frances-extended-state-emergency-what-new-powers-did-government-get

3. Amy Goodman with Denis Moynihan, "Fighting for the Climate in the Heart of the World," *Democracy Now!*, December 11, 2014. Accessed March 28, 2017: https://www.democracynow.org/2014/12/11/fighting_for_the_climate_in_the

4. Reece Jones, *Violent Borders: Refugees and the Right to Move* (Verso Books, October 2016).

5. Coral Davenport and Alissa J. Rubin, "Trump Signs Executive Order Unwinding Obama Climate Policies," *New York Times*, March 28, 2017. Accessed March 29, 2017: https://nyti.ms/2ovruhs

6. Paul Currion, "The Walls That Exist in Our Minds," *News Deeply*, June 27, 2016. Accessed March 28, 2017: https://www.newsdeeply.com/refugees/community/2016/06/27/the-walls-that-exist-in-our-minds

7. Arthur Neslen, "Paris climate activists put under house arrest using emergency laws," *The Guardian*, November 27, 2015. Accessed March 28, 2017: https://www.theguardian.com/environment/2015/nov/27/paris-climate-activists-put-under-house-arrest-using-emergency-laws

8. Alleen Brown, "Under House Arrest, a Climate Activist Waits Out the Paris Conference," *The Intercept*, November 30, 2015. Accessed March 28, 2017: https://theintercept.com/2015/11/30/under-house-arrest-a-climate-activist-waits-out-the-paris-conference/

9. David Ciplet, *Power in a Warming World* (MIT Press, 2015).

10. Andreas Malm, "Our Fight for Survival," *Jacobin*, November 29, 2015. Accessed March 28, 2017: https://www.jacobinmag.com/2015/11/climate-change-paris-cop21-hollande-united-nations/

11. "Filipino Climate Artist on COP21: If World Leaders Really Cared, Agreement Would Not Take 20 Years," *Democracy Now*, December 1, 2015. Accessed March 28, 2017: http://m.democracynow.org/stories/15732

CHAPTER EIGHT

1. Betsy Hartmann, "Rethinking Climate Refugees and Climate Conflict: Rhetoric, Reality, and the Politics of Policy Discourse," *Journal of International Development* (2010), Vol. 22, Issue 2.

INDEX

Abbott, Greg, 143–144
Abbott, Jeff, 90–91
Abrupt Climate Change Scenario and Its Implications for United States National Security, *An* (Schwartz and Randall), 28, 58, 166
ACLU (American Civil Liberties Union), 150, 154–155, 156
Adams, Brad, 46
Africa, 38–40
Agence France Press (AFP), 74–75, 182
Albright, Madeleine, 53
American Association for the Advancement of Science, 96
American Civil Liberties Union (ACLU), 150, 154–155, 156
American Exodus (Slade), 133
American Science and Engineering Inc., 78
American Security Project, 44, 76
Amnesty International, 219
Anderson, Brett, 19
Anderson, Kevin, 117–118
Aquino, Benigno, 192
Arizona, 54, 132, 139, 141, 144. *See also* Patagonia, Arizona; Phoenix, Arizona
Army Corps of Engineers, 54
Atlantic, The, 51–52
Austin, Valer, 233

Babeu, Paul, 144
Balogo, Philippines, 15–16, 24, 25
Banegas Barahona, Leonardo Lenin, 81, 93–94
Bangladesh, India, 45–47, 95
Barahona. *See* Banegas Barahona, Leonardo Lenin
Bautista, Elfleda, 192–193, 198
Beast, The (Martínez), 79
Benko, Jessica, 22
Bislig, Philippines, 179–182, 186–187
Black Fraternal Organization of Honduras (OFRANEH), 86
Border Patrol. *See* U.S. Border Patrol
Border Security Expo, 121
Border Strike Force, 144
Border Walls (Jones), 56, 138
"Border Wars," 125
Borkowski, Mark, 122–124, 126–127
BORTAC (Border Patrol Tactical Unit), 83, 160
Brady, Mary Pat, 56
Brooks, Arthur C., 175
Brown, Alleen, 219–220
"Bum Blockade, The" (Giczy), 139
Burke, Sharon, 116–117
Bush, George W., 57–58

Cabaljao, Marissa, 186–187, 192
Cabeza Prieta Wildlife Refuge, 102
Cáceres, Berta, 91, 197
California, 32–33, 137–141
California Supreme Court, 141
Campbell, Kurt, 114, 115
Campos, Lindolfo, 75
Carcamo, Cindy, 83

Carigara, Leyte, Philippines, 187–188
Carleton, H.A., 138–139
Carlos, Juan, 202
Carlos, Luis, 72, 77, 80
Carpenter, Scott, 127
CARSI (Central American Security Initiative), 82–83
Castro, Chris, 75
Castro, Raul, 155
CBP. *See* Customs and Border Protection (CBP)
Central America, 74–75
Central American Agricultural Council, 74
Central American Security Initiative (CARSI), 82–83
César (community leader), 83, 84–85, 86, 87–88
Cheney, Stephen, 43, 44, 45–47, 48–49, 62–63
Chess, Caron, 112
Chiapas, Mexico, 32, 79, 202
Chinese Exclusion Act (1882), 141
Christensen, Parley Parker, 140
Ciplet, David, 68–69, 221
Ciudad Inteligente, 93
Ciudad Trujillo, Honduras, 84
Clarke, Lee, 112, 190
Climate and Security Advisory Group, 61
Climate Cataclysm (Campbell), 115
Climate Central, 134
"Climate Change and Immigration" (American Security Project), 76
Climate Change and Migration (White), 120
Climate Interactive, 118
Clinton, Bill, 53
CLO. *See* Cuenca Los Ojos (CLO)
CNN, 161, 163
Coats, Daniel R., 62
Colibri Center for Human Rights, 99
Collins, Nora, 157–158
Colorado, 142–143
"Coming Anarchy, The" (Kaplan), 51–53
Common Science Climate Index, 22
Conference of the Parties (COPs), 220–222. *See also* COP21 (21st Conference of Parties)
"Contribution of Antarctica to past and future sea-level rise"(DeConto), 20
Cook, Ben, 137
COP21 (21st Conference of Parties), 108–110
Corrections Corporation of America, 105
Cuenca Los Ojos (CLO), 35, 231, 233
Currion, Paul, 212–213
Custodio, Jefferson, 187–189, 196, 198–199
Custodio, Rodolfo, 189, 193, 199–202
Customs and Border Protection (CBP), 29, 59, 73, 123, 148, 149, 150, 161–162, 164–165

David, Nellie Jo, 154
David, Yilian Maribel, 86–87
Davis, Angela Y., 96–97
Davis, James E., 139, 140
De León, Jason, 55–56, 103

deBuys, William, 132, 134
DeConto, Rob, 20
Department of Defense. *See* U.S. Department of Defense
Department of Homeland Security (DHS), 33, 41, 57, 66, 100–101, 102, 112, 150, 162, 178
Devil's Highway, The (Urrea), 133
Devoid, Alex, 200
Díaz, Juan, 84
DiSalvo, Joseph P., 64
Domenjoud, Joel, 219
Drug War Capitalism (Paley), 91
Dukes, John, 47
Duncan, Jeff, 65, 66–67
Dunn, Timothy, 33, 162
Dust Bowl Migration, 135–138
Dust Bowl: The Southern Plains in the 1930s (Worster), 136–137
Duterte, Rodrigo, 198
Dying to Live (Nevins), 99

Economic Development Zones, 86–87
Eggers, Dave, 162
18 de Agosto, 230–231
Elbit Systems, 126
Englander, John, 37–38
Enlace Zapatista, 31–32
Ethiopia, 225
EyeSite Surveillance, 127–128

Facusse, Miguel, 85
"Fatal Journeys" (International Organization on Migration), 56
Federal Emergency Management Agency (FEMA), 163
Fermia, Francesco, 44
Fernando, Santos, 72, 77
Fisher, Mike, 32
FLIR Systems, 64
Flores, Eleuterio, 74
Florida, 142. *See also* Miami, Florida
Foreign Policy, 43
Forward Operating Base, 98, 100–102
France, 205, 219. *See also* Paris, France
Frederickson, Keith, 163
French National Police, 206
FRONTEX, 125
Fuerth, Leon, 116

G4S, 103, 158–159
Gambia, 39, 95–96
Garcia, Joshua, 145–147, 149, 150–153, 158–160, 167–169
Garífuna people, 86
G-Boss (Ground-Based Operation Surveillance Systems), 102
Geglia, Beth, 87
Gentry, Blake, 103
Geo Group, 59
Germanwatch, 88, 89–90
Gerrard, Michael, 97
Giczy, Hailey, 139, 141–142
Gies, Heather, 89
Gilmore, Ruthie Wilson, 80
Global Trends 2025: A Transformed World, 120
Global Witness, 186, 197–198
Glowzecski, Barbara, 223
Golden Gulag (Gilmore), 80
González Castillo, Fray Tomás, 77–78
Goodman, Amy, 222
Gore, Al, 53

Goudreau, Jim, 47–48, 100
Gratton, Dave, 127–128
Ground-Based Operation Surveillance Systems (G-Boss), 102
Grupo Dinant, 85
GuardBot, 120–121
Guardian Centers, 163
Guillermo (OFRANEH member), 88, 89

Hagel, Chuck, 176
Hammer, Zoe, 227–228
Hampton Roads, Virginia, 20
Hansen, James E., 21, 113, 173
Hartmann, Betsy, 53, 228
Hayes, Ben, 34, 67
Hernandez, Gildegardo, 196
Hewsom, Marilyn, 45
Heyerdahl, Thor, 212
Hodges, David, 224, 231–232
Holland, Andrew, 61
Holthaus, Eric, 97, 119
Homeland Security. *See* Department of Homeland Security (DHS)
Homeland Security Quadrennial Review, 69
Homeland Security Research, 124, 125
Homeland Security Strategic Environment Assessment., 69
Homer-Dixon, Thomas, 53
Honduran Investigative National Police, 81, 83
Honduras, 74–75, 81–96, 197–198
Hope in a Changing Climate (2009), 224–225
Hope in the Dark (Solnit), 224, 239
Hopkins, Rob, 223
Humble, April, 29, 213
Hurricane Katrina, 160–162
Hurricane Mitch, 82, 89
Hurricane Odile, 26

"Ice melt, sea-level rise, and superstorms" (Hansen), 21, 173
Immigration Act of 1917, 141
Immigration and Nationality Act, 149
In Search of Shelter (Warner et al.), 22, 95
"Integrated Advance," 58, 63–64. *See also* Operation Vigilant Sentry
Internal Displacement Monitoring Centre, 22
International Organization on Migration, 40, 56, 96
Ismael (Honduran farmer), 72, 77
Israel, 114, 121–122

Jamail, Dahr, 135
Jarvis, Brooke, 21
"Joint Operating Environment, Trends and Challenges for the Future Joint Force Through 2030, The," 57
Jones, Reece, 56, 138, 210–211
Jorgensen, Randy, 86
Josue, Rollie, 17–18, 24
Juan, Amy, 151, 166–168

Kaplan, Robert, 52–53
Karapatan, 196, 197
Kelly, John, 42, 63
Kennedy, Jennifer, 85
Kerlikowske, Gil, 148–149

Kerry, John, 68
"*Killer Robots: The Soldiers that Never Sleep*" (Parkin), 122
Kimmelman, Michael, 22
Klein, Naomi, 119, 161
Klugmann, Mark, 87
Kolasky, Robert, 65–66
Kolbert, Elizabeth, 128–129
Kolesnikova, Lina, 107, 109
Kyte, Billy, 197

La Arrocera, 79
Lacson, Panfil, 192
Lambon, Marcel, 196–197
Land of Open Graves, The (De León), 55–56, 103
Leahy, Patrick, 156
Liu, John, 223–228
Lockheed Martin, 38, 45
Locklear, Samuel, 194–195
Loess Plateau, China, 225
Lopez, Barry, 35
Los Angeles Police Department (LAPD), 139, 140
Louisiana, 19. *See also* New Orleans, Louisiana
Ludwisgen, Kurt, 128

Malms, Andreas, 221
Manila, Philippines, 18
Marinduque, Philippines, 24–25, 238
Martínez, Óscar, 79
Mattis, James, 41, 43, 48
Mbalo, Ibrahim, 39
McCoy, Alfred, 177–179
Mead, Lake, 132
Mediterranean Levant region, 137
Melo Commission, 196
Merida Initiative, 73–74, 83
Mesoamerican Migrant Movement, 80
Mexico-Guatemala border, 73–74, 78
Miami, Florida, 20, 165
Migrant Trail Walk, 211
Milipol, 107, 110, 206, 213
Militarization of the U.S.-Mexico Border, 1978-1992, The (Dunn), 33, 162
Military Times, 84
Miranda, Miriam, 89–90
MIT Sloan, 118
Monterona, Marcelo, 196
Myers, Norman, 94

Napolitano, Janet, 59
NASA (National Aeronautics and Space Administration), 51, 137
"National Defense Strategy," 57
"National Intelligence Assessment (NIA) on the National Security of Climate Change to 2030," 57
National Intelligence Council, 57, 120
National Security Agency, 164
"National Security and the Threat of Climate Change," 57
NBC News, 215, 216–217
Nevins, Joseph, 99, 100
New Orleans, Louisiana, 33, 160–162
New York Times, 19, 133, 161
Nilsen, Alf Gunvald, 190
Norquist, Grover, 87
Nuñez (Honduran policeman), 81–82, 90–92

Obama, Barack, 49–52, 58, 143, 176, 194, 217
Obuson, Amalie, 18–19
OFRANEH (Black Fraternal Organization of Honduras), 86
Ogden, Peter, 115–116
Oliver, Mary, 238
Opall-Rome, Barbara, 122
Operation Streamline, 103–104
Operation Vigilant Sentry, 58, 163
Oracion, Edmund, 16–17
Organ Pipe National Monument, 98, 102
Ott, Herm, 113

Packard, Rose Marie, 138
Paley, Dawn, 91
Paradise Built in Hell, A (Solnit), 111
Parenti, Christian, 23, 231
Paris, France, 204–208, 215–220
Paris Climate Agreement, 61, 117–119
Parkin, Simon, 122
Parry, Chris, 111
Patagonia, Arizona, 224, 226
Peluso, Nancy Lee, 53
People Surge, 183, 187, 189–190, 192–193, 196
People's Pilgrimage, 203–206, 215–218
Pérez, Juan Manuel, 229, 231–232
Pforr, Chris, 173
Philippines, 18, 172–179, 191, 193–197. *See also* Tacloban, Philippines
Phoenix, Arizona, 131–132, 134, 165
Podesta, John, 115
Policing America's Empire (McCoy), 177–179
Politico, 41
Pomada, Andrew, 182
Posadas, Alfred, 179–183
Power in a Warming World (Ciplet), 17, 68–69, 221
"Prevention Through Deterrence" strategy, 54, 55, 77
Programa Frontera Sur, 72
Pruitt, Scott, 41

Randall, Doug, 28, 58
Rateau, Jacqueline, 104
"Record of Abuse: Lawlessness and Impunity in Border Patrol's Interior Enforcement Operations," 153
Ridgeway, James, 161, 162
Romm, Joseph, 113
Ross, Andrew, 132
Ross, Lindsey, 76
Rwanda, 225

San Bernardino Ranch, 229, 230
San Pedro Sula, Honduras, 93
Sandler Research, 124
Saño, A.G., 172–176, 183, 203–204, 209, 222
Saño, Yeb (Nadarev), 174, 183–186, 203–206, 208–212, 214, 220
Santos, Ana B., 198
Sarabia, Ignacio, 104
Satkhira, Bangladesh, 95
Scahill, Jeremy, 162
Schwartz, Peter, 28, 58
Schwenk, David, 217
Secure and the Dispossessed, The (Hayes), 34

Serraglio, Randy, 226
Sims, Alexandra, 134
Sims, Neil, 45
Singh, A.K., 114
Sixth Extinction, The (Kolbert), 128–129
Skousen, Mark, 87
Slade, Giles, 133
Smith, Sophie, 148
Smith, Thomas, 67, 69–70
Snowden, Edward, 164
Social Weather Stations, 18
Solnit, Rebecca, 111–112, 164, 224, 239
Sonora, Mexico, 26
South Carolina, 144
Special Economic Development and Employment Zones (ZEDEs), 86–87
Standing Rock, North Dakota, 157
Staton, Elisa, 21
Subic Bay Naval Base, 194
SunPower, 48
Super Typhoon Yolanda. *See* Typhoon Haiyan
Sustainable Palm Oil Transparency Toolkit (SPOTT), 82

Tacloban, Philippines, 173, 176, 182–184, 199–200
Tenosique, Mexico, 71–72
Teran, Alberto, 230, 231, 232
Texas, 144
Texiguat, Honduras, 74, 75
Third National Climate Assessment, 65–66
This Changes Everything (Klein), 119
"Threats, Challenges, and Change" (United Nations), 67
Three Points checkpoint, 149–150, 159–160
Tierney, Kathleen, 164, 190
Tillerson, Rex, 41, 62
TimberSpy, 128
Tohono O'odham Community Action (TOCA), 166
Tohono O'odham Nation., 147–148, 151, 152–154, 167
Trump, Donald, 31–32, 41–42, 58–62, 124–126, 141, 155–156, 198, 211
Trump, Ivanka, 62
Tucson Weekly, 235
Tuell, Cyndi, 102
21st-Century Border, 73–74, 78, 83
21st Conference of Parties (COP21), 108–110
Typhoon Haiyan, 16, 183–184, 187
Typhoon Ineng, 16

U. S. Geological Survey, 19
Undoing Border Imperialism (Walia), 30
United Nations, 22, 67, 95, 159, 220–222
Urrea, Luis Alberto, 133
U.S. Agency for International Development (USAID), 68, 176
U.S. Army Corps of Engineers, 54
U.S. Border Patrol, 54, 57, 153–160, 166
U.S. Border Patrol Tactical Unit (BORTAC), 83, 160
U.S. Coast Guard, 49–50, 58, 64
U.S. Customs and Border Protection. *See* Customs and

Border Protection (CBP)
U.S. Department of Defense, 43, 47, 48, 57
U.S. Department of Homeland Security. *See* Department of Homeland Security (DHS)
U.S. Global Change Research Program, 65–66
U.S. Green Building Council, 101
U.S. State Department, 68
U.S. Supreme Court, 141
USAID, 68, 176

Vallet, Elisabeth, 29
Vasquez, Lesly, 74–75
Vavages-Andrews, Tina, 167
Velázquez Navarrete, Marco Antonio, 77
Vigilant Sentry. *See* Operation Vigilant Sentry
Violent Borders (Jones), 210
Violent Environments (Peluso and Watts), 53
Vision Gain, 124

Wagner, Paul, 37
Walia, Harsha, 30, 96
"Walls Above, the Cracks Below (And To The Left), The," 31–32
Warner, Koko, 22, 23, 94, 95
Washington Post, 45
Watson, Kevin, 37, 38–40
Watts, Michael, 53
Weber, Max, 178–179
Werrel, Caitlin, 44
Western Resource Advocates, 132
White, Gregory, 120
Whitehead, John, 33
Wilson, Mike, 153
Wirth, Tim, 53
Work, Robert, 43
"Worldwide Threat Assessment of the US Intelligence Community" (Coats), 62
Worster, Donald, 136–137

Yee, Dakila Kim P., 174

Zapatistas, 31–32
ZEDEs (Special Economic Development and Employment Zones), 86–87

ABOUT THE AUTHOR

For the past 15 years Todd Miller has researched, written about, and worked on immigration and border issues from both sides of the U.S.-Mexico divide for organizations such as BorderLinks, Witness for Peace, and NACLA. He is the author of *Border Patrol Nation* (City Lights, 2014), and his writings about the border have appeared in the *New York Times*, *Mother Jones*, *The Nation*, *TomDispatch*, Al Jazeera English, and *Salon*, among other places.

NEW AND FORTHCOMING IN THE OPEN MEDIA SERIES

Loaded:
A Disarming History of the Second Amendment
By Roxanne Dunbar Ortiz

Breaking Through Power:
It's Easier Than We Think
By Ralph Nader

America at War with Itself
By Henry A. Giroux

I Couldn't Even Imagine That They Would Kill Us:
An Oral History of the Attacks Against the Students of Ayotzinapa
By John Gibler

Under the Affluence:
Shaming the Poor, Praising the Rich and Sacrificing the Future of America
By Tim Wise

The Meaning of Freedom
By Angela Y. Davis

CITY LIGHTS BOOKS | OPEN MEDIA SERIES
ARM YOURSELF WITH INFORMATION

MYSTERY UNRAVELED

Find the answers to the puzzles in last month's INTRIGUE titles!

Hidden Word
(Writing & Computers)

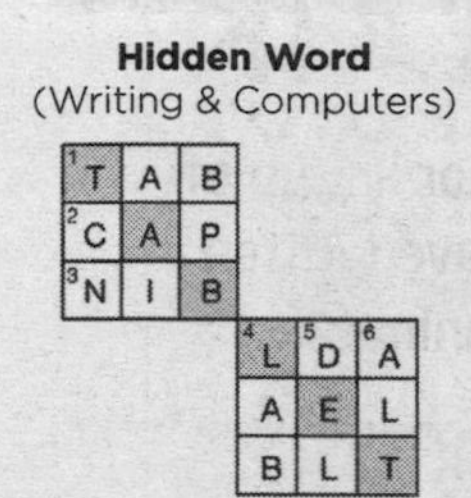

Hidden Word: TABLET

Hidden Word
(House)

Hidden Word: PANTRY

Figure Counting
(Squares & Rectangles)

Thirty-eight

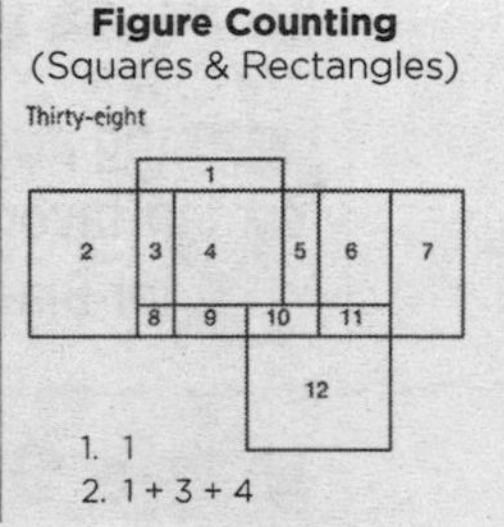

1. 1
2. 1 + 3 + 4

Figure Counting
(Triangles)

Eight

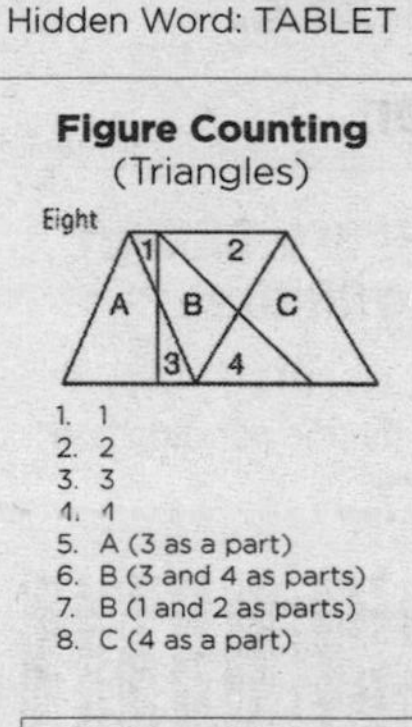

1. 1
2. 2
3. 3
4. 4
5. A (3 as a part)
6. B (3 and 4 as parts)
7. B (1 and 2 as parts)
8. C (4 as a part)

Matchstick Puzzle
(12-Matchstick Arrangement)

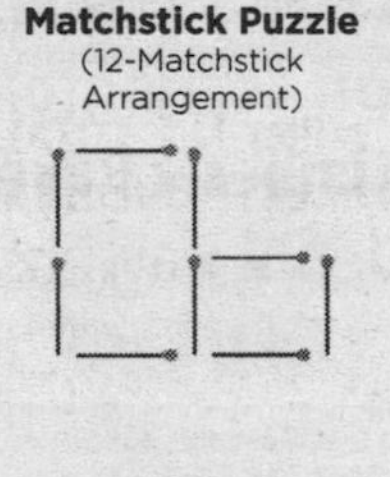

Matchstick Puzzle
(20-Matchstick Arrangement)

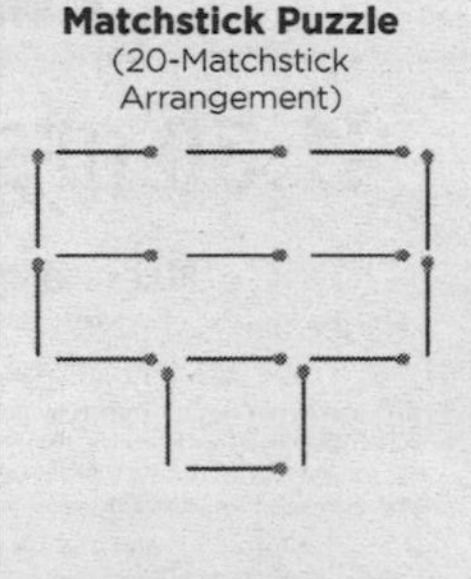

HNFPZAN2011MM

eyes were shut.

He looked oddly boyish. There was something innocent and unguarded in his expression. She felt a weakening in her resistance to him.

"Jon." She put her hand on his shoulder, intending to shake him awake. Instead, it rested there like a caress.

His eyes snapped open.

"You were asleep."

"No, I was, uh, visualizing something on this design." He gestured to the blueprint in front of him then rubbed his eyes.

That gesture dealt a bigger blow to her resistance. She realized it wasn't only animal attraction pulling them together. She took a step backward as if to get away from the knowledge.

She cleared her throat. "I'm heading off now."

He gave her a smile, and she could see his exhaustion.

"Yeah, I should, too." He stood and stretched. The hem of his T-shirt rose as he arched his back and she caught a flash of hard male belly. She looked away, but it was too late. Her mind had committed the image to permanent memory.

And suddenly she knew, for good or bad, she'd never look at Jon the same way again.

Find out what happens next in ONE GOOD REASON, available August 2011 from Harlequin® Superromance®!

HSREXP0811

Once bitten, twice shy. That's Gabby Wade's motto—
especially when it comes to Adamson men.
And the moment she meets Jon Adamson her theory
is confirmed. But with each encounter a little something
sparks between them, making her wonder if she's been
too hasty to dismiss this one!

Enjoy this sneak peek from ONE GOOD REASON
by Sarah Mayberry, available August 2011
from Harlequin® Superromance®.

Gabby Wade's heartbeat thumped in her ears as she marched to her office. She wanted to pretend it was because of her brisk pace returning from the file room, but she wasn't that good a liar.

Her heart was beating like a tom-tom because Jon Adamson had touched her. In a very male, very possessive way. She could still feel the heat of his big hand burning through the seat of her khakis as he'd steadied her on the ladder.

It had taken every ounce of self-control to tell him to unhand her. What she'd really wanted was to grab him by his shirt and, well, explore all those urges his touch had instantly brought to life.

While she might not like him, she was wise enough to understand that it wasn't always about liking the other person. Sometimes it was about pure animal attraction.

Refusing to think about it, she turned to work. When she'd typed in the wrong figures three times, Gabby admitted she was too tired and too distracted. Time to call it a day.

As she was leaving, she spied Jon at his workbench in the shop. His head was propped on his hand as he studied blueprints. It wasn't until she got closer that she saw his

HSREXP0811